# Dead Keen

*Denise Ryan*

For more information on other books
published by Piatkus, visit our website at
www.piatkus.co.uk

Copyright © 2000 by Denise Ryan

First published in Great Britain in 2000 by
Judy Piatkus (Publishers) Ltd of
5 Windmill Street, London W1T 2JA
email: info@piatkus.co.uk

This edition published 2000

Reprinted 2000

The moral right of the author has been asserted

A catalogue record for this book is available from the British Library

ISBN 0 7499 3180 9

Set in Times by Phoenix Photosetting, Chatham, Kent
Printed and bound in Great Britain by
Mackays of Chatham plc, Chatham, Kent

To Peter

And Mum, Michael, Elizabeth & family, Brian & Pat Clark

Mary & Arnold, for telling me about the ghostly monk,
a tale I never get tired of hearing – as they know!

And: Sigrid, Jose & Cees, Margaret, Famke and Panasse

# Part One

# Chapter One

'Come on, Justine!' he murmured. 'Move it!'

He stood tensely on the sunlit street corner, vigorously picking his nose as he darted glances from behind the dirty stone wall of an office building. He didn't want Justine to spot him from her window and be afraid to come out alone. He hoped some friend wasn't calling for her again.

'Hey, mate!' he called to a passing man in a suit. 'Got the time?'

The man glanced at his watch. 'Nearly six,' he said angrily, glaring as if to ask, Why haven't you got your own bloody watch?

'Ta, mate.' Miserable bastard, Matthew thought. 'Me Rolex is in for repair.'

Justine should be out of the advertising agency by now, in a hurry to drive home or go off with this or that friend. Although sometimes she worked late. She seemed to have a lot of friends – male as well as female. He looked at his finger and frowned, reached into his pocket for a crumpled pink tissue.

An elderly woman stopped and stared at him in disgust. He stared aggressively back and made a sudden flicking motion with his finger. She flinched.

'What are you looking at?' he asked slowly, menacingly. 'Nosy old bitch!' Small and thin, with resentful dark eyes, she reminded him of his mother.

The woman averted her eyes and walked on. There was something unnerving about someone who could stand in the street picking his nose in full view of passers-by and stare at them as if they had caused offence, though the tall skinny young man wearing beige cotton trousers with knife-edge creases, a crisp white shirt, polished but worn brown leather shoes and a navy blue jacket with shiny brass buttons, certainly didn't look like a dosser. If he had she wouldn't have dared glance in his direction.

Justine was coming out! Alone. Matthew tossed the pink tissue in a waste bin and followed her down the street of Victorian office buildings that sloped towards the Mersey as she left Brooks & Wilde and headed for her car. A warm salt-smelling breeze blew gently up from the river and the late-afternoon August sunshine illuminated her head of floating curly red-gold hair. She wore a long straight sleeveless turquoise dress and clumpy sandals, carried her black leather bag and a black linen jacket.

Justine had beautiful slender arms and smooth unblemished skin. Matthew could see the outline of her long legs through the light silky dress fabric. Her face was a perfect oval and she had a small nose, deep dark blue eyes with long lashes, straight darkish brows and a mouth that smiled easily. Not at him, he had to admit. Not yet. Her full lips were unpainted. Male glances lingered on her as she walked quickly down the street, car keys clutched in her left hand, her head slightly lowered. The glances made him feel angry and full of unease, although he liked the fact that she didn't return any of them.

'Justine!' he shouted, breaking into a run. 'Justine, wait!'

'Oh, my God!' she breathed. 'Not again!' She glanced back and stiffened with fear. She wished she could park her red BMW convertible right outside Brooks & Wilde's premises, but the spaces there were reserved. She also wished she could feel rage or at least aggression at the sight of Matthew. Anything except this hateful paralysing fear that made her body go cold and weak. Why me? she wondered guiltily. What did I ever do? Being polite to strange men was contributory negligence, it seemed.

'Hi, Justine!' He caught her up and fell into step beside her. 'How are you?'

'Oh, I'm fine,' she said grimly, hurrying along. 'I'm cool.' Get lost! she thought.

'Have you been in there all afternoon?' he asked in his nasal Scouse accent. He sniffed and pulled another pink tissue from his jacket pocket to blow his nose.

'You tell me!' Justine laughed nervously. 'You spend enough time hanging around spying. Of course I've been in there all afternoon. It's where I work.' Keep it polite, the scared little voice inside her warned. Don't antagonize him.

'Why wouldn't you talk to me then?' Matthew demanded roughly. 'I phoned you four times, Justine. That bitch of a receptionist practically told me to f—' He stopped. 'To get lost.'

'She isn't a bitch!' Justine protested, blushing. 'I was incredibly busy,' she said nervously. 'I'm writing the copy for a client's web page . . .'

He laughed. 'Say that in English!'

'I needed to concentrate on my work. I couldn't accept any calls.' Why am I explaining myself to this creep? she wondered, longing to feel angry with Matthew instead of with herself.

'I haven't spent all afternoon spying,' he said, suddenly aggressive. 'What you call spying, anyway. I just came from a job interview. Bloody stupid questions they ask! *Have you ever been psychologically challenged?*' He punched the air with his fist, startling her. 'That's life, being psychologically challenged.'

'Tell me about it.' She walked on, gripping the jacket and her sticky leather bag strap. 'A job interview?' she echoed hopefully. That explained the tragic jacket, which made her think of some retired commodore sipping gin-and-tonic as he cruised the river on his yacht. But Matthew's staggering lack of dress sense was the least of her worries. 'What kind of job?' she asked. If someone employed the bastard, he wouldn't have time to harass her anymore.

Justine's mouth was dry with fear, her palms clammy. She envied other girls and women walking past. Laughing, carefree, not knowing how it felt to be hounded by a man who gave you the creeps. She didn't know what the hell to do about it. She glanced at his scrubbed, jagged nails and then at his face, recoiling in horror as she noticed a blob of green mucus protruding from his left nostril. She felt sick, desperate to shake him off.

'Security work,' Matthew said importantly. Car park attendant didn't sound too impressive. 'The hours were crap and the pay was a joke. And those daft questions! I lost me rag.' He laughed angrily. 'Told them to stuff it.'

'Oh, I see.' Her heart sank.

Matthew had cropped brown hair, sickly white skin and deep-set angry brown eyes in a narrow skull-like face. He looked about thirty. He was clean-shaven and smelled strongly of soap, musky deodorant and some nauseating, cheap, in-your-face men's cologne. He had a receding chin, sloping shoulders and a mean, injured-looking mouth crowded with strong, yellowish teeth. The front teeth were crooked, as if they had been fighting one another for space over the years. He blinked and swallowed too often. There was a constantly aggressive, edgy air about him, as though he expected to be punched at any second. Justine wished *she* could punch him, beat him up so badly that he wouldn't dare come near her again. Why the hell wouldn't he leave her alone? He must know by now she didn't want him – she'd made it clear often enough.

This was something that happened to other women she heard about on the news or read about in the papers. Unlucky, unhappy women who lived in fear and couldn't take control of their lives. Not *her*. At least Matthew only hung around Brooks & Wilde. He didn't know where she lived. She couldn't stop him pestering her at work but her home phone number was unlisted, thanks to her and Adam's determination to avoid being plagued by people selling magazines, time-share holidays, double glazing, political parties.

'Come for a drink with me?' Matthew asked. 'We can go in your car. Mine's at the garage. I'll drive if you like,' he offered, grinning at her shocked expression. Justine shouldn't be at the wheel of a BMW, he thought. She belonged in the passenger seat. Lying back with no knickers on! He hadn't managed to pass his driving test after all these years, but she didn't need to know that. So what? Look at the way most people who had licences drove.

His uninsured white Ford Fiesta was parked outside the flat in Linnet Lane because he had no cash for petrol. Again. He felt in his pockets, hoped he had enough to buy Justine at least one drink. She probably liked white wine, or vodka with ice and lemon and lots of tonic. He gazed at her beautiful nervous face, the full bust beneath the thin dress. Her porcelain skin was flushed across the cheekbones. He loved her sweet clear voice, longed to lay gentle hold of a springy red-gold curl and twist it around his finger. Put his hands on her body. Matthew also loved the fact that he could sense, smell her fear.

'No, I won't come for a drink with you,' she said in a low angry voice. 'Leave me alone, Matthew. *Please!*' She hated herself for that 'please'.

6

'Hey, come on!' he said roughly. 'Don't be like that.'

'I mean it.' Justine steeled herself to look at him, at the staring eyes in his pinched face, the hideous blob of mucus. 'Stop following me! Three weeks now ... it's beyond a joke! If you don't leave me alone, I'll call the police.'

Fat lot of good that would do, she thought angrily. They would blame her for being female, twenty-eight and out alone. Or just plain paranoid.

'I only talk to you!' Matthew burst out, making her jump with fright. 'There's no one else in my life, I swear.' He wouldn't mention ugly fat bimbo Tracey. She was nothing. Not even a convenience, the way she nagged lately.

'I can believe that.' Bloody nutter, Justine thought. She turned and walked down the narrow side street where her car was parked, thumb poised over the remote control button. She hated the way he walked so close, hated the smell of his over-soaped and deodorized body. Maybe he had one of those washing manias – what did Adam call it? Ablutomania.

She reached the car, stopped and faced him. 'This is my last day at work for a month,' she said, breaking her rule about not revealing anything personal. Might as well tell him, make sure he got the simple message so far obscured by ego, stupidity, testosterone. 'D'you know why?'

'Course not,' Matthew said impatiently. He stared at her. 'Are you off on holiday?' Dismay swept over him. He didn't have the money to buy her a glass of white wine, never mind follow her abroad!

'I'm getting married,' she said coldly. 'Getting married to the man I've loved for two years. He's rich and handsome and successful. Not some sad bastard who hangs around dribbling over women who don't want him.' Being next to her car and seeing people walk by gave her courage. 'I don't want you, d'you get it?' She raised her voice. 'Leave – me – *alone*!'

'Getting married?' Shock flooded through him and he felt devastated, crushed by a terrible blow. 'You can't!' he exclaimed, horrified. His sickly white skin bloomed crimson.

'I can do what the hell I like! For your information.'

'You're lying,' he said. 'You're just saying that to get rid of me. It won't work.'

'This is unreal!' Justine's eyes held contempt for him, anger

7

and resentment warring with fear. 'So you know I want to get rid of you?' she flashed. 'You can't be all that thick then. I'm warning you for the last time.' Her voice shook. 'I mean it about the police.'

She unlocked the door, tossed jacket and bag on to the passenger seat. Matthew stared at her, stunned. His mind flashed back to the time he'd first seen her, on the train to Central Station that beautiful fateful July morning. Justine had looked bored, half asleep as she sipped coffee from a polystyrene cup. He recalled his shock of delight, the utter instant conviction that she was the one. The train was delayed in the tunnel and he started to talk to her. Of course she was shy, a bit cool and distant. Although polite. Justine was sweet, beautiful, respectable. Knew she had to be wary of strange men. He realized it would take time for her to trust him, open up to him a bit more. But that was weeks ago now. Surely he'd given her enough time. Suppressed anger and frustration rose in him, bubbled over.

'Hang on a minute!' He grabbed her arm, digging his bony fingers into the smooth flesh. Justine gasped with shock and pain.

'Don't you dare touch me!' She struggled furiously. 'Let *go*!'

'We've known each other long enough,' Matthew said hoarsely. 'I can understand you playing hard to get at first, but it's about time you gave me a bloody break!'

'I don't want you!' she shouted, on the verge of panic. She loathed his touch, his soapy, musky smell, felt she would faint or throw up or go crazy if she didn't escape. Her skin crawled and she broke out in a cold sweat. 'Let go of me, you bastard!'

'Hey! Don't you fucking talk to me like that!' Matthew grabbed both her arms and shook her hard.

'Help!' she screamed. 'Help me!'

People glanced nervously at them, averted their eyes, hurried past. This bastard could rape her, beat her up, kidnap her right here and obviously no one would do a bloody thing about it! Justine was furious, terrified, seething with outrage. She didn't try to knee Matthew in the groin. That wasn't as easy as it looked, and might only make him more angry. She lashed out instead and kicked his leg so hard she hoped his shin would crack.

'Ow!' His grip slackened and he let go of her left arm. Justine clenched her fist, keys tight between her fingers, and punched him hard on the nose. The keys cut him, drew blood. He let go and

staggered backwards, his eyes filling with tears. ⟨…⟩
the car, slammed and locked the doors, then screamed with ⟨…⟩
sion. The blob of green mucus had come off on her knuckle.

'Justine! Wait!' He banged on the window.

'Piss off!' she screamed. Her fingers trembled as she stuck the key in the ignition and started the engine. It choked and stalled. She swore, started to cry.

'Justine!' he yelled. 'Open this sodding door. *Now*!'

Matthew banged on the roof and bonnet, his face a mask of fury. His nose was bleeding. The thuds rocked the car, reverberated through her body. She revved the engine and tried desperately to concentrate as she manoeuvred out of the tight parking space. If the damn' thing hadn't been in the garage that sunny July day she'd never have got the train to work and been hit on by Matthew whatever-his-bloody-name-was! She accelerated away and narrowly avoided crashing into a middle-aged hippie on a Harley-Davidson.

'You stupid cow!' He swerved, stopped the bike and stuck his middle finger in the air, sunglasses glinting.

'This is a one-way street,' she shouted. 'Get an eye test!'

She was breathing hard, trembling, cold sweat prickling her breasts and armpits. Tears of fright rolled down her face. She glanced in the driving mirror and saw Matthew running after the car, fists clenched, his rabbit jaw rigid with fury. He stopped abruptly and doubled over, gasping for breath. She sped off, leaving him and the hippie behind.

Justine grabbed a tissue and scrubbed furiously at her knuckle as she drove, keeping an eye out for other morons who couldn't read road signs. Matthew was crazy, she thought, obsessed. Was she his first obsession or did he have a history that went way back? He might be a rapist or murderer for all she knew.

'Oh, great!' she whispered, screwing the tissue into a ball. 'That's cheered me right up, that has!'

Would Matthew stop now that he knew she was getting married? He viewed women as consumer items to be coveted and possessed by any male with sufficient physical strength or economic power. Or both. He might get bored and give up now that she was – according to his warped logic – another man's possession. If not, what the hell was she going to do? She wound down the window and threw away the tissue, grabbed another to wipe her tears.

9

the soft, grass-scented late-
...n the open window did nothing to
...y city centre behind, heading for leafy
...t. She tuned the radio to a classical station
...nish guitar music as she drove. It only made her
...e. She longed to feel Adam's arms around her
...er close, be comforted by his calm voice and his hard
... body. She could tell Donna that tonight was off, go to him
right now.

'No!' she whispered. 'I won't let that bastard get to me.'

Who was she kidding? Matthew *had* got to her. This time she'd
fought back, called him a bastard, lashed out and injured him. She
recalled his furious eyes, the blood on his face, his white corpse-
like fingers digging into her arm. Bruising the flesh, hurting her.

Panic gripped her again. Something had changed today. Battle
lines were drawn. All because she had broken her cardinal rule.

To keep things polite.

# Chapter Two

Justine was lying about getting married, Matthew decided. Women loved to lie, flirt, play games. But what kind of crazy game was a punch on the nose? Although it hurt like hell, the shock was worse than the pain. The humiliation was like a strange taste in his mouth, an indefinable physical sensation. How could she have done that to him? His nose dripped blood and his shin hurt so much he couldn't walk properly. She'd drawn blood there too. He swore.

He limped back to Lord Street and stood on the corner breathing traffic fumes, shading his eyes from the sun. He felt hot, frustrated, furious that she'd outwitted him and escaped. If only he had a flash car like hers! He would know every detail of her life by now. But a knackered Ford Fiesta couldn't compete with a BMW, even when the Ford Fiesta had a tank full of petrol.

Where was Justine going? To meet the man she said she'd loved for two years? Have sex with him? Matthew groaned, feeling agonized by the thought of some other man putting his dirty hands on her beautiful body. No. She was lying. Justine belonged to him, she had to realize that. He was her destiny. Fate, kismet, karma, whatever. She was testing him, wanted him to show her he was boss. Fine! He could play games too, if that was what she wanted. And win.

He blew his nose again and wiped more blood off his face. His nose throbbed and the cuts stung. He gingerly poked the bloodied pink tissue into a nearby bin that overflowed with crushed fast-food cartons. He needed to wash his face and hands. People darted curious, nervous glances at him and looked hastily away when they caught his angry eye.

'You hurt me,' he muttered, sniffing blood. 'You'll be sorry for that, Justine.'

So she was frightened – big deal! Not frightened enough. He'd had it with her bullshit. He couldn't even find out where she lived. She wasn't in the phone book. The receptionist at Brooks & Wilde refused to give out any information about Justine Flynn. Except that she was unable to take his calls.

Might as well get the bus back to Linnet Lane, watch telly and eat whatever Tracey was cooking that evening. Suddenly he remembered: Friday was her step class. She went straight from work and drank in the pub with her mates afterwards. Got home around eleven, wearing black lycra tights and a shiny pink leotard beneath her mac or long jacket. He'd have to dine on crisps and peanuts or microwave himself a salty TV dinner. He wasn't sure how the microwave worked. Watch *Star Trek* and *The Simpsons*. There were only a few beers in the fridge, half a bottle of inky French red on the kitchen table. He didn't have enough money to go to the pub and get pissed.

How could he find out where Justine lived? He thought for a moment then turned and walked slowly back to her office building. The advertising agency was on the second floor. You pressed a bell to gain entry, then took the lift or stairs. He'd never seen anyone who looked like a security guard. It was a small agency, as far as he could tell. Justine sometimes came and went with a blonde girl of about nineteen who favoured leather mini skirts, an older woman with dark hair and the same taste in clothes as the girl, or two middle-aged men in sharp suits. He'd never seen her with anyone else. The men skived off early on Friday, like most people. He'd seen them leave while he waited for Justine.

Matthew crossed the road, hesitated, then pressed the bell beside the gleaming brass plate with *Brooks & Wilde, Advertising Agency* engraved on it. He had no idea what he was going to do. He only wanted to see where Justine worked. He felt nervous, excited. Close to her. He sniffed the air like a hyena scenting prey. The pain in his shin had eased slightly. When the buzzer sounded he pushed open the door, walked into a cool dark hall and up two short flights of stairs. He didn't use the lift because there was a security camera in it.

'Can I help you?' The slim blonde girl in the small plant-filled reception area smiled politely at him. She wore a sleeveless black chiffon top with beading around the neckline, and her favourite black leather mini skirt. 'I'm just packing up,' she said. She glanced helplessly at the mess of papers and yellow cardboard files that littered her desk. In one corner of it was a security monitor and video. Three closed doors nearby presumably led to offices. Which one was Justine's?

'I've got an appointment with Mr Wilde,' Matthew said importantly.

She looked at him, surprised. 'I'm afraid Mr Wilde's gone home.' So had everyone else, but she didn't want this guy to know that. He looked like he'd been in a fight. Was that blood caked around his nostrils? 'Er – what did you want to see him about?' I don't believe that jacket! she thought.

'I've been doing a job at his house. Me and my mate. Repairing the gutters. He said to come to the office before closing time and he'd give me a cheque.' Matthew grinned unpleasantly. 'Here I am.'

She looked blank. 'I'm afraid I don't know anything about it.' She hesitated. 'Are you sure you've come to the right place?' This guy didn't look like he repaired gutters. There was something about him that bothered her. She couldn't imagine Anthony Wilde hiring a character like this in the first place, let alone telling him to come to the office for a cheque. It didn't make sense. Actually, it sounded crazy!

'This is Brooks and Wilde, the advertising agency, isn't it?' The girl swallowed, nodded. What was wrong with her? Matthew thought angrily. He looked clean, didn't he? Respectable. Just because he wasn't some arrogant sod in a three-piece pinstripe! 'Yeah, sure it's the right place! See if he's left the cheque on his desk, will you?' he asked casually. 'I've got another job first thing Monday morning, I don't want to have to come back here.'

'He's locked his door,' she said hesitantly.

'Got a spare key, haven't you?' This dozy bitch was beginning to irritate him. 'Come on,' he urged. 'I can't hang around here all night.'

Desperate to get rid of him, she took the spare key from the top drawer of her desk, walked self-consciously across the reception area and unlocked the middle of the three doors. Matthew glanced around, looked at the two filing cabinets behind her desk. How could he get what he wanted? A minute later the girl came out.

'I can't find any cheque on his desk,' she said nervously. 'Or in it.' She tossed back her long straight hair. 'I could phone him at home or on his mobile,' she offered. 'Ask him about . . .'

'That's no use,' Matthew interrupted. 'It's no good, I'll have to come back on Monday. Can I use the gents?' he asked, glancing around again.

'Down the hall on your left.' She pointed.

'Ta.' The receptionist watched as he walked slowly towards the men's toilet. Matthew opened the door, walked in and smiled as he looked around. He'd never been in such a posh bog before. It smelled of soap and expensive aftershave instead of stale pee. He studied his reddened nose and cheeks in the polished mirror, winced as he touched the two cuts made by the keys. What would Justine think if she knew where he was right now?

His nose looked sunburned as well as swollen. His white skin never tanned, only went bright red. He remembered a summer day when he was eighteen and his mother had told him malt vinegar mixed with salad oil made good suntan lotion. Of course he hadn't had money to buy proper stuff. His skin had burned and blistered in the hot sun, resulting in days of agony followed by days of being ankle-deep in huge skin flakes. He had a feeling his mother had done it deliberately.

Suddenly he had a brilliant idea that filled him with excitement, made him laugh out loud. So Justine thought he was a filthy bastard, did she? Thought he was stupid? She'd soon find out different. He peed, zipped up his trousers, carefully washed his hands and face, and went back to reception. The girl jumped, looked warily at him as he approached her desk. Matthew didn't like that.

'Ta, love.' He grinned. 'See you Monday.'

'Mr Wilde should be in around nine-thirty,' she said quietly, her eyes lowered. She couldn't wait for him to leave. There was something weird about him. Whatever it was, Anthony Wilde could sort out the guy himself.

She must be the bitch who'd given him the brush-off over the phone earlier this afternoon, Matthew thought. Her light voice sounded familiar. Maybe Justine had told her not to put his calls through. They probably made fun of him together, had a good laugh. Anger rose in him and constricted his throat. He turned and walked out.

14

The tired, nervous receptionist closed and locked the filing cabinet and sighed with relief as she heard the heavy door slam. She hurried into the adjoining cloakroom for her handbag and the plastic carrier bag full of shopping. Weekend at last! The phone rang and she swore as she snatched it up.

'Kevin? I know I'm late,' she said impatiently. 'Don't worry, I'll be there. Just got a few more things to do first, okay?'

Distracted by the phone call, she forgot to glance at the security monitor. If she had, she would have noticed that the departing visitor's cropped head and sloping shoulders did not appear on the black-and-white screen.

Justine pulled into the driveway of the big old house in Aigburth Drive, Sefton Park. A tall slim girl with long shiny dark brown hair who was lounging against one of the stone gateposts waved and ran laughing after the car. She had lively brown eyes, a heart-shaped face and smooth olive skin, and wore black cargo pants and a sleeveless lime green lycra top. She carried a canvas ruck-sack. She stopped laughing when she caught sight of Justine's tearstained face.

'What's wrong?' she asked anxiously as Justine got out of the car, white-faced and trembling. 'Oh, no!' she gasped. 'Don't tell me that creep was waiting for you again?'

'He was more aggressive this time.' Justine slammed and locked the car door. 'Wanted me to go for a drink with him right there and then. Of course I wouldn't have plans of my own, would I? I only exist for his convenience! He even wanted me to let him drive my car! When I tried to get away he grabbed me.' She sniffed and wiped her eyes.

'You're joking?' Donna exclaimed, staring at her in horror.

'I wish! I nearly crashed the car, I was so freaked out. What's wrong with men like that?' she asked wildly. 'I've told him God knows how many times that I'm not bloody interested! What does it take? If someone didn't fancy me I'd back off right away, develop an instant complex about being a charmless bore.'

'He's probably a pathetic loser who can't get a life. Or in the grip of some raving personality disorder.'

'Whatever it is, it's doing my head in! I suppose he set fires and tortured animals when he was little,' Justine said bitterly. 'No one spotted his psychopathic tendencies early enough.'

'Hey! What happened to your arm?' She winced as Donna carefully touched her bruised flesh.

'He did that.' Justine's voice shook. 'When he grabbed me.'

'My *God!* Justine, he's gone too far this time. You have to call the police.'

'I'll think about it. Have you got a cigarette, Donna?'

'You've stopped smoking, remember?' Her friend hugged her. 'Come on,' she said comfortingly. 'Let's go up to your flat and get you a nice big glass of wine. What time will Adam be home?' she asked.

A guilty pang of frustrated desire ran through her as she thought of tall, broad-shouldered Adam Shaw, Justine's flancé, with his low sexy laugh, gorgeous luminous brown eyes and head of dark tangled curls. He was the sexiest man she'd ever seen. Stop it! she told herself. Justine was her best friend. A very upset best friend. It was typical of her bad luck to be crazy about a man she could never have. This was one secret she could never tell Justine.

'He won't be home for hours.' Justine brushed away more tears. 'He doesn't finish at the surgery until seven, then he's being wined and dined by a couple of incandescently boring medical reps. They invited him to bring his *partner*,' she grimaced, 'but I declined. Anyway, I'd arranged to meet you. I'm not going to change my plans because of that creep!'

'Let's go up to the flat,' Donna urged. 'We can go out for that pizza later.'

'Okay.' Justine wiped her eyes, hesitated. 'Let me put the car away first.'

'It's all right here, isn't it?' Donna watched Justine as she glanced nervously around at the trees and bushes, the old iron railings and the high redbrick garden walls, the lush green park across the wide road. 'You always leave your car in the drive. So does Adam.'

'I want to put it away now,' Justine said, avoiding Donna's worried gaze.

'Fine.' Her friend shrugged.' I'll wait on your front doorstep.'

Justine got back in the BMW and drove slowly around the left side of the house, bumped the car down the long cinder path to the garages at the foot of the back garden. That was why the tenants usually left their cars in the driveway; it was a pain walking all the way back up the cinder path. Especially in the cold or rain or pitch dark, when you never knew who might be lurking amongst the trees and bushes. The basement flat had been burgled twice. It was almost September and there was a chill smoky whiff of autumn in the air, despite the warm sun. The nights were closing in. Normally she wouldn't have noticed it yet. She did now. Because of Matthew.

She felt better when the BMW was stowed out of sight in the big garage that had formerly been a coach house. As she walked back up the cinder path she waved politely to Marinda and Charley Bluff, the house owners, who sat drinking and smoking on their sunny walled-in terrace with its wrought-iron gate. They occupied the ground-floor flat. Beyond the terrace was Marinda's beloved rose garden, and acres of freshly mown green lawn.

'Hello, Justine!' Marinda, a slim sprightly tanned little woman in her seventies with long wispy dyed blonde hair, stood up and waved enthusiastically. Charley, her daughter, also waved. She was slumped on a flowered lounger, stomach and breasts bulging through her white nurse's dress. She was smoking a cigarette and swilling Scotch, thin eyebrows drawn together in her habitual scowl. Their rottweiler, Whitney, dozed at her feet.

'Come and have a drink,' Charley shouted.

'I can't right now,' Justine called back. 'I'm going out with a friend.'

'Pop in soon then, okay?'

'Thanks, I will. See you!' Charley and Marinda weren't exactly her and Adam's cup of tea, but Justine didn't mind having a drink with them occasionally. Right now she had other things on her mind.

'So it's my word against his,' she said to Donna when they were sprawled on the sofas in the living room of the big flat at the top of the house. The high-ceilinged room had a polished wooden floor and a tall grey marble mantelpiece. The walls were painted white. Three long sash windows overlooked the driveway and park. Justine was drinking a glass of white wine and smoking one of Donna's cigarettes. 'If I call the police he could say we had a fight. Which he got the worst of,' she added.

'*Yes!*' Donna clenched her fist and laughed. 'Good on you, giving him a bloody nose.' She raised her glass. 'Cheers! Okay, maybe that's true,' she admitted, 'but don't you think if you told

17

the police it might give him a fright? Make him realize you mean business? If he doesn't already!'

'I think it would just make him more angry. I antagonized him today.' She sipped more wine. 'I shouldn't have done that,' she said worriedly.

'For Christ's sake, Justine! *You* haven't done anything. This Matthew character hit on you. He's stalking you, projecting his twisted delusions.'

'Now I know why I gave up these things.' Justine coughed and stubbed out the cigarette, made a face. 'They taste horrible when you haven't had one for months. It's not *stalking*, Donna,' she said impatiently.

'What would you call it then?'

'Look . . .' Justine sighed, drank more wine. 'I've got a month off work. Adam and I will be married in a week and off to the Caribbean. When we come back we'll move into our new house in Childwall – once we've got rid of those bloody builders! Matthew pesters me at work, but he doesn't know where I live. He knows nothing about me – except that I don't want him! He'll get bored, give up. I won't call the police,' she said shortly. 'It wouldn't help. You hear a lot about stalking nowadays,' she went on as Donna opened her mouth to protest. 'The police might think I'm paranoid, jumping on some crazy bandwagon. I've got no evidence.'

'*What*?' Donna raised her eyebrows. 'He hangs around your place of work and pesters you when you enter or leave. He phones you there – the receptionist will verify that. He grabbed you today, bruised your arm. Have you heard of the Protection from Harassment Act?'

'Of course I have. Harassment is still very hard to prove. And even if I could prove it, he might end up with nothing more than a fine and a warning in the first instance. Next time around, six months in jail – *maybe*.'

'Okay, so they won't lock him up tonight. But you could take out an injunction.'

'Yeah, run up a load of solicitor's fees! And would he take any notice of it anyway? Besides, I don't even know his surname or where he lives. Donna, please don't go on about it,' Justine said in a low voice. She picked up the wine bottle and refilled their glasses. 'I want to marry Adam, go on honeymoon and forget all

18

about that lowlife.' She dumped the bottle on the coffee table. 'And that's what I intend to do,' she said firmly.

'Justine . . .', Donna looked at her friend's beautiful troubled face and smiled sadly. 'We've been friends ever since that freezing day in junior school when you thumped Terence Walsh because he pushed me and sent me flying on the ice. You're my best friend and a great person,' she said gently. 'I hate to see you like this. I'm sure Adam does too.' Justine was silent, staring into her wine glass. 'Being a nurse,' Donna went on, 'I get fed up when I see patients who wouldn't have needed major surgery if they'd had minor symptoms sorted . . .'

'Or hadn't kept screwing the wrong men because of warped judgement due to excess use of recreational drugs,' Justine teased. 'What are you on about?'

'Funny, ha-ha.' She tapped Justine's smooth cool bare arm with her finger. 'You know what I'm on about.' She paused. 'Get this sorted. Now!'

Justine sighed. 'I told you, Donna, forget the police. I don't want the hassle.'

'What do you think you've had these past three weeks?'

'It's over now. By the time I go back to work he'll have given up. I know you mean well but . . .' She gasped and flinched, turning pale at the sound of screeching tyres and blaring horns outside. 'My God! What's that?' She leapt up, one hand to her throat. Her wine glass crashed to the floor.

'Hey, take it easy!' Donna got up and went to the windows, peering out over Aigburth Drive and the leafy green mass of Sefton Park. The big chestnut trees along the drive met overhead. 'Can't see. Probably just idiots acting macho,' she said dismissively. She turned back to Justine and studied her pale frightened face. 'D'you know what that's called?' she asked grimly. 'Your reaction?'

'Jumping out of my skin?' Justine gave a nervous laugh.

'It's called exaggerated startle reaction. A symptom of continual stress or trauma. It wants sorting. Like your denial. Like the minor symptoms I was on about.'

'All right,' Justine said stonily. 'You've made your point.' She looked at the spilled wine spreading over the floorboards. 'Can we please go out?' she asked. 'After I've wiped up this mess, of course. I'd like to go for that pizza, as we arranged, then to the pub afterwards. I want to have a laugh, not talk about that Matthew bastard all evening.' She missed Adam, wanted him desperately. 'It's over, Donna,' she said firmly. 'Okay, what happened today was horrible. I admit, it really shook me. But there's no way he'll keep hanging around Brooks & Wilde when I don't appear. It's *over*,' she repeated.

She wished she truly could believe that. She had to if her life was ever going to be normal again.

# Chapter Three

Justine's small office overlooked the street. The room smelled of her, of the light fresh perfume she wore. A neatly folded pile of newspapers was stacked on a chair by the window. On the desk was a word processor and laser printer, a Bird's Nest fern with long curled bright green leaves, and a little green Connemara marble bowl. Nothing else. Matthew longed to steal the cute little bowl. But that would be a dead giveaway. He laughed. He couldn't believe he was doing this. It was better than *Star Trek* any day of the week!

He turned and walked back to the tiny cloakroom to stand over the prone figure of the bound and gagged receptionist. She lay on the floor, her hazel eyes staring up at him in panic. Long strands of blonde hair fell over her sweating, terrified face.

'Don't move!' he shouted, kicking her in the hip. 'Don't try anything stupid. I'll kill you if you do. Are you listening, you bitch?'

She moaned and nodded, flexed her tightly tied wrists. She'd thought he was going to rape her when he'd ambushed her in the hall before she could set the alarm, punched her to the ground and dragged off her tights and pants. He'd used the pants to gag her and the black tights to bind her wrists. Her ankles were tied with the silk designer scarf she'd so thoughtfully purchased during her lunchtime shopping expedition. Matthew checked that she wasn't wriggling out of her bonds the way victims in films always managed to do. He grinned. She wasn't going anywhere. He stared at her, wishing it was Justine lying there bound and helpless.

He went back to Anthony Wilde's poncy office with its beige

leather sofas and big framed pictures of various products and their slogans on the walls. A heavy mahogany block was propped on the desk, *Anthony J. Wilde* carved on it in ponderous gothic lettering. Next door to the office was a conference room.

'Wanker!' he murmured, staring at the block of wood.

Matthew had found Justine's personnel file in Wilde's office, aided by the terrified receptionist. He opened the yellow cardboard file and drew out the neatly printed curriculum vitae. His mouth was open, eyes shining with excitement. He sniffed, scratched his chin.

'Got you!' he whispered, smilling. 'You're *mine*, Justine!'

He stared at the passport-sized photo of her beautiful face. Justine's gorgeous dark blue eyes looked straight into his. There was a glint of humour in them and her red lips were pressed together, as if she was making a big effort to look serious. The wild curls were pushed back to reveal her cheekbones. He read the vital details: Justine Flynn was twenty-eight years old, birthday 25 May. There was a long list of academic qualifications. She had an MA in Metaphysics and a degree in Communications Studies.

Matthew's eyebrows shot up and he whistled contemptuously. What did she want to bother with that crap for? What the hell was metaphysics anyway? He grinned. He'd ask Justine before he screwed her into screaming, begging submission. He sniffed and his thin lips tightened. No more stupid lying games!

Before joining Brooks & Wilde she had been an executive officer in the Civil Service and, briefly, a rep for a pharmaceutical company. She had spent a lot of time travelling in Europe, the USA, Asia and Australia. He himself had never been further than Wales, the Lake District and the Isle of Man, dragged there by his parents on boring caravan holidays. Then his father had snuffed it, thank God, and the holidays had stopped. Justine's interests were listed as reading, writing, travelling, and various sports. Matthew laughed at that and nodded approvingly; he too would have lied about liking sports. He read her address and gasped with excitement.

'Aigburth Drive, Sefton Park. Bloody hell!' Fate kicking in again. She lived only ten or fifteen minutes' walk away from him, in one of those big old houses across the road from the park. Most of them had been converted to flats. Linnet Lane, where he lived with Tracey, was close to popular Lark Lane, with its shops and restaurants and pubs. Justine and her friends probably went to Lark Lane often.

'Seffy Park!' He laughed again, shook his head. He checked himself and glanced around nervously. He ran to the photocopier, switched it on and waited impatiently for it to warm up. He photocopied the A4 pages, folded them and stuck them in his inside jacket pocket, clicked the blue button off again. He replaced Justine's file in the top drawer and closed the filing cabinet.

He'd go to Sefton Park and hide behind one of the big leafy chestnut trees that lined Aigburth Drive, join the joggers, snoggers and dog walkers while he checked out Justine's house. Was she there now or out with friends? She wouldn't be with that rich, handsome, successful fiancé. He existed only in her lying, manipulative, game-playing feminine mind!

Matthew frowned. What to do about the receptionist? She didn't know his name or who he was but she would recognize him again, give a description to the police. He didn't want Justine to know he'd been here – not yet anyway. He wanted gradually to reveal what he knew about her life, let her torture herself with fear wondering how he'd found out. He would be in her head every minute of every day. Just as she was in his.

He froze in panic as the outer door slammed and slow heavy footsteps walked down the hall. Who the bloody hell was that? They mustn't see him or he was finished. He thought of the receptionist lying there waiting to be rescued. Waiting to talk. What he'd done would be labelled kidnapping, assault and battery. It would take more than a visit to the Magistrates Court and a few hours' community service to wriggle out from under that lot.

'Shit!' he breathed. 'Shit! Shit!' He glanced wildly around the office and his eyes locked on Anthony Wilde's carved block of mahogany. He grabbed it with both hands and darted behind the door, holding his breath. The wood felt very heavy. 'Hello?' a man's hoarse voice panted. 'I see you've all buggered off home and forgotten to set the alarm. Stupid sods!' he muttered.

There was silence, except for the man's laboured breathing. Matthew lifted the block of wood, gripped it as tightly as he could, and stepped out from behind the door. His heart raced, thudded against his ribcage. He saw the back of a short stocky man dressed in black trousers and a blue shirt, hands on his broad hips. He looked like a security guard from a private firm. Matthew bit his lips, swore silently. He should have let the receptionist set the alarm and de-activated it later. This wasn't supposed to happen. He was in big trouble now.

The guard looked at the receptionist's desk and the security monitor. He took off his cap and scratched his balding head. He was about to replace the cap when he heard grunting and mewing sounds coming from the cloakroom.

'Who's there?' he called. He put down his cap and the van keys, walked slowly around the desk and stood in the cloakroom doorway. The bound and gagged figure of the receptionist lay there, her shopping scattered around her. She wriggled furiously and stared up at him, eyes frantic with warning.

'Bloody hell!' he exclaimed, shocked. In eighteen months of security work this was his first emergency. What was going on? Should he untie her first or search the office? Whoever had tied her up might still be here. 'Okay, love,' he said. 'Hang on a sec, all right? I'll just . . .'

He turned to look around. Matthew leapt forward and brought the block of wood crashing down on his head. The guard caught a glimpse of panicked brown eyes, gleaming brass buttons and beige trousers with knife-edge creases; he smelled soap and after-shave as he collapsed like a stone. Matthew brought the block of wood down again and again, smashing it on the guard's vulnerable balding head as he lay prone, grunting with effort as he used all his strength to crush the man's skull. The receptionist winced, trembled and screwed her eyes shut as she heard and felt the horrible thuds. Jumbled snatches of prayers she hadn't said since childhood ran through her brain. She started to cry, her body shaking uncontrollably.

'You stupid bastard!' Matthew shouted at the dead guard. 'What d'you want to come in here interfering for? This is your own stupid fucking fault!' The beige carpet, the desk drawers, the block of mahogany, his own trousers, were spattered with dark blood. 'Think!' he muttered. 'Don't lose it!'

He had to wipe his fingerprints off whatever he'd touched. He grabbed the receptionist's empty carrier bag and dropped the block of wood and the security monitor videotape into it. He paused for a second, breathing hard. Suddenly he grinned and relaxed slightly. He'd just battered a man to death with a block of wood, but he could still think straight, cover his tracks. How many people would be capable of that?

'No flies on you, Matthew lad!' he whispered proudly.

He darted around wiping the photocopier, the filing-cabinet drawers and keys, door handles, the marble bowl on Justine's desk. He fished the guard's wallet out of his back pocket and unfastened the man's wristwatch, trying not to look at the hideous bloody raw mess that just a few minutes ago had been a human face. He shoved the wallet in his pocket, grabbed the van keys, and ran to look out of Justine's office window.

The street was quiet, a few people coming out of offices and heading for their parked cars or the nearest bus stop. A small dark blue van with the security firm's logo painted on it in gold was parked outside. What time was it? He glanced at the watch: 6.50. He'd use the van to make a getaway, dump it in some deserted spot miles from here. In the river, maybe. Matthew frowned, blinking furiously. There was one last problem he had to take care of.

He walked back to the cloakroom and stood over the helpless receptionist.

Tears were rolling down her face. His own panic was forgotten and he was hard, filled with excitement and a terrific sense of power.

He had always dreamed of killing, fantasized about it. In his fantasies he'd killed women, not men. The women were always beautiful, naked, terrified, screaming in pain and fear as he used them ruthlessly. Now all those anonymous female bodies had a face. Justine's.

He was doing this for her. So that they could be together. One day she would understand. He stooped and untied the scarf that bound the receptionist's thin ankles. Her bare feet immediately kicked up at him.

'Stop that, you bitch!' he shouted, enraged. He'd already been kicked like a dog today. No one, not even Justine, would do that to him again. He unfastened the girl's tight leather mini skirt and dragged it off. She moaned and struggled beneath him, her terrifed eyes pleading desperately as he knotted the scarf around her throat. Matthew unzipped his jeans and climbed on top of her, pulled out a condom and rolled it on. He didn't want his DNA inside her for some forensic pathologist to find. His bony fingers clenched the scarf around her throat as he used all his strength to pull it tight, tighter. He shut his eyes.

'Justine,' he panted. 'Justine!' He came, the strength of the orgasm making him tremble and cry out. He whimpered, blinked back tears. He was sweating profusely and his body felt weak, drained, like the time he'd got food poisoning from a dodgy hamburger. He slackened his grip on the scarf, slowly raised his head and looked down at the girl.

She lay still, staring beyond him into another world. The gag had worked loose and her tongue protruded obscenely.

Her eyes had stopped pleading.

# Chapter Four

Charley Bluff and her rottweiler came out of the house and down the dark, tree-lined driveway, crossed the wide road and headed for one of the dirt tracks that led into Sefton Park. Charley had changed into a peach-coloured cotton sweater and matching baggy cotton trousers. She lit a cigarette and inhaled deeply.

The moon and stars were out and there was a slight chill in the grass-scented air. Charley dreaded autumn and winter; no more hot afternoons baking her tits on the terrace while she drank Scotch or Southern Comfort and inhaled delicious cigarette smoke along with the perfume of roses. She and Marinda seemed to get on better outdoors, although her mother grumbled about her going topless and said her father would turn in his grave. As they reached the track Whitney stopped and growled low in her throat.

'What is it, baby doll?' Charley asked softly. She patted the dog's broad back and glanced around. She stiffened and her ciga-rette-free hand closed over the CS gas canister in her trouser pocket as she spotted a tall gangly figure a few yards away, standing by one of the chestnut trees. This was no jogger pausing to stretch seized up leg muscles. The man seemed to be hiding behind the tree, watching their house. She was instantly alert, filled with suspicion.

Charley wasn't too frightened, not with a rottweiler and CS gas canister for protection. She was strong and solidly built – fat, Marinda said! – and confident that she could fight off an attacker. She dropped her cigarette and trod on it, switched on her powerful C-cell, police-type, aluminium flashlight that held four batteries, and shone it in the man's direction.

'Hello?' she called challengingly. 'Can I help you?' He turned and walked quickly away, hands over his face. He wore light-coloured trousers and shirt, a dark jacket with gleaming buttons. Whitney barked at the retreating figure.

'Shh, baby doll. It's all right.' Charley patted the dog again. 'Definitely up to no good!' she muttered. She lit another cigarette and carried on down the narrow track into the park. An innocent person would have stood their ground, she thought, protested about the powerful flashlight trained on them. Was he some loitering mugger or drug addict? He didn't look like one, but you couldn't always tell. A wannabe burglar? There were a lot of break-ins around here. She peered at her gold Rolex. Almost eleven-thirty.

She removed the rottweiler's lead and threw a stick. Whitney dashed off, barking excitedly. Charley gripped the flashlight and stood watching and smoking. She smiled grimly. If some burglar tried to break into her and Mum's place they would get more than they'd bargained for! There was the alarm system, the didgeridoo – handmade by Aborigines in Australia's Northern Territory – that she kept by her bed, the terrifying *kris* dagger that Dad had brought back from his years in Malaysia. Best of all, his old army revolver with which he'd shot dead the escaping SS officer in 1945. Dad's gun was now deemed an illegal weapon – ridiculous! – but there was no way she would ever surrender it to the police.

Whitney squatted and peed against a tree, growled and barked at the distant sound of a fox. There were lots of foxes in the park; their cry sounded like a human scream. The lake shimmered in the moonlight. Tears pricked at Charley's eyes as she thought of her father, dead last year from a massive heart attack. She missed him on these walks; missed drinking with him in the drawing room at night, or on the terrace when the weather was sunny. It had always been the two of them against the world. She took a last drag on the cigarette, threw the glowing stub down and ground it into the earth with her heel.

She and the rottweiler were coming out of the park when she stopped and gasped with shock. The man was back, standing between the stone gateposts of their driveway. His hands were clenched in his jacket pockets, his sloping shoulders rigid as he stared at the house. She took a deep breath, marched to the edge of the pavement and glanced to right and left before crossing the road. Whitney growled and barked furiously. Startled, the man jumped and whirled round.

'Hey!' Charley shouted. 'What the hell d'you think you're doing?' She switched on the flashlight again and shone it at the man's face. He flung up his arms to protect his eyes from the dazzling beam, ducked and fled. 'That's right, get lost!' she shouted as he ran off down wide, tree-lined Aigburth Drive. 'I'll have the police on you, you scum!'

She marched up the driveway and climbed the wide stone steps to the front door, keys at the ready. Her legs felt weak and she was trembling, breathing hard. Charley suddenly felt very frightened and vulnerable, despite the rottweiler and her armoury of protection. Why was the prowler so interested in this house? *Was* he a burglar? A rapist? She shivered with fear.

There was more lowlife than wildlife around Sefton Park these days. Marinda refused to walk by herself in the park any more, when once it had been an everyday pleasure. Charley unlocked the porch door and the front door, taking care not to let Whitney race ahead of her. Rotties were darlings, but they had to know who was boss. In the long high-ceilinged hall she unfastened Whitney's lead and watched affectionately as the dog trotted off to the kitchen and her bowl of water. 'Mummy loves you!' Charley called softly.

She walked into the drawing room and sighed. Marinda was snoring in her armchair by the blazing gas fire, an empty glass and Amaretto bottle on the little table beside her. She wore her wine-stained peach satin robe, and her wispy dyed yellow hair fell over her delicate, lined face. Her mouth and chin were smeared with scarlet lipstick. The television was blaring; screeching tyres, gunshots, a woman's terrified screams. Marinda would watch any old rubbish.

'*Bloody* hell!' Charley went out of the drawing room, crossed the hall to her mother's bedroom and returned with a folded tartan blanket. 'You damn' well stay here this time,' she muttered crossly, draping the heavy blanket over the unconscious figure. 'I'm not doing my back in again trying to drag you to bed. Oh, Dad!' she sighed. 'Why aren't you here?'

She walked to the drinks table and poured herself a large cognac, paused to take a comforting swig. She switched off the television, turned the gas fire low and clicked off all the lights

29

except for one of the lamps on the tall mantelpiece. She went back into the hall and lit another cigarette, stood smoking and swigging cognac as she stared at the phone. Should she dial 999 or the local nick? Did the prowler qualify as an emergency? She decided he did. Dad wouldn't have hesitated. She put down her glass and grabbed the receiver.

'Police,' she said brusquely. 'I want to report a prowler.'

Adam Shaw's Jaguar swept into the driveway, headlights blazing. Justine's BMW wasn't there, he noted, as he drove past the front of the house and parked by the high brick wall. She would have put it in the garage and taken a cab. He hoped she and Donna hadn't gone into town. A couple of bouncers had been shot dead outside a club, and Liverpool city centre was crawling with drunks, ghoulish sightseers and armed response teams.

Adam was exhausted after his long day at the surgery and the boring dinner with the two medical reps, desperate to see Justine. He hoped she was all right and that the creep hadn't bothered her today. He wouldn't say it to her of course, but he was getting seriously worried about her safety.

He got out of the car and glanced up at the dark windows of the top flat. Justine wasn't home yet. Damn! Unless she was in bed already, warm and sleepy and naked. Ready for lovemaking. He smiled and his heartbeat quickened. He got out of the car and slammed the door, felt in his jacket pockets for the house keys.

'Adam!' a hoarse female voice shouted. 'Adam!'

'Oh, shit!' he groaned under his breath. His heart sank at the sight of beady-eyed, football-tits Charley Bluff as she stumbled down her front door steps, cigarette in one hand, tugging the growling lethal weapon by its lead. He couldn't seem to avoid her this past fortnight.

'You're working very late,' Charley called breathlessly. 'Who'd be a GP? Those patients never let you rest.' She dragged on her cigarette and burst out coughing.

What wouldn't I give for a night with him! she thought, looking at the tall, handsome, broad-shouldered man in his expensive suit. He wouldn't get any rest then either. She gazed hungrily at his sexy, generous mouth and strong, but not ridiculously strong jaw, his humorous dark eyes and the thick dark hair that curled over his high forehead. Adam was kind and friendly as well as heart-

30

stoppingly gorgeous. Otherwise she wouldn't have dared glance in his direction, let alone speak to him. Marinda never stopped singing his praises.

'Don't blame the patients.' Adam pressed the remote control device to lock the car. 'I'm not on call tonight. It was what you might term corporate hospitality.' He knew Charley Bluff fancied him, and was revolted by the thought. Justine loved to tease him about it. Although lately she had other things on her mind.

'How's Justine?' Charley asked. 'We saw her earlier, but she was on her way out. We're really looking forward to the wedding,' she said brightly. 'We've found someone to babysit Whitney for a couple of hours.'

'Oh, good.' Christ! he thought. At least she and the mad mother realized they couldn't turn up at the church with a rottweiler in tow. 'Justine's fine, thanks,' he replied. Charley came up close and he quickly stepped out of the line of spiralling cigarette smoke. He could smell her breath. As usual she'd had a skinful.

Adam could never get over his surprise that Charley Bluff actually liked Justine; he would have expected jealousy and criticism, surly resentment. Beauty and the Beast, he thought, grinning. Charley's thin, greasy, greying brown hair was dragged back in a ratty ponytail and secured with an elastic band, emphasizing her bulbous forehead and round fleshy cheeks and chin.

'I expect she'll be really busy next week, even though she's off work. But I told her to make time to pop in for a drink. Will you remind her?

'Yep, sure,' Adam promised. He backed away, fingering his keys.

'Come in and join me for a nightcap,' Charley offered. 'I'm afraid Mum's out for the count!' She was glad. She could have Adam all to herself for once.

'No, thanks,' he said firmly. 'I'm exhausted.' He had no intention of sitting in the gilt-mirrored crimson velvet drawing room that resembled some Victorian brothel, while Charley and the rottweiler stared at his crotch and the mad rat-arsed mother snored her head off. Or of listening to complaints about the bewildered old dears in the home where Charley worked as a care assistant.

'Oh, go on!' she urged, disappointed. 'You couldn't make it to my forty-third birthday barbecue a few weeks ago. Just a wee dram,' she pleaded. 'We've got everything.'

'I'm sure you have.' He hoped that didn't sound sarcastic. 'No, really.' He smiled. 'I just want to collapse into bed.' The hungry lascivious look she gave him made him wish he hadn't said that. 'Thanks anyway.' He backed further away. 'Give my regards to –'

'Adam,' Charley interrupted in a low urgent voice, 'I think we've got a prowler. I wanted to warn you and Justine.'

'A prowler?' Adam felt irritated at the way the hound from hell continued to growl at him. He and Justine had moved in more than a year ago; it ought to recognize him by now. It never growled at Justine. Maybe that was why Charley liked her so much.

'Whitney *darling* . . . shh!' Charley stroked the dog's huge head. 'I saw a man hanging around when I took Whitney for her walk earlier,' she said breathlessly. 'Hiding behind that tree across the road.' She pointed. 'I shone my flashlight at him and he ran off. When we came out of the park he was back, standing in the driveway staring at the house.' She glanced around, shivering in the dark chill air. 'I phoned the police, but they weren't much help. At least it's on record – I hope! They said they'd send a patrol car, but that was over half an hour ago and there's still no sign. I suppose they're too busy in clubland to bother with us!'

'The shootings? Yes, I heard.' Adam frowned. 'What did this prowler look like?' he asked warily.

'Tall – not as tall as you. Skinny build, sloping shoulders, short dark hair. Dressed in dark jacket and pale trousers, a white shirt. Clean clothes, but absolutely no quality, especially the jacket. *Cheap,*' she sniffed. 'Thirty-something. When I challenged him he ran off again. Might be the bastard who broke into the base-ment flat in June,' she said angrily. 'They never arrested anyone for that. Burglars often come back a few months later, don't they? When they think the victim's got new stuff.' She paused. 'Of course the police would be here in seconds if he'd broken in and I'd brained him with the didgeridoo – to arrest *me*! Typical!' she snorted.

'Sounds like the description of some creep who's been following Justine.' Adam felt anxious. 'He waits outside her office most days, pesters her for a date. Wears sad clothes. I can't be sure this prowler is the same guy,' he said quickly. 'I've never seen him and neither have any of Justine's friends – he always makes sure there are no witnesses. It's been going on for about three weeks now.'

32

'What, *really*?' Charley gasped. 'Oh, my God!'

'It probably isn't him. I hope to Christ it isn't! Justine's positive he doesn't know where she lives.'

'He might be smarter than she thinks.' Charley moved closer, causing the dog to growl jealously. 'Why hasn't she reported this to the police? Although I suppose she'd have to be raped or murdered before they got off their backsides! Even then . . .' She stopped as she saw Adam flinch. 'Sorry!'

'Justine says he's only a sad bastard and that he'll give up when she doesn't appear at work for the next month. I agree. Or I *did*. She'll freak when I tell her about this prowler,' he said anxiously. 'She's pretty upset and this is the last thing she needs. Even if it's not the same guy, it's still bad news. I have to warn her. *Shit!*'

Charley had never heard him swear before. 'Where is Justine now?'

'Out with a friend.' He glanced up at the dark windows of the top flat again. 'Unless she's already home and in bed. She probably had a great evening,' he sighed. 'Now I'll have to ruin it for her.'

'Not *you*, Adam!' Charley said indignantly. 'That swine, whoever he is. Look, it could be anybody,' she said, trying to reassure him. 'You get all kinds of lowlife hanging around the park, especially at this time of night. I should know!'

'True.' Adam nodded. 'But I can't risk not telling her.'

'He's been challenged twice, and now he knows there's a rottie waiting to rip his balls off.' Charley patted the dog's head. 'If he's got any!' she said contemptuously. 'I'll warn Mum, but that'll have to wait until the morning. She's been hitting the bottle a lot since Dad died.'

'It must be very difficult for her,' Adam said sympathetically. He had a feeling Marinda Bluff had been hitting bottles long before old Major Bluff popped his clogs. 'For you too.' He backed away, jangling the keys in his pocket. 'I'll say goodnight then.'

'Okay, Adam. Poor Justine,' Charley remarked. 'A stalker. What a nightmare!'

He nodded grimly. 'Let's hope it'll be over soon. In a week we'll be married and lying on some Caribbean beach. She'll feel better then. So will I.'

Married and lying on a Caribbean beach! Charley thought enviously as she waved goodnight to Adam and hurried back up the steps. Wouldn't mind some of that myself. She longed to find a gorgeous man who would fall in love with her, but there wasn't much chance of that now. To be honest, there never had been. Gorgeous men were thin on the ground and they didn't fall in love with the likes of her. She thought of Joan, one of the other care assistants, with her dyed auburn hair and coarse laugh. '*Let's face it, Charl, at our age men are like parking spots – all the good ones are taken and what's left is handicapped*!' Insensitive and politically incorrect maybe – but true! She looked lovingly down at the impatient rottweiler. At least she had Whitney. Whitney would kill to protect her, no question about that. 'Come on, baby doll!' she sighed. 'Time for bye-byes.'

Justine wasn't home. Adam switched on lamps in the bedroom and sitting room, noticed that there were two messages on the answering machine. He pressed the 'play' button; both times there was a kind of background roar, like heavy traffic, before the caller hung up without speaking. Puzzled and uneasy, he replayed them. He didn't think family, friends, anyone from the surgery or Brooks & Wilde would make hang-up calls. Had the creep somehow managed to get hold of their unlisted number? No! That was impossible. He dialled 1471. Caller had withheld number.

He shrugged and pressed the machine's 'erase' button, then walked to the windows and looked out over the moonlit park. Who might be lurking amongst that still, silent mass of trees? He felt spooked tonight, afraid for Justine. Where had she gone? He could have picked her up and driven her home.

He poured himself a small Scotch and paced the lamplit sitting room, put the drink down untouched. He became more and more agitated as the minutes passed, wishing desperately that Justine would come home. She and Donna were probably drinking in some wine bar, talking and laughing together like the schoolgirls they'd once been. Men would look at them and smile, admire. *Want*. Was the creep one of those men? Was he really a harmless sad bastard, or something more sinister? Adam felt restless, filled with anxiety and foreboding.

He was about to go down and wait in the drive for her when a shiny black cab drew up at the gates. Justine climbed out and called goodnight to the driver. Her mass of hair looked silvery in the moonlight. The cab didn't pull away immediately; she must have asked the driver to wait until she was indoors. She glanced nervously up and down the silent road, hesitated before entering the dark driveway. Justine was normally happy, relaxed and confident, Adam thought, didn't have a nervous bone in her body. This creep was destroying her peace of mind. He clenched his fists and swore under his breath as he strode out of the sitting room and downstairs. He had heard a lot about stalkers, none of it good. Fines, restraining orders, injunctions, arrest, jail terms, you name it. Nothing deterred them and their delusions.

The heavy downstairs front door slammed and he heard her clumpy sandals on the stairs. A minute later she was inside the flat and in his arms, the door locked, bolted and chained behind them. They went up to the sitting room.

'How are you?' he asked, kissing her lips and neck, smelling her perfume. 'Did you and Donna have a good time?' He hugged her tight. 'It's great to see you,' he said fervently. 'I missed you like hell all day!'

'I missed you too,' she gasped. 'I'm fine. Yes, Donna and I had a great evening.' She looked at him and smiled mischievously. 'How was the dinner?'

'Oh, that.' He'd forgotten all about it. 'Deadly!' he said. 'Nothing like the one where I met you.'

'I should hope not!' she laughed. 'Paul Melwood phoned me today.'

'The millionaire businessman? So, how are things at Melwood Materials?' Adam asked sarcastically. He frowned. 'What did he want?'

'To thank me for the copy I wrote for his company's new brochure and web page. He invited me to lunch next week.'

'I'll bet he did! You're a copywriter,' Adam said shortly. 'It's your job. You even get paid for doing it.'

'What's wrong?' she asked, disconcerted. 'You told me you liked Paul.'

'Yeah, he's okay. Fancies you rotten, though. Look, never mind Mr Melwood!' He hugged her again. 'Are you sure you're all right?'

'Yes.' Justine touched his lips and trailed her fingers through his thick dark hair, saw the anxious look in his dark brown eyes. 'What is it?' she asked nervously. 'Tell me, Adam. Has something happened?'

'No! Well . . . maybe.' He hesitated. 'There's no easy way to say this. I hate to worry you but –'

Nervousness escalated to alarm. 'What's *happened*?'

He kissed her again, looked into her glittering blue eyes. 'Charley Bluff saw a prowler tonight when she took the lethal weapon for a pee in the park,' he said, reluctantly, afraid of her reaction. 'He was watching the house. He ran off when she challenged him. I'm afraid he sounded like . . .'

'No!' Justine cried, eyes dilated with terror. 'It can't be Matthew! He doesn't know where I live – he can't, it's impossible!' She pulled away from him and burst into panicked tears. 'It isn't him!'

'Don't cry, Justine. Please!' Adam hated himself for upsetting her. 'All right, it probably isn't. But I had to warn you. Please!' he begged, torn by guilt and anxiety. 'It's okay.' He took her in his arms again, hugged and kissed her. 'You've got me, I love you. You're safe, I won't let anything bad happen.' He held her trembling body tight, his lips against her soft hair. 'Are you sure he doesn't know where you live?' he asked gently.

She raised her tearstained face and looked at him. 'Adam, with the evasion tactics I use, you'd think M15 had trained me! I make four right-hand turns then four left-hand turns to check no one's on my tail. I vary my route to and from work. You name it. There's no way he could have followed me here. I don't believe he's even got a car,' she went on. 'He keeps saying it's at the garage. He's full of *shit!*' she blurted furiously, then sniffed and wiped her eyes. 'Maybe this guy was an opportunist burglar. Or he could have been looking for someone and got the wrong house. Most house numbers around here are up a driveway and hidden by out-of-control foliage.'

Adam kissed her again, stroked her hair. 'Then why did he run off?'

'Wouldn't you run off if you saw that rottweiler? And you know how paranoid Charley is. Obsessed with security, always on about how she'd shoot or bludgeon or knife an intruder.'

'Yes.' Adam paused, gathering courage for his next upsetting question. 'Was he waiting for you again today? Did he hassle you?'

More tears filled her eyes. She stepped back and slipped off the black linen jacket, let it drop to the floor in a soft heap.

'The bastard did *that*?' Adam drew in his breath, fury rising in him as he stared at her bruised upper arm. 'Jesus Christ!' he exclaimed, horrified. 'I can practically see his fingermarks.' He gently touched her skin. 'He won't get away with this,' he said slowly. 'I'll kill him!'

'That won't help.' She smiled through her tears. 'Or would it?'

'What *will* help, Justine?' he asked, furious and disturbed. 'You don't want to tell the police. You don't want to do anything!'

'Not true. I kicked him when he grabbed me, punched him on the nose and cut his face with my keys. I told him once and for all to fuck off, that I wasn't interested. I handled it, okay? I *did* something.'

Adam stared at her. 'You punched him?'

'He's got the message now!' Justine touched her arm. 'You think this looks nasty? He was bleeding when I drove off. And what can I tell the police?' she went on. 'I don't know a damn' thing about him, not even if Matthew is his real name. I can't prove he hurt or hassled me.' She laughed shakily. 'No one stopped to offer their services as a witness. I'm the only one who's seen him.'

'Except for Charley Bluff. Maybe.'

'Yeah, *maybe*. Adam, it's over now.' She sat down and unstrapped her sandals. 'I'm sick of this,' she sighed. 'I'm so tired!'

He watched as she got up again and paced the room, her slim body stiff with tension. He noticed she didn't go near the windows. 'Look what he's doing to you,' he said grimly. 'To us.'

Justine stopped and wiped away tears, pushed back her mane of hair. 'Look, you were right to warn me about this prowler,' she acknowledged. 'I'll be careful ... *more* careful. I'll speak to Charley tomorrow, describe Matthew to her.' She grimaced. 'She'll love that!'

'Yes. She might even offer to kill him for you, ask which method you'd prefer. Knife, gun or hand-crafted didgeridoo.' He frowned. 'Or rottweiler! You realize she's completely demented, don't you? So's her mother. It's a *folie à deux* thing, one makes the other worse. All that alcohol doesn't help either.'

'They are a touch eccentric.' Justine stopped pacing. 'Charley tried to give me a CS gas spray once. I bet she's got a drawer full of them.' She shivered, rubbed her arms. 'Might take her up on that now!'

37

'As long as you remember to remove it from your pocket or stocking top before going through airport security next week. Otherwise you'll spend your honeymoon in jail instead of the Caribbean.' Adam stood up and loosened his tie, yawned and stretched.

'They wouldn't put me in jail.' She walked to him and slipped her arms around his neck, pressed her body against his. She felt comforted by Adam's strong body, loved the smell and feel of him. She kissed him and nibbled his earlobe.

'Okay, but you could forget leaving the country.' He unzipped her dress and unfastened her bra, stroked her smooth bare back. 'And I could forget fucking you on a Caribbean beach,' he murmured, kissing her smooth throat. Her dress and bra slithered to the floor.

'Adam, let's go to bed,' she whispered in his ear. 'I want you!'

'I'm all yours.' He touched her hardening nipples, stared into her dark blue eyes. 'I love you,' he said slowly. 'You're so bloody beautiful!'

'You're not bad yourself.'

He cupped her soft full breasts in his hands and she leaned her head back and writhed with pleasure as he gently kissed and stroked them and sucked her nipples. 'I've had a hard-on all day, thinking about what I wanted to do to you,' he murmured. She laughed as he swept her off her feet and carried her into the lamplit bedroom. She wriggled out of her pants and lay naked on the bed, watching as he quickly stripped off his clothes. She loved his smooth, hard, muscular body.

Justine forgot Matthew, forgot everything as Adam slowly and methodically played her body with his tongue, lips and fingers, taking his time to drive her wild with desire. She clung to him and groaned with delight as he slid deep inside her, kissing and licking her breasts. He stared down at her. He loved to watch Justine's beautiful face as she came, gaze into those deep blue eyes that held so much love, so much desire for him. Her hair fanned out over the pillow. She bucked under him and arched her back, cried out as the orgasm seized her and pulsed through her body, radiating to the tips of her fingers and toes.

'I can't get enough of you!' he whispered. He couldn't hold it any longer. He let go, shouted and trembled with the intensity of the climax. Justine clung to him and bit his shoulder, ran her hands

38

over his sweaty back and buttocks. She sighed and closed her eyes, laid her head on his shoulder. She felt completely relaxed.

The bedside phone rang, crashing into their silent intimate space. Adam raised his head and swore.

'No, don't!' she whispered urgently as he rolled away from her and sat on the edge of the bed. 'Let the machine pick it up.'

'Sometimes I think *I'm* a bloody answering machine!' Adam stood up and reached for his bathrobe. 'I'll do better than that,' he said. 'I'll unplug the phone. We want a good night's sleep and a lie-in. With sex, breakfast, newspapers and more sex!'

'Who can it possibly be at this time of night?' Justine sat up and pulled the heavy blue quilt over her breasts, glancing nervously around the big bedroom. Like the sitting room, it had a polished wooden floor, grey marble mantelpiece and three long sash windows that opened on to a stone balcony. There was a big wardrobe, a chest of drawers and an old dark green leather sofa by the fireplace. A carved oak chest at the foot of the bed had a portable television on top of it. Adam's bedside table held the phone, the alarm clock and a stack of medical journals. On Justine's table was a pile of unread paperbacks, mostly thrillers, a few sea shells, and a big smooth heavy pure white quartz stone.

'Whoever it is can go to hell!' Adam looked at her nervous expression and cursed silently. 'Might be my mother wanting to nag us about some massively trivial wedding detail. Don't worry, okay?' He pulled on his bathrobe, sat on the bed and kissed her. 'Relax.' He caressed her soft hair. 'You were relaxed a minute ago.' He grinned. 'Fancy a cup of tea?'

She nodded. 'I'd love one.'

'Lemon tea, m'lady? Earl Grey, Jasmine, the stuff that stinks of tar–?'

'You mean Lapsang Souchong.' She smiled. 'Lemon, please.'

'Coming up. Here.' He lifted the lump of quartz and put it in her hands. 'Have a play with your Inishbofin stone.'

'To think I found it in the cove on that beautiful island.' Justine looked at the stone, touched its coldness to her cheek. 'I read that quartz stones were always found in healing places.'

'We should go back to Connemara some time.' Adam ruffled her hair and got up. 'See you in a minute.'

The midnight caller had also hung up without speaking. He felt uneasy again. Who would call three times on the trot and hang up?

Assuming it was the same person. The 1471 voice repeated its infuriatingly unhelpful message.

'Fuck it!' Adam whispered. He unplugged the phone and answering machine, switched off the lamps and went down to the kitchen. While he waited for the kettle to boil he checked that the door opening on to the fire escape was locked and bolted. They had had new locks and bolts fitted after the basement flat break-in. The kitchen door had two bolts on the outside, a further deterrent.

He made the tea and stirred in one lump of sugar. Light from the kitchen window fell faintly on to the long back lawn three floors below. No light came from the terrace or ground-floor windows; Charley must have put Marinda and the rottweiler to bed before retiring herself.

He took the cup of tea, switched off the light and went back upstairs. Halfway up he stopped and turned, went back down and drew the bolts on the outside of the kitchen door. He felt ashamed of himself for doing that.

In the bedroom he looked at Justine and smiled. She was curled up, fast asleep, the white quartz stone clutched in her left hand. He put down the tea, gently prised the stone out of her grasp and laid it next to the sea shells. He sat on the bed and looked at her, felt a great rush of love and tenderness.

If that bastard came near her again – touched her! – he would get the kicking of his life. Justine was right. Even if harassment could be proved, the police didn't have the money or manpower to put alleged stalkers under constant surveillance. He wished he could take next week off, be with her all the time. But he had a conference in London, and a load of rubbish to attend to before the hapless-looking locum took over in his absence.

He dropped his robe, clicked off the lamp and got into bed. Moonlight slanted across the shiny wooden floor. Justine stirred, opened her eyes.

'Go back to sleep,' he whispered, kissing her. 'Everything's fine.'

'Adam?' she murmured.

'Yes?' He ran his hands over her smooth body, stroking her breasts and buttocks and between her legs, loving her soft, warm wetness. He wanted her again.

'Who was on the phone?'

'No one. Forget it,' he said firmly. He wrapped his arms around

40

her and they kissed passionately. 'On the other hand, don't go to sleep. Excuse me, Missis!' he said as he slid between her legs. 'I think I need to examine you again.'

'Oh, doctor!' Justine giggled and rolled on top of him. 'I was hoping you might say that!'

Matthew hesitated by the stone gateposts, then walked stealthily into the driveway. He stopped there and stared up at the dark house.

'Got you!' he whispered.

# Chapter Five

'You going to lie there all day, you lazy sod? Matthew! It's two in the afternoon.' Tracey Pearson stumbled over the Mount Everest of dirty jeans, leggings, T-shirts, socks and panties on the floor by the bed, and nearly fell on top of the inert lump beneath the pink-and-black striped quilt. Her stinking heap of laundry had lain there for weeks, she thought guiltily. But when was she supposed to find the time to wash tons of clothes? It was all right for Matthew, he didn't work. 'Move your arse!' she yelled.

He rolled over in bed and sat up, shot her a hostile glance. He felt sledgehammered by long hours of sleep and the sticky early-autumn heat, frustrated by fantasies of Justine. In his new one she was naked and tied up, wearing a leather collar like the bitches in his magazines. She cried and screamed, pleaded with him as he screwed her metaphysical brains out. She was afraid of him, but she wanted it. Only he could satisfy her.

'You look a right ghoul!' Tracey stared at his bony white shoulders and hairy, caved-in chest, the dark staring eyes in his pale unshaven face. What the hell did I ever see in *that*? she wondered. Good job I binned the Prozac. 'As if you've spent your life in a dark hole.'

'This flat's a hole.' Matthew yawned and stretched, blinked. 'A dirty hole.'

'Won't mind leaving then, will you?' she said shrilly. 'Along with the other cockroaches!'

'Shut it!' he groaned. 'I've got a headache.'

Matthew couldn't believe he had murdered two people last night. That he possessed Justine Flynn's life on three densely printed A4 sheets, had stood watching her house only hours ago.

42

From famine to feast in one jump! His life had changed, suddenly and dramatically. There was no going back now. He needed time to think and absorb the enormity of it all, plan his next move. How could he do that with this bitch in nag mode?

'Take your stuff and get out,' Tracey snarled. '*Now*! I've had it with you lying around being a useless bastard.' And the rest. 'You can sod off and be useless somewhere else.'

'I said, shut it!' He felt agitated. 'I'm not going anywhere.'

Tracey's bulging hips and sagging arse were emphasized by scarlet leggings. Why did fat slags like her always wear leggings? They had been out of fashion for years, even he knew that. Her out-of-control tits bulged through the white T-shirt with the sunflower motif. Step class! She had short frizzy blonde hair, dyed and permed, watery blue eyes and a round, pasty face. Her triple chin wobbled with anger and resentment.

He pushed back the quilt, crawled out of bed and headed for the bathroom, scratching his crotch and armpits. Tracey hated the sight of his scrawny white, hairy body. Matthew locked the door, peed noisily, then shaved and took one of his long showers, lathering himself with plenty of pink Camay soap. Tracey went into the living room and flopped on the sofa, barely able to contain her impatience. He always took ages in the bathroom, using up all the hot water. Today would be the last time he did that in her place.

Tracey was disgusted and ashamed of herself for ever having had anything to do with Matthew Casey. And now she was afraid. The other night he had come rolling back pissed from the pub and forced himself on her, tried to tie her up then put his hands around her throat, all the while mumbling some name she couldn't catch. She had managed to struggle free and lock herself in the bathroom until he passed out. Matthew was getting worse, always wanted to act out kinky scenes from his pervy S/M magazines. She wasn't having any of *that*. She had wanted him out for a while now, but the other night had been the last straw. She got up and went into the bedroom.

The small room was hot and stuffy, the flowered curtains drawn against the afternoon sun. Tracey reached up and dragged Matthew's cheapo blue nylon suitcase from the top of the wardrobe. The bondage magazines with their brutal pictures and crude unimaginative titles slid around inside like a coiled bunch of poisonous snakes. He thought she didn't know about them.

43

Tracey had laughed when her grandmother warned her that men were wild beasts dragged out of trees and forced into Y-fronts. After six months of Matthew she'd stopped seeing the funny side. He came out of the bathroom at last, wearing a frayed pink towel around his waist, smelling of soap and his horrible sweet, musky aftershave.

'D'you have to wear a gallon of that bloody stuff?' Tracey cried in disgust. 'Should be a law against it. Breach of the peace, or pollution or something.'

'I like to keep myself clean.'

'Don't you bloody just!'

'Not like some people!' He frowned. 'Shut up and do us a cup of tea.' He selected clean socks and underpants, a folded khaki-coloured T-shirt and a pair of neatly pressed pale blue jeans and pulled them on, balancing precariously on each spindly white hairy leg. Tracey noticed a gash and purple bruising on his right shin, the gash dark red as it oozed fresh blood after the hot shower and vigorous towelling. There was bruising around his nose, too, and his face was cut. Tracey wished she'd done it. She couldn't be bothered to ask what had happened; it wasn't as if she'd get a straight answer. Not my problem anymore, she thought.

'Bacon and eggs,' Matthew added. 'Toast.'

Tracey gasped with outrage. 'Didn't you hear what I said?' she shouted, tits heaving. 'You're *out* of here. I'm not typing my arse off forty-eight hours a week in that bloody estate agent's so you can lie around my flat like Lord Muck!'

'What's that doing there?' he asked angrily as he noticed his suitcase.

'What d'you think? I'm not getting through to you, am I?'

'*Shut it!*' he yelled suddenly, his fists clenched. He shoved her hard in the chest and she stumbled against the wall. He grabbed the suitcase and dumped it back on top of the wardrobe. 'Touch this again and you're dead meat!' he said hotly. If Tracey saw his magazines she really would freak!

He turned and went into the living room, switched on the tele-vision and sprawled on the lumpy brown velour sofa. There was a half-finished bag of cheese-and-onion crisps on the floor. He frowned again. The place was in a filthy state, Tracey never did any cleaning. She was a dirty slut. He grabbed the remote control and flipped channels, looking for local news bulletins. There

44

wouldn't be any at this time of day; he'd have to wait until five or six. A film was starting on BBC 2, a fifties bible epic starring Charlton Heston. He hated Charlton Heston, but it was either him or racing from Haydock bloody boring Park. They didn't have cable TV.

Tracey parked her body in front of the television, her face flushed with heat and fury. 'If you don't fuck off – *now!* – I'm phoning the police.'

Matthew's rage cooled and he felt nervous. The police were the last people he wanted to see right now. 'Look, I'll get a job, okay?' he said impatiently, munching crisps. 'I can get a job any time.'

'Yeah, right,' she sneered. 'In a freak show!'

'I don't want to move out.' He craned his neck so as to see the television screen. He felt like punching her stupid fat ugly gob, had wanted to do that for a long time. She should be careful, he thought, show some respect. She didn't know who she was dealing with. 'Where can I go?'

'That's your problem. Back to Mummy in Old Roan, I suppose. Though she won't want you either. Poor sad cow had thirty-two years of you – six months was enough for me! You were dead keen at first,' she said bitterly, hands on hips. 'Thought it was Christmas with soft girl Tracey, didn't you?' She glared at him, rubbed her sweaty hands on her thighs. 'Right!' she said grimly. She turned and marched out of the room.

Matthew sighed angrily, got up and went into the kitchen for a beer. The sink was full of dirty mugs and plates. Black-specked lard had solidified in the frying pan. He took a can of Heineken out of the fridge and pulled the ring. The cold lager made him feel better.

The police would never nail him for the advertising agency murders, he thought confidently, not in a million years. Even if by some incredible stroke of bad luck they got on to him, how could they prove anything? He'd wiped his fingerprints, removed all traces of his presence. Ditto with the van. He'd kept the guard's wallet and sixty quid cash. The van was at the bottom of the Mersey, dumped in the river at a deserted stretch of dockland. It would be a while before they found that – if they ever did.

He had no form, the plods didn't even know he existed. One day he would tell Justine what he'd done for her. By then they would be together and she would belong to him properly. He imagined her fear and awed admiration. Justine was the only link between him and the killings. But she loved him and he had total control over her; she would be incapable of betrayal. He was safe. He gulped the rest of the lager and reached into the fridge for another can.

'What the bloody hell's this?' Tracey came into the kitchen, startling him out of his reverie. She held up the huge black-and-gold dildo. 'A present for your dear old mum?' She laughed nervously.

'Give me that!' Matthew snatched it off her, his face and neck crimson with embarrassment. 'It's not mine,' he muttered. 'It belongs to a friend.' The dildo was a present for Justine. He'd left it under the bed, forgotten to hide it in his suitcase. Fury at Tracey boiled inside him. She needed a lesson – had it coming!

'You don't have friends, you mental case! Christ!' Tracey exclaimed, suddenly afraid again. 'I don't know a thing about you, do I? Tell you what, I don't bloody want to either. Take your filthy pervy magazines and *go*!'

Matthew flinched. 'You've been in my suitcase! I told you not to.' He charged past, shoving aside her soft, sweaty bulk. She shouted something he didn't hear.

His suitcase lay open on the bed, magazines spilling out. The top cover had a photo of a naked blonde girl lying hog-tied on her stomach, wrists and ankles chained together. The girl was also gagged and blindfolded. 'You interfering bitch!' he yelled. 'I warned you not to touch my stuff.' He ran out and collided with Tracey in the tiny narrow hall.

'For the last time – sod off!' she said. She was breathing heavily, her face as scarlet as her leggings. 'Before I call the police. I'm not joking!'

'Neither am I.' His temper flared and he smashed her across the face, drawing back his arm like a tennis player preparing to hit a cross-court forehand. Tracey cried out and staggered backwards, one hand to her cheek. Her short stubby nails were painted purple and she wore an antique turquoise ring, a gift from a former boyfriend. She said.

'You never bloody shut it, do you?' Matthew yelled, infuriated. He grabbed hold of her and dragged her into the sitting room, shoving her viciously. She fell, scrabbling among biscuit, cake

46

and crisp crumbs on the dirty bottle-green carpet. He kicked her hard on the thigh, wishing he had boots on.

'You mad bastard!' she shouted, staring up at his contorted, reddened face. His sunken brown eyes blazed. 'You've done it now!'

She began to scramble to her feet, desperate to reach the phone. Matthew clamped an arm around her waist, grabbed a handful of dry frizzy hair and dragged her towards the bedroom. She struggled and screamed in pain.

'Want me out, do you?' he panted. 'Not before I've taught you a lesson.'

'Let go of me!' Tracey cried, twisting and struggling. 'Stop it!'

She was terrified now. Matthew was so quiet and withdrawn most of the time, brooding in a dark world of his own. You never knew what he was thinking. When people like him lost it, they really lost it. He let go of her waist and punched her in the stomach. She doubled over, winded. Tears poured from her eyes. He yanked her head back and kicked her legs from under her. She fell forward on the unmade bed, face buried in the smelly quilt.

'No!' she gasped. 'Stop it!'

Matthew laughed. 'Not so mouthy now, are you?' He shoved the suitcase out of the way and went on laughing as he dragged off her trainers, white socks and leggings, used the leggings to tie her hands tightly behind her back. He shoved a pair of her dirty underpants into her mouth. Tracey gagged in fear and revulsion. He rolled her on her back, knelt between her legs and stared down at her, enjoying the look of terror in her eyes.

'You're a fat, ugly slag, Tracey,' he panted. 'I've seen you look at other men – not that they'd look at you! I'm sick of you making an arse of me. I was going to leave anyway,' he lied. 'I've met a girl.' He smashed her across the face again. 'She's so beautiful she'd blow you out of the water!' he shouted. 'She loves me. She'd beg me for what you're going to get now.'

He unzipped his jeans and stroked his erect penis. Tracey moaned and shook her head frantically, her body tense with fear as he dragged off her pants and pushed up her T-shirt, exposing her big sagging breasts. He plunged inside her, grunting and gripping handfuls of her dry frizzy hair. He thrust away roughly, hurting her. His bony sweating hands closed around her throat.

'Justine!' he moaned. 'Justine, Justine!'

He's going to murder me, Tracey thought. I'm going to die in this crappy little bedroom with the drawn curtains and pile of stinking underwear. He pounded away inside her, his hands clamped around her throat. She began to feel faint, and the room went black around the edges. Matthew's face blurred and there was a red mist in front of her eyes. She gasped for the breath that wouldn't come. Her tongue felt enormous in her mouth.

'Justine!' he shouted as he came, a terrific climax that made his body shake. He took a deep breath, opened his eyes and looked down. Tracey's eyes were bloodshot and bulging from her head, and her skin was dark crimson, suffused with blood. Shocked, he saw that his hands were tight around her throat, still squeezing. She was almost unconscious.

He let go of her, scrambled off the bed and zipped up his jeans. He was frightened at what he'd done – or nearly done. Unlike with the security guard and the receptionist at Brooks & Wilde, there would be lots of clues for the police to pick up here. Tracey's mother and girlfriends knew him too – the feeling that existed between him and them could best be described as toxic. He had to get out of here. It was bloody inconvenient, a pain. But there was no alternative.

He pulled out the gag and Tracey gulped for air like a distressed goldfish, ran her swollen tongue over her lips and around her dry mouth. Her throat felt so sore she could barely swallow, let alone cry for help. Just go, you crazy bastard! she thought, trying to get her breath back. He might still murder her. She looked at his white hairy hands with their bony knuckles and bitten fingernails, trembling with shock and fear.

Matthew crammed his clothes into the suitcase, covering the black-and-gold dildo and the bondage magazines. He zipped it up and dragged it into the living room, grabbed two bottles of French table wine and four cans of Heineken from the fridge and shoved them into a carrier bag. He had no books or CDs. He fetched his bottle of aftershave from the bathroom.

He wasn't sorry to leave the bitch in her pigsty. He and Justine would be together soon. He looked in Tracey's greasy green suede purse; forty-two pounds and sixty-eight pence. Not much, but better than nothing. What with her cash and the dead security guard's, he was richer than usual. He could buy petrol for starters.

He put on his navy blue jacket and stuffed the notes and coins into the guard's wallet, slid his feet into the polished brown leather shoes and carefully laced them. They were his only good pair, bought for thirty quid in St John's Market in the city centre.

He went back to the bedroom to check on Tracey. She lay on the bed crying and trembling, staring at the peeling blue rosebud wallpaper. Did blue roses exist? He thought she was in shock. He'd be well away by the time she recovered. He rolled her on her side and untied the leggings. Her wrists had deep red marks around them.

'I'm off now,' he said loudly. He felt shaken. What if he'd gone too far and strangled her? Three murders in less than twenty-four hours wasn't a good idea. He had to watch himself. At the same time he couldn't help feeling proud. He was strong, he had a temper. Where had this strength come from? He felt like it had always been a part of him. Why hadn't it come out sooner? Justine, he thought, smiling. She was the reason. She was the focus of his entire life now.

'Don't call the police,' he warned Tracey. 'We had a row, I left. It's my word against yours. If you cause me trouble I'll come back and kill you. I'll finish the job, Tracey – that's a promise! Are you listening?' he shouted. 'You know I mean it, don't you?'

She nodded weakly, her eyes full of tears. He went back to the living room, picked up the heavy suitcase and left the tiny flat. His mother would take him back if he shoved her a few quid. She was a nag too, money being the only thing that shut her up. He'd stay with her while he looked for a job. Justine had to respect him. He was finished being dependent on some bitch who thought she could push him around because she earned a wage and he didn't.

Linnet Lane was quiet, sleeping in the afternoon sunshine. The hot, sticky weather had been going on for weeks now, summer's last gasp. Matthew slung the suitcase on to the back seat of his rusting, white Ford Fiesta, got in and drove off down the narrow street. He glanced at the petrol gauge. There was just enough fuel to make it to the garage on the main road.

Tracey hauled herself into a sitting position, coughing and choking. Tears poured from her eyes and she couldn't control the awful trembling that made her feel utterly weak and helpless. Her heart was pounding, hurling itself around inside her chest like a trapped, terrified bird desperate for freedom.

The bastard had nearly strangled her! She could have died. Her neck and throat hurt so much she didn't think she would be able to talk properly again. Her eyes in the toothpaste-specked bathroom mirror were bloodshot, wide with shock and terror, and her neck was covered with dark red contusions.

She staggered into the kitchen and poured herself a glass of wine from the half-full bottle on the cluttered drainboard. Swallowing was agony, and the wine tasted warm and sour after standing uncorked in the sun all morning. She slowly sipped it, then went into the living room and picked up the phone. Her hands shook so much that she dropped the receiver twice.

'Mum?' she croaked when a woman answered at last. 'It's Tracey. Can you come round right away? I need help.' She collapsed on to the sofa, more tears spilling down her cheeks and dripping into the wine.

'What's up?' her mother asked warily. 'Sounds like you've got the 'flu. Or tonsillitis. What sort of help? I'm off out with the girls from work tonight, I was just going down the hairdresser's. I'm not being funny, Trace, but I can't afford to catch whatever you've picked up. I'm already knackered as it is, and I've got double shifts next week.'

'It's not 'flu. It's him – Matthew.' An enormous sob shook her body. 'Mum, please help me!' she whispered desperately. 'Come now!'

'Trace? What the bloody hell's wrong?'

'The bastard tried to murder me!' she cried weakly. 'He's gone now – for good. Said he's met some girl who loves him. Oh, Mum!' she sobbed. Her cracked voice broke into a high-pitched, anguished wail of panic that seared her raw throat. 'I thought I was going to die!'

# Chapter Six

'Anna raped and strangled! *Dead!*' Justine sat white-faced and stunned, her hands clenched in her lap, as Adam drove out of Merseyside Police headquarters car park and turned into the crowded street. 'That security guard battered to death – it's unbelievable!' She shuddered as she stared out of the window. Adam glanced at her, knew what she was thinking.

'It wasn't *him*,' he said grimly. 'It's just coincidence you had that fight with him yesterday. At least you've reported the harassment now, given a description of the bastard and voiced your suspicions. The police will check him out.'

'Will they?' Her voice trembled. 'They didn't seem all that interested. And how can you check someone out when you don't know their surname or address or place of work or anything? I got the impression the police thought I was trying to distract attention from Anna's murder for my own selfish purposes!'

'They don't have much to go on and it's a long shot.' Adam left Canning Place and headed out of the city centre. 'They'll concentrate on the victims' families and friends first.' He changed gear, glanced at her and squeezed her hand. 'I realize it's not much consolation,' he said, 'but they'll soon get whoever did it. Most murders are solved pretty quickly. Christ!' he sighed, shaking his head. 'What a bloody Saturday!'

It had got off to a great start. A lie-in and a sexy breakfast in bed, shopping followed by a pub lunch with friends. A couple of hours at their house in Childwall. The renovation was almost finished. They had made love in the house, warm skin against bare floorboards, every cry of passion echoing through the empty rooms. His denim shirt and jeans, Justine's tight black silk sweater and black-and-gold Italian designer jeans, were covered with white plaster dust. She had been happy and relaxed, her beautiful eyes full of laughter. She hadn't mentioned the stalker-cum-prowler once, and it didn't seem as if she was thinking about him either. Then they had got home to find the shocking message from Ian Brooks on the answering machine. He requested that Justine contact the police – they wanted to interview everyone who had seen or spoken to Anna the day she died.

Adam was stunned and sorry for the murdered receptionist and security guard but his main concern was for Justine. Anger burned beneath his calm, controlled exterior as he drove. Three weeks of being hassled by some delusional dickhead who couldn't get a life – and now this! It was the last thing she needed. He was desperate to protect her, stop this whole business from blowing up into a nightmare.

'The police said there were no signs of a break-in? Nothing was touched?' His foot came down hard on the brake and he swore as a lorry pulled out in front.

'Not as far as they know. Of course they're still checking.' She shrugged. 'We may not find out exactly what happened until after we get back from honeymoon.'

'Suits me. Tell you what,' he said grimly, 'let's *not* come back!'

Justine ran her hands through her hair, studied her long shiny nails. 'Anna loved going out and enjoying herself,' she whispered. 'She and Jacqui and I were laughing about that the other day. Anna said she'd have to get in as much clubbing as possible before she started college in September. She wanted to be a designer, she was really talented. It's such a waste!' She paused, brushed away tears. 'How can I go back and work there again? How can any of us?'

'Look, you've got a month off,' Adam said firmly. 'That's just as well. Don't call in on Monday to see the others, or talk about it with them over the phone. You'll only upset yourself more.'

'I should go in,' she argued. 'If that creep's hanging around waiting for me again I can have him arrested.'

'Justine, please don't go anywhere near the office,' he said anxiously. 'You'd be putting yourself at risk. The police will probably make an arrest soon. I'm sure the murders are nothing to do with this Matthew character!' At least he hoped not. 'Sounds horrible, but there's a strong possibility that Anna knew her

52

killer,' he went on. 'Most murder victims are killed by someone close to them.' He pulled up at traffic lights and grasped Justine's hand again, leaned across and kissed her. 'Think about *you*,' he urged. 'Be selfish for once in your existence!' Justine looked puzzled, distant. 'Did you hear what I said?' he asked gently.

'Yes. Adam, don't worry about me.' She looked at him, tried to smile. 'I'm okay.'

'Are you? What are you thinking?' he asked, kissing her again. He hoped to God that the stalker, last night's prowler and this murderer weren't the same man. Otherwise Justine was in terrible danger. He didn't need to say it – she was thinking the same thing. But there was no concrete reason to suspect Matthew. Not yet. Get a grip and stick to the facts, he told himself sharply. He had to be calm for Justine's sake.

'Jacqui told me Anna had something going with Ian Brooks,' she said hesitantly. 'She said they'd been screwing each other for months. I don't know if that's true, I never suspected anything myself.' She shrugged. 'Okay, so what? Besides, it's irrelevant. Ian would never . . . ' She stopped, shook her head.

'The teenage receptionist and the married, male menopausal managing director?' Adam smiled cynically. 'Not very original. But is it ever?' He let go of her hand and shifted back in his seat as the lights changed to green. 'So why didn't you include that information in your statement?'

'It's not information, Adam, it's gossip! I didn't think it was a terrific idea to repeat gossip to the police, especially not in a written statement. Ian Brooks is a right hard case,' Justine said nervously. 'He'd sack me or sue me for slander if he found out I'd spread unsubstantiated rumours about him. Jacqui can tell them if she wants. It's *her* rumour, and she's always been a shit stirrer.' I've got enough to worry about, she thought.

'That's right,' Adam nodded. 'Stay out of it.' They cleared the city-centre traffic and he increased speed as they headed for Sefton Park. Dusk descended and the clear blue sky turned to violet. 'Let's take a shower and get changed,' he said. 'Think of somewhere to go for dinner.' He glanced at her. 'Okay?'

'I don't think I can eat much.' Justine's voice was subdued. Red-gold curls fell across her face as she looked down at her lap. Her body was tense, aching with fear. There was no room in her stomach for food.

'Well, try!' Adam longed to hug her, comfort her, shield her from the horror. He hated to see Justine like this: frightened, upset, filled with anxiety. He pulled up behind a shiny black Mercedes S300. 'Look,' he said suddenly. 'Even if last night's prowler and this Matthew turn out to be one and the same, it doesn't necessarily mean he's dangerous,' he argued, trying to convince himself as much as her. 'And it *certainly* doesn't mean he . . . ' His voice tailed off.

'I know you're right,' she said quietly. 'I *hope* so anyway.'

Back at the flat Justine poured herself a glass of white wine, stripped off her dusty clothes and got under the shower. Adam checked the e-mail and his latest bank statement, then walked into the sitting room and pressed the 'play' button on the answering machine. He listened, frowning.

Three more messages, all hang-up calls. There was silence each time, as if someone were listening, eavesdropping almost. Adam thought he heard faint breathing, a gasp that sounded like laughter. Unease escalated to alarm. He dialled 1471, knowing it was pointless. Fury rose in him. How dare the bastard harass them like this! Assuming it was him. If it was, how the hell could he have got hold of their number?

'Thanks for fucking nothing!' he muttered to the supercilious 1471 voice. He crashed the receiver down in frustration. Could someone be thick enough to dial the same wrong, unlisted number five times? It was possible, if unlikely. The calls got on his nerves and he didn't want to have to tell Justine about them. He quickly pressed the 'erase' button as she strolled in, sipping white wine and rubbing her hair with a towel. She wore her thick white cotton bathrobe. Smells of citrus shower gel and fresh flowery perfume invaded the big room.

'Any messages?' she asked anxiously. 'I thought Donna or Stephanie might have phoned.' She put her wine glass down on the coffee table.

'There's nothing,' Adam lied. He looked out of the windows into the violet dusk. The dark mass of trees was still and hushed, as if exhausted by the day's heat. 'Thought about where you'd like to go for dinner?'

'I fancy going to Chinatown. I could manage a few dim sum, maybe share a crispy Peking duck with you.' She dropped the towel and came and stood next to him, put her arms around his waist. 'I'll miss living by this park,' she said. 'Even if it is full of rapists and rottweilers and rat-arsed Bluffs half the time!'

Adam smiled down at her and they kissed. She ran her hands over his broad shoulders, gazed into his warm dark brown eyes. 'One more week, my fairy princess,' he teased, hugging her so tightly that she gasped. 'Sure you want to marry a stressed-out GP?'

'Sure *you* want to marry a stressed-out copywriter?'

'I've never been more sure of anything in my entire life,' he said seriously. 'It'll be great. We'll pour each other huge gin-and-tonics when we come home knackered. I'll fend off clients who've never heard of evenings and weekends, and you can fend off disturbed patients who get crushes on me and start losing it. Sorry!' he sighed, kicking himself for stupidity as Justine tensed in his arms. 'I'm sorry. What am I *like*?'

'Forget it. Adam ...' She shook back her hair and her face turned pale as she gazed up at him. 'I know there's no proof, nothing concrete to go on, but suppose Matthew did murder Anna and that guard?'

'Okay, suppose he did? The police will get him.' Adam gripped her shoulders, his eyes furious. 'Listen to me,' he said fiercely, 'you've had a shock, you're upset. We both are. But that's no reason to jump to wild conclusions. Why the hell would he murder them? It's crazy, it doesn't make sense.'

'Why should it have to make sense? He might have gone there to ask about me. After the fight. He was furious, I know he was! Maybe Anna let him in.' Her lips trembled. 'If he murdered them, it's down to me,' she whispered. 'I should have reported him sooner, but I thought he was a harmless sad act.'

'I'm sure that's exactly what he is! Justine, you've got to stop torturing yourself like this,' Adam said angrily. 'You'll end up ill, stressed out. He can't be a harmless sad bastard one minute then a murderous maniac the next.'

'He could be anything,' she said slowly. She turned and walked back to the coffee table, picked up her glass of wine. 'What do we know?'

'It's up to the police now. You've done all you can. And please don't blame yourself, for Christ's sake, you can't possibly be responsible for anything he does. That's crazy!'

'Why did he pick on me?' she whispered brokenly. 'What did I do?'

'You didn't *do* anything!' Adam walked over and pulled her against him. 'Don't torture yourself like this,' he said, anguished. 'You had the misfortune to be on the same train as him that morning. It was bad luck, Justine!'

'I know you're right.' But knowing wasn't the same as believing. She laid her head on his shoulder and he stroked the back of her neck, smelled the delicious citrus odour of her damp hair.

'And it's going to be his bad luck if he comes near you again,' Adam said grimly. 'I've had enough of this. I'd murder the bastard myself if I thought I could get away with it!' He kissed her lightly on the lips and smiled to hide his anxiety. 'Get dressed, okay? Or we'll never make it to Chinatown. I'm starving,' he lied.

He showered and changed into beige chinos and a dark blue shirt, while Justine finished the white wine and blow-dried her hair. She sprayed on more perfume and put on a flowered silk slip dress, high-heeled sandals and the black linen jacket. Her soft hair floated and curled around her slim shoulders. They left the flat and linked arms as they came down the stone steps in the warm, grass-scented darkness.

'The nights are closing in already,' Adam remarked, desperate to talk about something safe and normal, shake the anger and frustration he felt. He couldn't wait to marry Justine and fly off to the Caribbean, get away from everything. When they came back they would move into the Childwall house. Maybe it would be better if she never returned to Brooks & Wilde, he thought suddenly.

Justine glanced around. 'I hope the good weather lasts until next Saturday.'

'It will.' Adam smiled. 'Mrs Shaw!' He kissed her and felt in his pocket for the car keys. The gleaming, metallic burgundy Jaguar was parked near the wall. A few leaves had drifted down and settled on the bonnet. He brushed them off.

'When you next speak to Donna,' he said, 'tell her she'll have to get the train to London next week. I won't be going to that conference.' He pressed the remote control button to unlock the car.

Justine stopped and pulled at his arm. 'Why not?'

'You think I'm going to leave you alone for two nights with all this shit going on? No way!'

'But, Adam, I want you to go,' she protested, dismayed. 'It's important. You're giving that paper, you've worked so hard.'

'Forget it. Nothing's more important than you.' He leaned her gently against the car and slid his hand up her smooth thigh and inside her silk panties. 'I love you,' he murmured, nuzzling her earlobe. 'I'm not going anywhere.'

'Please, you must go to London.' Justine gasped as he pulled her against him, his warm hand stroking her buttocks. She felt the hardness of his erection against her belly. 'I'll be fine,' she said. 'I don't want you to change your plans because of – Oh, no!' she breathed. '*No!*' She went rigid with fright, gripped Adam's arm as she stared over his shoulder into the dusk.

'What the hell's wrong?' He took his hand away.

'He's there – it's Matthew!' Her voice rose to a sob. 'Across the road, spying from behind that tree. Oh, my God!' Shock flashed through her, making her heart pound. 'How the hell did he *find* me?'

Adam turned, followed her terrified gaze. Across wide, potholed Aigburth Drive a thin, shadowy figure darted behind the broad trunk of a chestnut tree, the dark mass of the park at his back. The street lamps cast an ineffectual pale light and were dwarfed by the massive trees.

'There's definitely someone there.' He hesitated, glanced back at Justine. 'Are you sure it's him?'

'Of course I'm sure!' she flashed. 'I'm imagining it, is that what you think?'

'No,' he said sharply. 'Take it easy, okay?' He held the car door open for her but she backed away and took the house keys out of her jacket pocket. 'Where are you going?' he asked.

'Back inside to phone the police, of course! Let's forget going out. It must have been him Charley saw last night. I don't understand,' she said, her voice shaking. 'He's *never* followed me home before.' She dropped the keys, stooped and picked them up.

'He'll know he's been spotted and he'll run off,' Adam said quietly. 'Besides, even if they catch him there's not a lot they can do. You know what they said – there's no proof he committed any crime.'

'He's committing one right now, isn't he? Stalking me! They can arrest him, check him out.'

'Maybe. But there's not enough to convict him.' Adam's

suspicion that the creep had made the five hang-up calls hardened to certainty. His heart raced with fury. How had he got hold of their number? 'They'll charge him with harassment – if we're lucky. And he'll be back here tomorrow morning!'

'Then what do you suggest?' she hissed. 'Shall I wait for him to break in and rape me next week while you're at that conference?'

'I told you, I'm not going to the bloody conference!'

'Make sure I get plenty of stab wounds, preferably his finger-marks around my neck instead of my arm? End up in intensive care – or dead? Will that be *enough* for them? He might have killed Anna . . . we *have* to call the police!'

'He'll be long gone by then. Justine, calm down.' Adam stepped forward and slid one arm around her slim curved waist. 'Get in the car.'

'Why?' She struggled. 'What are you going to do?'

'I'm as pissed off as you are,' he said. 'There's only one language his sort understands – and he won't hear it in a Magistrates Court. He needs a reality check. Get in,' he repeated.

Terrified, she got in the car and slammed the door. Adam slid into the driver's seat and started the engine. 'I thought I was safe here,' she whispered. She was shaking with fright.

Adam slowly backed the car out of the drive. 'You are safe,' he said calmly. 'I promise.' He would get some answers out of the bastard, teach him a lesson he would never forget.

Matthew, flattened against the trunk of the chestnut tree, breathed freely and relaxed his taut muscles as the Jaguar reversed between the stone gateposts into the wide quiet road, tail lights glowing red. It was okay. For a second he'd thought Justine had spotted him.

*Adam Shaw*, he thought furiously, clenching his fists. That calm, confident voice on the answering machine, a voice used to giving orders and expecting them to be obeyed without question. Justine might lie and play flirtatious games, but she hadn't lied about having a man. This Adam was tall, handsome and broad-shouldered, the type women fancied. He looked rich and successful, like she'd said. Kissing her like that in public, putting his grubby paw up her dress! The bastard thought she was his plaything, his property. Justine didn't have a clue. She let herself be used, helpless and terrified. That was why she had punched and kicked Matthew yesterday. She had been desperate to get away in case Adam caught them together. Everything was clear. Of course he forgave her now he understood. It didn't stop him feeling sick to his stomach at Adam's existence.

Matthew felt tired and hot, burning with disappointment and the half bottle of Mexican brandy he'd nicked from the assortment of dusty sticky bottles on his mother's sideboard. He had drunk the beer and wine last night. He breathed hard, clenched his fists again. He'd murdered two people for Justine, risked his life and freedom for her. She didn't know, didn't appreciate him. It wasn't fair!

The Jaguar slid past then suddenly screeched to a halt. Adam sprang out of the driver's seat and lunged at him. Shock and brandy slowed Matthew's reflexes. The breath was knocked out of him as he found himself slammed against the tree trunk, rough bark scratching his face and filling his mouth. He yelled in pain and surprise as his arms were pulled behind him and twisted viciously up his back.

'Hurts when someone grabs your arm, doesn't it?' Adam's voice in his ear was steely, cultured, full of barely controlled fury. 'What the fuck are you doing, spying on my fiancée?' he demanded, wrenching Matthew's arms so hard that he howled in pain. 'She's not happy about it and, neither am I.' He shook him. 'Who are you? Where do you live? How did you get our address and phone number?'

Fiancée! 'I wasn't spying,' Matthew choked, his mouth full of bark. 'Me and Justine are friends. She told me where she lived – gave me the number.'

'You're lying!' Adam said furiously. 'Stay away from her,' he warned. 'Or you're dead. That's a promise! How did you get the number?' he repeated.

'I phoned her work,' Matthew gasped. 'Said I was a friend. They told me.'

'Liar!' His head was yanked back and smashed twice against the tree trunk. Blood gushed from his nose and mouth and tears poured from his eyes. His ears were ringing and he couldn't breathe properly. He sagged and grunted in agony as Adam began punching him in the stomach and then around the face and head.

'You followed her home, didn't you?' he panted. 'Where's your car?'

'Haven't got a car any more. Borrowed one from a friend. Okay, I followed her!'

His legs were kicked from under him and he collapsed, dizzy and winded, gulping for breath. A passing jogger in shorts and vest speeded up as she ran past, eyes firmly averted. In the car Justine watched in horror as Adam dragged Matthew to his feet and butted him.

'Stay away from Justine!' he repeated. 'If you don't, I'll kill you.'

Matthew's face was covered in blood and tree bark, his injured nose and lips and eyes already swelling. Adam grabbed him again and shook him like a rag doll, punched him twice on the jaw then kicked him to the ground. Matthew's idea of what constituted terrible pain changed for ever when Adam's booted foot slammed into his vulnerable groin as he lay helpless.

Agony flashed through him like an electric shock. He doubled over, his mouth wide open in a silent scream. He couldn't even groan. If he hadn't been sprawled on the ground he would have fainted.

'I want your name and address,' Adam said calmly. He stood over Matthew, kicked him again. 'Answer me, you piece of shit!'

'Doyle,' Matthew gurgled. 'It's Doyle!' He remembered the name from a billboard propped outside a bookshop in town, advertising some author who would be going there to sign copies of his latest novel. He had tripped over the board in his haste to avoid a drugged-up, tattooed scumbag screaming at him to buy the *Big Issue*. He knew he was finished if he told Adam his real name. He tried desperately to think of an address. His mouth was full of blood and he bit down on something hard. A filling? He sprawled against the tree trunk, tried to curl up and protect himself from the next kick.

Adam bent and grabbed him by the hair. 'Address!'

Matthew thought of his mother's favourite flowers. 'Marigold Street.' There was an area off Westminster Road in Kirkdale where the streets were named after flowers. His grandmother had lived in Crocus Street. There might be a Marigold Street. 'In Kirkdale. Number twelve,' he stuttered.

'Twelve Marigold Street, Kirkdale?' Adam didn't know the area and it wasn't on his patch. 'You'd better not be lying!' He tightened his grip and Matthew gave a choked cry. 'Justine

60

wanted to call the police, do it by the book,' Adam said matter-of-factly. 'But I've had enough of you screwing up her life . . . *our* life. I told her shits like you only understand one language.' He let go and stood up. '*This!*'

Matthew gurgled and choked again as Adam's foot slammed into his ribs and stomach. He rolled on his side and vomited, knew he couldn't hold out any longer if the beating went on.

Justine pressed the button and the window slid down. 'Adam!' she called, her voice shaking. 'Someone's coming – let's *go!*'

'Okay.' He turned back to Matthew.

Matthew coughed blood and spat bark and vomit, curled his body tight in terror. Another kick like that could land him in intensive care. He was dizzy, in agony, had a blinding pain in his head and groin and a horrible sour taste in his mouth. This maniac could kill him!

'The police know you murdered Justine's colleague and that security guard.' Adam squatted beside him, hands on his knees. He had broad strong hands, long slender fingers. The skin looked pale in the rising moonlight. His knuckles had dark shiny blood on them. 'Justine told them about you today, filed a complaint. You're going down for years. Unless you die first. Oh, and no more hang-up calls,' he warned. 'Or I'll hang you myself!'

He pulled a folded handkerchief from his pocket and wiped his bloodied knuckles, brushed dirt off his clothes. Matthew stared at him, memorizing his features. Square jaw, calm expression, thoughtful dark eyes, a mass of dark curls that strayed over his ears and forehead. How the hell did he know about the murders? He couldn't know, he must be guessing! Matthew made a final effort.

'I don't know what you're talking about,' he whispered. 'I never killed nobody!'

What did he mean, she'd told the police about him? The bastard was bluffing, he thought. You didn't *file a complaint* if you thought someone had committed two murders! It didn't work like that. Besides, Justine would never betray him, not even if she knew what he had done. She loved him, she could never hurt him.

Matthew watched, hugging his injured ribs, knees bent against his stomach, as Adam stood up and walked back to the Jaguar, got in and accelerated away down Aigburth Drive. Then he vomited again, this time from fear. He groaned as he retched blood and vomit, tried not to cough because it hurt so much. After a few minutes he slowly pulled himself into a sitting position.

He had terrible shooting pains in his ribs and groin, didn't need a mirror to know that his face was a bruised, swollen, bloody pulp. His head hurt like hell. His clothes were stained with blood and vomit, filthy with dust and tree bark. The sour stink was horrible. The few joggers and dog walkers gave him a wide berth. One dog, an inquisitive golden retriever, trotted across to sniff and lick the bloodied object sprawled at the foot of the tree. Matthew swore and hit out at its warm wet nose. It yelped and jumped back.

'Crystal!' its bald, middle-aged owner hissed. 'Get over here. Now!' He was short and stocky, wearing trainers and a shell suit. He looked away from Matthew and hurried on, the dog trailing reluctantly in his wake.

It was obvious no one would help him. Fucking bastards! He would have to get himself to hospital. Could he walk? Drive? He hadn't expected Justine to help him. She was under the control of the swine who'd given him such a kicking. She was terrified of him, did whatever he told her. She had to be rescued.

It took another few minutes before Matthew could stagger to his feet. He leaned against the tree trunk, groaning in pain as he got his breath back and gathered strength for his next move. He felt dizzy and nauseated. Gasping and groaning loudly, he staggered from tree to tree in the direction of his white Ford Fiesta. The car was parked further down the road, out of sight of Justine's house.

'I can't believe you did that!' Justine stared at Adam as he drove towards town in his calm, efficient manner. 'I never imagined you could beat someone up!'

'It's easy when you've had the right button pressed,' he said grimly.

'You won't do it to me after we're married, will you?'

He smiled, took her hand and kissed it. 'Only if you put ice in my gin-and-tonic.'

'What if he goes to the police?' she asked. 'You could be struck off for this. You shouldn't have done it,' she said wildly. 'You might have made things worse. God knows what he'll do now!'

'Stop hassling you, for starters.' Adam let go of her hand to change gear. 'It doesn't matter if he goes to the police,' he said.

'Although I doubt he'll be that stupid. I'll deny everything. Who do you think they'll believe?'

'But –'

'What did you expect me to do, Justine?' he interrupted. 'Give him the phone number of a rational emotive behaviour therapist? Write him a prescription for the latest anti-psychosis drug?' He pulled up at traffic lights, laid a warm hand on her bare knee. 'Don't worry,' he said. 'He's had his wake-up call and he won't come near you again. Now we can tell the police his name and address. If he's guilty of murder as well as harassment, he'll soon be banged up.' Adam decided not to mention the hang-up calls. What was the point? There wouldn't be any more.

'He could have given you a false name and address. You might have kicked the shit out of him, but not the truth!'

'We'll see.'

'I still can't believe he followed me home,' Justine said nervously. 'I was so careful! I got such a shock when I saw him standing there . . .'

'Now *he's* had a shock. He'll have to be content with hand relief and gynaecological manuals from the newsagent in future. Aren't you glad I did it?' Adam asked, stroking her knee. 'Don't you want me to protect you?'

'I suppose,' she said reluctantly. 'As long as you don't end up in trouble. It would be typical if that happened.'

He drove off again. 'I know it's easy to say,' he began, 'but please try to relax, stop being so frightened. It's been a nightmare for you lately – especially today. But it's over now. This time next week we'll be married and sipping champagne in the first-class lounge. Don't go back to Brooks & Wilde. You're good, you can easily get another job. Or start your own agency.' He glanced at her. 'You'd like that, wouldn't you?'

'I'd love it,' she said, her voice subdued.

'We just have to get through next week,' he went on. 'Stay busy, concentrate on the wedding, on each other. You'll have a great time on your hen night. Donna's organizing it, isn't she?'

'Yes.' Justine smiled. 'I told her no strippers!'

'We've got a lot to look forward to,' he said. 'Everything's going to be great.'

'You'll go to that conference now, won't you?'

'I'll think about it.'

Adam wouldn't admit it to Justine but he felt exhilarated by the slapping he'd given that tosser. He was hard again, raring to go. After their Chinese dinner he would take her back to the flat and screw her up a tree. She was so beautiful and sweet, so bloody sexy! He loved her, could never get enough, wanted to be with her all the time. She felt the same way about him. They would have a great life together.

Matthew told the polite solemn young Asian doctor in Accident & Emergency that two skinheads had kicked the crap out of him for trying to defend a black woman against their racist taunts. No, he hadn't had a tetanus jab for as long as he could remember. There was no point calling the police; it had been dark and he wouldn't recognize either of them again. Skinheads all looked alike anyway. The doctor ordered a tetanus jab and carried on treating his wounds. He'd come off worst in the fight, there was no doubt about that.

So why didn't she believe a word he said?

Tracey had slowly swallowed one-and-a-half litres of red wine, attended by her anxious irritated mother, who had reluctantly given up her ladies' night out to Blackpool. Tracey's throat felt better, but it was still very sore. It would take a few days before the shock wore off and she recovered. Yes, she would change the locks. But Matthew wouldn't be back. No, she didn't know his mother's address. He was gone and she was well rid of him. That was the main thing. She pitied his new girlfriend though, this so-called beautiful *Justine* he'd mentioned. Wished she could warn her what she was letting herself in for. Then again, would she listen?

Poor bitch must be desperate!

# Chapter Seven

'Where've you been all night? Holy Mother of God!' Paula Casey exclaimed, clutching her pink wool dressing gown around her slight figure. 'What on earth's happened to you?'

She quickly lit a cigarette and stared in horror at her only son as he lay slumped on the sofa watching television, the thin yellow ochre living-room curtains drawn against the morning sun. Matthew wore his pale blue, threadbare towelling robe, his skinny white hairy legs stretched out in front of him. Clean but worn black-and-yellow trainers served as slippers. He had severe bruising on his shin. His face was a bruised, purple, swollen mess, both eyes almost closed. He had a fluffy dressing on his forehead, a surgical collar that gave him a double chin, and his left wrist was bandaged. In the kitchen the old Bendix shook as his vomit and blood-stained clothes tumbled around inside it.

'I wanted a wash earlier.' Matthew looked accusingly at his mother. He would have preferred a bath or shower, but the doctor and nurses had told him to make sure he left the collar and dressings on for now and kept them bone dry. 'But there was no hot water.'

'I can't afford to keep the boiler on all the time. What's happened?' she repeated, blowing out smoke. 'D'you get in a fight?' Her nasal Scouse accent was low and wheezy.

Matthew's suitcase still stood by the piano where he'd dumped it yesterday. A foil pack of painkillers lay on the coffee table, next to his car keys, the telly guide and the empty bottle of Mexican brandy.

'Mind your own business,' he said irritably. 'And don't gawp at me.' He looked at her cigarette. 'D'you have to do that at this time of the morning?'

'I'll do what I like in me own house. Don't think you can just turn up after six months and start laying down the law!' Paula picked up the brandy bottle and tutted. She glanced at the television screen. A Mass from Rome, a dozing bishop slumped on his throne surrounded by hordes of priests and altar boys. Clouds of incense rising. There was no way Matthew was interested in *that*.

'It is my business, now that you've dumped yourself on me again because your girlfriend gave you the elbow. You look for a new place tomorrow,' his mother ordered. 'I'm not having you under me feet again. It's bad enough being stuck with that lot next door. Drugs, loud music, screaming kids . . . she says those dogs aren't pitbulls, but I swear they are! They'll rip me throat out one of these days.'

If I don't first! Matthew thought, irritation rising in him. Why couldn't she shut up, get out of his face? Same old, same old! Tracey telling him to sling his hook, now her. He didn't want to move back here, but where else could he go?

Paula Casey had the same brown staring eyes as Matthew, bitter and injured, and her thin grey hair was scraped back in a girlish ponytail. Her mouth was a tight line, her little rabbit's jaw tense with distaste and disapproval. Matthew had been nothing but a pain to her since the night old Dermot had knocked her up with him.

'I don't want the police round,' she said aggressively. 'That Jackson woman next door'll think I'm complaining about her. She'll barbecue me!'

'The police?' Matthew started and looked at her in alarm. 'Why would they come here?'

'Because you've done something, that's why.' His mother stood in front of him, puffing on her cigarette, blocking his view of the bishop. 'What is it?'

'I haven't *done* anything!' He glared at her. 'I was mugged, if you must know,' he lied, looking aggrieved.

Paula nearly laughed but stopped herself just in time. 'Who'd mug you, for God's sake? You don't look like you've got two pennies to rub together.'

'A gang of skinheads kicked the crap out of me,' he said angrily. 'I had to wait hours in Casualty. I told the nurses I'd been mugged, but they didn't give a shit. There were loads of drunks and drugged-up tossers who'd been in fights or crashed stolen cars. They got seen to before me, of course! I had no money for a hot drink. I asked one nurse for a cup of tea and she looked at me like I was barking. Don't know why they're called angels,' he muttered. 'Hard bitches, most of them!'

'You *are* barking,' Paula said contemptuously. 'Retarded! No wonder you get beaten up and kicked out. No one can stand you. First girlfriend at thirty-two,' she sighed. 'I knew that'd end in tears. I'm surprised it lasted six months.'

Matthew winced and flushed at his mother's barbs. 'I've got another girlfriend now,' he muttered. 'She's beautiful.'

'Move in with her then, can't you?'

'It's not the right time,' he said uncomfortably. 'Not yet.'

'You mean she doesn't want you any more than I do. If she exists!' Paula stubbed out her cigarette and went to draw the curtains.

'Don't do that!' he said, sitting up. 'I'm watching telly. And me head hurts.'

'You want to sit in the dark watching telly twenty-four hours a day, you can do it in your own place. Or your beautiful girl-friend's,' she sneered.

Matthew looked away and shut his eyes as sunlight flooded the mean sitting room with its faded flowered wallpaper, thin grey carpet and cracked brown mock leather sofa and armchairs. The scuffed piano in the corner hadn't been touched since his father died. When pissed, Dermot Casey had sat there banging out Irish revolutionary ballads about barbed wire and Thompson sub-machine guns. In between belting his wife and son. There were no ornaments or family photographs in the room, only Paula's favourite gilt-framed print on top of the piano, the sad, half-starved little Victorian match girl.

She looked out of the window and gave a cry of dismay. 'Oh, my God! Look what she's done! Look!' She pointed a trembling finger at the back garden, a rectangle of lawn surrounded by a wooden fence. There was a dilapidated shed at the end with a dead cherry tree leaning over it.

Matthew sighed and hauled himself out of the armchair, gasping at the pain from his bruised ribs. His whole body was stiff, sore, hurting. It even hurt to breathe too deeply. He felt more like eighty-two than thirty-two. He joined his mother at the window. 'What's up?'

The middle of the dried-out lawn was heaped with shitty nappies, bloodied tampons and sanitary towels, old newspapers, takeaway pizza and hamburger cartons, dog turds, empty dog food and soft drink cans. He stared in shock, his skin crawling with revulsion. Paula staggered away and collapsed on the sofa. She started to cry, thin shoulders shaking.

'I can't stand living next door to that woman and her brats any more!' Her voice was harsh, choked with tears. 'Sixty-six, I am! She'll be the death of me. The noise of them dogs and kids . . . and music doing me head in all day and night. Six kids she's got, by four different fathers! Gets hundreds of quid a week income support. It's the likes of *me* who's paying for her.' As if on cue, drums and throbbing bass started to pound through the thin living-room wall. 'Effing and blinding at me, even the little ones.' She reached for a tissue and blew her nose. 'I came back from Tesco the other day and she stood there laughing her fat head off while three of the lads poked at me with yellow plastic swords and them toy Russian guns . . .'

'Kalashnikovs,' Matthew interrupted tonelessly. 'AK-47 assault rifle.'

'One of them jumped at me, bit me on the arm.'

'One of the kids?'

'One of the dogs, you stupid . . .' Paula looked up and glared at him. 'I had to go down the doctor's and he gave me a tetanus injection. I didn't dare phone the police! Her over the road – Mrs Ellis – called the police about the noise, but they wouldn't do anything. Said it was the council's job. Next thing, she got a brick through her window.' His mother bent her head, started crying again. 'Why don't *you* help me? Get me out of here, find yourself a good job and make some proper money? I need someone to look after me,' she moaned. 'I'm sixty-six!'

'I know,' he said. 'You keep telling me.'

She and his father had neglected him from the moment he was born, never wanted him, didn't care whether he lived or died as long as he went to Mass every Sunday. Paula expected him to help her now, though, act the loving caring son. Wanted a daughter-in-law, grandchildren, Sunday lunch, the works. Bloody nerve of her! Old bitch! he thought furiously. She thought he was useless, made him feel it. He stared at the awful mess in the back garden, shivered with disgust and turned away. Hopelessness swept over him.

Justine was engaged and her big strong man had punched his lights out. She might even get married soon. He couldn't bear the thought of it. The odds were stacked against him; he would have to fight hard to rescue her. He also had to make damn' sure his and Adam's paths didn't cross again.

'Why don't you stop whingeing and get some breakfast on? I could murder a cup of tea!' *Murder*. That made him smile, despite himself. 'I won't take just any job. I'm waiting for the right offer,' he said pompously. 'I've got one or two things in the pipeline.'

'The only thing in your pipeline is sewage!' Paula sneered. She wiped her eyes.

'You had a good job as a security guard with that computer firm a couple of years ago – what was it called? Hayland Software. You could still have had it if you hadn't gone and ruined everything.'

'I can't stand injustice,' he said hotly. 'Betrayal.'

'Grow up,' she snorted. 'Torching the place because they wouldn't give you that couple of hundred quid wages you said they owed you! You were lucky they couldn't prove you did it,' she went on. 'People get banged up for years for arson. A million quids' worth of damage! It was a miracle no one got killed.'

Matthew felt extremely proud of having caused a million quids' worth of damage and got away with it. He kept newspaper clippings about the fire in an old pigskin wallet that had belonged to his father, got them out to gloat over whenever he was feeling down. He didn't want to talk about the fire now, though, and certainly not with his mother. One day he would tell Justine about it.

He slid one hand inside his dressing gown and gingerly felt the bandages around his ribs. It was horrible to be back in this tip of a house, to have to unpack the suitcase and put his clothes in that child-size wardrobe. What was Justine doing now? he wondered. Still sleeping? Being fucked senseless by Adam? He couldn't bear the thought of her lying naked in that bastard's arms. Bass throbbed and vibrated through the wall.

'The only peace I'll get is when I'm carried out of this dump,' Paula moaned. 'Feet first!'

He'd bury her in the garden if he had his way. Or sling her on the council tip along with the rest of the garbage, let the seagulls peck out those miserable accusing eyes. The thought gave him great satisfaction.

Grimacing with pain, he dragged his suitcase into the hall, unzipped it and took out the heavy bloodstained block of wood wrapped in a carrier bag. He went out the back door and down the garden to the shed, carefully skirting the stinking heap of garbage. Ruby Jackson's boys were screaming in their back garden now, the dogs yelping and growling. Bloody kids, he thought, up at the crack of dawn ready to cause chaos. He laid the block of wood on top of the pile, leaving it in its plastic wrapping. It would burn better.

The two jerrycans of petrol were still in the corner of the shed where he'd left them six months ago, covered with dust, dead, dried-out spiders and their cobwebs. He took one can and emptied it over the rubbish, taking care not to get petrol on his hands; it made his skin itch like crazy. He struck a match and tossed it, jumped back. Flames and black smoke billowed into the sunny air.

The morning was cool and autumnal. It was 30 August. Matthew watched with satisfaction as the purifying flames took hold, licking around the block of wood and consuming the horrific filth. It didn't matter if the block didn't burn through. As long as it was sufficiently charred, unrecognizable as a murder weapon. He stamped his feet and shivered. He should have got dressed first.

Bonfires weren't allowed around here, but so what? Everyone else had a contemptuous disregard for petty council regulations. Why not him? Out of sight behind the fence, the pitbulls barked furiously. He saw a pink blur through the frosted glass of the back door and hoped his mother was making tea instead of feeling sorry for herself.

'What the fuck d'you think you're doing, soft lad?' Ruby Jackson's round red bespectacled face and sunburned gorilla shoulders appeared over the fence. She stared indignantly at him as she brushed back lank greying mousy hair. Ruby looked about fifty, but she was probably ten or even fifteen years younger. Someone with six kids was bound to look prematurely aged. 'Hey!' she shouted. 'My kids and the dogs can't breathe with all that smoke.'

'Excellent!' He didn't want to look at her gruesome gob. 'I hope it chokes them.'

'You *what*?' she shouted, enraged. 'Put that fire out right now or I'll bloody have you!' She sounded like the air raid warden from *Dad's Army*. 'Jesus Christ!' Ruby stared at his injured face. 'Someone gave you a right good seeing to, didn't they? Want another one? Tell that old cow the dogs'll do more than bite next time. I'll make sure she gets a heart attack. Put that sodding fire out now!' she screamed, furious at being ignored.

Matthew's anger flared. Ruby Jackson was like all the others who despised him, laughed at him, thought he was a nobody. He wanted to throw her on the bonfire, watch her burn. The fat would melt and run out of her, fuel the flames as she died a slow, agonizing death. In the Middle Ages they'd strangled people before they were burned at the stake. Unless they were witches. Like her.

He breathed a sigh of relief as Ruby suddenly disappeared. He was exhausted, fed-up, sick of the ugliness all around him. He had to see Justine again. Church bells rang in the distance and a jet aircraft droned miles overhead, leaving white trails in the clear blue sky. The acrid bonfire smoke made him cough, and he groaned at the pain in his ribs. His eyes stung and watered. Everything except the block of wood was nearly burned, the empty dog food cans blackened and crumpled in the heat. Black smoke spiralled upwards.

How was he going to follow Justine with Adam guarding her every move? Another beating like last night's would land him in intensive care. Adam would be watching for him – would definitely string him up if he got the chance! And there was that big fat bitch with the rottweiler. He had to really watch his back.

Matthew cried out in shock as cold water from a garden hose was suddenly trained on him, soaking him instantly. He flung up his arms and staggered backwards.

'Told you to put that fire out, didn't I?' Ruby Jackson laughed shrilly. 'No one in this road does anything I don't like. Get it?' Five evil little laughing faces popped up beside her, screaming abuse. The dogs barked and he could hear a baby crying. 'Soft lad!' she taunted. 'Wanker! Get back to Mummy!'

Matthew ran inside, coughing and spluttering. He slammed the back door and turned the key in the lock. In the kitchen the radio was on and there was a smell of toast. Paula stared at him, the contemptuous critical stare that had unnerved him as a child. Still did, although he hated to admit it. She picked up the kettle and poured boiling water into the brown teapot with the chipped spout.

'What are you looking at me like that for?' he shouted. He shook himself like a dog; he was wringing wet. 'What was I supposed to do, pick up all that bloody awful crap with my bare hands?'

'Don't use language like that in my house!' Paula stirred the tea. 'What did she say?' she asked, the anxious look returning. 'I heard her shouting.'

'She said if you don't get a heart attack soon those dogs'll rip you to pieces,' he said brutally.

Paula put one hand to her throat. Matthew took clean underpants and socks, a black sweatshirt and blue jeans out of his suitcase and got dressed in the hall, wincing in pain as he pulled on the clothes. He draped the dressing gown over the cold radiator. Then he went back to the kitchen and poured himself a mug of strong tea, added milk and three sugars. He dabbed at the soaked dressings with a tea towel. The hospital hadn't given him any spare, and Paula didn't keep such things in the house. There had been no plasters for his bloodied knees as a child. He took a gulp of the hot sweet tea and warmed his hands on the mug. He walked into the living room and sat in the armchair.

'She'll do it again.' Paula came in carrying a cup of tea and a plate of toast.

'She won't,' he said, and gulped more tea. No one treated him like that and got away with it. He had an idea. 'I'll sort it.'

'Oh, will you?' she sniffed. 'That'll be the dae-woo!' She sat back on the sofa and lit another cigarette, ignoring the toast. 'You couldn't sort anything,' she said. 'Not even those kids at school who beat the hell out of you.' Matthew gasped and his hand tightened around the mug. 'The number of times I had to take you up that hospital! The nurses were sick of the sight of you.' Paula laughed harshly. 'The time those lads threw you off that bus, I thought you'd be dead.'

'Hoped, you mean!' he said bitterly. 'You never stood up for me.'

'You never stood up for yourself. And nothing's changed.' She took another drag on her cigarette. 'Hitler had the right idea,' she said, eyes narrowed. 'Get rid of the useless ones. A quick injection, and Bob's your uncle!'

'Don't let me keep you chatting,' Matthew said. 'You'll be late for Mass!'

He leaned his head back and shut his eyes, felt pain wash over his battered body. His mother's cruel words battered his psyche. He saw himself lying bruised and beaten in the school playground, his body curled up as he tried to shield himself from the kicks. He was surrounded by shouts and laughter, gleeful malicious faces peering down at him.

'Mental Case, Mental Case! We're gonna kill you, you fuck!'

After beatings they held him down and took turns to pee on him. Girls included. He'd never forget the sight of Kimberley Bowen's pale hairless crotch inches from his face. The teachers weren't interested; they sat smoking and swilling instant coffee in the staff room, joking about how Hitler and Stalin's educational methods could be applied to modern Britain. Half of them couldn't spell their own names, had only landed in teacher training college because their 'A' level grades weren't good enough for university. Matthew attracted aggression by being quiet and withdrawn, they said. He was a hostile loner who hated sports. His father said he was a wimp, a weirdo who couldn't find mates. There was something about Matthew that pissed people off, he said as he unbuckled his old black leather belt. Himself included.

Matthew was delighted when his father snuffed it. Dermot came staggering home drunk one rainy November night and accidentally washed down fourteen Paracetamol and a handful of strong sleeping pills with half a bottle of Scotch. That had cured his headache, all right! Paula was shocked and frightened but stayed in control, waiting in the bedroom with the radio playing until her husband fell into a coma and choked on his own vomit. Her years of being raped and slapped and punched, afterwards cleaning up his puke, were over at last. She checked his non-existent pulse, called an ambulance and assumed a grieving widow act. 'I'll admit he wasn't the perfect husband, but what man is? I loved him. You do, don't you?'

Privately she said that being a widow was the best thing for any woman. You got shut of one slob and had the perfect excuse not to

73

hook up with another. Widows got a lot more sympathy than wives or mothers. The only difference between a single mother and a married mother was money, she said. Because men had all the money.

People looked on Matthew's indifference as stunned grief that he was unable to express, made crass remarks about how it was all right for boys to cry, how he should talk to his mates. That made him laugh. He had no mates, didn't want any. The lads at school and in his road were thick. All of them.

He became more withdrawn and failed every exam he took. Left school and got a job folding boxes at the cardboard factory. After that came a step up stacking supermarket shelves, followed by promotion to serving behind the cold meat counter. Since then there had been more crap jobs interspersed with long periods on the dole. But things would change. Once Justine was his.

Bitches like Ruby Jackson were a drain on society. They couldn't even be quietly useless but had to shout and scream about their rights, about how everyone owed them a living. Well, they had no rights. They were scum. Matthew opened his eyes and drank the rest of his tea.

'I'll sort it,' he repeated, staring at the nodding beringed bishop on his throne.

Paula got up and looked out of the window at the smouldering pile of garbage on the scorched blackened grass. She crushed the cigarette stub in the white china ashtray. She'd hardly slept all night and felt worn out. Indigestion burned her stomach. She always had it lately. Having Matthew back was the last thing she needed.

'I want you out tomorrow, you hear?' She went and stood over him. 'Don't get your backside stuck to that armchair. My God!' she sighed as the bass from next door throbbed through her body. It made her ears go funny.

'Why can't you be a normal mother?' he said through clenched teeth. 'You hate me. You always did.'

'Normal?' Paula threw back her head and laughed. 'You're a great one to talk about normal! I want some peace in me old age,' she said furiously. 'I did cleaning for years, paid tax, put up with your useless father. And I end up with that scum next door – and now you again! It's lucky for you abortion's against me religion,' she shouted as Matthew got up and walked slowly out of the room. 'I would have done it meself with a knitting needle if I'd had the nerve. Let you bleed out of me, flushed you down the bog with the rest of the . . .' She stopped. She wouldn't swear, lower her standards because of him. Although Matthew would make the Pope himself use the 'f' word!

Matthew turned pale, felt sick again. She could say things like that, then murmur prayers at Mass. His body ached and throbbed and he shivered with cold. He had a blinding headache. He went into the hall, picked up his suitcase and began to slowly drag it upstairs. His mother followed.

'Don't bother unpacking!' she called after him. 'You won't be here long enough.'

She turned and hurried to the living-room window as she heard a car outside. The rusted red Escort belonged to one of Ruby Jackson's boyfriends. A short, thick-set man in a shiny lime green tracksuit got out carrying a box. His hands looked like bunches of bananas covered with tattoos. He stopped as he noticed Paula, gave her a hard stare. Then he put the cardboard box on the car bonnet, turned his back on her and pulled down his pants, exposing a big pale bottom with dagger tattoos on each buttock. Paula gasped in horror and turned away.

Matthew dragged the suitcase into his old room and pushed it under the bed. The room was unchanged since he'd left it. The peeling dirty white woodchip wallpaper had been there since he was five years old. He lay on the hard, narrow bed and slowly stretched out his sore limbs. His chest felt like someone was sitting on it, bearing down on him.

He couldn't remember ever feeling this bad. He needed a couple of days in hospital, but of course they'd thrown him out on his ear. What if it was true? he thought suddenly. What if Justine really had told the police about him, filed a complaint? She couldn't know about the murders. That was Adam bluffing, trying to frighten him, turn Justine against him.

'No!' he whispered, his eyes filling with tears. 'I'd have to kill you if you betrayed me. I don't want you to die, Justine!'

Justine opened her eyes, rolled over in bed and stretched her naked limbs. Sunshine poured into the big bedroom and dancing wave patterns from the park lake shimmered over the white walls and the ornate ceiling with its cherubs and plaster grapes and vine wreaths. Birds sang and ducks chattered and squabbled at the edge of the lake. Her nipples were tender and she felt slightly sore, but it wasn't an unpleasant kind of soreness. It was as if she could still feel Adam's touch, feel him inside her. She smiled. A kind of phantom penis effect!

She closed her eyes and hugged the pillow. After dinner in Chinatown they had come home and gone straight to bed. Adam was so hungry for her but he had taken his time. Kissing, licking, sucking, stroking, thrusting inside her until she thought she would faint if she came again. Sometimes it scared her to think how much she loved and needed him.

The door opened and he came in, dressed in jeans and a black T-shirt, balancing Sunday papers and magazines and a tray of coffee and croissants. His dark curls were damp from the shower.

'Breakfast in bed again! You're spoiling me.' She smiled and sat up, pulling the quilt over her bare shoulders. There was a touch of autumnal chill this morning, despite the sunshine. It would warm up later.

'You deserve it.' He carefully set the tray and newspapers in the middle of the big bed. Then he pulled the quilt away and gently kissed her lips and smooth throat, her breasts. She gasped as she looked down at his tongue circling her pink nipples, felt her face go hot.

Adam looked at her and smiled with delight. 'You're blushing, Justine!'

'I was thinking about last night,' she said shyly. 'You were unbelievable!'

'I can never get enough of you,' he whispered. 'You know that.' They kissed, clinging together. A minute later he let go of her, stripped off his clothes and got back into bed.

'Guess what?' He picked up his mug of coffee and took a sip. 'I decided to walk to the newsagent on the main road for the papers. I took a good look round on the way there and back. No sign of that bastard.'

'Did you think there would be yet? After what you did?'

Adam put down his coffee and kissed her. 'He's gone,' he said triumphantly. 'You'll never see him again. Unless the police want you to identify him, of course. I told you it would be all right.' The bedside phone rang. 'Bugger!' he groaned. 'Oh, well, I am on call.'

Justine slipped her arms around his neck and rested her head on his bare shoulder as he listened to the male voice at the other end of the phone. She stroked his broad, muscled back and kissed his warm skin, breathed in the wonderful comforting smell of fresh ground coffee. She hoped Adam wouldn't have to go out on a visit; she didn't want to be alone. Even if Matthew had learned his lesson. Hope sprang eternal. But so did doubt.

'I see. Yes, I understand that. No, it probably doesn't mean anything. Thanks for letting us know anyway.' Adam replaced the receiver and turned to her, his handsome face grim.

'Who was that?' she asked. 'Someone wanting a visit because they've got a sore elbow?' She knew it wasn't.

'It was the police – the inspector you saw yesterday. You were right,' Adam said gloomily. 'I didn't kick the truth out of that bastard! They checked the name and address. He doesn't exist.'

'Oh, no!' she whispered, immediately terrified again.

'Don't look like that,' Adam said, stricken. 'I still think he's out of our lives.' He put his arms around her, hugged her tight. What the hell next? he wondered. 'It doesn't mean he's a murderer either.'

'I know.' I should have stopped Adam last night, she thought, insisted on calling the police. So what if Matthew had escaped? There would have been a next time. But what was the point of dwelling on that now? And hadn't she wanted Matthew to get a kicking, wished she could have done it herself? She could only hope the price of vengeance wouldn't be too high.

# Chapter Eight

'So Adam kicked the bastard's head in?' Paul Melwood raised his eyebrows and smiled grimly. 'Good!' he said. 'I only hope he doesn't get charged with assault.'

'If that was going to happen we'd know by now.' Justine glanced nervously around the crowded restaurant, looked out of the window into the sunlit street. 'It's Tuesday and I haven't seen Matthew since Saturday. Adam thinks he's got the message.'

'But you don't, do you?'

Paul found it difficult not to stare at her. Justine was so beautiful! Today she looked fantastic in a silk-mix purple shift dress and spike-heeled satin sandals with ankle straps. Her smooth slim legs were bare. She had taken off the matching jacket and draped it over the back of her chair. He loved her dark blue long-lashed eyes and the wild, curly red-gold hair. Her soft skin was flushed pink across the cheekbones. She wore hardly any makeup; she didn't need it.

'No.' She gazed at the white tablecloth, the candle flame, the bottle of champagne in its ice bucket. 'I'm terrified,' she confessed. 'But I don't want to go on about it too much in front of Adam. I didn't realize how freaked out he was by all this. Adam really went for that creep,' she said in a low voice, her eyes downcast. 'Battered him! Afterwards he was *exhilarated*. We had dinner in Chinatown and when we got home he . . .' She blushed and picked up her glass of champagne, emptied it in two gulps.

Paul could imagine. 'Maybe you should tell Adam you're terrified,' he said gently. 'I understand you want to protect each other, but secrets in this situation could be dangerous. Don't let that stalker come between you.'

'That's exactly what I'm trying to avoid!' Justine looked upset. 'I want us to have a normal life, Paul. Adam's leaving for that London conference later, when he finishes afternoon surgery. I had a hell of a job persuading him to go! I won't let Matthew spoil any of our plans,' she said emphatically. 'He'd have won then.'

Paul nodded. 'I see your point.' He watched as she fished the dripping champagne bottle out of the ice bucket, poured herself another foaming glass full and drank it down as if it were lemonade.

'Hey!' he exclaimed jokingly. 'Go easy on that stuff! I'm responsible for you while you're out with me.'

She smiled briefly then the troubled, hunted look returned. His concern for her increased. The advertising agency murders were front-page headlines in the local papers, the first item on every news bulletin. Brooks & Wilde was besieged. Justine might not have to go back to work for another month, but she couldn't get away from it.

By this time next week she would have been married three days. The thought depressed Paul slightly. He hoped Justine and Adam's marriage wouldn't deteriorate into the disaster his own had become. He still hadn't told Sara he wanted a divorce. He was waiting for his solicitor to work out the final details of the generous settlement he planned to offer.

'Give us five minutes, will you?' he said to the hovering waiter.

The man smiled and hurried to a nearby table. Justine picked up her menu and put it down again.

'I'm losing confidence,' she said miserably. Her eyes were filled with fear. 'I can't have a normal conversation with a good friend like you. I can't even concentrate on reading a menu! All I can do is obsess about *him*, keep wondering why he picked on me. Whether maybe it's my fault.'

'Of course it's not your fault,' Paul said indignantly. 'He's in the wrong, he's responsible for his own actions. Nothing to do with *you*!'

'I know, but . . . I took a cab into town today,' she went on. 'I was too frightened to drive myself. I'm jumpy all the time, looking over my shoulder like some paranoid Cold War secret agent planning a drop!' She sighed and picked up her glass of champagne again, blinked back tears.

Without realizing what he was doing, Paul reached across the table and took her hand. 'I wish there was something I could do,' he said quietly.

'Know any contract killers?'

He smiled and squeezed her hand. 'I'm afraid not. Besides, I don't imagine a real live contract killer would be anything like the cool, skilled professionals you come across in films. He'd probably bungle the job and you'd be arrested within five minutes. Or end up being blackmailed.'

'Oh, well,' she said lightly. 'Bad idea!'

His hand felt warm, comforting. Paul was so nice, she thought, looking into his warm grey eyes below the dark straight brows. His face was thin and tanned, a longish oval. He was tall and broad-shouldered, with a slim body. He didn't look thirty-eight. He wore an expensive dark grey suit with a white collarless shirt. He had nice lips, a sexy smile, and his short straight dark brown hair was parted on one side, a few threads of grey at the temples. They had met through her work, about nine months ago, and hit it off immediately.

'He looks so ordinary,' she said. 'That frightens me too. 'I keep thinking he should have horns, a tail and an evil expression.'

'They don't usually look like wolves in wolves' clothing.' Paul frowned, shook his head. 'People like this Matthew character don't get it,' he said thoughtfully. 'He never has and never will. He'll have created an entire fantasy relationship with you in his head. He probably believes you love him, tries to rationalize away any evidence that doesn't fit the theory.'

'That's what I think,' she said eagerly, glad that he understood. 'He couldn't give up the fantasy if he wanted to.'

Paul let go of her hand and she reached for her bag and opened it. 'No tissues,' she said. 'Typical. Of course I've got at least twenty packets lying around the flat!'

He quickly passed her a folded white handkerchief and she took it and dabbed at the corners of her eyes. The handkerchief was warm and soft and smelled faintly of his aftershave.

'Shall we order?' Paul asked, seeing the waiter glance at them again.

'Okay. Some lunch this is turning out to be,' she sighed, picking up the menu for the second time. 'I'm sorry for boring you with all my problems.'

'You're not boring me,' he said sharply. 'Stop apologizing!'

The waiter reappeared, took their orders and poured more champagne. Justine wanted two starters instead of starter and main course. 'What do the police say?' he asked

'Not a lot. Being female and twenty-eight and not quite resembling the back of a bus on a rainy day doesn't help my case much either. They think it's my fault.'

'Great!' he said, annoyed. 'What's how you *look* got to do with it? Stalking's a crime now, isn't it? I thought the police took it more seriously.'

'So did I,' Justine said gloomily. She drank more champagne. 'According to the Protection from Harassment Act, he hasn't caused me to fear violence. Or not enough! So far, his behaviour doesn't constitute *enough* harassment. It's very hard to prove. Adam could have ended up in more trouble for defending me!'

'So what the hell are you supposed to do now?'

'Keep a log of incidents. Call the police if I see him again. Paul, don't let's talk about this any more,' she pleaded. She unfolded her napkin and shook it out. 'It dominates every conversation I have lately. I'm sick of it!'

'You're upset,' he said. 'Frightened. You've got every reason to be.' He felt anxious and afraid for Justine, felt a strong desire to protect her. Stalkers could wreck their victims' lives and the lives of the people around them. Destroy the strongest relationship. This bastard was an unknown quantity. He might be harmless and sad. But what if he wasn't?

'Adam's a great guy,' Paul said, and looked closely at her. 'I think you should tell him how you feel. If he knew you were this frightened . . .'

'I can't, Paul!' she said despairingly. 'I don't want him to worry about me any more than he does already. He thinks Matthew's got the message – he could be right. Adam and I had a long talk on Sunday,' she went on. 'When we come back from honeymoon everything will be better. We'll have our new house, a new life. I've decided to resign from Brooks & Wilde. It isn't solely because of the murders, although I won't deny they've affected my decision in a big way. I've wanted to start out on my own for years,' she said. 'Why wait any longer?'

'That's great!' he exclaimed, and raised his glass. 'Here's to your new career move! I'm sure it'll be a big success. I'll network like mad for you.'

'Thanks, Paul.' She smiled. They clinked glasses.

Their starters arrived, a salad of wild leaves topped with parmesan shavings for her, smoked salmon with tagliatelle and caviar for him. Paul's company and the champagne made her feel more relaxed. You just have to get through this week, she reminded herself. Four more days!

'Let's talk about you for a change.' She picked up her fork. 'Tell me how you are. Adam and I were in Mawdsley a few Saturdays ago,' she said. 'We went to visit a cousin of his who's just had a baby. We drove past your posh farmhouse.'

'Really?' he asked, surprised. 'Why didn't you bang on the door?'

'We did, but there was no answer. We thought if you weren't there we could introduce ourselves to your wife. Sara, right?'

'Right.' He felt depressed at the mention of her name.

'Isn't it a bore commuting from there to Liverpool every day?'

'Tell me about it! Sara had to fall in love with a stone and oak-timbered mausoleum in the middle of nowhere.' He would find an apartment in town now.

Justine laughed. 'We didn't think it looked like a mausoleum.'

'You haven't been inside.' The smoked salmon was delicious but Paul didn't have much appetite. 'I'm sick of Hansel and Gretel furniture, lead crystal and dried flower arrangements,' he said abruptly. 'Cold stone floors and little mullioned windows that keep out the light: I'm sick of the ghost too!'

'What ghost?' She looked at him, an interested gleam in her eyes.

'I don't believe it myself. Sara's never seen it either. It's supposed to be some sixteenth-century monk who got grassed up for saying Mass and was hung, drawn and butchered at the nearest Assizes. We get groups of confused people knocking at the door asking for a guided tour, telling us how they've seen a short figure in a brown habit –'

'With the hood up so that you can't see the face?'

He nodded. '– glide across the garden and melt through the sitting-room wall.'

'Sounds wonderful.' Justine ate a mouthful of salad. The fresh wild leaves and lemony dressing tasted delicious. 'Except for the furniture and the dried flower arrangements. And the horrible fate of the poor monk. I do hate dried flower arrangements,' she said thoughtfully.

'Then you're my kind of woman! Sorry,' he muttered, embarrassed. 'That sounds a bit cheesy. I didn't mean . . .'

'Don't worry about it,' she laughed. Paul was a touch unsure of himself, despite his wealth and good looks and business success. It was one of the reasons she liked and trusted him. Paul liked her and she thought he fancied her too, although he would never do anything about it in the circumstances. Nor would she. She loved Adam too much.

'What does the ghostly monk do?' she teased. 'Drag chains over the floor at night? Chant plainsong? Some very mundane things seem to go on in the spirit world, if the stories are to be believed.'

'We hear strange noises during the small hours.' Paul laid down his fork and pushed his plate away. 'Personally I blame the dried flowers rustling in the icy draughts.'

Justine laughed again and drank more champagne. 'I feel better now,' she said happily. 'You've cheered me up.'

'Have I? I'm glad I'm good for something.'

'That sounds rather gloomy.' She leaned forward and he caught a whiff of her sensuous flowery perfume. 'So, have you got any tips for Adam and me?'

'Tips?' he asked, startled.

'About marriage.'

'Oh! Apart from don't do it, you mean?'

'You're so cynical!' She smiled her dazzling smile and his heart flipped. The waiter removed their plates and refilled their glasses.

'Seriously.' Paul shook his head. 'I'm not the best person to ask. You're getting married,' he said, 'starting out. And I want a divorce.'

'Divorce?' she echoed, dismayed. 'Paul, I'm so sorry!'

'Don't be,' he said abruptly. 'I wish I'd done it years ago.'

'It's still a horrible ordeal, though, isn't it? I knew you were unhappy, but I didn't realize things were this bad. How long have you been married?' she asked. 'Or should I shut up?'

'No.' He picked up his glass. 'I don't want to bore you, that's all.'

'Come on! I must have bored you a lot more.' His handsome

face looked gloomy and she felt sorry for him. She also felt slightly pissed. 'How long?'

'Nineteen years,' he sighed. 'Sara's ten years older than me – not that that means anything. We met when I was at uni and she was a legal executive. Our children, Andrew and Rebecca, are away at uni now. Sara always says she wanted to be a barrister and that we stopped her. But I encouraged her, was ready to support her all the way. It's harder for women, I know, but it seemed to me she wasn't prepared to do what it took.' He paused, looked into Justine's incredible eyes. 'I don't necessarily expect you to believe my version of the story.'

'Go on with your version.'

'God knows why we got married!' he said bluntly. 'Sex, inexperience, the fact that Rebecca was on the way . . . You only know better when it doesn't bloody matter any more. The business took off, I've been very lucky. Sara had various jobs over the years, but the legal career was binned. She just *talked* about it a lot.'

The waiter put a plate of *gambas* grilled in garlic butter in front of Justine. Paul had ordered sole.

'I realize this sounds boring and self-indulgent and totally lacking in originality,' he said, 'but we've got zero in common. I'm not sure we ever really had anything. Sara's only interested in me for my economic worth.'

'*What?*' Justine looked at his broad shoulders and strong elegant hands, his handsome face. His grey eyes met hers. 'Paul, I can't believe that,' she said slowly. They stared at one another for a few seconds, then she blushed and lowered her gaze.

'She's had numerous affairs,' he went on. 'A string of young lightweights, each of whom dumped her after an embarrassingly short interval. She thinks I don't know about them.'

'How did you find out?' Justine asked curiously. 'Hire a private investigator?'

He smiled. 'Nothing that tacky. I'm afraid Sara isn't as clever and discreet as she likes to think. Rebecca and Andrew are grown up now – they've turned into a couple of strangers. They don't need me. Andrew's barely spoken to me since he was twelve. I think they regard me more as a financial backer than as a father,' he said bitterly, his eyes full of sadness. 'Do you and Adam want children?' he asked suddenly.

'It's never been an issue for us.' She shrugged. 'I realize

Adam's supposed to be desperate for a male heir and I'm expected to spend every spare minute worrying about my biological clock ticking away – it's just not something we ever think about. That seems to annoy a lot of ex-friends.' She laughed. 'Are you going to tell me I don't know what I'm missing?'

'No. D'you want pudding?' he asked as the waiter collected their plates again.

'Just coffee, thanks. Espresso.'

'Two espressos, please,' he said to the waiter. 'And the bill.' He reached into his inside pocket and drew out a red envelope. 'Here,' he said, handing it to her. 'I'm sorry I can't be at the wedding on Saturday. But I got you this.'

'You didn't have to buy me a present.' Justine ripped open the envelope and burst out laughing. 'A book token!'

'You said you didn't want boring things like towels and cutlery and casserole dishes. And I know you love reading. So . . .'

'It's perfect!' she laughed. 'Thanks very much, Paul.'

'You're welcome.' He raised his glass again. 'Congratulations! All the best to you and Adam. I'm sure you'll be very happy together.' He grinned. 'Although, to be honest, I can't really picture you as a GP's wife.'

'What's your picture of a GP's wife then?'

'Oh, I dunno. Someone who likes pine furniture and Laura Ashley dresses and curtains. Who doesn't sound sexy over the phone.'

'I couldn't live without pine furniture,' she joked. 'And it's great to have Laura Ashley dresses and curtains because I can hang the dresses at the windows and go out wearing the curtains and *nobody* will know any different!' She took a sip of espresso and glanced at her gold wristwatch. 'My God!' she exclaimed. 'It's after two. I have to leave in a minute, I've got a dress fitting. A friend's meeting me there, she's going straight from work.'

'I'll give you a lift,' Paul said, thinking of the stalker again. He could tell by Justine's altered expression that she was too. The relaxed jokiness had gone and she looked nervous and hunted again, her slim shoulders stiff with tension. She stood up, slipped on her jacket and they left the restaurant. In the sunlit crowded street she stopped and looked fearfully around.

'Any sign of the creep?' Paul took hold of her arm protectively. 'I'd like to do some damage to him myself!'

'I can't see him,' she said, scanning faces. 'But that doesn't mean anything.' They walked towards Paul's Mercedes. 'I thought I was too flash a driver for him to follow me home, didn't I?'

'Maybe he didn't follow you,' Paul argued. 'There's loads of ways to get someone's address. Or their phone number. Even if it's private.'

'That's another thing that scares me!'

Ten minutes later he dropped her off outside the dress shop and watched as she walked gracefully down the narrow street, mellow sunlight glinting on her beautiful hair. He had wanted to kiss her on the cheek when they said goodbye, but he'd restrained himself. He sighed.

He could easily have attended Justine and Adam's wedding, but he didn't want to go. Sara didn't care one way or the other because she had never met them. He thought of the look that had passed between him and Justine over lunch. It wasn't only that he felt so attracted to this beautiful, warm, exciting woman who liked him but unfortunately loved someone else. He was depressed by the idea of being amongst happy people celebrating a wedding when his own next major life event would be divorce. His phone rang and he sighed again before picking it up. He felt bored and sleepy, frustrated and fed-up. Psychically exhausted, as Rebecca would have said.

'Paul, when are you coming back to the office?' Linda, his secretary, sounded frazzled. 'Your two o'clock lady arrived five minutes ago. Ms Terekhova?'

'Oh, right.' The beryllium deal, the cool polite, female voice on the phone. 'Apologize for me, will you?' he said. 'Tell her I'm on my way.'

He replaced the phone and started the engine. He had done business with people from the Russian Federation, but he had never come across Ms Terekhova before. He couldn't remember her first name.

Would Justine be all right? Paul wondered. Adam Shaw was a great guy, he would look after her. Paul frowned as he pulled out into the traffic. He had to stop thinking about Justine, see less of her in future. His business with Brooks & Wilde was concluded. He had to concentrate on this promising-sounding beryllium deal, on the rare earth products and metals his company dealt in. Not on

86

things that could never happen. He had to think about Sara. About divorce.

The Mercedes sped past the Liver Buildings and headed for Melwood Materials on the Dock Road.

'The dress is fantastic!' Donna exclaimed as she and Justine came out of Stella's Bridal Creations. She lit a cigarette. 'Gorgeous ivory silk, such a lovely simple, off-the-shoulder design. I love it!' Donna wore her dark blue staff nurse's uniform beneath a light beige mac, and she had removed the big clip that held up her hair. Her hair and clothes smelled of formaldehyde. She could never quite wash or shower away the hospital odour.

'It's good, innit?' Justine smiled. 'I didn't fancy some frilled, billowy, rosebudded, footballer's wife type thing. Aren't you hot in that mac?' she asked.

'It was cold when I left home at the crack of dawn. And I can't walk the city streets in my uniform, I'd get besieged by perverts and hypochondriacs. My God, I was dying for a fag!' Donna breathed, blowing out smoke. Come on,' she said. 'We'll go back to your place and have a quick drink while I get changed. Then I'll take a cab to the surgery and wait for Adam.'

'You'll come back from London, won't you?' Justine teased. She glanced sideways at her friend. 'I don't want you lying in Cal's flat in a sexual stupor, forgetting about my hen night and the wedding. I can't believe you're travelling hundreds of miles just for a stupid birthday party of some guy you hardly know.'

'I'd like to know more,' Donna laughed. 'I really fancy him, Justine.'

Not as much as Adam, of course. Cal would do for now, screw away some of her pain and longing. Shame he lived in London. Donna did fancy Cal, but felt more excited at the thought of three or four hours alone with Adam in his car. Was he in a hurry to get to London, or would they stop off somewhere? Maybe they could have dinner together. She wasn't in too much of a hurry to get to Cal's. Let him wait!

'No problem,' she said. 'I'll be back. Everything's under control. The club, the balloons, the strippers . . .'

'No strippers! I warned you.'

'Well, what's your idea of a hen night? Bring Mum along and

87

count the number of tea towels? Is your mother coming to the wedding?' Donna asked.

'Yep. She phoned a couple of weeks ago. There's no phone in that tumbledown cottage, so she had to go to the pub – *not* a problem for her! I told her to leave Swithin the eco warrior behind. How did you meet this Cal?' Justine asked.

'At a party. He works in London, he came up to Liverpool for the weekend. His family live in Crosby.'

'What does he do?'

'He's a probation officer.'

'Bloody hell!'

'Listen, we can't all be friends with sexy millionaire businessmen who buy us book tokens and champagne lunches and chauffeur us to dress fittings in their S300 Mercedes!' Donna sighed and dropped her cigarette. 'I tell you what, Justie babe, I'm in the wrong job!' She paused. 'I'm sorry to be a bore . . .'

'Then don't be,' Justine said briskly. 'Yes, Donna, I'll be *fine* on my own. You're as bad as Adam. Hey! Quick, there's a cab.' She waved and broke into a stumbling run. 'Damn these shoes!'

Neither girl noticed the dirty white Ford Fiesta in the stream of rush-hour traffic that clogged the city centre. Matthew frowned and clenched his fists, gripped the wheel as if he were choking the life out of the receptionist all over again.

A wedding gown shop! The nightmare was becoming reality. When was she getting married? It might be this coming Saturday! Who was the bitch with long dark shiny hair and lying eyes, a fag stuck in her gob? The tall guy in the sharp suit who Justine had had lunch with? There was so much he didn't know, so much that wasn't on that elaborate curriculum vitae of hers.

The idea of Justine getting married and becoming Adam's official property was intolerable to him. Not only intolerable, it would make her rescue that much harder. She looked even more beautiful today, he thought, pained. She should wear short sexy dresses and high heels all the time. He would make her wear high heels when he fucked her. The lights changed to green and the long line of cars edged forward. He let in the clutch and moved slowly off after the black cab.

'I'm your fantasy and your nightmare, Justine!' he said aloud. He hated the sticky heat, the noise, dust and traffic fumes. The fact that she had told the truth all along. Except about wanting him to leave her alone, of course. She loved playing hard to get. They all did.

His head ached and his ribs hurt, although the pain wasn't as bad any more. His face still looked a mess. Adam Shaw was going to be very sorry for that! He punched the wheel in pent-up frustration, causing the Ford Fiesta to swerve to the right. Several drivers blared their horns and swore at him through open windows. Matthew blared back at them.

'You won't marry him, Justine!' he shouted, enraged. 'No fucking way!'

# Chapter Nine

Justine could not remember the last time she and Adam had spent a night apart. He and Donna were halfway to London now, and the thought of spending the next two nights alone in the flat frightened her. She stepped out of the shower and wrapped herself in a big towel, then went down to the kitchen and poured herself a glass of white wine.

She stood sipping the chilled, flowery-scented Riesling and gazing out over the back garden. The sun was fading; long shadows slanted across the lawn. Water droplets rolled off her hair and skin and fell on the floor. It was almost seven, but she wasn't that hungry and didn't feel like cooking. What should she do this evening? She was too restless to watch television or lose herself in a novel. She had gone off thrillers – and no wonder!

I'll go out, she decided. It was pointless to cower at home with an overactive imagination and a fridge full of wine. She wouldn't lead a crippled existence controlled by fear. Anything was better than that.

She felt very lonely without Adam, and the silence in the big flat was oppressive. Music, she thought. She took her glass of wine, went up to the sitting room and put on her favourite CD of the moment, *The Best of George Michael*. The phone rang and she jumped out of her skin.

'Justine? It's Charley.'

'Oh, hi!' Justine closed her eyes and breathed a sigh of relief. 'How are you?'

'Fine, thanks. Mum and I thought you'd be missing Adam,' Charley said in her deep, authoritative voice. 'We're no substitute, of course,' she said, 'but we wondered if you'd like to join us for drinks and dinner – if you haven't got any other plans? I could order us a big *lasagne al salmone* from the Italian place.'

'That sounds great. Thanks, I'd love to join you both.' A boozy evening with Charley and Marinda was the perfect solution. It would give her a laugh, take her out of herself. And she would be out yet close to home. 'I'll be down in about ten minutes, okay?'

'Excellent,' Charley said. 'See you soon. Whitney's missed you,' she added.

Justine went into the bedroom and dressed in a short black top and khaki combat trousers, vigorously towelled her damp hair and fluffed it out. It curled even more when it was left to dry naturally. She didn't bother with makeup. She got a bottle of Gewurztztraminer as her contribution to the dinner, put on a pair of trainers and looked for her keys. She whistled, feeling more cheerful. The phone rang again and she snatched it up, hoping it would be Adam.

'D'you like me present?' Matthew asked. 'Have you tried it yet?'

Justine froze. The receiver felt as though it were glued to her hand and right ear. She stared out of the window at the stone balcony, the green tree tops and darkening blue sky. Some of the leaves were turning brown already. Adam's wristwatch and thick black notebook were missing from his bedside table. Time seemed suspended. It felt as if she had been rooted to this spot, stuck in this terrifying moment, for eternity. She opened her mouth to ask, How the hell did you get my phone number? What present? No words came out.

'Say something, you bitch!' he demanded, angered by her silence. 'D'you know where I've been for the past couple of days?' he shouted. 'Recovering from the damage that big bastard did me!' I'll do him more damage, he felt like saying. But why give advance warning? 'Come on, Justine.' He lowered his voice. 'Put it inside you now, tell me what it feels like. Wait until it's me doing it to you! Who was that man you were with today?' he asked. 'I don't like you seeing other men behind my back. I'm sick of your games . . .'

Justine crashed the phone down and hit the 'recall' button. No

91

use, he'd dialled 141 beforehand. She stood up, trembling with fear, and walked into the sitting room. Matthew had followed her again today, seen her and Paul together! He wasn't going to stop. He would never leave her alone.

'What *present*?' she whispered, one hand to her mouth. Her glance flew to the carrier bag on the sofa. Marinda had thoughtfully scooped up her and Adam's post, put it in the bag and left it outside their door after showing a workman in to mend a light fitting in the downstairs hall. Justine had forgotten all about it. She grabbed the bag and shook its contents on to the coffee table, moving aside the lavender-scented candles.

Cards, junk mail, a phone bill. A strangely shaped package, gift-wrapped in tacky flowered paper with a crumpled card clumsily sellotaped to it. Her name was scrawled on the card in blue biro. Justine hesitated, feeling sick with fear. She didn't want to touch it. She ripped off the paper and gasped in horror at the sight of the huge, obscene black-and-gold dildo.

'Oh, no!' she whispered. 'Oh, my God!' She pulled the card from the envelope. It was a postcard of a naked woman lying on her back clutching her breasts, her legs wide apart, a cat's face where her vagina should have been. The woman's face wasn't visible. Justine turned the card over.

*Soon it'll be the real thing. You're mine and I need you in my life. You belong to me. No more games, Justine. You've tested me enough and I've come through with flying colours.*
*Love from Matthew xxxx*

*Love!* What did he know about love? He was sick, twisted, an evil presence spreading a suffocating black cloud over her life. Sobbing with rage and fear, Justine hurled the dildo across the room and tore the card up, scattering the pieces. What the hell did he mean, he'd come through with flying colours? She grabbed her keys and rushed out of the flat in panic as the phone rang again and kept on ringing. She closed and double-locked the flat door, her fingers shaking.

She slammed the downstairs front door and ran round to the front of the house, dashed up the steps and rang the bell. She heard the rottweiler barking in the hall. Charley answered the door. She wore baggy blue cotton trousers and her enormous breasts bulged through a tight black T-shirt. Her bulbous cheeks and forehead were flushed bright red.

'Hi!' she said. 'We're having drinks on the terrace while we soak up the last rays of sun. What's wrong?' she asked in consternation, seeing Justine's pale, shocked face. 'You look like a vampire's had a go at you!'

'Same difference! It's that creep again, he sent me . . . oh, God!' Justine's eyes filled with tears. 'I need to call the police,' she said. 'Can I phone them from here?'

Matthew staggered out of the Victorian pub with its panelled walls, stained glass windows and old-fashioned shiny brass taps and stood swaying on the pavement, breathing in the cool early-autumn dusk. A faint smell of burning wood hung in the clear night air. Lark Lane was as busy in the evenings as it was during the day. People came from miles around to enjoy the pubs, restaurants and wine bars. He had been drinking since he'd called Justine from the phone box nearly four hours ago, pints of a beer called Old Peculier. Its strength certainly made him feel peculiar.

For once he'd felt like talking to people, having a laugh. But the young women and men he smiled at averted their eyes and turned their backs on him, acted as though he were invisible. Maybe his bruised face and bandaged arm, the surgical collar, put them off. He had tried to tell the group of snotty students what he was going to do but they had jeered and shouted at him to get lost, looking at him like he had two heads. It made him furious. He began to walk along the pavement, jangling the car keys in his pocket, bumping into people. The smell of woodsmoke grew stronger as he walked in the direction of the park. He stopped and leaned against a wall. When he closed his eyes he felt dizzy, as if he were flying backwards at about a hundred miles an hour. He liked the sensation.

He imagined Justine naked, on all fours, crying out and pleading with him as he pounded away inside her, the mass of curly hair falling over her tear-streaked face. Her blue eyes were wide with pain and fear. 'I'm sorry, I'm sorry!' she screamed. 'Matthew, I swear I didn't look at that man. Don't hurt me, please!'

She was telling the truth. She was sweet, submissive, faithful to him. She would never look at another man because he would make sure she didn't! He grabbed a handful of hair and yanked her head back, tightened the leather collar around her neck and pulled it so tight that she started to choke . . .

The tall young man with pale tangled hair and a denim jacket slung over his shoulder caught the word 'sorry' as Matthew collided with him.

'S'all right, mate!' he smiled. 'I wasn't looking where I was going either.'

'Got the time?' Matthew mumbled. '*Mate!*'

'Quarter to eleven.'

There was no way Ruby and her pitbulls and brats would be asleep yet. She probably had visitors again, the shaven-headed tattooed thugs who sat up all night drinking and laughing while music shook the walls. He got into his car, which was parked near the old police station, and sat listening to Radio City, trying to clear his head. The Old Peculier was better than painkillers, and certainly a lot more enjoyable.

Justine didn't want to marry Adam. She was only doing it because she was terrified of his threats and violence. She was praying to be rescued and Matthew wouldn't let her down. She must have hung up on him earlier because Adam had come into the room. Matthew belched loudly and laughed. Then he started the car and slowly reversed out of the parking space.

Aigburth Drive was dark and quiet, the street lamps barely penetrating the mass of foliage around the big Victorian houses. A full moon rose in the starry sky and he could smell grass and earth as well as woodsmoke. He parked the car out of sight and walked slowly to Justine's house. A skateboarding teenager in baseball cap and baggy clothes careered past him and crashed headlong into the unforgiving trunk of a chestnut tree. Matthew laughed at the groans and curses of the injured boy, then winced as he remembered how it had felt when Adam slammed his head against the tree trunk, just three nights ago.

He was about to cross the road when he saw the police car. It was cruising, headlights dimmed. He gasped and darted behind a tree, flattening himself against the trunk. It was coincidence, he told himself. They weren't after him, they were just patrolling Sefton Park. He risked a glance. The car slowed and stopped outside Justine's house. Two plods, a man and a young woman, got out and walked up the drive, climbed the steps to the front door.

Matthew was alarmed at the sight of the police. But it couldn't be anything to do with him. That wasn't Justine's flat they were going into. The hall and sitting-room lights were on, long red velvet curtains partially closed. He glimpsed the sparkle of a chandelier in the massive room. A light was on over the front door.

An old woman with a sharp eagle's face and swept-up dyed yellow hair appeared at the windows, smoking a cigarette and staring suspiciously into the darkness, a big glass of red wine clutched in one claw. She wore a tight black dress that exposed bony raddled arms and shoulders. She put the glass down and drew the curtains fully. The plods came out by themselves about five minutes later and sat in the car for another minute before finally driving off.

What was going on? He needed to see Justine right now. Was Adam home? His poncy Jaguar wasn't there. Neither was Justine's BMW. Matthew swore, felt helpless and frustrated. Suddenly the front door opened again and the mad, wall-eyed Amazon came out with her rottweiler. She wore the same kind of trousers and sweater as the other night, only blue this time instead of peach. The dog strained at the leash in its eagerness to get into the park and rip someone or something's throat out. He backed quickly away and hid behind another tree further down the road.

'Steady, baby doll!' the woman panted, her deep voice audible in the still air. 'Hang on, wait for Mummy!'

If it hadn't been for the tits you'd have thought it was a man. *Baby doll! Mummy!* Matthew suppressed a snort of incredulous disgust, watched anxiously as the unholy pair crossed Aigburth Drive and headed into the park. He was too far away for the dog to smell him. Rottweilers were the psychopaths of the dog world, he thought. Normal and friendly for years, then suddenly they ripped your head off. Nothing personal.

He shivered in the cooling air, wishing he'd brought a jacket. He darted across the road, went up the driveway and around to the side of the house, keeping himself hidden in the bushes. He pressed the bell and stood breathing heavily over the intercom, ready to run off if Adam answered. Trees and bushes lined the narrow cinder path that led to the back garden. He pressed the bell again, hard. Justine was out – or pretending to be. She hadn't picked up the phone again, and the answering machine wasn't on. He didn't think Adam was home. Desperately he pressed the bell a third time, so hard that his finger hurt.

Anger boiled in him, fuelled by the beer he'd drunk. He'd warned Justine about stupid games, but she'd ignored him. She needed to be taught a lesson. He kicked furiously at the unyielding door. He pressed the other bell, but no one answered that either.

'Justine!' he shouted. He ran down the steps and round to the front of the house. 'Justine!' he screamed up at the dark windows of the top flat. 'Get down here now! You'll be sorry if you don't.'

He flexed his fingers and clenched his fists, sore eyes blazing. His jaw was rigid with pain and fury. He had to tell Justine what he'd done for her. What he was going to do. She had to understand.

'What the *hell* d'you think you're doing?'

The scrawny old bat stood at the top of the steps, glowing cigarette held gracefully in one hand. Matthew stared at her. The black velvet dress belonged on a woman Justine's age, not someone who collected her pension and bus pass. Her rouged cheeks, black eyeliner and thickly glossed red lips looked ghoulish in the strong overhead light. She was stick thin, her arms and legs like twigs.

'I need to see Justine,' he shouted. 'It's an emergency.'

'Is it really? Well, I'm afraid you're out of luck.' Marinda Bluff's supercilious gravelly voice was slurred after she'd drunk about a litre of wine. She took a last drag on her cigarette, threw it down and crushed it beneath her elegant high heel. 'Justine went out,' she lied. 'Hours ago.' In fact Justine was behind her in the hall, shaking with fear as she phoned the police for the second time that evening. Unfortunately the two officers on patrol who had called back to check on her had left only minutes ago.

'Where is she?' Matthew shouted. 'When will she be back?'

'I have absolutely no idea,' Marinda answered belligerently. The brazen impudence of him! she thought. Astonishing that he wouldn't keep away even after Adam had given him a good hiding. 'If you don't know either, you're obviously not meant to.'

'She's my girlfriend!' Matthew yelled, enraged. 'I've got a right!'

96

'Oh, yes! Lowlifes like you are always shouting about your *rights*.' She eyed him contemptuously. 'Don't care about other people's rights, do you? Justine isn't your girlfriend,' she said angrily. 'She never was and she never will be. You're nothing but a stalker, a criminal! She hates the sight of you – as do most people, I imagine. Get off this property now!' she ordered. 'You're trespassing. My daughter will be back from walking our dog soon, and neither of them takes kindly to finding dossers hanging about!' She peered down the driveway and across the road, trying to see into the park. Where was Charley? She was taking ages tonight.

'Don't you call me a dosser!' Matthew clenched his fists, incandescent with rage and humiliation. Had Justine described him as a stalker, a criminal? Told them she hated him? He couldn't believe it. 'If I want to wait here I will,' he shouted. 'You fucking old bitch!'

Marinda raised a twiglet arm and he gasped in shock as he found himself staring down a gun barrel, some kind of big pistol pointed right between his eyes.

'D'you know what this is?' she asked breathlessly. 'It's my husband's army pistol. He taught me to shoot and it's still in excellent working order. So am I.' Her arm trembled slightly with the weight of it. 'I assure you, I won't hesitate to use it.' She cocked the safety catch and took a step forward. 'I'd love to shoot a miserable criminal like you,' she said. 'I don't get much fun nowadays.'

'That's not a real gun.' Matthew backed away, his eyes fixed on the barrel.

'Isn't it?'

'You won't shoot!'

'Won't I?' Marinda laughed drunkenly. 'I suppose it's like Mr Clint Eastwood says, it depends on whether or not you feel lucky.' Charley adored Clint Eastwood and drooled over videos of his films. She might as well drool over something; a middle-aged Amazon who didn't wear makeup and bought her clothes in job lots from catalogues wasn't likely to land a husband.

'You mad bitch!' Matthew shouted nervously.

'Mad, bad and dangerous to know!' Marinda laughed again and levelled the gun, gripping in both hands. 'Well, do you feel lucky? I'd love to blow you away!' she cried gaily.

'Yes, he's outside now. Please hurry!' Justine replaced the receiver and walked to the front door. She was trembling all over and wished with all her heart that Marinda would carry out her threat and shoot Matthew. She could plead alcoholism and bewilderment, totter away with a suspended sentence. Be celebrated in the tabloids as another diehard, have-a-go senior citizen who wouldn't stand for any nonsense.

'*Mum!*' Charley hurried up the drive, Whitney panting after her, surprised and disgruntled by the sudden burst of activity. 'What the hell are you doing with Dad's pistol?' she called, horrified. 'Put it away, for God's sake, you'll kill somebody! We'll get done for . . .' She saw Matthew and stopped dead.

'It's the stalker,' Marinda called, waving the gun at Matthew who ducked. 'Justine's inside, phoning the police again.' She clapped a hand over her mouth.

'Oh, dear!' she giggled. 'I shouldn't have said that!'

'Justine!' Matthew yelled, furious and alarmed. 'Come out of there! Justine!'

She came out and stood at the top of the steps, shielding Marinda, the overhead light glinting on her hair. Her face was pale and her beautiful eyes were filled with rage. Marinda stepped back and lowered the gun.

'Leave me alone, you bastard!' Justine blazed. She shook back her hair. 'I hate you, can't you understand that? I've had enough,' she shouted. 'I told the police about you – handed over your *present!*' How long would they take? Thank goodness Marinda had the gun.

'You called the police?' he gasped. 'You betrayed me? You don't know what I did for you,' he choked, eyes filling with tears. 'You fucking bitch!'

'What did you do for me?' Justine stepped forward, hands on her hips. A verbal confession in the presence of two independent witnesses would come in very handy. 'Tell me!' she shouted desperately.

Charley and Marinda were watching him intently. Charley longed to set Whitney on him, but was afraid of the consequences; for the dog more than herself. The rottweiler barked, then growled steadily and menacingly. Matthew heard a car approaching at great speed. No siren, they didn't want to announce their arrival. He had to get away – now! He looked wildly around like a trapped animal. He couldn't believe Justine had done this to him.

'I'll be back!' he shouted. He pointed at Justine, stabbing the air with his finger. 'I'll have you! You'll be sorry for this!'

He stumbled down the cinder path to the back garden. His bruised ribs and sore muscles ached and he could hardly breathe. It was pitch dark. Fear of arrest, the desire for vengeance, drove him on. He would show Justine – he would show them all!

'The police are here,' Charley cried. 'Mum, get inside and put that gun away, quick! You okay, Justine?' She nodded, white-faced.

Matthew ran panting across the long back lawn and came up against a high brick wall. Even if he could climb it, he would break every bone in his body when he dropped down the other side. He ran backwards and forwards, swearing furiously, his hands scrabbling over the rough brickwork. Justine wasn't sweet, submissive, terrified, waiting for him to rescue her. She despised him, hated him, thought he was nothing. It was unbearable.

He breathed with relief as his scrabbling hands touched a solid wooden door. He managed to undo the two stiff rusty bolts, sleeves over his hands to avoid fingerprints and cuts. But the door was locked and there was no key in the lock.

'Fuck!' he whined. He dropped on all fours and scrabbled desperately in the loose dry soil. His fingers touched what felt like a big tile to one side of the door. Underneath was a rusted key. Thank Christ! He took the key, twisted it in the lock and pulled the door open. He could hear distant male voices, the rottweiler barking. He pulled the door shut and locked it behind him, dropped the key.

He ran down a long narrow alley and turned left down another one, wishing he could run faster. His legs and shoulders and ribs hurt like hell and his breath came in short harsh bursts. He found himself in a dark, quiet, narrow tree-lined road with smaller houses, the lights of the main road ahead. Police sirens wailed in the distance. He pulled off the surgical collar and shoved it down the front of his black sweatshirt, wiped his face. He was boiling hot, covered in sweat.

He reached the main road with its shops, chippie and Chinese takeaway and stood at the bus stop, flinched as a police car raced past. Then he crossed the road to the other bus stop. He would get a bus back to town, then walk to Central Station and get a train to

Old Roan. The police would comb Aigburth Drive and the surrounding streets, look for lone men acting suspiciously. He didn't dare go back for his car. He would have to wait until tomorrow to retrieve it.

'Fucking *bitch*!' he muttered, his eyes full of tears. How could Justine humiliate him in front of those two women, betray him so cruelly, spew those words of hate? She had crucified him, and now he had lost all faith in her. She was just like Paula, like Tracey. Like all the rest. She didn't know how much she had hurt him, wouldn't care if she did. She was a demon, not an angel.

The bus came and he got on, went up to the empty top deck and sat at the front. He buried his head in his hands and let pain and disappointment, the unbearable agony of loss, burn through him. Justine Flynn was the only person he had ever loved. And she had scorned that love, flung it back in his face.

Matthew wiped his eyes and sat up, took a couple of deep breaths. The bus lurched towards the centre of Liverpool, through streets full of pubs, boarded up houses and brightly lit shop windows. Traffic fumes irritated his nose and throat.

So be it, he thought. If he couldn't have Justine's love he would take her fear.

Then her life.


Adam hung up the phone and lay back in bed, frowning. Three times he'd called now and Justine still didn't answer. The machine was switched off. She must have gone out with a friend, probably Stephanie, and she was all right, of course she was! He had to stop worrying. He reached for his Scotch and took another sip, picked up the remote control and switched off the television.

It had been a relief to escape the tension at home although he felt guilty admitting that to himself. Now he missed Justine like hell, and longed to be back in Liverpool with her. She'd probably stay the night at Stephanie's place, or get her friend to stay with her. That made him feel better. He began to relax.

He and Donna had had a laugh on the drive down to London, talked about all sorts of things. He was glad Justine had a friend like her. Donna hadn't been in any hurry to get to her new boyfriend's party so he had invited her to have dinner with him and Simon, an old friend from medical school. Simon's interest in Donna was undisguised, as were the embarrassing blokish grins and winks he kept giving Adam. He had never thought of Donna as a sexy, attractive woman in her own right, simply as Justine's best friend. Justine was so beautiful that beside her Donna usually didn't get a look in. But Simon's interest had revealed her in a new light. Adam liked her though he wasn't interested, of course, not that way. For him there could only ever be Justine.

He picked up *The Lancet* and flipped over a few pages. Great bedtime reading! He sighed and tossed the journal on the floor, yawned and stretched his arms above his head. He missed Justine desperately, wished she was in bed with him now. He loved it when she fell asleep in his arms after sex. He had to get some sleep; tomorrow would be a long, busy day. The presentation was at ten.

He was about to switch off the bedside lamp when someone knocked frantically at the door. He sighed and got up, put on the scratchy white hotel bathrobe and peered through the door's spyhole. Donna's tearstained face loomed. He unlocked the door and opened it.

'What are you doing here?' he asked, astonished. She stood there clutching her rucksack, her pretty face twisted with misery. 'What's wrong?'

'Oh, Adam! I'm really sorry to bother you at this hour.' Donna bowed her head, crying bitterly. 'But it's too late to catch a train back to Liverpool, and I'm too scared to spend the night sitting around Euston station. I didn't know what to do,' she sobbed. 'Where else to go.'

'It's all right. Come in,' he said, holding the door wide. Donna walked in and stopped outside the bathroom, holding on to the rucksack for comfort. Her shiny brown hair fell around her face. She had exchanged the navy blue lycra crop top and black cargo pants for a short sleeveless flowered dress and high-heeled pale pink slingbacks. Adam shut the door and turned to her.

'I presume things didn't work out with Cal?' he asked sympathetically.

She shook her head miserably. 'I got to the party but he wasn't there. His mates said he'd gone out to buy some extra booze.' She could hardly speak for crying. 'They were all looking at me, laughing and sniggering. It was obvious something was going on. I had a couple of drinks then I thought I'd go and dump my stuff in his bedroom. Cal was there . . . in bed with some girl!' She dropped the rucksack and burst into floods of tears. 'He just laughed! Told me to fuck off. I'm so unhappy,' she sobbed. 'I can't bear it! Nobody ever wants me!'

'Hey, come off it! That's not true.' Adam stepped forward and took her in his arms, smoothed back her shiny slippery hair. Donna clung to him, her slim body shaking. He felt concerned, sorry for her. 'You don't need a tosser like that,' he said, hugging her. 'You're too good for him. His loss!'

'You're so kind, Adam!' Donna wailed. She didn't really care about Cal, but she was humiliated and felt very sorry for herself. 'It's nice of you to say that.'

'It's the truth,' he said firmly. Her bra-less breasts were jammed against his chest and her nipples were hard. He shifted away slightly.

Donna shut her eyes and clung tighter, loving the feel of Adam's arms around her. She wanted him so much she could hardly bear it. In a few days he would be married, forever out of her reach. It wasn't fair! 'I'm sorry,' she repeated, her voice muffled. 'I shouldn't have turned up like this.'

'Don't worry about it.' He stroked her back, one smooth bare shoulder. The thin dress strap slipped down. 'It's late, you're upset. You did the right thing. We don't want you wandering around London all night, do we?' He patted her arm. 'Try to calm down, okay? He's not worth it.' He glanced over her head towards the mini bar. 'I'll get you a drink,' he said. 'Gin-and-tonic?'

'Thanks.' Donna raised her tearstained face and looked at him. 'Adam, can I stay here tonight?' she pleaded. She glanced around the double room. 'Just let me sleep in that armchair – or in the bath. I'll leave early before you're awake. I'll be really quiet, I'll try not to be too much of a nuisance.'

'You're not a nuisance,' he said. 'Although you will be, if you go on like that!' He handed her the drink, watched as she drained it in one go and put the empty glass on the bedside table. 'Of course you can stay.'

'It's very kind of you. Are you sure?' She looked at him, her eyes glittering with tears and lust. The strap slipped further down her arm and she didn't bother to yank it up. Her nipples were visible through the thin, silky dress fabric. Adam swallowed, glanced away. I should throw her and her bloody rucksack out, he thought. Right now. He didn't move.

'I'm sure,' he said awkwardly. 'And you don't have to sleep in the bath. It's a king-size bed, there's loads of room.' He was nervous, embarrassed, out of his depth. 'Which side do you want?'

Donna didn't answer. She slipped the dress off and stood naked in front of him. Adam stared unwillingly at her breasts and slim waist, her long, smooth tanned legs. She stepped forward, slid her arms around his neck and gazed longingly into his eyes.

# Chapter Ten

The dark house stank of chip fat and the street was silent except for the throb and boom of bass coming from guess where. Shame Ruby and her visitors were still awake, but it couldn't be helped. At least they would be drunk, tired and slow. It was three in the morning and he couldn't wait any longer. Matthew got slowly off the bed and stretched his stiff, sore body. He pulled up the black sweatshirt hood and fastened the strings.

The pack of latex gloves and two jerrycans of petrol were at the bottom of the wardrobe, covered with neatly folded clothes. He crept into the spare room, parted the curtains and stared out into Wordsworth Avenue. No one else was up as far as he could see, no insomniac gawping from bedroom or sitting room windows. Of course there was always a risk. He took a pillowcase from the airing cupboard on the landing, then went back to the bedroom and pulled on a pair of latex gloves. He felt nervous and excited; it was hard not to laugh out loud. He carried the heavy petrol cans downstairs.

In the sitting room Paula's green plastic lighter lay on the coffee table next to her cigarettes. He took the lighter and put it in the pocket of his sweatpants. In the kitchen he unbolted and unlocked the back door and went down the garden. It was annoying to have to stumble around in the dark, but he dared not switch on any lights. He unbolted the fence gate and hurried along the alley that ran between the back gardens of the houses. A pitbull growled as he passed the Jacksons' garden. He swore. He was sick of the sight and sound of bloody dogs!

He came to the cul-de-sac that separated one row of houses from the next and hurried through to the front of the street, glancing around as he went. There was nobody about. He smiled to himself and his confidence rose. It would be okay.

He squatted in Ruby's porch and unscrewed the cans, praying that no one would come to the door. Thank God the dogs were in the back garden! He lifted the letter flap and peered inside. Light came from the back room and there was a smell of sweet smoke and stale urine, the damp stink of dogs and people who were no better than dogs.

'Come on, Rube!' There was a burst of male laughter. 'Shag it or rag it, you soft bitch!' Cards were slapped down and beer can rings pulled. The throb of bass went right through Matthew, did his head in. How could they stand it?

He listened for a few more seconds then lifted a jerrycan and carefully poured petrol through the letter box, as slowly as possible so as to avoid loud glugging noises. He sweated with fear trying not to drop the damn' thing. A pool of petrol formed on the uncarpeted hall floor and flowed in a silent deadly stream towards the kitchen and living room.

Please God, let them not notice! He mouthed the words silently. There were more shouts and he drew a sharp breath as Ruby Jackson suddenly screamed with demonic laughter. Matthew emptied one jerrycan and started on the second. He didn't mind the fumes; he liked the smell of petrol. Once the second jerrycan was emptied he relaxed slightly. The fumes were incredible. How could they not notice? Of course they had their own smells. And they were well pissed.

He twisted the pillowcase into a rope and shoved it through the letter box, leaving the end bit sticking out. There would be a lake of petrol now and it would move quicker because there were no carpets. He was brimming with laughter and excitement, had to fight down a whoop of delight. The buzz was fantastic! His temples throbbed with the bass.

He snapped the lighter and the pillowcase end flared. When it was burning properly he poked it through the letter box, jumped up and grabbed the empty jerrycans. He would have loved to stay and watch but it was too risky. He stepped out of the porch and sprinted away down the alley.

A river of flame whooshed through the hall and up the stairs. Clouds of acrid black smoke and flames billowed into the kitchen and the front and back rooms. Ruby Jackson and her brothers,

Keith and Martin, didn't stand a chance. They looked up from their cards and beer to find themselves engulfed by scorching flame and dense black smoke. The window was double glazed with a small opening at the top left. Too small. Keith grabbed a chair and tried to smash the windows. It was no use.

'The kids!' Ruby screamed, panic-stricken. 'Get me kids out!'

Upstairs the children screamed and cried in panic, their small feet frantically pattering on the bare floorboards. In the back garden the pitbulls, Thor and Wodan, jumped up and ran around in circles, barking frantically.

'Mam! Mam! Help us!' Neil, the eldest boy, grabbed the screaming baby from her cot and huddled in the bathroom, shutting the door. The others were driven back by the flames and trapped in their bedrooms.

In the living room Keith, Martin and Ruby's clothes caught fire. Ruby's last thought before she passed out from shock, third-degree burns and smoke inhalation was that the smoke smelled horrible, like when you were trying to get a barbecue going. From the other room she heard an explosion and shattering glass as the front window was blown out.

Matthew regained the safety of Paula's back garden after having tossed the cans into a nearby skip. It didn't matter, his fingerprints weren't on them. So what when the police realized the fire was deliberate? There were any number of pissed off people who could have torched the Jacksons-from-hell. He had done what those miserable cowards only dreamed about!

He bolted the fence gate and locked the back door, ran upstairs and stripped off pants, sweatshirt and latex gloves and stuffed them in a carrier bag under the bed. He pulled on his pale blue threadbare towelling robe over his tartan underpants and knotted the belt. It was still damp because Paula wouldn't put the radiators on. He couldn't smell petrol on himself. He'd been ultra-careful.

Matthew was hot and sweaty and wanted to take a shower, but thought it might look weird at that time of the morning. He crept into the spare room. An orange glow penetrated the thin curtains.

'Yes!' he whispered fiercely. 'Yes!' He shook with silent laughter, clamped one hand over his mouth as he suppressed a yell of pleasure and excitement. Wait until Justine found out what he'd done! This would get her attention, all right. He wasn't a nobody, to be scorned and ignored.

He suddenly realized his hands, face and neck were itching like crazy. He swore; he must be allergic to latex. He went into the bathroom and splashed cold water over himself. It didn't help. He drew the blinds and switched on the light. His face and neck and hands were covered with pink blotches. He dried himself with a rough frayed towel and rubbed on some of his mother's Nivea cream. That made it worse. He'd nick one of her Valiums – that would help him relax, might stop the crazy itching. He went back into the spare room and peered out.

A murmuring crowd had gathered outside the Jackson house, uselessly standing and gawping, their shocked faces lit by the orange glow from the flames. Matthew pushed his sweaty bare feet into his trainers, ran downstairs and out the front door.

'What's going on?' he shouted at the blank faces. 'Has anyone called the fire brigade?' He didn't intend to call them himself; he'd heard that the first person to report a blaze was usually suspect number one as far as the police were concerned.

'Yeah, I called them.' Suspect number one, a big bearded man in a dark-coloured shell suit, stepped forward. 'They're on their way. You should get out quick, mate,' he warned. 'Your place could go up too. Anyone else in there?'

'Me mum! I'll get her.' Matthew dashed back inside and up to Paula's bedroom. She was snoring away on a bloodstream full of sleeping pills.

'Wake up!' he yelled, shaking her roughly. 'The Jacksons' place is on fire.'

'You what?' She turned over in bed, blinked sleepily and stared up at him. The orange glow in the room reminded her of the Liverpool blitz. 'What d'you say?' she faltered. Her face was even more sunken without her false teeth, and her voice was slurred and muffled. Matthew was revolted. She looked like a corpse.

'Get up!' he shouted. 'You dozy old cow! I *said*, next door's on fire.'

'Oh, my good God!' she gasped. She pushed back the bedclothes, sat up and shuffled her feet into slippers. She wore a long cotton nightgown buttoned up to the neck. 'How did it start?' she asked fearfully.

'I don't fucking know, do I?' Matthew shouted, enraged by her slowness and stupid confusion. He'd like to let her burn if this house went up too, but it wouldn't look good. The role of concerned son was highly appropriate just now. 'Come on,' he urged. 'Move your arse!'

Paula stared at her son, suddenly frightened of him for the first time in her life. Matthew's thin lips were drawn back in a snarl and his eyes shone and glittered with excitement. His bruised face was covered with strange blotches. He looked completely mental. She hauled her dentures out of the glass and slipped them into her mouth, then stood up and pulled on her dressing gown.

'Where's me handbag?' she quavered.

'Never mind your sodding handbag!'

A horrible thought flashed into her brain. 'You did this!' she hissed. 'Didn't you?'

'Shut *up*!' Matthew clenched his fists. 'Or I'll leave you to burn!'

'Is this your idea of sorting it? I might have known! You've had it this time,' she said. 'They'll put you away for years and I won't be sorry! Don't expect me to visit you in the slammer and bring you sweets and filthy books.'

A massive blow landed on the side of her head and she found herself on the floor. Coloured stars exploded in front of her eyes and she tasted blood in her mouth. Her head spun and she gulped for air, thought she would faint. Matthew dragged her up and threw her on the bed.

'You open your big gob and I'll fucking kill you!' he yelled, his hot stinking breath in her face. She flinched away from him. 'I won't take any more crap from you – I'll break your bloody neck first! D'you hear?' His eyes were furious, manic. Terrified, Paula nodded weakly. He gripped her arms and pulled her into a sitting position. 'Come on!'

She struggled to her feet and Matthew manhandled her out of the bedroom and down the dark stairs. At the front door he stopped and turned to her.

'Remember!' he warned, gripping her arms so hard that she cried out in pain. 'Keep it shut or you're dead! I mean it,' he said fiercely. 'I've got sod all to lose.'

Paula gasped in horror and clapped one hand over her mouth as she saw flames and smoke shoot and billow from the Jacksons' windows. Were they all in there? She trembled with cold and fright and a tear ran down her cheek. She'd hated the abuse, noise, harassment and fear Ruby and her brats had caused her. But that didn't mean she'd wanted them dead! She just wanted to feel safe, to be left in peace. She glanced at her son's ugly bruised face, clenched hands and exultant expression. He was loving every minute of it!

He was a nutter, an evil murdering bastard, but if she grassed him up she would only make trouble for herself. She didn't want to be notorious as the mother of a murderous arsonist. They always blamed the mother. And Matthew would kill her as he'd threatened. If he was capable of this, he would stop at nothing.

The distant siren grew louder and two fire engines turned into Wordsworth Avenue, blue lights flashing and sirens blaring. Firemen jumped out and unrolled the long hoses.

'How many are in there?' one of them shouted at the crowd.

'Six – no, seven. A woman and six kids.' An exclamation of horror went up. 'Oh, God! The kids!'

They trained hoses on the burning house and donned breathing apparatus. No one could get in yet, the flames were too fierce. The occupants were almost certainly dead. Smoke inhalation killed within minutes. A police car and two ambulances pulled up.

Matthew watched the horrible scene raptly, eyes shining with pleasure and excitement. This was bound to be on the telly, might even make the national news. Justine would see it! He wished he could be there when she did.

Paula clutched her dressing gown around her and shivered violently. He wants locking up, she thought. What can I do? She was too scared to open her mouth. Matthew gave her a hard, warning look as a policeman approached them.

'Someone told us you live next door,' he said. 'Mrs Casey, isn't it?'

'That's right,' he interrupted. 'This is my mother.' He put one arm around Paula's shivering shoulders, felt her stick-like body go rigid with fear. 'D'you think it'd be safe for me to go inside and make her a cup of tea?' he asked solicitously. 'I'm a bit worried. It's chilly out here and she's had a terrible shock.'

Paula could warm herself on the Jackson fire! He bit his lips, fought back a burst of laughter. The policeman shrugged.

'Dunno about that, mate. You'd better check with the fire brigade. I'd wait a bit if I were you. D'you know how many people were in there?' he asked.

'Seven, I think. Maybe more. She had a lot of visitors. Men.'

They looked round as the crowd moaned. A few women started to cry as a fireman struggled out of the flame and smoke-filled house carrying the limp body of a small boy in pyjama bottoms, his lifeless little face blackened by smoke. The boy was lifted gently into the waiting ambulance. The next body to be brought out was that of Ruby Jackson. She didn't look any better in death than she had in life. Except that she was silent, not screeching obscenities as the body bag was zipped over her blackened face and charred hair.

'There's a baby,' a young girl sobbed. 'She's called Katrina. Where's little Katrina?' she screamed.

The room was lit by one lamp and the heavy flowered quilt had been kicked to the floor. Donna's head pressed against the ludicrous pink shell-shaped headboard as Adam furiously fucked her, his hands on her breasts and his tongue in her mouth. Her long dark hair cascaded over the pillow. Her moans turned to cries as another orgasm started and she clung to him, her hands sliding down over his buttocks. Adam was unbelievable, better than in all her fantasies. He made her crazy. She felt his body go rigid for a second, then he shuddered and groaned as he came, his eyes tight shut, strands of her slippery hair twined around his fingers. She felt his pounding heart against her breasts, his warm breath on her neck, sweaty skin against skin.

'I love you,' she gasped.

Adam raised his head and looked down at her. A bead of sweat dripped off his chin. 'Come off it, Donna!' he whispered sharply, his dark brown eyes cold. 'I thought you were a grown-up.'

Was he? He had betrayed Justine, a few days before their wedding. With her best friend, in a hotel room. The ultimate sordid cliché that he'd never even dreamed he would be capable of! What the hell was he playing at? Justine was alone, terrified by a stalker, and here he was hundreds of miles away shagging her best friend. Nice one, very blokish! He raised himself on one elbow and turned away, filled with remorse.

'Will you get me another drink?' Donna asked quietly, hurt by the sight of his broad smooth muscled back, the turning away that signalled rejection. Did Adam hate her now? She felt guilty about Justine. But not that guilty.

'What d'you want?' He got off the bed and walked to the mini bar, paused to look down at the lights of Park Lane. You don't deserve Justine, he thought. You don't deserve anyone, you miserable bastard!

'Gin-and-tonic again.' Donna laughed nervously. 'Make it a large one. Can I smoke?' she asked.

'If you must.' He got two little bottles of gin and a can of tonic out of the fridge, kicked the door shut. He felt self-conscious as she looked hungrily at his naked body. He poured the drink, handed it to her and pulled on the white bathrobe.

'Don't you want a Scotch or something?' Donna smiled at him as she lit her cigarette. Don't panic, she told herself. It'll be all right.

'No,' he said shortly. 'I've had more than enough to drink for one evening.'

There was an awkward silence. Donna took a gulp of gin-and-tonic and smoked her cigarette, tried to think what to say. Adam sat on the edge of the bed.

'Look –' He paused. 'I hope you didn't mean what you said just now.'

'That I love you? Sorry, but I did mean it.' She stared at the chilled, misted glass and took another gulp. 'It's my problem,' she said sadly. 'I know that.'

He looked warily at her. 'So what are you planning to do about your problem?'

'I won't tell Justine, if that's what you mean!' Donna dumped the glass on the bedside table and stubbed out her barely smoked cigarette. 'All I can *do* is suffer in silence. Don't worry,' she said sulkily, 'I won't become one of those crazy obsessed women who follow men around, bombard them with letters, phone calls and e-mails . . .'

'Not funny,' he interrupted coldly. 'Especially in view of *recent events.*'

'No.' She sighed. 'Sorry, sorry!'

'I love Justine.' He stared at her. 'I really love her, she's everything to me. We're getting married this Saturday, for Christ's sake!'

'I know. I'm a guest, remember?' Donna pulled the sheet over her breasts. 'Or would you rather I didn't attend? In view of *recent events!*'

'Don't be silly,' he said abruptly. He ran a hand through his dark hair and the robe fell open. She felt another pang of painful desire. 'I'm not angry with you,' he said. 'I blame myself. This should never have happened. I don't know what the hell came over me!' He shook his head despairingly. 'I love Justine,' he repeated.

'I know you do.' Donna smiled sadly. 'Put it down to wedding nerves.'

'It was a one-off,' he said. 'An aberration.'

Donna winced and tears of hurt filled her eyes. 'Is that what I am?'

'No! I'm sorry. I didn't mean it like that.' Adam got up and walked around to her side of the bed, sat down and took her hand. 'Don't cry,' he said awkwardly. 'Please, Donna. I feel enough of a bastard already.'

'I didn't mean to fall in love with you,' she sobbed. 'It just happened. I never would have said anything. Justine's my best friend.'

'And I'm her future husband!' Adam let go of her hand. 'Justine must never find out about this,' he said fiercely. 'She'd be devastated.' The feeling of guilt was horrendous. He felt as though he had violated their relationship, stained and soiled something precious, personal, intimate. 'I don't think she could handle it. Certainly not now.'

'I won't say anything.' Donna's voice was low and subdued. 'I promise.' Musn't hurt the beautiful, fragile, fairy bloody princess! she thought furiously. Darling Justine, who had stolen the best men and left her with the dregs ever since they'd both grown tits and started bleeding every month! She kept her eyes lowered so that Adam wouldn't see her rage. She stretched out one arm and picked up the glass of gin-and-tonic, causing the sheet to fall from her breasts. They were high and rounded, the nipples hard. Her belly was smooth and flat. Adam looked at her and she smiled through her tears.

'I wish I could find someone I really loved – who wasn't spoken for,' she whispered. 'Sometimes I feel so insecure. I don't think anyone will ever want me. Except for the occasional shag!' she said bitterly.

Adam took her hand again, squeezed it. 'You don't need to be insecure. You're beautiful, Donna. You've got a great personality.'

112

'You don't mean that.' She sniffed and wiped her eyes. 'You're just being kind.'

'I'm not!' Donna was manipulating him, even though she really was upset. But her breasts looked beautiful and he was getting hard. He hated himself, but he wanted her again. She saw the look in his eyes.

'Please, Adam.' She knelt up in bed and slipped the robe off his shoulders. 'I want you so much! This won't happen again, I accept that.' Like hell! she thought. She kissed him, pushed her breasts against his chest. 'Let me have tonight,' she begged tearfully. 'It's our secret. I promise you, I'll never tell anyone as long as I live!'

'I don't love you,' he said. 'I never will. I don't think I'll even like you after tonight. Any more than I like myself!' he added bitterly.

She took his hands and laid them on her breasts. 'Touch them,' she whispered, her dark eyes pleading. 'Make love to me again. Please!'

Adam shrugged off the robe, pushed her down on the bed and slid between her legs, roughly stroking her breasts. Donna cried out as he entered her. She tried to put her arms around him, but he gripped her wrists painfully and held her down.

He looked into her eyes. 'I love Justine.'

Justine woke at seven and went down to the kitchen to make coffee. She felt exhausted and depressed. The sun was shining and the long back lawn glittered with frost. The whole Matthew situation was escalating, had become a nightmare. She couldn't even think about the wedding. Tonight was her hen night; she wished Donna would forget it and stay in London with Cal. This was supposed to be the happiest time of her life and Matthew bloody no-name was ruining it. Fear and hatred pumped adrenalin through her bloodstream, made her dread that she would never again feel safe or happy.

The dildo and ripped up card had been bagged as evidence; she hoped the police wouldn't lose it. They had found the key Matthew had dropped in the alley and taken it away for analysis. Charley said she would put a spare one beneath a flowerpot at the foot of the fire escape, in case they needed to use it. She was supposed to keep the answering machine on, tape any calls Matthew made. She still couldn't think how he had got her phone number. What else did he know? *Had* he murdered Anna and that security guard? Not knowing was driving her crazy. If only the police could arrest him, a search of wherever he lived might reveal all kinds of evidence. Unless they caught him in the act of stalking her, she didn't see how they were going to pick him up. But if they did, what then? She couldn't see Matthew obeying an injunction or restraining order, or being deterred by a jail sentence. He was getting angrier and more unbalanced all the time. Adam's beating had made things worse. Stalkers regarded their victims as one hundred percent good – or bad. Now she had fallen off her pedestal.

The smell of fresh ground coffee filled the kitchen, and she poured herself a cup. She decided to have a proper breakfast for once, a boiled egg with buttered toast, some beautiful ripe Victoria plums to follow. She put everything on a tray, carried it up to the bedroom and drew the curtains. Sunlight poured into the room and the sky above the tree tops was blue and cloudless. She switched on breakfast news and got back into bed, took a sip of hot sweet coffee.

The Good Friday agreement was in trouble – again. She cracked the top of the egg and bit into the toast, thought how lonely it felt to wake up without Adam beside her. She couldn't wait for him to get back. The regional news came on.

A terrible fire in a council house near Old Roan had killed nine people, three adults and six children, one of whom was a baby. The children were all under ten. Justine stopped eating and stared at the screen. The family dogs, left in the back garden, had survived the inferno. New homes were being sought for the traumatized pitbulls, and many people had already phoned in. Nobody had wanted anything to do with the children when they were alive, but they were willing to give a couple of dogs a loving home.

'My God!' Justine sighed and shook her head despairingly at the hideous sight of the burned out smoke-blackened house with its gaping windows. The householder had been a thirty-eight-year-old woman named Ruby Jackson, who had died along with her children and two visiting brothers. The fire had started in the early hours of the morning. Arson was suspected. The house was cordoned off, forensics experts and fire investigation teams picking over the debris. Ruby's bereaved mother and the fathers of the children were expected to appear at a press conference later that day.

Justine picked up her mug of coffee and took another sip. Then she stiffened, staring at the screen. Standing in the early-morning crowd of moronic scruffball ghouls outside the burned out house was Matthew, dressed in the same black sweatshirt and pants he'd worn last night. His face was a bruised mess and covered with red blotches. He was biting his lips and smiling, looked as if he was bursting with manic energy. He literally tore at his skin as he scratched it.

Justine gasped with shock. Coffee spilled on to the white quilt with its gold embroidery. Matthew looked directly at the camera and smiled broadly. His angry sunken brown eyes glittered with excitement and his thin lips formed words she could not decipher. He shouted something.

Her name.

He was grinning straight at her.

# Chapter Eleven

'So you're one of the new Russian entrepreneurs?' Paul said, looking at Adriana Terekhova. 'Well, relatively new!'

Capitalism with a vengeance. They would buy and sell anything and everything and many of them had organized crime connections. He was normally a good judge of character, but so far Adriana was proving something of a mystery. That intrigued and disturbed him at the same time. She was about thirty, slim and beautiful and very blonde, with cool blue eyes and a fair complexion. She wore a black trouser suit and high-heeled black ankle boots. Her long nails were painted shell pink. She didn't use much makeup, and favoured some kind of tinted gloss in place of lipstick. She sat back on the sofa, with her long elegant legs crossed and her hands folded in her lap. A faint smell of perfume drifted towards him. She was doing a good job of hiding her nervousness and impatience. Although not quite good enough.

'That's correct, Mr Melwood.' Adriana nodded and smiled slightly. She had a faint American accent. 'My Moscow commodity trading firm is doing very well.'

'I know. Please, call me Paul.' He had told her that at their first meeting, but she remained polite and formal, rather reserved. 'You don't sound very Russian,' he commented. 'If you don't mind my saying so.'

'Of course I don't. I spent some years in the States,' Adriana explained in her soft, light voice. 'My father was a diplomat posted to Washington. I attended Harvard Business School,' she lied. The accent was in fact the result of a two-year affair with a New York businessman, who had dumped her when his wife

116

inherited a million dollars from an aunt and used her new financial clout to bring her husband to heel.

'I'm impressed.' Paul didn't necessarily believe her. 'Your firm specializes in minerals, metals, alloys and – what was it?' He raised his eyebrows. 'Consulting on questions of foreign economic activity?' That sounded suitably vague and all-encompassing.

'Correct.' Adriana shook back her long silky blonde hair. 'So, you see, Mr – Paul – I'm very well placed at the centre of the export action in Russia.'

'Yes, I can see that.' Her credentials were impressive and she came recommended. But he still wasn't sure about this deal. Adriana uncrossed her legs and sat up straight.

'So, have you considered my offer?' she asked tentatively.

'To pay you two million dollars for three tons of beryllium?' He nodded. 'Yes.' It was a serious amount of money, but he could locate a possible buyer who would pay ten times that amount.

'And you've reached a decision?'

'I'm afraid I need more time to think about it,' he said cautiously. His checks hadn't revealed anything untoward. But Adriana Terekhova had come out of nowhere. He wished he could reach Ivanovich, the Moscow business acquaintance who had given Adriana his name. Or so she said.

Adriana smiled again to conceal her impatience. 'Is there a problem, Paul?'

'The export licence makes no mention of what the consignment could be used for,' he replied. 'Frankly, I'm not completely happy with it. Beryllium is on the list of dual-purpose items that your government, as a member of the International Nuclear Supplies Group, agreed in 1993 to start restricting.'

Beryllium. Discovered in 1797 by Vauquelin in Paris. A hard greyish metal found in coal, soil, mineral rocks and volcanic dust. Cancer-causing agent. Very pure gem quality beryllium was better known as aquamarine or emerald. Beryllium and its alloys were used in electronic components, fibre-optic components, nuclear reactors and nuclear weapons. Beryllium reflectors significantly increased the explosive power of modern nuclear bombs. It was also used in air satellite space vehicle structures, mirrors, ceramics – bicycle frames! – and as an additive in solid-propellant rocket fuels. Amongst other things. A kilo of the stuff could fetch US $600 on the open market.

The enormous mineral resources and military-industrial complexes of the former Soviet Union were a rich source of supply. Plenty of redundant scientists and nuclear physicists trying to get rich quick by laying their hands on 'surplus' material. The best way to make money was to deal in commodities. Pay for your goods in roubles, ship them out of the country and sell them for dollars. Profits could be ballistic. Foreign businessmen were often approached, either in the Russian Federation or in their own countries.

Paul was very tempted by this deal. As long as it was legal. The buyer he had in mind was a Korean businessman named Lim-Taek Han, based in Paris. He had spoken to him last night; Han was enthusiastic.

Adriana nodded calmly. 'I admit, Russian export regulations can be confusing.'

'They seem pretty clear to me. In this instance, anyway.'

'It's not illegal to export beryllium,' she argued.

'I know it's not *illegal* . . .'

'How could I have got the purchase order, the export licence?' He shrugged. 'You tell me!'

'It's all perfectly in order,' she assured him. 'I obtained permission even though, strictly speaking, I didn't need it. You've seen the paperwork. I don't anticipate any problems.'

She finished her glass of mineral water and sat back on the sofa. Paul got up, strolled across the room to his desk and opened a window. Melwood Materials was near the old Canada Dock, and his big light office overlooked the Mersey. The river sparkled in the morning sunshine. Paul's grandfather had headed Canada Dock Goods station during the war; Paul had a large black-and-white photograph of him on his desk, standing by a shipment of American tanks that had been transported across the Atlantic ready for the D-Day landings. He had put the photograph of Sara in the top drawer.

'I'm very interested,' he confessed, strolling back to the sofa. He sat down opposite Adriana. 'Would you like another of those?' he asked, pointing to the empty glass. 'Some tea or coffee?'

'Oh, no thanks. Our Russian nuclear materials are half the price of yours,' she said, pressing her case. Adriana thought again how handsome and sexy Paul Melwood was. She knew he wanted this deal, but she had to be patient, serious. He wasn't the sort of man who could be led by the dick. If he had been she wouldn't have wanted him. But it was a shame to feel so attracted to someone you might have to kill. 'Russia alone could cover the world's demand for nuclear fuel – oh, more than twice. Isn't that incredible?'

He smiled again. 'Terrifying, more like! Especially if it falls into the wrong hands. We all know some of it has, unfortunately.'

'Yes,' she said thoughtfully. 'Organized crime is a great problem in Russia. And not only there, of course.'

He was looking at her cynically. 'It's often impossible for legitimate businesses to operate outside its control.'

'Not my business,' she said firmly. 'You've seen the paperwork,' she repeated. 'Everything's in order.'

Not quite everything. Adriana would not tell Paul, for instance, that her ex-husband, Gregor, was chief of the Material and Technical Supply Department of the local nuclear institution in the town of Sverdlovsk, about eighty miles from Moscow: the Institute of Physics and Power Engineering. Gregor had known who to come to when he'd heard about the consignment of beryllium 'going spare'. He thought it would be his passport to riches and freedom. But he needed her help, and Moscow money to get things going. Adriana had obtained the bogus purchase order and phoney export licence, provided the finance. Gregor would not get his big profit, though, she would see to that. He had treated her and their two daughters like dirt for years, beaten her up, called her a whore. Well, that was true. But not until after she had escaped from him and gone to Moscow.

Adriana had sold first herself then other women. After that there had been the video game hall, the marriage bureau, the sports club that was little more than a front for drug deals. Gregor knew she would never take him back, but still he thought he could make money out of her. He was wrong. The little girl from Sverdlovsk had grown up. Her father, dead from tuberculosis, had been a farmer not a diplomat. But Paul Melwood did not have to know that. With this beryllium deal she would hit the big time; money would work for her from now on, not the other way round. She intended to leave Russia and take her mother and two daughters to live in America. Her contact at the American Embassy in Moscow would see to it that there were no problems about visas.

Paul leaned forward and rubbed his chin. 'I'd like another day or so to think about it. If that's all right?'

*No!* 'Yes, of course,' she said politely. 'I understand.'

She looked down, tried to hide her annoyance. She needed to get rid of the beryllium consignment as soon as possible and collect her two million dollars. After that it was Paul's problem. He didn't know that the beryllium was contaminated with highly enriched uranium, which meant it was illegal under Russian law to export it without permission. She would disappear, of course. If Paul Melwood didn't want it she would try somebody else. The longer she had the consignment, the more dangerous it became, the greater the risk of others finding out and wanting a slice of the action. Ivanovich, her ex-lover, was storing it for her – at a price, of course. The beryllium consignment had been transported to Moscow and now lay hidden in the vaults of a disused bank on Tverskaya Street.

'The answer's almost yes,' Paul said. 'I just need to finalize one or two things.'

Like get in touch with Ivanovich, the Moscow banker whom she said had given her his name. Ivanovich was out of town but would be back this evening, his cagey secretary had said. If he vouched for Adriana, the deal could go ahead.

There was a knock at the door and Linda entered. His secretary was forty and had long light brown hair, brown eyes and a flushed, unhappy face. She wore slimming black trousers and a lilac silk shirt. Adriana looked at her and smiled. Surprised, Linda smiled back. Most visitors treated her like part of the furniture, to be sat on and ignored.

'I'm sorry to interrupt, Paul,' she said, embarrassed. 'Sara's on the phone. I told her you were in a meeting, but she insists on speaking to you.' It was nice to be smiled at by the Russian lady after Sara – or Mrs Melwood, as she insisted on being called – had given her an earful. She didn't know how Paul put up with his wife. Well, she did. He was *nice*. 'She says it's urgent.'

It always was. 'Okay, put her through,' he said. 'Thanks, Linda.' He stood up and smiled at Adriana. 'Excuse me one minute.'

'Sure!' She stood up too. 'I'll wait outside.'

'No, please,' he said. 'No need.' He crossed to his desk and picked up the phone. 'Hello, Sara.'

'You should sack that bloody bitch,' she said aggressively. 'She tried to stop me speaking to you – she thinks she's your wife, not me! I know she's got the hots for you –.'

'I asked Linda to hold any calls because I was in a meeting.' Paul turned away and stared at the sunlit river. Maybe he should have let Adriana wait outside. Sara sounded drunk as well as angry. 'What d'you want, Sara?'

'Oh, charming! Busy, are you? Okay, I'll tell you what I *want*,' she said. 'I went shopping this morning and my credit card wouldn't work. I felt like a right prat! What the hell are you playing at, you bastard?' she shouted. 'The big businessman indulging in a bit of power play? You're bloody pathetic!'

'Check the date on the card,' he said coldly. 'It's expired. There was a letter from the bank the other day asking you to call in to collect the new one. I told you I couldn't pick it up because you have to sign for it. I thought you knew.'

'Oh!' There was a brief silence while she studied the card. 'Okay.'

'Anything else?' he asked. Of course he didn't expect an apology.

'No, that's it. Right,' she said angrily, 'I'll go to the bloody bank after lunch. Then buy something sexy to wear tonight. I'm off to Elaine's later, we'll have dinner and go clubbing afterwards.'

'Nice of you to let me know. I hope you both have a wonderful time.'

'Fuck *you*!'

Sara crashed the phone down and Paul replaced the receiver. He felt the familiar unhappiness and frustration wash over him. The thought of a solitary dinner in the big silent kitchen of the lonely old farmhouse would once have been depressing. Now it was pure relief.

'My wife,' he explained as he crossed the room and sat on the sofa again. Adriana looked at him, noted the gloomy expression on his handsome face.

'I was married once,' she said quietly. 'I got divorced about five years ago. My mother looks after my two young daughters while I work and travel. It's not easy being alone but it's much more lonely in a toxic relationship, don't you think?'

'That's true!' Paul thought longingly of Justine Flynn again. He felt like calling her one more time before the wedding day to ask how she was doing. But that wasn't a good idea. He might phone when she got back from honeymoon, see her and Adam together as friends. For dinner, perhaps. Really, it was best not to see her at all. And right now he had enough to think about. Adriana tossed back her silky hair and picked up her small black handbag.

'Shall we meet tomorrow?' she asked. 'When you've had more time to think?'

'Yes,' he said. 'Say, back here at three tomorrow afternoon?'

'That's fine.' He escorted her to the door and they walked into the outer office. Linda's busy fingers flew over the word processor keyboard. Adriana walked up to the desk and held out her hand.

'Goodbye,' she said. 'Thank you for the drink.'

'You're welcome.' Nice woman, Linda thought. 'Enjoy the rest of your day.'

'I'll try,' Adriana laughed. 'All alone in the big city of Liverpool!'

'Are you?' Paul shook hands with her. 'Listen, why don't we have dinner later?' he suggested. 'If you're free.' It would be a good chance to probe Adriana for more information.

'Thank you! I'd like that very much.'

Once upon a time he would have asked Sara to join them. He looked at his secretary. 'Linda, you're invited too.' *What?* Adriana thought.

Linda blushed with pleasure. 'I'd really love to, but I'm afraid I can't,' she said regretfully. 'Colin's out tonight, and there's no one to look after the boys.' Her husband had a darts match again. If it wasn't darts it was snooker, pool, or boozing her money away while he and his double sad, brain-dead mates put the world to rights. Slagging off women, of course. They liked that best of all.

'How old are your sons now, thirteen and fifteen?' Paul grinned. 'I bet they'd be delighted to have the run of the house for an evening.'

'I'm sure they would, but I shudder to think what I'd come home to!'

'Point taken. Well, that's a shame. Another time, maybe. Okay, Adriana,' he said. 'I'll pick you up at your hotel. Is seven-thirty all right?'

'Perfect.' She smiled. She felt hopeful again. One more day

122

would surely clinch it. He wouldn't invite her to dinner if he intended to reject her offer. Or was he being kind? No, men are never *kind*, she thought contemptuously. Did Paul Melwood possibly want to fuck her? If so, she certainly wouldn't fight him off!

Maybe she had organized crime connections that stretched across most of Europe, Paul thought as Adriana left. He wouldn't know until he'd spoken to Ivanovich. This was a fantastic deal and he didn't want to miss out. He could buy off Sara, retire at the tender age of thirty-eight, do whatever the hell he liked. Anything except have Justine Flynn, he reflected sadly.

'Nice lady,' Linda commented.

He laughed. 'Let's hope so!' He glanced at his watch. 'Come on, I'll take you out for lunch, seeing as you can't make dinner.'

'I've got a load of shopping to do,' Linda said sadly. 'There's only my lunch break to do it in.' *Break*, that was a laugh.

'You can do it afterwards,' he said. 'Take a couple of hours.' He felt sorry for Linda, knew she had a rough time with her unemployed husband and the two boisterous boys. The elder boy had recently been in some sort of trouble with the police for dealing at school.

Adriana took a cab back to the Adelphi, hurried up to her suite and poured herself a double Scotch, sipped it while she dialled the Moscow number.

'I think it's okay,' she said when Ivanovich answered.

'You *think*?'

'Well, I'm pretty sure,' she corrected herself. She sat on the bed and pulled off her ankle boots. 'He wants one more day.'

'To talk to me. He called a few times. I thought I'd stall him a bit before I sing your praises. Being instantly available would look very suspicious.'

'He'll bite,' she said. 'I know it. The consignment must be ready immediately.'

'It will be. You're a clever girl, Adriana,' he said. 'You've done well.'

'Don't *clever girl* me!' she said furiously, sipping Scotch. 'This is my deal, not yours. Show some respect!'

Ivanovich chuckled. She was so touchy. 'You can have all the respect you want,' he said, 'when you get back here with my share of Paul Melwood's two million dollars. He's an attractive man, isn't he?' he said slyly.

'Very,' Adriana admitted. 'Eager, too. Nothing will go wrong. Otherwise . . .' She sprawled on the bed and stretched out, stared at the ornate ceiling. 'What a shame if he had to die!' she said softly.

# Chapter Twelve

'For Christ's sake, Justine!' Donna said agitatedly. 'Lighten up, will you? It's your hen night, you're supposed to be happy. Don't give me any more old chat about cancelling it! The others will be in the pub by now.'

She felt frantic with hurt and frustrated desire. Adam had been horrible that morning. He was cold and distant, turned his back on her, pushed her away when she tried to kiss him goodbye before leaving to catch the train. He had shaken her awake at some unearthly hour and practically shoved her out of bed, did not even ask if she wanted coffee. She was to stay away from him, he warned, he didn't want to see her in any capacity except that of wedding guest. Unwelcome wedding guest!

Last night Adam had blamed himself; now the blame seemed to have shifted to her. She had cried all the way back to Liverpool. The thought that she might never again make love with him was unbearable. She didn't know what the hell to do. All she wanted now was to go out and get wrecked! She picked up her glass of white wine and drained it, lit another cigarette.

'What about *my* good time?' she demanded. Her breasts and bottom stood out in a purple, metallic, off-the-shoulder dress. 'I didn't wear this to sit home and count tea towels. Don't be such a bloody misery,' she added aggressively. 'You're zero fun these days, you know that? I'm sick of you.'

Donna fought the spiteful desire to tell Justine about last night, shatter her delight and trust in Adam. That would devastate her all right, blast her precious illusions sky high! She didn't care any more that the stalker was making

Justine's life hell. She had Adam, didn't she? She had too bloody much!

'Donna, what *is* wrong with you?' Justine sat at the dressing table sipping white wine, wearing a black Wonderbra and black lacy panties. She stared at her friend in the mirror, her eyes full of hurt. 'You're in a terrible mood. So *angry*! I've never seen you like this.' She hesitated. 'I can understand you're pissed off about Cal but . . .'

'It's not Cal,' Donna interrupted, blushing. 'I don't give a toss about him. He's history,' she said bitterly. 'Not even that! He never happened.' She turned away, chewing her lip, blinked back the tears that came suddenly. Why should I keep quiet? she thought furiously. Make sure everyone but me gets to stay happy?

'Then what is it?' Justine asked anxiously. 'You're so different! Miserable . . . desperate almost. Tell me what's wrong,' she begged.

'Nothing, okay?' Donna walked to the windows, looked out at the darkening sky. An autumnal smell of burning leaves hung over Sefton Park. 'Forget it,' she said abruptly. 'I'm just fed up lately, that's all. With everything.'

A thought occurred to Justine. 'Are you worried things won't be the same after I'm married?' she asked. 'Don't be,' she said earnestly. 'You're my best friend, Donna, nothing will ever change that. Adam likes you a lot, but I wouldn't care if he didn't. I won't disappear into marriage and become a spare body part that goes by the name of Mrs Dr Adam Shaw!' She laughed uneasily. 'And those are *not* famous last words!'

'I believe you.' Donna crossed back to the dressing table and poured herself more wine, stubbed out her cigarette. She glanced at her watch. 'Come on, get dressed. It's nearly eight-thirty.' She turned to the open wardrobe, riffled through the rack of clothes. 'What are you wearing?'

'Matthew could have torched that house . . .' Justine's voice trembled.

'Oh, don't start going on about *him* again!' Donna sighed and reached for her wine. 'A house fire, any kind of disaster, always attracts crowds of ghouls and mental cases,' she said impatiently. 'They love a good blaze! He probably lives nearby or saw it on telly and went to have a gawp. The police said they'd check it out, see if he does live in the area. You have to give them time to do their job.'

'Maybe I haven't got time! He was looking into the camera. Laughing at me.' Justine took another sip of wine. 'Stalkers often start out as arsonists,' she said slowly. 'I read that somewhere.'

'It's the other way round with him then, isn't it? Finish your makeup, get dressed and stop playing the frightened female. You'll end up in a psychiatric unit if you carry on like this.' Donna grabbed another cigarette and lit it. 'Look at the state of you!' she said angrily. 'That stalker would laugh his head off, he'd love it. He's turning you into a fucked-up recluse!'

'What can I do?' Justine asked desperately. That was the one argument that could get to her. One more night without Adam! She longed for him.

'Come out, get wrecked. Like I said. You'll feel tons better.'

'That's your answer to everything!'

'You know what?' Donna blew smoke in her face. 'It works!'

'Okay,' Justine said despondently. 'I'll come out.'

'Excellent! Now, cheer up!' Donna ordered. 'Sure you don't want an e?'

'Positive.' Justine got up and went to the wardrobe. Her heart pounded and her breathing was shallow. The anxiety she felt was like a premonition. That was crazy, of course. She felt this way because of Matthew. She had to go on fighting until this nightmare ended. But when would it end? And how?

'You're not wearing *that*?' Donna pulled a disgusted face at her choice of dress, a long, tight, crushed black velvet with chiffon sleeves and a round neckline. 'It's your hen night, not a bloody funeral!'

'Adam thinks it's really sexy. Besides,' Justine said lightly, 'tonight is a kind of funeral. Of my swinging single life.'

'You can have a swinging married life! Especially with a husband like Adam.'

Justine glanced at Donna curiously and she blushed and turned away, stubbing out her cigarette. 'I'll call a cab, shall I?'

'There's a card by the phone in the sitting room, I always use that firm.' Justine sat on the bed and put on high-heeled black shoes with an ankle strap. 'If the police cruise past again we could ask them for a lift,' she said sarcastically. She glanced at the bedside phone, wished Adam would call. But right now he would be dining with colleagues in some Michelin-starred London restaurant.

Donna went into the living room, picked up the phone and paused. Should she tell Justine about her night with Adam? Justine might be so devastated that she would cancel the wedding and throw him out. And guess who would be around to comfort him? Adam might hate her at first, but he would come crawling back when Justine rejected him forever. Men didn't throw away sex on a plate.

What if Justine and Adam didn't split up, though? That was a risk she had to take. If she did nothing she would never get another chance with him. This way there was at least hope. She didn't relish the thought of losing Justine's friendship. But if she had to sacrifice Justine, so be it.

Donna stared out of the windows at the dark sky, saw Venus glitter light years away. Her eyes shone. I don't know, she thought. It may not work. I might cause a disaster! Have I got the bottle? She closed her eyes, remembered the feel of Adam's hands on her breasts and his tongue exploring her mouth, the feel of him moving inside her as she came. She gasped, bit her lip. She had the bottle!

'Have you called the cab?'

She jumped. Justine stood right behind her.

'Yes! No.' She blushed. 'Where did you say that card was?'

'Right under your cute little nose.' Justine picked up the card and held out her hand. 'Shall I phone?' she asked. 'You seem a bit confused.'

'No,' Donna said lamely. 'I'll do it.' Her guilty blush deepened under Justine's suspicious gaze. 'What are you looking at me like that for?'

'Donna – are you *sure* everything's all right?'

'Of course it is!' She held up the receiver. 'D'you want me to call this bloody cab or what?'

'If you think you can manage! Go ahead, I'll get my jacket and keys.'

Justine turned and went back to the bedroom. Her instincts screamed at her to watch out, take care, guard herself against God only knew what! The bad feeling was getting stronger every minute. But she had to fight that feeling, otherwise she would never go out again. She put on her jacket, finished the glass of wine and sat on the bed, waiting like a prisoner about to be led to execution.

Donna called the cab, hung up and danced into the bedroom. She looked better, Justine thought, almost high all of a sudden. What was it with her? Maybe she had something special planned for tonight. Her heart sank.

'Come on, then!' Donna smiled at Justine as the door bell rang, her brown eyes sparkling with malice. 'I'm going to give you the hen night of your life!'

'Well, I only intend to have *one*.' She stood up and followed Donna downstairs, double-locked the flat door behind her. Her heart resumed its awful pounding as they went down the stone steps and got into the waiting cab.

She had never felt so frightened in her life.

In town the autumnal earth and woodsmoke smell was obliterated by exhaust fumes, fast food and stale beer odours wafting from pub doorways. The pub was bright, packed and noisy. They pushed through the crush of bodies towards the corner table where their friends Kate, Ingrid, Louise and Stephanie sat laughing and talking. Their table was crammed with bottles, glasses, crumpled crisp packets and an overflowing ashtray. They cheered at the sight of Justine and Donna.

'Here she comes at last, the blushing bride! Where the hell have you been?'

Justine whirled round in shock as someone tapped her on the shoulder. A tall, powerfully built man with a white-blond fuzz of hair and narrow mean hazel eyes in a thin face grinned down at her. His pale skin was rough and pockmarked and he smelled of booze and sweat. He wore a white shirt and crumpled beige cotton trousers.

'Fancy a drink, luv?'

'No.' I don't believe this! thought Justine furiously.

'You're with your mates? So'm I. Okay.' He stared at her. 'Later, eh?'

'Not now. Not later.' She turned away and he grabbed her arm.

'What's up?' He leered. 'Not posh enough for you, am I?'

'Leave her alone,' Donna said angrily as Justine twisted,

shuddering, out of the man's grasp. 'She said *no*, can't you understand that? It's not rocket science!'

He glared at them. 'Lesbians' night out, is it?'

'Oh, piss off!'

It's starting, Justine thought as she sat down next to Stephanie. This is going to be the worst night of my life. She wanted to run out of the pub and take a cab home, lock herself in with the telly, a glass of wine and a hot water bottle. Tragic, but what the hell! She wished Adam would come home tonight.

'What a caveman!' Ingrid commented as the man retreated. She took out her wallet and stood up. 'My round, ladies,' she announced. 'What's yours, Justine? And don't tell me mineral water!'

'I'll have white wine.'

'Come on, you can do better than that!'

'Okay. Vodka-and-tonic.' She nervously scanned the crowded pub, searching for Matthew, and caught the hostile eye of the creep who had grabbed her arm. He stood at the bar, drinking with his mates. She looked quickly away. Donna nudged her.

'He's not here,' she whispered. She took out a cigarette and snapped her lighter. 'He wasn't outside the house either.'

'You mean, we didn't see him!' Justine shrugged off her heavy leather jacket.

'Is that stalker still harassing you?' Stephanie asked worriedly. She was a tall, thin girl with long straight blonde hair and pale green eyes. Like Justine, she wore a tight black dress, only hers was short and skimpy. 'Have you called the police yet? I was thinking about you while I was in Rome.'

Justine pulled a face. 'All they've done is warn me to lay off pepper and mace sprays. They're looking for him, but there's not much to go on. Did you have a good time in Italy?' she asked, desperate to get off the subject of Matthew. Donna was right. He would be thrilled to know how much he dominated her life.

'Brilliant, except for Italian men. What about this Protection from Harassment Act?' Stephanie asked. 'It's been in force for more than two years now.'

'Will you tell them or shall I?'

'Oh, I get it. Being female and out alone after dark is contributory negligence.'

Justine laughed suddenly. 'If only you could be sure it would happen after dark! You'd know where you were then.' She took a sip of the drink Ingrid handed her.

'People blame the woman,' Stephanie said indignantly. 'You're either too nice or too nasty, you give out mixed messages, that kind of bullshit. They judge your behaviour, not his. It's so unfair!'

'Can we drop this?' Justine smiled, too brightly. She felt she would burst into tears if Stephanie went on. 'Please?'

'Okay,' her friend said, seeing her expression. She slid one arm around her shoulders and hugged her. 'I understand. I'll tell you all about my trip to Italy and my brilliant career as a certified accountant, shall I?'

'Hey, come on!' Donna laughed. 'We want Justine to stay awake.'

'Shall we go somewhere else after this round?' Stephanie nodded cautiously towards the bar. 'The caveman keeps giving Justine evil looks.'

'Ignore the silly bastard,' Ingrid said contemptuously. She laughed as Justine drained her vodka-and-tonic. 'See! She agrees with me.'

'I've hurt his fragile ego and now he wants to kick the shit out of me!' Justine put down her glass. 'Actually, I wouldn't mind going somewhere else. We weren't planning to stay here long anyway.'

Tonight she hated Liverpool. The city's atmosphere was tense, edgy, unpredictable, threatening violence. Gangs of marauding males roamed the streets. Justine felt that she couldn't drink, dance, have a laugh, without being watched menacingly or curiously by hostile male eyes, disapproved of or coveted like a consumer item. It would be a huge relief to get home in one piece. Was Matthew watching her now? she wondered. What would he do next? What did he do to her in his fantasies?

'Let's go,' she said, suddenly desperate to get out of the pub. 'Now!' The crowd, the noise and laughter, made her feel trapped, suffocated. For a split second she nearly panicked, thinking she couldn't get her breath. She knocked over the empty vodka glass as she jumped up and pulled on her jacket. Stephanie touched her arm and she flinched.

'You all right, Justine?' Stephanie's green eyes were full of concern.

'I'm fine!' She tried to smile. 'Really.' Stephanie raised her eyebrows and glanced at Donna and the others. Donna shook her head slightly.

In a different, quieter pub after several more drinks Justine began to relax as far as she could relax. She still hadn't spotted Matthew. Maybe he wasn't following her. What could he do anyway, amongst all these people? She felt safe surrounded by her friends. It was going to be all right. Adam was back tomorrow. She couldn't believe how much she'd missed him. She never wanted to be separated from him again.

'Get that down your neck.' Stephanie dumped another vodka-and-tonic in front of her. 'Feel better now?' she asked, smiling.

'Great.' Justine picked her the glass. 'Cheers!'

'Ready for the next stop?' Donna winked at the others, burst out laughing and nearly fell off her leather stool.

'Whatever that is!' Justine laughed and stood up. 'I'm off to the loo.'

In the ladies' toilet a drunken girl lay groaning and sobbing on the floor, surrounded by her solicitous friends. 'Breathe, Karen, just *breathe*! Karen, that bastard's not worth it! Come on, try and sit up. Put your head between your knees. I know that sounds disgustin'!' Laughter.

Justine fluffed her hair in front of the mirror and painted on more red lipstick, determined to ignore them. Imagine getting in that state over some man, she thought irritably. She decided not to use the toilet; the blue-tiled floor was wet and slippery, the locks on the doors broken, and there was no loo paper. She sprayed perfume on her neck and wrists, fastened the clasp of her handbag and turned to leave.

The door swung shut behind her and she froze. The aggressive, white-blond man who had hassled her earlier was standing some distance away, propping up the bar with his mates. Don't panic, she told herself. It could be coincidence. This pub was just a few minutes' walk away from the other one. But Justine didn't believe in coincidence anymore.

She stood there uncertainly, the handbag clutched to her chest. A couple of girls jostled her as they pushed past. My God! she thought, horrified. Is he following me? Or am I being paranoid? The man slowly turned his head and gave her a long, hostile stare. His blond-lashed hazel eyes bored into hers, flickered over her face and body, and she knew he was trying to imagine her naked.

Then he licked his thin lips and laughed, raising his glass in a mocking salute.

'Paul, I really had a great time tonight!' Adriana smiled at him as he brought the car to a stop at the foot of the Adelphi steps. 'The dinner was delicious. Thank you very much.'

'You're welcome.' He toyed with the ignition key, wondering whether or not to switch off the engine. The warm dark interior of the Mercedes was filled with the mingled sensuous smells of her perfume and the leather seats. 'So, I'll see you at three tomorrow afternoon,' he said. 'My office.'

'Yes.' Adriana looked up at him. 'What are you going to do now?' she asked flirtatiously, playing with a long silky strand of hair.

'Do?' he echoed. 'Er . . . drive home.' He wondered if Sara would be back tonight. He doubted it; she would probably sleep over at Elaine's. Or somewhere else that he preferred not to know about. 'I don't want to rush you but I can't stay here long,' he said, glancing in the driving mirror. 'I'm on double-yellow lines.'

'Then why don't you park your car? Come up to my suite and have a coffee before you go.' She smiled again. 'Or *don't* go!' She shifted towards him and kissed him lightly on the lips.

Shit! Paul thought. Adriana was beautiful, sexy and intelligent, but for whatever unfortunate reason he didn't feel remotely attracted to her. Men were supposed to think about sex every second of every day, be able to shag at the drop of a hat any woman who didn't look like the back of a bus on a rainy day. He smiled. Justine's words! But the thought of sex with Adriana interested him not one bit. She aroused no warmth or desire in him, ignited no sparks. He had a feeling that there was nothing behind the beautiful polished façade. Only an aching, terrifying void where a personality should have been.

He would accept her business offer, having managed to get hold of Ivanovich earlier that evening before he called to take her out for dinner. The Russian had said all the things he'd hoped to hear; Adriana's company was legitimate, she had worked very hard for her success. The beryllium hadn't come from the Russian mafia. Everything was all right. More than all right. So why couldn't this be the icing on a delicious cake?

Her soft, full lips kissed his throat, nibbled his earlobe then returned to his mouth. Her fingers touched his cheek and her breasts pressed against him. Adriana kissed him harder, tried to part his lips with her tongue. Her hand slid down to his crotch. Her coolness and reserve were melting like spring snow, Paul thought. Or had the coolness been a pose?

'Sorry, Adriana.' He disengaged himself and held her gently by the shoulders. 'You're very beautiful and I like you a lot,' he said awkwardly. 'I'm flattered. But this doesn't feel right.'

'It does to me!' Adriana felt insulted and disappointed. 'What's wrong?' she asked lightly. 'Afraid to mix business with pleasure, Paul?'

'Let's just say I don't think it's a great idea.' I must be losing it! he thought. Why don't I want her? So what if she hasn't got a personality? But he knew what was wrong. She didn't have crazy red-gold hair that smelled like flowers in a meadow, dark blue eyes that could look sad, humorous or dreamy by turns, a smile that pierced his heart and kept her image constantly before him. She wasn't Justine.

'Can't you make an exception in my case?' Adriana leaned forward again, tried to slip her arms around his neck. 'Come on,' she murmured, kissing him. 'I want you very much, Paul. Give in to me!'

'No!' he said sharply. His grip on her shoulders tightened as he held her at arm's length. 'I'm very flattered,' he repeated. 'But I don't want to sleep with you. I'm sorry,' he said. 'I have to go now. I'll see you tomorrow.'

He let go of her shoulders and she didn't try to kiss him again. She glanced away, her face burning with humiliation in the darkness. No man had ever rejected her before. She felt insulted, belittled, confused, filled with frustrated desire. She wanted to cry like a hurt child. Who the hell did this bastard think he was? She grabbed her handbag off the dashboard and swung the door open.

'Goodnight!' she said icily.

'Adriana . . .' he called. 'Wait a second . . .'

The passenger door slammed so hard it rocked the car and reverberated through his body. Paul watched her walk gracefully away on her high heels, her slim shoulders rigid, the silky blonde hair hanging straight down her back. She climbed the steps and entered the brightly lit hotel.

'Bloody hell!' he murmured. He leaned back and sighed. Adriana was furious. He hadn't handled that very well.

He had a nasty feeling he was going to regret it.

# Chapter Thirteen

They ended up in a club. Donna had gone against Justine's wishes and hired a stripper. She recoiled and pushed away a disgustingly sweaty, over-pumped grinning himbo in a bit of black leather as he tried to squirt baby lotion in her face. She watched him gyrate and play with his penis, listened to the screams and laughter around her. Why did anyone think this was *fun*? She didn't care that Donna and the others thought her a spoilsport. Although Stephanie didn't seem amused either.

She was on her way to being drunk, but not drunk enough. Bored, but also tense. The act finished amidst screams and applause and the stripper disappeared. She turned thankfully away and looked around the crowded club again. She couldn't see Matthew, but kept getting that nasty eyes-between-the-shoulder-blades feeling. At least the caveman seemed to have got the message and disappeared.

'Come on, Justine!' Kate, Ingrid, Louise and Stephanie jumped up and ran to the dance floor. Justine half rose, then sat down and picked up her latest vodka-and-tonic. She didn't want to dance, risk being hassled again. The music pounded through her head and she felt hot and slightly dizzy. Donna came out of the Ladies, stumbled across the dance floor and collapsed beside her on the banquette. The black leather was cracked in various places, looked as though it had been slit with a Stanley knife.

'Having a good time?' Donna's voice was slurred and her eyes glazed. She picked up her glass and gulped Scotch.

'Yep,' Justine said curtly. 'Great.'

'You're lying, you miserable cow!' Donna flung out an arm and knocked over several empty glasses. 'I arrange all this for you and you don't appreciate a bloody thing! Do you?'

'I told you I didn't want a stripper. You ignored my wishes.'

'*My wishes!*' Donna sneered. She finished her Scotch and banged the glass on the wet table. 'Who the fuck do you think you are?' she demanded. 'The universe doesn't revolve around you and your bloody wishes!'

'I'm acutely aware of that, don't worry.' Justine looked at her friend. 'Donna, why don't you tell me what the hell is wrong with you?' she asked slowly. 'I mean, apart from the fact that you're so pissed you can barely remain vertical. Something's happened,' she said. 'What is it?'

'Okay.' Donna nodded heavily. 'All right.' She glanced towards the crowded dance floor. The others were laughing and dancing wildly. Her own glass empty, she picked up Stephanie's iced vodka and took a swig. 'You asked me, so I'll tell you.' She paused. 'I didn't go to London to see Cal,' she lied. 'He doesn't exist.' Good opening line, she thought admiringly. Very creative.

Justine stared at her in bewilderment, shook her head. 'I don't understand!'

'No? Then let me spell it out for you. Adam asked me to go to London with him. Begged me, in fact.' Donna smiled, a cruel smile. 'So that we could spend an entire night together. For once!'

'*What?*' Justine did not know whether to burst out laughing or feel very annoyed. Donna had really lost it tonight.

'Don't look at me like I'm fucking crazy!' her friend said viciously. 'I'm pissed, but not that pissed.' She swigged more vodka. 'I spent last night with Adam,' she said loudly. 'In his hotel room. D'you get it now? We made love over and over. It was fantastic! He said he couldn't get enough of me.'

Unexpected tears came into her eyes and spilled over, dripped off her chin into the vodka. She watched shock and disbelief register on Justine's beautiful face. 'I love him, Justine!' she cried brokenly. 'I love him and we spent all last night fucking!' She suddenly felt very drunk and very sorry for herself.

'I don't believe you!' Justine felt weak, cold with shock. 'You're lying.'

'Why would I lie?'

'I don't know! Donna, what have I ever done to you?'

whispered Justine. 'You're my best friend. Why do you want to hurt me with such terrible lies?'

'They're not lies!' Donna shouted, startling her. 'I've loved Adam ever since I met him,' she sobbed, fuelled by drink and frustration. She had opened her mouth now – there was no going back. 'We started seeing each other a few months ago. He feels the same way.' I bloody wish! she thought miserably.

'Really?' Justine's head was whirling. 'So why's he going to marry me?'

'I felt so guilty, but I couldn't resist him.' Donna hadn't meant to delve this deep into the realms of fantasy, but what the fuck? 'We couldn't resist each other. The London conference was a chance for us to get away together. Adam needed a break, he's been so stressed out by all your problems.' Justine gasped. 'He wants to go on seeing me after –'

'Stop!' Justine stood up and stumbled backwards, knocking over a stool. 'Stop it! It's not true!' She covered her ears with her hands.

'Ask Adam!' Donna shouted defiantly. 'He'll admit it if you confront him. He swore me to secrecy, but I'm pissed off with secrets. Mouth shut, legs open! Why should I only have responsibilities and no rights? He's bored sick with you and your bloody stalker!' she added viciously. 'He says you encourage that creep.'

She cried out and flung up her arms as Justine grabbed a pint glass and showered her with cold lager. Her nipples poked through the thin, soaked metallic fabric. People looked at them, laughed and cheered.

'Catfight!' a man yelled. 'Any bets, lads?'

Justine dropped the glass and stood over her. 'I never want to see you again,' she said quietly, her voice shaking. 'Our friendship is finished.' Tears rolled down her cheeks. 'Don't bother phoning or coming round to apologize once you've sobered up. I don't want to know!'

She turned, grabbed her handbag and jacket and fled, skirting the packed dance floor. Stephanie spotted her, stopped dancing and followed.

'Justine, where are you going?' she called. 'What's up?'

She turned. 'I'm leaving,' she cried. 'I can't talk now. Please, Stephanie!'

'But–' Stephanie stood there, bewildered. 'You look terrible! What's *happened?*'

'I can't talk about it. Sorry, but I really have to go!' She darted away and left Stephanie behind, lost in the crush of clubbers. Adam! she thought. You didn't betray me with Donna. You couldn't!

'Wanna dance?' She gasped with horror as the caveman blocked her path and leered down at her. His hot breath stank of alcohol and nicotine.

'Get lost!' She tried to shove past him but he grabbed her shoulder.

'Okay, forget the dance. What you drinking? Come on,' he said angrily. 'Give us a break! I haven't followed you all night to get the big E!'

'You *what*? Leave me alone!' She twisted out of his grasp, furiously shook him off. 'What the hell d'you think gives you the right to follow me?' she shouted, enraged.

'Take it easy, you mad bitch!' His grin faded and he looked at her with hatred. 'What d'you come out for if you don't want to cop off?'

'Oh, spare me your retarded fucking reasoning processes! I was stupid enough to think I could enjoy myself,' she said wildly. 'I was wrong. Now, get out of my way!' She shoved past him, ran through an arch and down the red-carpeted staircase to the exit. Three fat, shaven-headed, blank-eyed bouncers in evening dress regarded her silently.

'Goodnight, love!' one of them called sarcastically as she ran out crying. They weren't called bouncers anymore in fact but 'door supervisors', members of a respectable profession well versed in politically correct behaviour. Especially towards distressed females.

The night air was cool after the smoky, sweaty club. Thick clouds had gathered, hiding the moon. Bright Venus glittered briefly then disappeared. Justine stopped and looked around for a cab. The quiet narrow street of Victorian buildings oppressed her. She began to walk towards Hope Street and the Philharmonic Hall. Plenty of cabs cruised there.

Justine was crying bitterly and clutching her bag as she stumbled along, the heavy leather jacket slung over her shoulders. The fiancé and the best friend! she thought. A theme so tedious and tacky and boring it wasn't even a joke anymore. She had never remotely suspected that anything could be going on between Adam and Donna. Or had she been too wrapped up in herself – in the problems Adam was so stressed out by! – to read the signs and signals? As well as the hurt and shock and devastation there was another feeling: humiliation. She felt like a bloody idiot. She hoped Donna wouldn't call her or have the nerve to turn up at the wedding on Saturday.

*What* wedding? She stopped, sobbing wildly, taking deep, gulping breaths. How could she marry Adam now? 'It's not true!' she whispered. But why would Donna lie? Jealousy? She recalled her friend's tears, the desperation in her voice as she'd made her shocking confession. The miserable, aggressive, drunken state she had been in all evening. Why else was Donna so unhappy?

She needed to talk to Adam. Tonight. It wasn't the ideal conversation to have over the phone, but she couldn't wait in agony until he got home tomorrow evening. *Home* . . . where was home? She hitched up her jacket and carried on walking. No wedding, no Caribbean honeymoon, no new life in a beautiful house filled with love, sex and sunshine. Only the harsh reality of ugliness, betrayal, fear. Loneliness. She could not even begin to comprehend the nightmare that was her existence.

Hope was all she had now. Hope that, for whatever twisted reason, Donna was talking bullshit. She cursed the tight dress and clumpy shoes as she heard running feet behind her. Was it Donna? No, the feet were too heavy. *Matthew?* She hitched up the dress and tried to run. Terror gripped her. Hope Street was ahead, less than a hundred yards. People, street lighting, shiny black cabs. Could she make it in time?

'Where d'you think you're going, bitch?' a hoarse angry voice panted. 'I haven't finished with you yet!' Her head was jerked back as the caveman grabbed a handful of her hair and twisted it around his fingers. Justine screamed in pain and the leather jacket slid from her shoulders. She kicked him in the shin and tried to elbow him in the solar plexus, but that didn't work. He swung her round.

'Why wouldn't you have a drink? Eh?' His fist shot out and he punched her in the stomach. She doubled over and retched, fighting for breath. He kicked her legs from under her and she fell,

140

grabbing at nearby railings for support. He dragged her up, breathing heavily, and twisted her arms painfully behind her back. 'Who the fuck d'you think you are?' he shouted in her ear.

'Help!' she screamed, getting her breath back. 'Somebody help me!'

'Shut it!' he panted. 'I've watched you all night, I saw you looking at that stripper's dick – couldn't take your eyes off it, could you? Fucking slag!'

The dark narrow street was deserted. Groups of clubbers one minute, nobody the next. Justine tried to grind her heel into the man's foot, but he dodged away and kicked her again. Her pinioned arms stopped her falling.

'You're dead, you are!' he panted as he wound and knotted the thin leather handbag strap tightly around her wrists. 'I'll cut you up after.' *After?* 'Who d'you think you are?' he shouted again. 'Eh?'

'Let me go!' she cried. Her wrists bound, he grabbed her shoulders and spun her round, smashed her twice across the face. Justine sagged against the cold rusted railings, her head spinning with pain and shock. She was bleeding, somewhere in her mouth. Her wrists hurt like hell as the thin strap cut into her flesh and restricted circulation. She screamed in agony as he grabbed her by the hair again.

'Say you're sorry,' he ordered. 'For ignoring me.' He started to drag her towards a pitch dark Jack the Ripper alley. 'You made me look a right twat in front of me mates! Now I'm gonna kill you!'

'No!' she moaned, struggling. 'Let go of me!'

'Say you're sorry!' He yanked her head back and she yelped with terror as she felt a cold blade against her throat. 'Or you're dead – *now!*'

'Sorry!' she screamed, sobbing. For being female, for thinking I could go out and have fun, for thinking I could ignore you and your sad bloody ego. The handbag dangled from her wrists and bumped her bottom. She flexed her wrists, desperately trying to loosen the strap. Her legs went weak and she felt pure terror as the blackness of the alley loomed. He'll kill me, she thought. I'm going to die in this awful place.

'What's wrong with me anyway?' he shouted, shaking her viciously.

141

Oh, God, an inferiority complex! That was all she needed. The alley was so dark she could hardly see. The man's white-blond head gleamed faintly in the darkness. There was only the stink of sweat, nicotine and stale urine. The alley was obviously an open-air bog for drunks after chucking out time. If only one or two of them would come along now! Or maybe not. They might want to join in. The perfect end to a perfect evening.

'What's wrong with me?' He slammed her against the brick wall, the knife jabbing her throat.

'Nothing,' she whispered.

'Give us a kiss, then.' He bit savagely at her lips, shoved his tongue deep into her mouth. Justine gagged and choked with revulsion. Furious, he punched her twice on the side of the head and pinioned her body with his to stop her falling. Blows to the head could cause brain damage, hearing damage, detached retina. Her ears were ringing and she could barely breathe. She knew she would pass out if he punched her again.

'I'll kill you, you slag!' he shouted. 'Why wouldn't you have a drink?'

'I was tired,' Justine gasped. 'I wanted to go home. No, don't!' she begged, shaking with fear as he dragged down her dress and used the knife to slit her bra straps. She felt chill night air on her bare chest and shoulders. His damp sweaty cruel hands squeezed her breasts, twisted and pinched her nipples so that she cried out in pain.

'Nice tits!' He laughed angrily. 'You could be in *Playboy*.' He ground his pelvis against her as he reached down and pulled the dress up over her thighs and hips, pinning her against the wall. Her stockings tore. Justine lifted her face to the dull sky, desperate for air, her mind and heart racing.

In a movie she would try to reason with her attacker, ask about his mother, did he have sisters? He would drop the knife and sob out the story of his abused childhood in a dysfunctional family. In life he was intent on causing her pain, humiliation and degradation. After that he would murder her. All because she didn't want a drink! He ripped off her black silky pants and forced her legs apart.

'Gagging for it, aren't you?' he panted. He laughed angrily again. 'Tell me you want it, you bitch!'

Was this to be her fate? To die at the hands of a rapist, knowing

142

the man she loved most in all the world had betrayed her with her best friend? After being stalked by some loathsome sad act for weeks, her freedom and peace of mind stolen from her? In that split second Justine decided it wasn't good enough. It was as if her mind and body had suddenly shut down, refused to take any more trauma. She decided to survive. If only to spite Donna.

'I'm not a bitch!' she gasped. He pushed her to the ground with such force that her head banged against the wall, nearly knocking her out. She twisted her wrists, frantically trying to work the handbag strap loose. He knelt between her legs and slashed the inside of her left thigh. Warm wet blood flowed. She cried out and bit her painfully swollen lip, her fingers tugging at the knotted strap. He dropped the knife and unzipped his fly.

'Tell me you want it!' He grabbed her by the hips and pulled her towards him. 'Go on!'

'No!' Justine screamed and writhed as she tried to close her legs. 'I don't want it – let me go!'

'Shut it!' he growled. The knot suddenly loosened and circulation flowed again. Justine lifted her buttocks, fingers inching towards the knife. He misunderstood the small movement, and laughed with satisfaction.

'Slag!' he said triumphantly. 'You do want it, don't you?'

Her fingers closed around the knife handle and she gripped it. His dark shape loomed over her. 'Keep still,' he shouted, spreading her legs wide. 'Or I'll . . .'

Justine brought up the knife and thrust it under his ribcage, using all her strength to drive it in. It felt like cracking a wishbone. He caught his breath and his whole body went rigid as the knife plunged deep into his heart. It seemed an eternity before he let out his last breath in an enormous sigh and collapsed on top of her, his blood flooding over her breasts and belly.

Justine lay there paralysed with terror. He's dead, she thought. I've killed him. Good! said the protective primeval voice deep inside her. She had to get out of here – now! She fought and struggled out from under his warm dead weight, crying with fear and the horror of it all. She was soaked in his blood, saturated with the warm, sticky, metallic-smelling fluid. She sobbed, screamed in shock and revulsion.

She got to her feet and adjusted her dress, groped on the rough concrete for her jacket, handbag, ripped bra and pants. She couldn't put the bra and pants back on. Her knees were scraped and the stockings torn to shreds. She stuffed them into her handbag, picked up the bloody knife and stuffed that in too. It had a long, viciously curved serrated blade and a broad handle. She had no idea what she would do with the hideous thing, except that it had her fingerprints all over it and therefore couldn't be left here.

She cried out as she stumbled over her attacker's dead weight and nearly fell on top of him. She found tissues in her bag – for once! – and scrubbed frantically at her hands, *à la* Lady Macbeth. The blood-soaked tissues fell apart. The smells of blood and stale pee filled her nostrils and she felt sick to her stomach.

'He didn't rape you,' she whispered, trying to calm down, pull herself together. 'It's okay, you're all right!'

A chill breeze swept the alley and heavy raindrops began to fall. The cold air smelled fresh. The raindrops became a steady downpour. Justine pulled on her leather jacket, slung the bag over her shoulder and stumbled out of the alley towards Hope Street. She was sick, dizzy and hurting all over. She had shooting pains in her head and stomach, and her inner thigh stung where he'd slashed her. She tried to stop crying, fought back the urge to scream and bawl out her shock and pain and terror. A man had tried to rape her and she had killed him!

She already knew she wouldn't report this to the police. How could she prove self-defence? There were no witnesses. She was beaten, bleeding and traumatized, but you had to be battered almost to death, preferably with a hammer or a length of pipe, before the police and courts would believe you. And even if he'd raped her, that still might not have been enough evidence for them. She could end up on a murder or manslaughter charge, be forced to relive the horror in court for public entertainment. No doubt there would be family and friends to testify what a great guy her dead assailant was, how passionately he had loved his wife, girlfriend, child, dog, boa constrictor. It would be the beginning, not the end of her ordeal.

She could imagine what would happen, visualize it as clearly as if she were watching a film. She deserved to be punished, didn't she? Out clubbing with a gang of mates, drinking, laughing, watching strippers. Wearing a black Wonderbra and black stockings! Prosecuting counsel would think she had fallen off the

Christmas tree. They would have more fun with her than they would portraying some murdered woman as a nagging, vicious, ball-breaking wife who had richly deserved every blow of her unmanned husband's spanner.

The rain came down hard and soaked her, flattening her hair. Coloured lights were reflected in puddles. People stayed in pubs and clubs, waiting for the weather to ease off. In Hope Street Justine hailed a black cab and it swished to a halt alongside, spraying her bare legs with cold rainwater. She climbed in and collapsed shaking on to the back seat. Her legs felt so weak she didn't know how she had made it this far. The pitch dark alley would haunt her dreams for ever.

'Nasty night, eh, luv?' The driver eyed her curiously in the mirror. He was a thin, middle-aged man with a moustache and thick glasses. This one looked in a right state, he thought. Why was she shivering so much? It wasn't that cold.

'Lark Lane,' Justine said tersely. She would walk home from there, it was only ten minutes. She didn't want the cab driver knowing her address, he might remember it. Disjointed thoughts raced through her brain. *Cab driver recalls picking up young woman in dishevelled state* .... . Her teeth chattered and she twisted her hands together, wished she could control the terrible shaking. She felt freezing cold.

Justine couldn't believe she had killed a man. Even in self-defence. She couldn't face the thought of going to hospital for a check-up, having to explain what had happened to brisk, over-familiar nurses and doctors who would look at her like she was just another tissue sample from the pathology lab. They might want to call the police, become suspicious when she tried to stop them. She bent her head and choked back a cry of anguish, shoulders shaking as more tears rolled down her cheeks.

How the hell could this happen? How could she be unlucky enough to fall foul of two psychos within such a short time span? It was crazy, unreal, statistically impossible! Less than a million to one, less than the risk of being killed in a plane crash. And why *her*?

Was it merely breathtakingly bad luck or was she doing something wrong? Did she seem too girly, polite, vulnerable? Too free? Was it a spider and fly thing, victim and persecutor drawing each other like magnets? Maybe it was her fault, maybe she gave out the wrong signals without even realizing. *Hi! I'm a victim, punish me!* Don't think like that, she told herself fiercely. You're not a victim, you survived. You stopped him raping you. You can get through this, deal with it. You have to!

The cab left the city centre and sped through dark, deserted streets of seedy pubs and boarded up shop windows. Justine furtively wiped her eyes, avoided looking in the mirror and encountering the driver's curious gaze.

'Listen, love, he's not worth it, you know,' he said in his strong Scouse accent.

She started. 'What?'

'The fella,' he grinned. 'Your fella. Don't upset yourself over him.'

'I'm not upset,' she said stonily, and took a deep, shuddering breath.

'All right, love.' He shrugged. 'None of my business.'

'So why don't you bloody well mind it then?' Justine said fiercely.

'Hey, take it easy, love! I'm sorry I opened me big gob, okay?' He glanced nervously in the mirror at her blazing eyes. Her hair was wringing wet and her makeup smudged by the rain. Her long eyelashes looked like spider's legs. What was she on? They were all on something nowadays. The girls were worse than the lads. He hoped she had cash for the fare. He turned into Lark Lane and drove slowly past pubs, restaurants and lighted shop windows. Justine leaned forward.

'Drive to the end,' she ordered brusquely. 'By the park gates.'

'Right you are, madam!' He drove down past the old police station and stopped. Justine dropped several pound coins into his hand and climbed unsteadily out of the cab. Rain and wind blew in her face. She walked quickly away, knowing the driver was watching her. The cab moved off a minute later, reversed and headed back towards the city centre.

Justine wasn't scared to walk alone along dark Aigburth Drive. It could hardly happen again – forget statistics, even she couldn't be that unlucky! If Matthew appeared she would kill him too. She had a knife, didn't she? She'd done it once, she could do it again. I won't phone Adam, she thought suddenly. I can't talk to him while I'm in this state. After what had just happened, being cheated on by your fiancé and best friend had suddenly dropped way down the scale of traumatic life events.

The rising wind moaned around the house, rustling the trees and creaking the branches as she opened the downstairs front door. Justine was so upset that she didn't notice the flat door wasn't double-locked, the way she'd left it. She ran upstairs, desperate to rip off her bloodied clothing and get into a hot bath. On the kitchen landing she stopped, breathing heavily, and looked fearfully around. The lights were on and she could smell coffee. A shower of rain hit the huge stained glass landing window. Adam walked out of the sitting room, wearing his white bathrobe and holding a mug of coffee in one hand.

'Hi there!' He laughed. 'My God, you look rough!' He came to the top of the stairs and grinned down at her. 'Like a drowned rat. You obviously had an interesting hen night,' he commented as she climbed the stairs. 'What did they do, stick your head down the bog then throw you in a skip? Very lad-*ette*!'

'What are you doing here?' Justine gasped. 'No, don't!' She jumped back as he took a step towards her. Adam stooped and put the coffee mug on the floor.

'I was worried,' he said slowly. 'I decided to come back early. Are you okay?' He looked closely at her. 'Your lip's bleeding. How did you do that?'

She touched a finger to her lip, didn't answer him. Adam wondered what was wrong. He had spent all day in an agony of guilt and self-loathing, couldn't believe he had let Donna seduce him like that. He never wanted to see her again, certainly not hanging around Justine pretending to be her best friend! That thought sickened him. He would look after Justine properly from now on, never leave her again. She wouldn't find out about last night. Donna had promised to stay silent. He had no option but to trust her.

'Aren't you glad I came back early?' he asked anxiously. 'I missed you like hell.'

'Missed Donna after your night of passion, you mean!' Justine watched him flinch, turn pale. 'So it is true!' She started to cry again. If she told him about the attempted rape and how she had stabbed her assailant dead, he might call the police. How could she trust him now?

That bloody bitch! Adam thought furiously. Donna couldn't

147

keep it shut, not even for five minutes. He had rejected her and now she wanted to destroy him. She didn't love him or Justine, only herself. Why had he not realized sooner what a callous, vengeful, manipulating cow she was?

'How could you do this to me?' Justine screamed. 'To *us*?' Nausea welled up in her. 'You and my so-called best friend . . .' She couldn't go on.

'Justine, you've got to listen to me!' he said desperately. 'It was a terrible mistake, I must have been crazy. I don't know what came over me.' He stepped forward and tried to take her in his arms. He had tears in his eyes. 'I love you.'

'Liar! Don't touch me.' She slapped him across the face, a stinging blow that left a bright red mark on his cheek. 'Get out! Leave!' she shouted. 'Right now.'

'No,' he said, anguished. 'We have to talk.'

'Talk?' She burst into hysterical laughter. 'You only talk with your dick!'

'*Please*, Justine –' The phone rang and she stopped laughing and gulped with terror. They stood frozen to the spot, their eyes locked on one another. The answering machine in the sitting room bleeped into action.

'I like your tits, Justine.' Matthew's voice was loud and harsh in the big, silent space. 'That bloke was right, you could be in *Playboy*. Did you like the stripper? Put you in the mood for a shag, did it? You dirty whore!' he shouted angrily. 'Why did you kill him? He was only trying to give you what you wanted. What you deserved. Shall I tell the police you murdered him? Hey!' He laughed. 'What's Metaphysics?'

The phone went dead. Shocked, Adam stared at Justine. He saw that her face was bruised and her lips swollen as well as bleeding. Why were her legs bare? She always wore black stockings with that dress. There was dirt in her hair and her face was soaked with tears, not rain. She couldn't stop shivering and her beautiful eyes were filled with panic.

'What the bloody hell's happened?' he whispered. A tidal wave of guilt and fear crashed over him. He should never have left her, not for one second. 'Tell me!'

'No!' she shouted, tears streaming down her face. 'What do you care anyway?'

'Of course I care!' He grabbed her arm.

'Leave me alone, you bastard!' Justine screamed and hit out furiously at him, wrenched her arm away. 'Get out of here – don't ever touch me again!'

Her handbag and jacket fell on the floor. Sobbing wildly, she stumbled into the bathroom and threw up.

# Chapter Fourteen

The body might have been discovered by now. What would happen next? Justine climbed out of the bath and stood under a hot shower, vigorously shampooing her hair and rubbing more foaming citrus shower gel over her sore body. The bathroom was filled with steam. She would never forget the sound of her attacker's last sigh, the feel of his warm blood flooding over her bare breasts and belly. That hideous knife against her throat . . . slashing the inside of her thigh . . . Tears poured down her face along with the hot water. She couldn't stop crying.

'Justine?' Adam called again. He knocked at the door. 'Please, come out.'

She had been in there half an hour and he felt like kicking the damn' door in, but that would only increase her terror. She had been attacked and assaulted, he'd gathered that much. Ironically enough, not by Matthew. He had just stood back and enjoyed the show. He must have followed her all night. How the hell did the bastard know Justine had studied Metaphysics?

Adam felt shocked to the core, overwhelmed with guilt and horror. He should have stayed with Justine, protected her. If he hadn't gone to London this would never have happened. He shook his head and swore under his breath, impatiently brushed away tears. He would never forgive himself. He couldn't stand the thought of losing her, being helpless to do anything about the agony she was going through. Agony that was his fault. Justine had to let him help her now.

He went into the bedroom and quickly dressed in jeans, trainers and a dark blue sweatshirt. They would have to spend the rest of the night sitting around some grim police station. He shuddered at the thought of the questions Justine would be asked, the humiliating medical she would have to undergo. They might want to examine her even though she said she hadn't been raped. He walked out of the bedroom and knocked at the bathroom door again.

'You shouldn't be washing away evidence,' he warned. 'It won't help your case. You need to be examined by a police doctor.'

'That's the last thing I *need!*' She sobbed. 'I won't go to the police,' she shouted. 'They've done sod all to help me so far!'

She switched off the shower and reached for a towel. The knife slash on her inner thigh stung. It wasn't much deeper than a scratch and probably wouldn't leave a scar. She was lucky, very lucky! She took a smaller towel and rubbed at her wet hair. I mustn't let this turn me into a fucked-up recluse, she thought, recalling Donna's words. I've got to hold myself together. She had the stupid impossible desire to turn the clock back a few hours and start afresh, do something different so that the attack and killing would not have happened. She longed for Adam and Donna's betrayal not to have happened. But it had, and there was nothing she could do about it. She could only go forward, not back. Fall apart and play the victim role – or deal with it. Her choice.

'Justine, you have to go to the police,' Adam said frantically.

'I don't have to do bloody anything,' she cried. 'Go away, get lost!'

'Please try to calm down and see sense.' He knocked at the door again. 'Can I get you a drink?' he called. 'Some tea?'

'Tea!' She laughed hysterically. 'How about a litre of vodka?'

'Did you really kill him – the man who attacked you?' Adam closed his eyes as he remembered Matthew's words. 'How did . . .?'

'Leave me *alone!*'

'I can't. Justine, you've got to tell me what happened.' He rattled the doorknob. 'Let me in, please!' he begged desperately. 'We have to sort this out. You need help.'

There was no answer. She ran the cold tap, started to brush her teeth for the third time. Adam leaned against the wall and sighed heavily. He felt confused and filled with anxiety, wished he could do something to assuage the terrible guilt that was so strong he almost felt he could taste it. He wished he had killed Matthew. A

151

few years in jail would have been worth it! He clenched his fists then straightened up and faced the door again.

'You've got to report this assault,' he said, his voice low and urgent. 'Especially if you killed your attacker. It was self-defence, you won't be charged with anything. But if you don't report it you'll be in big trouble. No matter how traumatized you are.' He paused. 'Talk to me, for Christ's sake!'

Her toothbrush clattered in the sink. Adam's foot touched the leather jacket lying on the floor. Justine's black leather handbag lay next to it. He stared at the bag then squatted down and undid the gold clasp, shook out the contents. A lipstick in a gold case, a small perfume spray and a sticky, bloodied knife with a serrated blade fell out, entangled with her torn bra and pants and ripped black stockings, bits of sodden, bloodied tissues. Adam froze again, gasped in horror. The bathroom door opened and he leapt to his feet.

Justine stood there wearing her white bathrobe, her long, curly hair damp and her smooth skin flushed from the hot bath and shower. Adam flinched at the look in her eyes. She glanced away, shuddering as she caught sight of the bloody knife and torn underwear. Her shoes and the damp, crumpled velvet dress lay on the wet bathroom floor.

'Good job I wore black, isn't it?' she said harshly.

'The knife,' Adam stammered, dry-mouthed with shock. 'Is it . . .?'

'The *murder weapon*?' She pushed past him, her blue eyes icy. 'Yes. It's his. A charming gentleman's fashion accessory for the perfect night on the town!'

'Why did you bring it home?'

'I had to, it's covered with my fingerprints. He was going to kill me with it,' she said, 'but *he* was the one who ended up stiffed. Makes a change, doesn't it? Why don't you marry Donna on Saturday?' she shouted, as she ran downstairs. 'She can have my wedding dress. She loves it. She loves *you*!'

'I don't want her!' Adam experienced a moment of pure hatred for Donna. And himself. He glanced again at the bloody knife nestling in its bed of ripped black underwear. It looked like the cover for some thriller or crime novel. He followed Justine downstairs and into the kitchen. Rain beat against the long sash window. 'I only want you,' he said desperately. 'Justine, please! I love you!'

'Stop saying that!' she flashed. 'You'll make me throw up again.'

'You've got to let me help you.'

'Okay, fine. You can spend tomorrow cancelling the wedding.'

'No!' Anguished tears filled his eyes again.

'I'll be too busy,' she said, ignoring his reaction. 'I mean, I've got to get over this, haven't I? Keep out of Matthew's way, guess his next move. Get a new life without you, come to terms with everything, concentrate on staying sane.' She grabbed a bottle of white wine from the fridge and poured herself a big glass full. 'Why me?' she shouted suddenly. 'What the hell have I ever done to deserve all this shit? I've never hurt anybody in my life. He hated me,' she cried, staring at Adam. 'Matthew hates me too. *You* must hate me. Why?'

'Justine, I don't hate you. Calm yourself, please!' He tried again. 'You've got to report this,' he repeated gently. 'I'll come with you to the police, I'll stay with you while you're examined. I won't let them ask you any horrible questions.'

'Asking horrible questions is their job, or haven't you heard?' She dumped the wine bottle on the kitchen table. 'Look, I realize doctors have a problem listening to lesser mortals, but will you please get your head around the fact that I am *not* going to the police!' she blazed. 'It's got sod all to do with you anyway. We're finished. You destroyed us.' She wiped her streaming eyes on her sleeve. 'Why are you still here? I told you to go!'

'I'm not going anywhere,' he said, white-faced. 'I won't leave you alone when you're in this state.' He watched her gulp the cold wine. 'You shouldn't be drinking,' he pointed out. 'You're in shock.'

'Don't tell me what to do, Dr bloody Shaw!'

'Okay,' he said quietly. 'I'm sorry.' He couldn't even begin to imagine her terror, the grief and trauma she was going through. And all he had done was make it ten times worse. 'But this is an emergency,' he pleaded, his voice choked. 'You're hurt. We've got to do something.'

Justine stared at him, her brilliant eyes glittering. 'That bastard deserved to die,' she cried. 'And I'm glad I killed him. Are you going to grass me up?'

'For Christ's sake! You haven't done anything to be grassed up for!' Adam crossed to her and tried to take her in his arms, but she

153

furiously pushed him away. 'It was self-defence, they can't charge you.' He felt stunned, helpless, sledgehammered by shock.

'Can't they? His wife or girlfriend, his family, will say what a great guy he was. I'll be ripped to shreds in court . . .'

'You won't have to go to court,' he interrupted.

'You don't know that! You're a doctor, not a bloody lawyer! My whole life dissected by the media,' she went on. 'For their fun. It'll be like some witch hunt from the Middle Ages. I'll be made to look a lying slag. Don't give me any bullshit about how things have changed! I won't stand a chance.' She gulped the wine and poured another glass. 'If you think I'm going to go through that torture after everything else that's happened, you can bloody well forget it!' she said fiercely. 'I've had enough. Anyway, he's dead, isn't he? He won't hurt any other women.'

'All right, Justine.' Adam longed for a big Scotch, but restrained himself. 'If you don't want to go to the police that's your choice,' he said, hoping she would change her mind if he dropped the issue for now. He looked at her beautiful tearstained face. 'At least tell me what happened.' He reached out and took her hand. It felt icy.

'Don't!' She pulled away, trembling with fear and panic. 'What am I going to do?' she screamed. 'I'm so frightened!' She snatched up the bottle of wine, pushed past him and ran out of the kitchen. He followed her back upstairs. She went into the lamplit bedroom and collapsed on the bed, curled her shivering body up tight. Rain lashed the windows, and tree branches creaked in the wind. Adam sat on the edge of the bed.

'Justine, you'll get through this.' He stretched out one hand, let it fall. He wished she would let him touch her, comfort her. 'You're going to be fine. you're strong.'

How strong? She was traumatized, devastated, and now she couldn't trust him any more. She could have been murdered tonight, could have died knowing he had betrayed her with her best friend. He had wrecked everything. For one stupid fuck!

'I was in a club with Donna and the others.' More tears spilled from her eyes and rolled on to the pillow. 'This guy had been hassling me, he'd followed us to a few pubs.' Her voice trembled. 'Yes!' she said, seeing Adam's shocked expression. 'Another one. I don't understand, I must be some kind of magnet for lowlife psychos! I was thinking about it in the taxi on the way home, how it's statistically impossible and that I'd have more chance of dying in a plane crash.' She sniffed and brushed away her tears. 'I didn't see Matthew in the club although I kept looking for him. Donna was acting weird all night, totally out of character. She seemed angry, bitter. I couldn't think why. She wouldn't talk about it. Later on she got really pissed and told me about your night together. Said she loved you and you loved her, that you wanted to go on seeing her after we were married . . .' She stopped and shut her eyes, her whole body shaking with sobs.

'That's bullshit!' he exploded, furious and horrified. 'She's lying!'

Justine opened her eyes. 'Why would she lie?'

'Because I told her I wanted nothing more to do with her. That I'd made a terrible mistake and it would never happen again. She's jealous now – wants revenge. You must see that,' he said despairingly.

'I ran out of the club . . . I had to get away from Donna. The guy followed me. He beat me, dragged me into an alley, put a knife to my throat. He said he'd kill me and I believed him. Then he tried to rape me. I managed to grab the knife and stab him before he could . . .' She paused. 'He died instantly, it must have gone straight into his heart. I didn't mean to kill him!' Her voice rose to a wail. 'I only wanted to escape.'

'Jesus Christ!' Adam breathed. 'I'm sorry, Justine, I'm so sorry.' He shifted towards her and wrapped his arms around her shivering body, kissed her soft hair and tearstained face. This time she didn't resist. 'No one saw anything?' he asked grimly. 'I mean, apart from . . .?' He couldn't speak Matthew's name aloud.

'*Him*. Adam, I'm so scared!' she wailed. 'What if Matthew goes to the police?'

'There's no way he'll do that. Don't think about him now. You're going to be all right,' he said, hugging her to him. 'I promise! I'll look after you.'

'How can I ever trust you again?' she wailed. 'You betrayed me.' She pushed him away and turned over, crying bitterly. 'What if I'm HIV-positive?' she sobbed.

'Put that out of your mind,' he said sharply. 'Right now. He didn't rape you, so at least you don't have to worry about that.'

'He bit my lips, slashed my thigh with the knife. His blood was all over me!'

'I told you, don't even think about it! The chances of contracting HIV like that are so remote . . .'

'More remote than dying in a plane crash? Or being attacked by two psychos?'

'*Yes!*' Adam wished desperately that he could calm her; he might have had more success if he hadn't spent last night screwing her best friend. He pulled the quilt over her shivering body and tucked it around her.

'Justine, please listen,' he begged. 'Donna came to my hotel room late last night. She was upset because she said she'd found her boyfriend in bed with another woman. She asked if she could stay the night because it was too late to catch a train back to Liverpool.'

'She told me Cal didn't exist.' Justine's voice was muffled, her face buried in the pillow. 'She said London was your chance to get away together, that you were stressed out by my problems. That you think I encouraged the stalking.'

'*What*? She's lying!' he exclaimed, stunned. If Donna had walked into the room that minute he would have killed her. 'I never said that – I never thought it,' he said hotly. 'There was nothing going on, I swear! Think about it,' he urged. 'We're together nearly every evening, every weekend or else I'm stuck in that bloody surgery or doing visits. When was I supposed to find time for an affair, even if I'd wanted to? What she says is bullshit! I realize I've fucked everything up,' he said bitterly. 'Destroyed your love and trust in me. But it was one stupid night, Justine, no more. That's the truth! Donna wanted to see *me* again, not the other way round. Don't listen to her lies!'

Justine was silent, staring at her Inishbofin stone on the bedside table. The white quartz gleamed in the lamp light. She raised herself on one elbow, stretched out her arm and picked up the smooth heavy object. She shifted on to her stomach, held it in both hands and stared at it, feeling the weight and coldness. Her tears dripped on to the pure white stone and rolled off.

'I wish I'd never gone to that sodding conference.' Adam looked at her, heartbroken.

'I knew something terrible would happen tonight,' Justine whispered. The stone warmed in her hands. 'I told myself I was being paranoid.' She turned over in bed and faced him, put the stone down and wiped her streaming eyes again. 'Matthew sounds different now.'

'What d'you mean?'

'Terminally angry. He turned up here last night.'

'*What?* I tried to call you, but –'

'I spent the evening with Charley and Marinda, they invited me for dinner. Matthew sent me a dildo, then phoned to ask if I liked his present! The police bagged it as evidence. God knows how he got our phone number,' she said dully, 'but that's another story. He turned up later, drunk and shouting. I called the police again, but he escaped. This morning I saw him on television,' she went on. 'Outside a council house in Old Roan where nine people had burned to death in a fire. He was laughing at me. Maybe he set the fire!'

Another electric charge of shock shot through Adam's taut body. 'What makes you say that? How can you possibly know?'

'He did it to show off, prove what he's capable of. Because I rejected him.'

Adam took her hand, gently stroked it. 'Justine, we have to call the police.'

'No!' She snatched her hand away and sat up in bed. 'He'll say I murdered that man who attacked me.'

'I don't think he'll confess to the police that he's been stalking you for weeks, or that he witnessed a crime take place and did nothing. You were followed by this bastard who tried to rape you?' Justine nodded. 'Did the others see him?'

'They saw him hassle me during the evening. Stephanie might have seen him again when he tried to stop me running out of the club.'

'The police will probably want to question everyone there,' Adam said gently. 'You'll have to make a statement anyway.'

'No!' she cried, panicked. 'I can't!'

'Listen to me – your friends witnessed that guy hassle you, it was obvious you'd never seen him before. There's no way you'll be charged with murder or manslaughter! We've got Matthew's call on the answering machine tape. It proves he was stalking you, that he watched you being attacked and did nothing. The Bluffs witnessed his stalking last night – not for the first time either. The police will realize you killed in self-defence, they'd have to be insanely stupid not to! They'll arrest Matthew and you'll be safe. You're too traumatized to think straight now, of course,' he said. 'But when you calm down you'll see I'm right.'

'No, you don't understand . . .' Justine was crying and shaking again. 'I can't take any more, Adam!' She gripped his arm so tightly that he winced in pain. 'I can't go to some awful police station and be interrogated, let some brusque police doctor examine me! Appear in court, have everyone know what happened. They'll judge me, wonder if I'm a liar, maybe deny what I went through – I'd feel even worse then. And I *could* end up in jail. I'll have no control over my life ever again. I'd rather be dead!' she screamed. 'I can't do it, Adam. Don't try to make me, please, please!'

'All right,' he said, alarmed. She was hysterical, and no wonder. 'Shh!' He pulled her into his arms again and hugged her tight. 'It's okay,' he whispered, kissing her forehead. He gently took hold of her wrist; her pulse was racing. It was no use, she was too upset. He couldn't possibly force her to go to the police. Certainly not tonight.

'Why is my life such a nightmare?' she wailed. 'I thought we'd be so happy!'

'Shh!' he whispered, stroking her back. 'We will be,' he said soothingly. He blinked away tears. 'I've hurt you so much and I know it'll take a long time before you can trust me again, but I love you and I'm here for you. I won't mention the police again, okay?' He couldn't bear Justine's terrible shock and grief, his own guilt at betraying her. 'We'll get married on Saturday,' he said, kissing her again. 'Leave all this shit behind. Two more days. Then we can relax, be alone together. Sort everything out.'

Justine stopped crying and went quiet. She believed Adam when he said he had spent no more than one night with Donna. But it didn't make a hell of a lot of difference. How could he mention marriage now?

'Let me get something to relax you, help you sleep,' he said, hugging her. 'We can talk in the morning. Sleep is what you really need now.'

'Okay.' That was a good idea. She wanted oblivion. 'Adam,' she whispered, 'I can't marry you now. Marriage would make everything worse, not sort it out.'

'Don't let's talk any more tonight,' he said, anguished by her words. 'I'll make you some tea, get a hot water bottle.' He kissed her and she slid out of his arms. 'I won't be long.' He got up.

Justine turned away from him and huddled beneath the quilt.

158

On the landing, he stopped and trembled with revulsion at the sight of the knife and Justine's ripped underwear. He couldn't leave them lying there. He opened his bag and pulled on latex gloves, then went downstairs and got two bin bags from the cupboard under the sink. He went back upstairs and put everything in one bin bag, including Justine's dress and shoes. He stuffed one bag into the other. His gloves were stained with the dark, sticky, clotted blood of her dead assailant. For the first time in Adam's life, the sight of blood made him feel sick.

In the kitchen he shoved the bin bag with its horrible contents into a bucket in the cupboard under the sink. He would decide where to dump it tomorrow. He took off the gloves and thoroughly washed them and his hands, threw the gloves in the pedal bin. He realized he was breathing hard, almost panting, shaking with horror. His legs felt weak.

He put the kettle on, went next door to the dining room and poured himself a big Scotch, gulping it down. It made him feel better. In his bag he found a packet of Diazepam five-milligram tablets, the lowest strength. They'd do for Justine. She'd never taken a sedative in her life. He put them in his pocket. The phone rang and he dashed into the kitchen and snatched it off the wall.

'Justine?' Donna's voice was distraught. 'Please don't hang up,' she begged. 'Listen, I'm so sorry for what I said! I don't want to wreck our friendship –'

'You already have. Fuck off!' he said icily. 'Don't you come anywhere near me or Justine again. You evil lying bitch!'

'Adam!' She hadn't expected him to be back from London yet. Donna shivered; she could feel his hatred and contempt. 'How's Justine?' she asked fearfully.

'How do you fucking think she is?' Fury burned in him. 'Why did you have to make her pay too? I made the biggest mistake of my life last night,' he said. 'And let me tell you, you weren't worth it. You're not worth shit! Stay away from us,' he ordered. 'Don't dare turn up at that church on Saturday. Oh, yes!' He smiled grimly at Donna's look of shocked dismay. 'Of course there's going to be a wedding. Justine and I love each other, we're going to spend the rest of our lives together. You surely didn't think a sad piece of crap like you would have the power to break us up?'

Donna started to cry. 'Adam, I never wanted to hurt Justine! Or you. I'm so sorry for what I said.'

'You will be,' he interrupted, 'if you don't leave us alone. Go to hell!'

He crashed the phone back and stood there breathing deeply, trying to compose himself. He had to stay calm for Justine's sake, persuade her to go through with the wedding. Tomorrow they could have a long talk.

He made tea and filled the hot water bottle, poured a glass of water. He switched on the radio then switched it off again. There wouldn't be any news yet. The man's body might not be discovered until morning. He went back upstairs. Justine was sitting up in bed clutching the quilt around her shoulders.

'Who was on the phone?' she whispered. She looked terrified.

'Donna,' he said grimly. 'She wanted to check that she'd split us up. I told her to fuck off. Here.' He handed her the glass of water and a tiny yellow tablet. 'This will help you sleep.'

Justine washed the tablet down then took a few sips of hot, sweet lemon tea.

Adam tucked the hot water bottle in beside her.

'What if I'm HIV positive?' she whispered again.

'Justine!' He sighed. '*Please* don't worry about that. To use a totally crap analogy, you've got more chance of hitting the lottery jackpot!' He sat on the bed and took her hand again. 'Try to get some sleep now.'

She lay down, the hot water bottle against her stomach. Adam lightly stroked her hand as he gazed down at her. She yawned, suddenly overwhelmed with exhaustion. 'Adam?'

'Yes?' He felt slightly more hopeful. She seemed calmer now. And she wasn't rejecting him completely. She would get over this terrible ordeal, with his help, and together they would fight Matthew. He had to make her feel safe. Loved.

'I don't want you to sleep in this bed with me tonight.'

'I understand,' he said quietly, hope crushed. He nodded, swallowed hard. 'I'll be in the spare room. Call me if you need anything, okay? I'll leave the door open.' He kissed her hand, held it tight. 'Justine, please tell me one thing?'

'What's that?' She lay looking up at him, too tired and drained to cry any more.

'I love you,' he said desperately. 'I want to be with you for the rest of my life, I couldn't bear to lose you now.' He looked at her, his eyes brimming with tears. 'Donna hasn't split us up, has she? Tell me she hasn't?'

'No.' Justine's face was pale and exhausted and her dark blue eyes glittered.

She pulled her hand out of his grasp. 'Not Donna,' she whispered. '*You!*'

# Chapter Fifteen

When Adam woke up he felt all right for a split second. Sunshine warmed his face. The rain and wind had passed with the night and it was a beautiful calm clear autumn morning. Then everything flooded back. He got out of bed, pulled on his robe and looked down at the trees and drive. The spare room alarm clock showed 6.50. His body was stiff and he ached all over. He felt exhausted, leaden, as if he'd taken ten sleeping pills after running a marathon.

The nightmare had blown up, whirled out of a clear sky, caught Justine and him and torn their lives apart. Adam felt murderous rage as he thought of Donna again. He wanted to beat her, hurt her like she had hurt Justine. Who was he kidding? he thought. Without his own betrayal there would be no pain, no hurt, no assault. No killing. Justine might never get over this. And what if the police found out she hadn't reported the assault and stabbing? Anything could happen then.

He crossed the landing and crept into the bedroom to check on her. Justine was deeply asleep, curled up and hugging the pillow. Adam moved nearer to the bed, his eyes filling with tears as he looked down at her. She was peaceful now, but she would wake soon and feel terrible again. He couldn't believe he had risked losing the love of this beautiful, intelligent, spirited woman by giving in to a stupid, crazy, momentary itch! What *had* he seen in Donna?

He crept down to the kitchen and shut the door quietly, crossed to the window and looked out over the garden. The trees and lawn glittered with frost and he could hear the lethal weapon barking and growling on the terrace below. Adam spooned coffee beans into the grinder and poured water into the filter. He yawned and stretched. He looked at the cupboard under the sink and shuddered. What could he do with the knife and Justine's ripped, blood-soaked clothing? Right now he didn't think he could bear to touch or look at them again. He switched on Radio City for the 7 o'clock news bulletin and turned the volume low.

*Merseyside Police have launched a murder investigation after one of their colleagues, Detective Constable Ronnie Davis, was found dead in an alley near Hope Street in the early hours of this morning. DC Davis died from a single stab wound to the heart. Police have appealed for witnesses to come forward, especially anyone present at the Crystal Cave club in the city centre, where DC Davis was enjoying a night out with friends and colleagues. Ronnie Davis was thirty-two years of age, married and the father of two young children . . .*

'Shit!' Adam breathed, horrified. His heart pounded with shock. Justine's attacker had been a policeman! He switched off the radio, walked back to the window and stared down at the sunny, frost-covered garden again. The coffee machine hissed and gurgled in the silent kitchen.

Justine couldn't go to the police now. They would be baying for her blood, wouldn't believe a word she told them. She didn't know how right she'd been last night. He had to try and keep her away from television and local newspapers until they were married and off to the Caribbean. Justine had to marry him now, even if later she decided she couldn't live with him any more. A policeman! Adam was stunned with shock and disbelief by this latest terrible blow. He poured himself a cup of coffee and slowly sipped it.

He had to protect her now. Together they could ride out this storm. He made toast, sliced a sweet juicy orange, poured coffee into a mug and took it up to her on a tray, hoping she wasn't already awake and watching the news. The national as well as local media would seize on this 'murdered' policeman, delight in another opportunity to spread terror and confusion about the so-called epidemic of crime and general lawlessness. Fiction and speculation would be regurgitated as hard fact. If the killer turned out to be female, that was icing on the cake.

Justine stirred and opened her eyes as he came in. She turned

163

over in bed and gazed sleepily at him as he set the tray on the bedside table. Adam looked haggard, she thought sadly, unshaven. His dark brown eyes were sorrowful and anguished. Then her whole body tensed, shrank from him. She sat up, immediately full of fear and despair.

'Good morning.' Adam tried to smile. 'You managed to get some sleep?'

'Yes. Thanks.' She took the mug of coffee he handed her.

'How are you feeling? I mean – no headache, disturbed vision, any other symptoms?'

'No. I'm sore and aching, though. Did you hear anything yet?' she asked anxiously. 'Switch the TV on, will you?'

'I just listened to Radio City news. There was nothing,' he lied. He sat on the bed. 'Staring at television waiting for news won't do your nerves any good.' He picked up the plate of toast and offered it to her. 'Eat some breakfast,' he said. 'Try to relax.'

'I don't want that!' She pushed the plate away. 'How the hell can I relax?' She took a sip of hot sweet coffee and put the mug back on the tray. 'Who was he? I've got to know!' Her eyes were wide with panic. 'They must have found the body by now. And what about Matthew?' She buried her head in her hands. 'Oh, my *God!*' she groaned.

'Look ...' Adam felt panicked himself. He reached for the Diazepam tablets and glass of water. 'Have another of these.'

'They're not strong enough,' she complained. 'They don't knock me out.'

'They're not supposed to. They calm you, promote rest. You don't want to be a drugged-up zombie.'

'Yes, I do!' Justine swallowed the tablet then picked up the mug of coffee and took a few more sips. She looked him in the eye. 'I can't marry you.'

Pain flitted across his handsome features. 'Justine, if we start our new life the way we planned – we can work things out,' he said desperately. 'I know we can.' He blinked back tears. 'We love each other!'

'You don't love me,' she said, her voice trembling. 'You can't!'

'I do love you!' He gripped her bare shoulders and the quilt slid down, exposing her breasts. She gasped with fright. 'You've got to marry me,' he said urgently. 'Please, Justine! It's our only chance.'

'*Your* only chance!' She lashed out at him. 'Take your fucking hands off me!'

Shocked, he let go of her. She scrambled out of bed and grabbed her robe to cover her nakedness. 'I'm going to take a shower and get dressed,' she said breathlessly. 'Will you cancel this farce planned for Saturday?' she asked, pulling the belt tight. 'Or do I have to do it?'

She wanted to go back to sleep and never wake up. Oblivion was the only thing that would kill the agony, the terrible, unbe-lievable pain, pain like she'd never known. But that was victim behaviour, and she wouldn't act the victim. Or let herself be treated as one. She wished she were dead, but she was alive and she just had to get on with it. What hurt most was that she still loved Adam with all her heart and soul, still wanted to marry him despite everything. But trust had disappeared, leaving a cold, empty, dark space inside her.

Adam stood up and came towards her. ' 'It's all right,' he said as she backed fearfully away. 'I'm not going to touch you. Cancelling the wedding would be the worst thing to do,' he said gently. 'Don't you think? Apart from the fact that Donna would be delighted.'

'I don't care about her! She's history.'

'Okay. But wouldn't it look odd . . . suspicious?'

'Why? Of course, I realize you don't want your family and friends and adoring patients to know what a cheating arsehole beloved, respected Dr Shaw really is!' she flashed.

'I wasn't thinking of my reputation, believe it or not.' Adam hated the way she backed off, kept her distance. He might be a cheating arsehole, but she had no reason to be afraid of him. 'It's you I'm worried about. The police will have discovered the body by now, launched an investigation. You were in that club with your friends, they saw the dead man follow you, hassle you. You left the club alone – in an upset state.'

'What the hell's that got to do with cancelling the wedding?' Justine felt sick and faint as the awful scenes flashed back, replayed themselves in her mind. Cold and dizzy, she held on to the door to steady herself.

'He followed you out of that club, and the police will want to ask you a number of questions,' Adam went on. 'If you have the bad luck to attract their attention. There's a high probability you will, if you stick around Liverpool. And there's Matthew,' he said slowly, 'the most unpredictable element in the equation.'

'What is this, a chemistry lesson?'

'All I'm saying is that you might have a lot of explaining to do. If you don't come forward when the police get around to interviewing everyone who was in the Crystal Cave club last night, and they find out you were there but didn't tell them, it's going to look very odd. Unless you're thousands of miles away on honeymoon, of course. Wouldn't you rather be?' He paused. 'I know I would.'

Justine stared at him, pale-faced. 'I didn't tell you the name of the club we were in. You know something, don't you?' she cried. 'Tell me!'

'All right.' Adam swore, kicking himself for his stupid slip. 'I listened to Radio City news earlier. That bastard was a policeman,' he said reluctantly, dreading the effect of his words, 'a detective constable named Ronnie Davis.' He left out the bit about Davis' wife and two young children; Justine was right, there would be a family to testify what a great guy he'd been. Adam was spooked – it was happening exactly the way she had envisaged. 'They've launched a murder investigation.'

'Oh, my God!' Justine breathed. She let go of the door and turned away from him. Her hands felt cold against her face and her head whirled so that she thought she would faint or throw up again. Her legs buckled under her.

'Justine!' Adam's voice seemed to come from miles away. She felt his strong arms lift her, half carry her to the bed. She collapsed, shivering with cold and terror. He picked up the mug of coffee and held it to her lips. 'Drink some of this.'

'I don't want any,' she whispered.

'Come on, drink it!' he said harshly, frantic with worry.

She raised her head, swallowed the lukewarm coffee and lay back on the pillow, tears running down her face. 'I've had it now,' she moaned. 'I could get banged up for twenty years. If Matthew doesn't murder me first!'

'Neither of those things will happen. I promise you.' Adam sat on the bed and looked at her, grim-faced. 'Justine, listen to me,' he said, with a firmness he didn't feel. 'I want you to stay here and rest. Sleep as much as you can. We'll get married on Saturday and fly away. We love each other!' he repeated. 'Please don't let one crazy mistake destroy that love.'

166

'I might forgive you, Adam,' she sobbed. 'I don't know if I could forget.'

'I don't expect you to. When all this has blown over . . . if you decide you can't live with me, fair enough. I won't stand in your way. But you really need me now, Justine. Please give it a try,' he begged. 'It can work!' He took her icy hands in his and rubbed them.

'I don't know, I don't know.' Justine felt so frightened and freaked out that she was tempted to do what he wanted. She hated herself for still loving him so much.

'I'll go to the surgery and arrange for that locum – or someone – to take over from today instead of next Monday,' he said. 'Take care of a few other things there, get some shopping on the way home. I won't be long. When I get back we can talk properly.' He leaned over and kissed her tenderly. 'Okay?'

'Okay,' she whispered. She closed her eyes, wishing the second pill would work quicker. Why me? she thought again. What did I ever do? Or not do!

Adam stood up. 'I'll be about an hour.' He patted her shoulder. 'Rest.'

He left the flat and double-locked the door behind him. Made sure the heavy downstairs front door was locked too. He stopped the Jaguar at the gates and looked searchingly up and down leafy, sunny Aigburth Drive as he revved the engine. No sign of that scum. If he showed his ugly face again he would be as dead as DC Davis! Adam sped off, the screech of his tyres startling Marinda Bluff and Whitney out of their post-breakfast coma. Charley had an early shift at the residential home and had left an hour ago.

Justine had to go through with the wedding on Saturday, he thought, gripping the steering wheel. For both their sakes.

It was the only way.


Matthew ran back to his Ford Fiesta that was parked illicitly in someone's drive further down the road, jumped in and raced after the Jaguar. It was hard to keep up but also keep his distance. Trailing somebody wasn't as easy as it looked in movies and police series. He glanced proudly in the driving mirror at his new bleached cropped hairdo. It was a symbol, something to celebrate the new person he'd become. He'd done it himself yesterday, in between watching news bulletins about Ruby Jackson and her dysfunctional existence. An existence he had cut short. He had done society a big favour; no more taxpayers' money wasted on that fat cow and her brats. The police would never catch him. He was too clever for them. Let's face it, who wasn't! They were all thick, had minds like long narrow tunnels with no light at the end. No wonder they only caught shoplifters and speeding motorists.

He laughed out loud. The news bulletins were not only about Ruby-Rube. This morning's was even better.

'You're in big trouble, Justine,' he sang gleefully as he drove. 'You killed a plod and I watched you do it. You'll bloody do what I want now!' He increased speed to keep up with the Jaguar, turned the radio louder and sang along with The Verve.

Adam, worried sick about Justine, didn't notice he was doing ninety as he sped along the dual carriageway towards the city centre. He also didn't notice the white Ford Fiesta tucked in behind him in the stream of traffic. Shops, libraries, trees, pedestrians, supermarkets, flashed past. Matthew swore as he tried to keep up. He wanted to force Adam off the road, smash him and his fancy Jaguar. The Fart Fiesta wasn't much better than a shopping trolley. He felt alive, really alive, for the first time since the night he'd watched Hayland Software go up in flames. He would get Adam today, pay him back for Saturday night's beating.

'I'll kill you!' Matthew shouted, convulsed with rage. 'You're dead, you bastard!' He swerved out of the lane of traffic and into another one without indicating. The driver of a battered red Escort blared his horn in fright.

Adam cursed the rush-hour traffic as he headed for the surgery. He hoped Rosemary Elliott, the practice manager, would be in early. He needed her help to arrange everything. He would stay with Justine, take care of her, make her feel safe again. She needed him. Everyone else could go to hell.

He reached the busy street where the surgery was located, and swore as he saw a grey Volvo parked in his reserved space. Couldn't the stupid bastard read? Luckily there was a space on the opposite side of the street. He drove further down, reversed, and drove back. He parked and grabbed his bag off the passenger seat, got out and locked the car.

He hoped Justine was asleep now. She was traumatized, exhausted and terrified. He wished she would let him comfort her, show how much he loved her. What if she'd died last night? What

168

if he lost her now? He couldn't bear the thought of it. His eyes blurred with tears.

'Morning, Adam!' a cheery female voice called.

He swallowed hard, glanced up and waved. Rosemary Elliott was walking briskly along the pavement on the opposite side of the road. Her smooth, straight, shoulder-length grey hair looked immaculate as usual, and she wore a long flowered dress and a beige jacket with matching beige pumps and handbag. It was one of Adam's casual days, Rosemary noted, smiling at his crumpled jeans and navy blue sweatshirt. Tomorrow it would be an Armani suit. It was all part of his charm. She reminded herself to ask him how the London conference had gone.

'Morning, Rosemary,' Adam called back. Thank goodness she was early! He glanced to right and left and started to run across the road. He was seized with irritation at all the stupid trivial things he had to sort, felt desperate to get back home and be with Justine.

'Adam, look out!' Rosemary stopped and gasped in terror as she saw a white Ford Fiesta suddenly swerve out from the line of traffic and speed straight towards him. 'No!' she screamed. 'Adam! Oh my God, *no*!'

Adam saw Rosemary's cheerful expression turn to horror, saw her mouth open wide in a scream. He was puzzled. Why was she screaming? Then he saw the car. Everything suddenly slowed down and went quiet, seemed suspended in slow motion; he felt as though he had all the time in the world to leap out of the path of the white Ford Fiesta heading straight for him. He recognized Matthew's bruised face hunched over the wheel, bloodshot eyes glaring at him. Matthew, with a new cropped bleached hairdo that made him look mental. Adam saw the hatred in his eyes.

The bastard's going to kill me, he thought. No! *Justine!* I can't leave Justine! He felt a terrible jolting impact that knocked him off his feet and jerked his body every which way, forcing the breath out of his lungs. He heard a shout and realized it was his own. Everything went black.

'*Yess!*' Matthew yelled with triumph as the car slammed into Adam's body and hurled him high in the air, crushing the doctor's bag he'd been carrying. Adam landed with a horrific bang on the bonnet of a grey Volvo, rolled off and fell on the road, arms and legs splayed, his body limp like a rag doll. Blood trickled from his nose and mouth.

Cars swerved, horns blared, passers-by stopped and gazed, horror-struck. A middle-aged woman in a flowered dress and beige jacket was crying and screaming her head off, waving and pointing at him. Matthew wanted to reverse over Adam's body but there wasn't the space and he had to get out of here fast. He sped off down the road, swerved left and drove down another road. He pulled into a parking space beside a row of shops, in between two lorries, and sat there with the engine running. He was panting, sweating, trembling with excitement.

No one could have survived that impact. Shame it wasn't a Range Rover instead of a Ford Fiesta. But the job was done. Matthew wanted to go back and watch the scene, gloat at the sight of Adam being zipped into a body bag. But that was too risky. He hoped the screeching old bitch in the flowered dress hadn't got a good look at him.

He wasn't a nobody, a ripple on the grey ocean of life's sad onlookers who just took it up the arse instead of fighting back. He had sorted it. Ruby Jackson and her family were stiffed. Adam would never fuck Justine again. Matthew sat back and laughed loudly. He felt exhilarated, triumphant, awed by his own death-dealing powers.

Now there was no one to keep him from Justine.

# Part Two

# Chapter Sixteen

'Last night was fantastic, darling!'

Sara Melwood leaned over her lover Daniel, kissing his handsome face and smoothing her hands over his broad, bare tanned chest. She smiled tenderly; he was still half asleep. Daniel was thirty – a bit old for her! – and an estate agent, of all things. Not her usual bit of rough. He was great in bed, though – she hadn't felt so excited by a man in years. He made her feel like a teenager again. Or how she would have liked to feel as a teenager. In two words, properly fucked!

'Sara, it's nearly eight.' Daniel blinked in the shaft of pale gold morning sunlight that slanted across the grubby white pillow. Like a lot of men, he changed bedsheets about as often as he would a piece of furniture. 'You've never stayed all night with me before,' he said, sitting up and shifting away from her. 'Your enraged husband will be rampaging round here with his Remington Woodmaster.'

'Oh, don't get out of bed! And Paul's not the type to *rampage*. That's the last thing he'd do. What's a Remington Woodmaster?' she laughed. 'Some kind of dildo?'

'It's an American sporting rifle.' Daniel stood up, pulled on a pair of baggy khaki shorts and looked down at her. Sara had short, straight blonde hair with a fringe and sarcastic, predatory blue-grey eyes in a longish tanned face. Her breasts were small and round, the nipples hard. He looked at her thin hostile mouth, the deep lines around her tired, sun-strained eyes. Thirty-eight? Last night in the club, maybe. This morning – no way! Sara was a laugh and he had found it flattering to be fancied by a rich, mature, sophisticated woman. Now he felt awkward and bored. He'd had

173

enough mature sophistication. Daniel also felt guilty because he had an idea Sara liked him more than she let on. She would be upset, no matter how gently he tried to let her down. He didn't like hurting people's feelings.

'Come back to your whiffy bed.' Sara laughed at his frowning expression. She sat up and stretched out her arms. 'Don't worry, darling,' she said, misunderstanding. 'Paul doesn't own any rifles and even if he did he wouldn't be jealous enough to shoot you.' She patted the grimy pillow. 'I don't have to leave for hours yet,' she said eagerly. 'Paul thinks I'm at Elaine's. He won't expect me before lunchtime.'

Daniel's heart sank. 'Who's Elaine?' he asked, not giving a toss.

'My friend who introduced us, remember? Small, dark hair, big tits. That was her party we met at last month. What's the matter with you?' Sara teased, concealing her nervousness. Daniel was different this morning, restless. Maybe it hadn't been a good idea to spend the whole night with him. She didn't look human at this hour of the morning. But she'd been too pissed to drive home.

'Sara . . .' Daniel sat on the bed and looked at her, embarrassed. 'I think you should leave now,' he said gently.

'Charming!' Nervousness escalated to panicked dismay. 'Don't I even get a cup of your disgusting instant espresso?' she asked. 'Or a lovely hot shower with you under it?'

'I'll make you some coffee if you want.' She knelt up in bed and stretched out one hand to caress him. Daniel moved away. 'Look,' he began awkwardly, 'we've had a really good time, but we both knew it was never going to be –'

'I thought we were still having a good time?' Sara broke in, hurt. She looked at his light brown eyes and wavy fair hair, his broad shoulders and long muscular legs. Daniel was trying to be kind, and that made it worse. He felt sorry for her. Three weeks and already she was being dumped! She was old, pathetic, losing it. Her throat tightened and hot tears stung her eyes.

'Daniel, I really like you,' she said in a low voice. 'I thought you liked me.'

'I do,' he said. He sat down and kissed her lightly on the lips. 'You're a terrific lady. Look, I still want to see you now and then,' he lied. 'We can be friends, meet for a drink.'

Her eyes narrowed. 'But you don't want to fuck me any more!'

174 .

'Well,' he said uncomfortably, 'if you want to put it like that . . . no, I don't think it's a good idea.' He flushed.

Sara glared at him. 'You're pathetic, you know that?' she said viciously. 'Why can't you have the guts to say you're bored with me and think I'm a clapped-out old slapper?'

'Because I don't think that! Sara – I'm trying to make this as easy as possible. For both of us.'

'How kind!' she sneered.

'To be honest,' he said, 'I never thought you treated me like a person.'

'You what?' she asked, astonished.

'You fancy me so you don't want us to split up. But you're not interested in *me*, in my work or anything I do.' He looked at her resentfully. 'You just used me for sex. All we talk about is what you want to do in bed.'

'I don't believe I'm hearing this!' Sara didn't know whether to laugh or cry. 'I thought being used for sex was every red-blooded male's fantasy?'

'Well, it's not mine,' he said quietly. 'I need more.'

'I really *am* past it!' Sara scrambled out of bed and pulled on crimson lace pants, a short sleeveless glittery crimson dress and strappy, high-heeled matching sandals. Coffee and a shower would have to wait. She wished she had worn bra and stockings and brought a jacket; it was cold this morning. A tear fell on her red varnished toenail as she bent to fasten the sandal straps. 'Can't bloody win, can I?' Her voice trembled.

Daniel's embarrassment increased and he couldn't wait for her to leave. She straightened up awkwardly and rubbed her aching lower back. He shoved his hands in the pockets of his shorts, looked down and shuffled his bare feet.

'You're right, of course, darling!' Sara sniffed furiously and reached for her handbag, took out her cigarettes and car keys and lit a long thin cigarette before Daniel could object. 'It wasn't your intellect or your boring sodding existence showing sad bastards around sad houses that intrigued me,' she said, brushing away tears. 'I never could get my fluffy little head around the idea of an estate agent being a *person*!' She laughed her high brittle laugh. 'Know what I mean?' She took a huge drag on the cigarette and tossed it into the centre of the bed as she swept past him. ''Bye, darling!' she said, blowing a mouthful of smoke into his face and making him cough. 'It's been fun. Although I've had bigger and better fuckmeat than you!'

Daniel swore and dived for the cigarette, too late to stop it burning a hole in the beige quilt. He picked it up gingerly, opened the window and threw it out. He coughed again. The cigarette landed on the bonnet of her red Porsche and rolled off. Sara's spike heels echoed on the bare wooden staircase, making tiny dents that would last forever. She slammed the front door behind her and came out into the lane, stared defiantly up at Daniel as he stood watching from the bedroom window.

'Don't think you'll sell another property around here!' she shouted, eyes wet with tears. 'You miserable little shit! You won't get to fuck any of my friends either.'

'No worries, Sara! I've given up necrophilia!' He shut the window and turned away, sighing with relief. The burning smell in the stuffy bedroom reminded him of cinder toffee. Fuck it, he thought, looking at the burned hole. Now I'll have to change the sheets.

Sara started the engine and raced along the twisting, tree-lined country lane, tears of hurt and humiliation running down her face. How dare Daniel throw her out like that? He was nothing! Wait until she told Elaine what had happened. She would spread the word, make sure his up and coming business went to hell in a handbag.

At least she still had Paul, his money, her beautiful house and car and other possessions. Status, respect. For when there was nothing else left to care about. She shivered with cold and put the heater on full blast as she sped along the narrow lanes.

'Sod being forty-eight!' she cried, blaring the horn at a clumsy, low-flying pheasant. 'Sod Daniel! Sod bloody *everything*!'

Paul woke up and stretched, turned over in bed and glanced at the clock radio. Eight-thirty on the morning of Justine Flynn's wedding day. Would she be awake by now, happy and excited as she did her hair and makeup? She wouldn't think of him. And why should she? No reason at all. Adam Shaw was a great guy – and a lucky bastard!

He got up and drew the curtains, looked out at the sunlit, stubbly fields, pockets of mist lying in the hollows. He shivered slightly. The sixteenth-century farmhouse always felt cold, despite its log fires and central heating. He disliked the stone floors, dark panelled walls and twisty little passages, the grim mullioned windows that kept out the light. Sara would be in her bedroom across the passage, sleeping off her hangover. Paul wondered what time she'd got in last night. He hadn't heard the front door bang or her heels on the oak staircase.

All that remained was to tell his wife he wanted a divorce, get the sordid tedious legal formalities sorted. She might go into shock – or go ballistic – but in time she would accept it. She would have plenty of money, unlike many divorced women. Or men! That would ease the shock considerably.

He could never be with Justine. But her beauty and wit, her sweetness and laughter even under grim circumstances, had acted on Paul like a catalyst, made him realize how intolerable his own situation was. Better to be alone than go on living this farce with Sara. He no longer wanted to think about how or why. They shared a roof, the occasional silent dinner and two children who were now people with lives of their own. Sad, but it happened.

He went into the adjoining bathroom and showered, looking out over the back garden as he dried himself. He would miss the huge oak. The tree at the bottom of the garden was ancient, older than the farmhouse itself. Rebecca and Andrew had played around it as children, hidden giggling in its hollow to eat crisps and chocolate bars and bags of sticky sweets. He'd loved to sit or lie beneath it on hot sunny days and gaze up through the branches. Now pale green acorns littered the frosty grass.

Paul dressed in jeans and a black sweater and went down to the big stone-flagged kitchen. The original range, which Sara had insisted on keeping, took up most of the space. The microwave on the nearby marble counter looked silly next to it. Or did the range look silly next to the microwave? He made coffee and stood sipping it while he half listened to the radio. An off-duty policeman had been found dead in Liverpool city centre in the early hours of the morning and a murder hunt launched. They would go to more trouble for one of their colleagues than some ordinary member of the public, he thought idly.

He wondered when Adriana would phone. She was back in Moscow, arranging the shipment of the beryllium consignment. She had been perfectly polite and friendly at yesterday's meeting, the cool composure back in place. But he was worried, didn't like it that she had his home phone number and knew where he lived. He couldn't reach her at the number she had given him. Of course that could be due to the hit-and-miss Moscow telephone network.

His associate, Lim-Taek Han, had already located a mystery buyer in Zurich who would pay twenty million dollars for the beryllium. Han was in his early thirties and favoured black suits and flashy ties. Unlike many Koreans he laughed a lot, at anything and nothing. He was ruthless and efficient, totally reliable. Stop worrying, Paul told himself impatiently. This was the perfect deal and after it he would never have to think about money again as long as he lived. Apart from how to spend it.

Divorce might be the making of Sara, he thought hopefully. She was bored, depressed, spent her days doing nothing very much. Forty-eight wasn't too old to start afresh. She was intelligent and good-looking. All she needed was a goal in life. They might even end up friends. He poured a cup of coffee to take up to her, steeling himself for what would be a nasty scene. He took the coffee and walked into the hall, glanced nervously at the silent phone.

A car pulled up outside and the door slammed. Feet crunched on gravel and he heard Sara swear breathlessly. He stopped. She had been out all night. He felt sad because he didn't give a damn any more. The studded front door that looked like the entrance to some medieval torture chamber swung open and they faced one another. Sara shivered in her glittery dress.

'Good morning!' he said mildly. She looked like she'd been crying.

'I stayed the night at Elaine's.' She stared at him defiantly. 'We went to a club. I'd had a few too many so . . .' She shrugged. 'Oh, thanks!' She took the coffee he held out. 'Just what I need!'

'Can I talk to you?' he asked.

Sara looked warily at him. 'About what?'

'Us. Everything, basically. I'd really like to talk now, if possible.'

'Well, it's not bloody possible,' she said shrilly. 'You don't half pick your moments! The last thing I want to do now is *talk*. I'm going to drink this coffee, take a long hot shower and get some sleep. I'm exhausted – I'm also freezing my arse off in this dress.'

'It's important, Sara,' he said quietly.

'Yeah, I'm sure it is – to you!' She pushed past him and went up the creaking stairs. 'The great businessman snaps his fingers and all the minions come running,' she sneered. 'I'm not your fucking secretary!'

'I want a divorce,' he said bluntly. He had meant to lead into it, sound her out, break the news as gently as possible. But that wouldn't cut it. Her attitude, her sneering tone, had angered him. Sara stopped at the top of the stairs and turned.

'You *what*?' she gasped.

'I said, I want a divorce.' He stared up at her. 'I won't go on with this farce of a marriage any longer. I can't imagine you want to either.'

Sara experienced a tremendous flash of shock and insult that left her body weak and made her heart pound. She felt herself blanch then blush. The white china coffee mug crashed on the oak staircase and shattered, splashing hot coffee on her bare ankles.

'No!' she whispered, shaking her head. 'You can't do that to me!'

Panic took hold. She had been dumped by Daniel and now Paul wanted to dump her too! She would be fifty in two years' time, was losing her looks, confidence, the ability to pull. The menopause was on top of her. Horror gripped her as she thought of life as a divorced abandoned woman, the joke of the neighbourhood, the hot flushing spectre at everyone's dinner party! If she even got invited to any dinner parties. Elaine wasn't really a friend, just someone to have lunch and go out on the pull with. She would have nobody, nothing. All this, and it wasn't even nine in the bloody morning! Did Paul mean it? She looked into his calm grey eyes. He meant it.

'You bastard!' she screamed, shivering and hugging herself. 'You can't dump me just because it suits you!'

'I thought it would suit both of us.' He stepped back, one hand on the polished banister, as she hurried downstairs and swept past him. He smelled her eighties in-your-face perfume and a whiff of sweat. Male sweat. Sara still had the smell of a man on her. He followed her into the dark chilly panelled sitting room.

'I'm warning you, I won't tolerate this!' She lit a cigarette and headed for the sideboard, poured gin and a splash of tonic into one of the horrible heavy lead crystal glasses. The oil paintings on the walls were so darkened by years of her cigarette smoke that it was impossible to guess their subjects. Paul sometimes wondered what his own lungs must look like. 'Don't think I'm going to lie down and roll over,' she said furiously, swigging gin and dragging on the cigarette. 'I'll fight you every inch of the way! I suppose you've got some brain-dead, under-age slapper lined up to take my place?'

He saw the panic in her eyes, her hand tremble as she gripped the glass. 'You deal in clichés, Sara,' he said calmly. 'I don't. I'm not leaving you for another woman.'

'You expect me to believe that?' she shouted, bursting into tears.

'No.' The tears surprised and disconcerted him. He sat in the bottle-green leather armchair by the fireplace, glanced at the dried flower arrangement in the grate. 'You use your own behaviour and motivation as a yardstick for others. You think because you've been screwing around for years ...' He paused as she gasped and turned away, took another swig of her drink. 'Come on, Sara!' he said angrily. 'Don't tell me you didn't think I knew?'

'I won't tell you anything, you fucking bastard!' She faced him again, smoke spiralling from her cigarette. 'Except the name of the best divorce lawyer in England. You'll be sorry you started this.' She paced the stone flags, stumbling slightly on her high heels. 'I don't want a divorce,' she cried.

'Sara.' He sighed, leaned forward. 'We're not happy together, we haven't been for years. This is a crazy situation,' he argued. 'I don't want it to go on. Why can't we be civilized about this?'

'*Civilized?*' She finished her drink and poured another, dropped the cigarette on the stone flags and trod on it. 'You want to dump me for some slapper ...'

'I told you, there's nobody!'

'... then talk about being *civilized*? Get stuffed!' she spat.

Paul stood up. 'You don't love me,' he said bitterly. 'Why the hell do you want to go on being my wife in name only?'

'Arsehole!'

'There's no love, friendship, support.'

'Not for me any more, obviously.' She swigged the gin-and-tonic. 'What do I do now, throw myself on the tender mercy of the DSS?'

'I didn't mean financial support,' he said icily.

'What about Andrew and Rebecca?' she asked, tears falling into her drink.

'What about them? They're two not very friendly people who only visit when they've got nothing better to do. Phone or e-mail when they want extra money.' Sara's tears were from panic, he thought, shock. She'd get used to the idea. She banged the glass down on the sideboard and whirled round.

'What the fuck am I going to do?' she shouted.

'You'll be fine, Sara. Don't worry about money, you'll have plenty to live on for the rest of your life. You don't need to work, although you might like to have a job. Maybe you could resume your legal career.'

'Yeah, right. At my age. What legal career?' she cried. 'I didn't have what it takes. I'd never have become a Cherie Booth.'

Paul softened suddenly, feeling very sorry for her. It was the first time he'd heard Sara blame herself, after years of accusations that she'd been stifled by husband, children and domesticity.

'You can keep this house,' he went on. 'Or buy another if you like. I'll be there for you if you need help. We could be good friends one day,' he said hopefully. 'You'll meet another man who can make you happy.'

'Nobody's going to want a divorced, menopausal woman,' she wailed. 'Despite what all those bloody stupid magazines tell you.' She grabbed the glass and smashed it on the stone flags. 'I'll be alone, I'll have nothing!'

'You're defining your own boundaries, Sara,' he said sharply. 'It doesn't have to be that way. You won't miss me. You're shocked and angry right now, your pride's hurt. Divorce is a big life change, for both of us. But I don't believe for one minute that you're so sad you think you'll be nothing without a token husband on your arm. You've got more self-respect than that.'

'Ditch the wrinkled old bag and set up with your new slapper!' Sara shouted, deliberately disregarding his words. '*You'll* have a new life, not me. What's your hurry anyway?' She grabbed another glass and poured more gin. 'Pregnant, is she?' she sneered. 'Got a lovely big new house ready for her and the foetus?'

He flinched with disgust. 'Would you like there to be another woman?' he asked. 'Would that make you feel better?' He stepped forward, his whole body tense with anger. 'You fuck other men, you're just back from spending the night with one of them, and you have the nerve to tell me you don't want a divorce!' She was silent, wouldn't look at him. 'I've had it with your cheating, lying, greedy, cold indifference. All you care about is money. Fine. You'll get it, a damn' sight more than you deserve. You can accept it or fuck off. Go on, get pissed,' he said bitterly, watching as she drained her glass for the third time in ten minutes. 'That'll really help, won't it?' He watched horrified as she suddenly crumpled before his eyes, collapsing on to the sofa in floods of tears.

'Please don't divorce me, Paul,' she moaned. 'Don't leave me. I need you, I can't stand being alone!'

'So that's it. You don't want to be alone.' He looked down at her, disgusted and embarrassed by her performance. 'You don't need *me*.'

'I do!' Sara felt terrified, freaked out with panic. 'Paul, you can't leave me,' she sobbed. 'We've been together for so long!'

'Too long,' he said sadly. He hadn't expected her to fall apart like this. He preferred her cold and contemptuous any day of the week. 'I'm sorry, Sara.' In all this she hadn't once said she loved him.

'Don't leave me!' his wife screamed. She looked up at him, her face streaked with tears and mascara. 'I'll be different from now on. I won't screw anymore idiots, I swear! I only wanted to prove I could still pull. It was just a bit of fun.'

'I can't believe you've got so little self-esteem!' He had to raise his voice to make himself heard. 'The truth is, you'll be perfectly all right.'

'No!' she sobbed wildly. 'I'm finished!'

He turned away, agitated. He suddenly realized he had given no thought to finding another place to live. He had stupidly assumed they would go on sharing this house, continue a kind of armed détente until he found somewhere else. He should have looked for an apartment in Liverpool while Alan was drawing up the settlement. The phone rang and he swore and snatched it up.

'Paul Melwood.' He couldn't hear the caller or make himself heard over Sara's drunken panicked sobbing. 'Hold on a second, please.' He went out of the sitting room and down the hall to the kitchen.

'Good morning, Paul,' Adriana repeated. 'Sorry, is this a bad moment?' She smiled at his grim harassed tone. What was going on in that house? Paul could have had her, but he preferred his crazy, screaming wife. 'Shall I call back?'

'No, it's all right.' He took a deep breath. 'What's happening?' he asked. 'Where are you calling from?'

'My apartment in Moscow. I've arranged for the shipment of the consignment,' Adriana said coolly. 'The flight is scheduled for tomorrow evening at nine. There will be a few hours' delay because the aircraft has to go via Heathrow first. But that's not a problem.'

'You work quickly,' Paul said. He put the unease he felt down to the horrible scene with Sara. But he knew it wasn't only that.

'I don't like to waste time.' Adriana gripped the phone. 'I'll be back on Monday,' she said briskly. 'I've got some other business to attend to here first. You'll have the money ready?' she asked. 'Two million dollars in cash?'

'As long as everything's in order.' He glanced nervously around the kitchen, down the hall. 'The buyer will want a sample first, to check the purity.'

He had found a buyer already? *Shit!* 'How long will that take?'

'Shouldn't be more than a couple of days. Why?' he asked. 'Does it matter?'

'Paul, I've got other deals. I don't have time to hang around Liverpool indefinitely.' Especially after a man she really wanted had rejected her! Adriana still burned with fury after the other night.

'I understand that but –'

'Are you his slapper, you bitch?' Sara screamed down the sitting-room extension. Adriana jumped. Her mother came into the elegant high-ceilinged room carrying a tray of tea, and she brusquely waved her away. 'Don't think being pregnant with his bastard will make any fucking difference . . .'

'Adriana, please allow me to apologize for my wife,' Paul broke in, his voice strained. 'She's hysterical and she's had too much to drink.'

'Whose fault is that?' Sara shouted. 'You bastard!'

Adriana frowned, even while she enjoyed Paul's discomfiture. Did he have some other woman? she wondered. Was that why he had rejected her?

'Whore, prostitute, slut!' Sara raged, her voice slurred. 'Wait until I get my hands on you! I'll kick the crap out of you, you cheating, conniving bitch!'

Adriana suddenly felt very angry. She was already stressed out waiting for this beryllium deal to go through; she didn't need to be screamed at by Paul's hysterical wife.

'Adriana, I'm very sorry! I'll call you back,' he said. 'Give me your number.'

'No,' she said sharply. 'It's safer if I contact you.'

'Safer?' Sara paused, breathing hard. 'What the fuck is going on?' she shouted. Adriana quickly hung up. Paul put the phone down then walked slowly back to the sitting room, trying to hold on to his temper.

'That woman is a business acquaintance,' he said coldly. 'We're in the middle of a deal. If you don't believe that, fine. I'm leaving now. I'm not going to argue with you any more. I've had enough.'

He turned, went into the hall and ran upstairs. Why had he imagined his wife would be civilized about this? About anything? He would go to the office and make some calls, find a hotel and stay there until he could move into an apartment. He got a suitcase from the attic, went into his bedroom and began packing clothes and business papers. Sara could stay here and drink herself stupid for all he cared.

Paul wished he were moving in with Justine. But she wasn't for him, never had been and never would be. He pictured her red-gold curls and incredible blue eyes, her beautiful smile, and felt overwhelmed by sadness and futility. What did the future hold for him? He would have money, of course, more than he could ever spend. But what else?

Sara ran out of the sitting room, glass in hand, as he lugged his suitcase downstairs. She had taken off the spike-heeled sandals and her feet were bare.

'You can't treat me like this!' she blazed. 'I'm not some sad act nobody you can shove aside. You're going to be very sorry.'

'I already am,' Paul said grimly. He picked up his briefcase and laptop, pulled open the front door and felt the sun on his face. He breathed the cool autumnal air as he walked to the car. He slung the suitcase into the boot of the Mercedes then ducked as her empty glass whistled past his ear and smashed on the gravel. The glass was followed by a spike-heeled crimson sandal. Sara was

184

crying noisily, her face ravaged by gin and tears. Paul opened the car door and put the briefcase and laptop on the passenger seat, then straightened up and looked at her.

'I'll be back to see you,' he said abruptly. 'Get the rest of my stuff.'

'You fucking won't! You don't set foot in this house again. I'll burn your bloody stuff. I hate you!' she shouted. She ran forward then stopped and gasped with pain as gravel cut into her bare feet.

'Goodbye, Sara!' Paul got into the car, slammed the door and started the engine. He glanced in the driving mirror as he headed down the curving, tree-lined drive that led to the lane. Sara stood there in the short glittery red dress, hands clenched, eyes blazing with hurt and fury. Her pale thin lips moved as she yelled insults he couldn't hear.

Paul was breathing hard and sweating, filled with rage and anxiety. He had no idea what the next few days, what the future, would bring. Beneath all that, however, he felt relief, a kind of peace after years of anger and sadness and futile rows, constantly wondering how and why things had gone so wrong. Now the mourning, the healing, could begin.

He was in pain, nearly as much pain as Sara. Maybe more. It wouldn't go away anytime soon. But he had taken the first giant step at last.

His marriage was over.

# Chapter Seventeen

'My Ronnie was a lovely fella!' The young widow's husky voice rose over the clicking cameras. 'A great dad to our two kids. I dunno what they'll do without him. If anybody's got any information, if you saw Ronnie that night or were in the Crystal Cave club, please come forward.'

The words nearly choked her. Chantelle Davis bowed her head and cried tears of relief, unable to believe her incredible good fortune. After nine years of being raped and beaten and shouted at, constantly told what a useless slag she was and having her life totally controlled, someone had actually killed the bastard! Every time Ronnie left the house to go to work or go boozing with his mates, she had wished fervently he would never come back. Now that wish had come true and the miracle had scared the hell out of her!

Chantelle was glad that she'd been too frightened to tell anyone, even her mother, what Ronnie was really like. They might have arrested her! She had the best motive for murder of anyone she knew, felt as frightened and hunted as if she had stuck the knife in herself. She had made excuses for her visible cuts and bruises, blamed last year's miscarriage on pushing a pram loaded with children and shopping up the hill, instead of his boot in her vulnerable belly. She felt guilty and ashamed of herself for allowing the abuse to keep happening, for being too frightened to just take the kids and run somewhere, anywhere. But Ronnie had threatened to kill her if she grassed him up or left him. Chantelle knew he'd meant what he said.

The press and public thought her tears were for Ronnie, but they were for her own years of misery and terror, for the poor little baby girl he had kicked to death in her womb. After the miscarriage she had started to dream, fantasize about Ronnie's death. In her dreams he had died slowly and agonizingly. Death from a single stab wound to the heart must have been quick and painless – too bloody quick! She wished he had suffered terror and pain, realized he was going to be killed and that there was nothing he could do to stop it. She tensed at the flashbulbs, the cameras, the stares and questions. Why should I be put on show? she thought furiously. I've had enough!

'Mrs Davis was at home with her children at the time of the murder,' she heard the Assistant Chief Constable say approvingly. More murmurs.

Of course she was at home! Where else would she be? She was never out with any mates, the few she had managed to hang on to after nine years of her marriage from hell. Ronnie wouldn't let her go to the pub or out clubbing or even to bingo, wouldn't let her go bloody anywhere except her mother's or Tesco. Why? What was he scared of? He always said no one would fancy an ugly knackered old slapper with a gob like a dog's arse. Old! Chantelle was twenty-nine, three years younger than him. Her ragged, bitten nails dug into her palms as she clenched her hands. Well, I've seen you out, you fucking bastard! she thought. You can rot in hell now.

The press conference over, she got up and stumbled out of the brightly lit room, guided by the sympathetic hand of the Assistant Chief Constable in his black uniform. Outside, little Billy and Yasmin dashed up to her, shouting and laughing. Three-year-old Billy threw his arms around her legs and Chantelle felt his little white teeth playfully nibble her leg through the thin trouser material. She had a bite mark on her thigh; Billy had once got carried away and really bitten her instead of just pretending. Yasmin's brown eyes shone with delighted anticipation. She was five going on thirty. She wore a tartan dress with a black velvet collar and cuffs, and her long straggly white-blonde hair was tied up with a huge red velvet bow topped by a plastic strawberry. Billy was in jeans and his favourite sweater that her mother had knitted him, black with little yellow chicks on it.

'Shh, you two!' Chantelle stooped and gathered them to her. 'Calm down,' she whispered. 'Your dad's dead,' she said hesitantly. 'You know what that means, don't you?' she asked, acutely conscious of the policemen and reporters grouped around them. Ronnie's parents and two brothers hovered a few feet away, stern controlling expressions on their ugly gobs. The Davis family thought they were the bee's knees, though God knew why! She had never been good enough for their precious Ronnie.

'Yeah, Mam, 'course we know!' Yasmin looked impatient, reproachful at this insult to her intelligence. Already she was brighter and more outgoing, less fearful. 'It means he won't come home again. It's great, isn't it?'

'Shut up, Yasmin!' Chantelle hissed under her breath.

'Yeah,' Billy echoed. 'He won't come home again. He won't nark at us no more. Can we go to Florida now, Mam?' Billy had a thing about Florida. 'Dad never let us go on holiday, did he?'

Chantelle closed her eyes in despair, straightened up and gently freed her trapped legs. The wife was always the first suspect. Billy and Yasmin would have her banged up with the cockroaches and buckets of piss by dinner time if they didn't shut up. Despite her fear Chantelle had a crazy desire to laugh out loud, shock the shit out of all these stupid bastards crowding her. But if she started laughing she would never stop.

'Poor little buggers.' The Assistant Chief Constable shook his head gravely. 'Don't have a clue what all this means, do they? Just as well.' He took Chantelle's elbow again. 'Come on, love,' he said quietly. 'Let's get you a nice cup of tea. Then we'll run you home.'

Tea! She wanted a bloody big vodka-and-tonic, her favourite drink that she hadn't tasted in ages. What about pension rights? she wondered.

'Anything we can do, just let us know,' the tall, grey-haired man went on. He had a long purplish nose and mournful brown eyes. 'Okay? Your Ronnie was a great lad.' He patted her shoulder. 'Never forget that. He'll be missed. This is a terrible loss for all of us.'

Not quite all. Chantelle nodded obediently. Stupid, sentimental, patronizing bastard! She wiped her eyes with a damp tissue.

'We'll get the lowlife who murdered him. Don't you worry!'

She nodded again, her head bowed. She didn't believe it was murder, but she would keep her dangerous thoughts to herself. Ronnie had had his knife with him when he went out the other night, the horrible-looking one he'd kept hidden in his sports bag

188

in the cupboard under the stairs. She wasn't supposed to know about it. She'd hated it being in the house, had been terrified that one day he would murder her with it. A couple of times during the past year a mate of his had phoned to ask where he was, on the very nights he and Ronnie were supposed to be out playing snooker together. Both times Ronnie had come home hyper, burning with rage and excitement. He had raped her on the living-room floor and beaten her afterwards, told her how much he would like to kill her, how he would if she ever took one step out of line.

Ronnie did that to her so why not to other women? He'd been free, could do what he liked, knew she was too terrified to open her mouth. Chantelle hadn't heard about any rapes, but that meant nothing. So what if his victims went to the police? Ronnie *was* the police! Had he attacked some other poor girl or woman, tried to rape her? Had she somehow managed to stick him with his own knife and get away?

Wishful thinking, maybe. But the more Chantelle thought about it, the more likely it seemed. They hadn't found his knife or any other weapon at the scene. The woman Ronnie had attacked might have taken it. It must have been covered with her fingerprints. She would know by now that he had been a policeman, and was probably terrified of being hunted down and arrested for a 'murder' she hadn't committed. She'd know she wouldn't stand a chance if she went to the police and tried to tell them what had really happened. That had never been an option.

Chantelle Davis longed to meet the woman, whoever she was. Talk to her, help her, be her friend.

Thank her!

That woman had saved her life.

Justine stared at Chantelle Davis as she finished her appeal and stood up to leave the press conference. The woman's long thick auburn hair was wild, her hazel eyes swollen and reddened from weeping. Her dark brown pinstripe suit and brown top looked new or barely worn, carefully preserved for special occasions that never arose. Until now.

So this was the widow of the man she had killed! Was Chantelle really heartbroken, or just acting out the expected role? Justine couldn't believe the woman's marriage had been happy. Did

Chantelle guess what had really happened? The old man watching television with her in the day room outside the intensive care ward sighed and shook his head.

'Killing coppers!' His voice was loud and nasal. 'Stop at nothing nowadays, do they?' He took a gulp of tea and looked at Justine expectantly. 'Poor sod probably went in that alley to take a leak. Don't expect to get murdered while you take a leak, do you? Bet it's something to do with those drug gangs. Liverpool's crawling with them! They'll soon nick the killer,' he said confidently. 'Or killers. I mean, it's one of their own, isn't it?' He grinned at her, flashing a row of brilliant white dentures. 'They wouldn't give a monkey's if it was you or me, eh, girl?'

'No,' she said in a low voice.

The next item on the lunchtime news was the road rage hit-and-run doctor case. A young blond man driving a white Ford Fiesta, witnesses said. Police were treating it as attempted murder.

'Jesus Christ!' The old man shook his head again. 'Got their work cut out, haven't they? Well, we know which case'll get priority!'

Justine quickly got up and left the day room to stand in the quiet deserted corridor. She was shaking. She couldn't take in what they'd told her about Adam being run down outside his surgery. *Had* Matthew done it? He didn't have blond hair and she didn't know if he drove a white Ford Fiesta. But he would have wanted revenge for Saturday night, wouldn't he?

She looked at the wall of colourful 'thank you' cards from grateful patients and their relatives, mechanically read a few of the scrawled inscriptions. She felt cold all the time and couldn't stop shivering. She looked down at her short black sweater and the black-and-gold jeans. The last time she had worn these Adam had pulled them off her and tossed them on the bare floorboards in the empty house when they were both desperate to make love. Tears filled her eyes and she clutched the wad of damp tissues in her hand.

Justine felt that her life was over. Tomorrow, next week, were meaningless concepts. Adam was in a coma and might stay in it indefinitely. Or die. Matthew or the police would get her, or she'd be driven crazy by the terrifying flashbacks she kept getting. Knives, the dark alley, blood. Blood everywhere. She wept for Adam, for his betrayal, for the terrible events that had caught and crushed them. This time last week they had been sure of each other's love, looking forward to a bright future. Now their lives had crashed. Literally.

'Adam!' she whispered, clenching her hands and squeezing her eyes tight shut. 'Please, please wake up!'

She hadn't contradicted comments about how tragic it was that the wedding had had to be cancelled because of this awful hit-and-run. Who knew? She might have donned the ivory silk dress, washed down a diazepam with a glass of champagne and gone through with it, the state she was in. The thought of any explanation was too exhausting and draining; let people think what they liked. It took all her strength to get through each hour. The longer Adam remained unconscious, the worse it looked. Justine felt desperate, stunned with shock and disbelief. It was another beautiful September day. She glanced at her wristwatch: 1.30. She should have been due at the church in half an hour!

'Justine!' She jumped with fright and turned. It was the staff nurse, a woman in her thirties with short, straight brown hair and piercing blue eyes, in a navy uniform. 'You can come back now,' she called. 'We've replaced the tube.' Justine nodded and followed her back inside the intensive care unit.

Adam looked heartbreakingly helpless lying there, so vulnerable that she could hardly bear it. It was warm in the yellow-curtained cubicle, but his hands felt cold. The life support machine forced harsh breaths in and out of his lungs. He had a tube down his throat and a dark blue blood pressure cuff attached to his left arm. His right arm was hooked up to a saline drip and a bleeping green monitor measured his heart rate. He had a broken pelvis, multiple fractures and contusions, and his right leg was broken, the knee smashed. A CAT scan hadn't revealed brain damage, but it was too early to tell. They would do another scan in a few days' time. Justine had listened silently to insensitive remarks about how Adam was lucky his injuries weren't worse, that he would have been killed outright if the hit-and-run driver hadn't been prevented from getting up speed in the busy street. Maybe they were right. But if anyone used the word *lucky* again, she would land them one!

She stroked his chestnut brown hair, still dirty and tangled, covered with grit from the road. Keeping Adam alive took precedence over washing him. His bed was near a window that overlooked a courtyard full of green plants three floors below. Justine took his hand in both of hers and kissed it, wept silent tears.

The nurse hovered. 'How are you doing?' she asked awkwardly.

Justine held on to Adam's hand and didn't reply. How did they think she was doing! She was tired of asinine questions, unrequested advice and patronizing sympathy, thick white chipped cups of disgusting tea and coffee. She wanted Adam to open his eyes, smile at her and get up so that they could walk out of this bloody hospital together and go home. She would marry him, lock Donna in a dark recess at the back of her mind, do anything if only he would open his eyes and whisper her name!

'We're making some more tea, would you like a cup?'

'No, thanks,' she said politely. The nurse went out then reappeared.

'There's someone outside wants to see you. She says she's a friend of yours and Adam's.'

Another nuisance with flowers and sympathy and questions! If people wanted to help, why didn't they just keep out of the way for now? Her physical and mental energy were draining away fast. The only friend Justine would have liked to see right now was Paul Melwood. Was this woman a reporter? she suddenly wondered. Thank goodness the ward doors were kept locked and visitors had to state their business over an intercom before gaining entry. Otherwise they would probably burst in here and crowd around Adam's bed.

'I don't want to see anyone,' she said firmly. 'No reporters, that's for sure!'

'She says it's important . . . urgent. She's not a reporter.'

Justine sighed and reluctantly let go of Adam's hand. She would get rid of this woman, whoever she was, in thirty seconds flat. If that seemed rude, tough! She parted the yellow curtains and left the cubicle, pushed through the double doors and stopped abruptly. Donna stood in the corridor by the wall of cards, her big dark eyes shining with tears. She wore her navy blue nurse's uniform and her smooth slippery dark hair was done up in a bun.

'Get lost!' Justine turned away, trembling. 'Now. How dare you come here?'

'Justine, wait! Please!' Donna dashed forward and grabbed her

192

arm. 'I'm so sorry about Adam,' she cried. 'I can't believe it! How is he?'

'That's none of your business. Take your hands off me!' Justine violently shook off Donna's grasp. I said, get out!' she repeated stonily. 'I never want to see you again and neither does Adam. I thought we'd made that clear.'

'Justine, please don't go! Tell me how he is?' Donna begged tearfully. 'It's terrible about the hit-and-run. Who would do that to Adam? I can't bear it!'

'*You* can't bear it!' Justine shook her head in disbelief. Then suddenly she smiled. 'I won't say I don't believe I'm hearing this because . . .' The smile made Donna think of her grandmother's oft-repeated and largely ignored warning to beware of people who smiled when they were angry.

'Listen, I'm really sorry about me and Adam.' She took a step backwards.

'There is no you and Adam!' Justine hissed, agonized. 'There never was.'

Donna started to cry. 'Justie, we've been friends since we were little,' she wailed. 'I feel so guilty. Don't let this split us up, please! I didn't mean to hurt you, I swear!' She saw the pain in Justine's eyes. 'I really do want to help you.'

'Is that right?' Justine stared at her. 'Then have one tiny decent impulse, and *leave us alone*.' She pointed down the corridor. '*Go!*'

The sight of Donna penetrated Justine's numbed shocked brain, brought all the horrors back into terrifyingly sharp, agonising focus. She had built her life around Adam, she loved him and would stick by him now. But was she fooling herself? Did Adam love her, had he ever really loved her? Were Matthew and her dead assailant the only realities? She couldn't think about that now. It was too dangerous.

'You bitch!' She glared at Donna, clenching her fists. 'I hate you! All this is your fault!' If it hadn't been for Donna she would never have run crying out of that club into the arms of a murderous, hate-filled psycho.

'Hey, come on! I realize you're in shock.' Donna wiped her eyes, smearing browny-black mascara on her fingertips. 'You must be really upset right now. But you can't blame me for the hit-and-run,' she protested, misunderstanding. 'I didn't land Adam in intensive care!'

The blow across her face took her completely by surprise. Dazed, she staggered backwards against the wall of cards. Justine came after her and Donna saw the blur of her fist, flying red-gold hair and furious blue eyes. She gave a cry of fright as Justine grabbed her and slammed her against the wall. Donna bit her lip and tasted blood. Several cards came unstuck and fluttered to the floor.

'*Upset* doesn't cover it!' Justine's voice was loud in her ear. 'What would you like me to say?' she asked viciously. 'Let's watch over him together until he wakes up – *if* he wakes up! You hold one hand, me the other. Very touching! I suppose you wish it was me lying in there – or preferably dead! Shall I go out and get myself stiffed by that stalker so you can have Adam all to yourself?' She gave Donna a enormous shove. 'Get out!' she screamed.

Donna was unnerved by Justine's hatred and fury, full of pity for herself as well as Adam. Her gamble had failed pathetically. She had lost him for sure – not that she'd had him to lose in the first place! And now she had lost Justine, her oldest and best friend. Let's face it, her only friend. It was way too late for damage limitation.

'No! Don't!' she cried as Justine charged at her and shoved her viciously again. Donna stumbled backwards and collided heavily with two men entering the corridor.

'Watch it, love!' one of them, a balding, middle-aged man in a grey suit, said angrily. He stared at her with distaste. The younger and better looking one, dark-haired and wearing a dark blue suit, smiled slightly. The men stopped as they sensed the violent, emotionally charged atmosphere, looked curiously at her and Justine. Then they walked on and entered the ward manager's office. Donna ran away, crying bitterly.

Justine pressed the button for re-admittance to the ward, walked back to Adam's bed and took his hand again. She was trembling and breathing hard. She felt shocked at herself; she had never hit anyone in her life. Except Matthew when he tried to grab her. Adam might die, she had nearly been raped and murdered herself, and now she was being hunted by the police and a stalker! It couldn't be called a nightmare – you woke up from those. The staff nurse reappeared.

'Adam's mum and dad just phoned,' she said. 'They said

they'll be back soon and you should go home and rest. And . . .' She glanced at Adam, lowered her voice to a whisper. 'The police are here. They want to talk to you. I know!' She grimaced as Justine stared at her, horrified. 'We fended them off before, told them you weren't up to answering questions. But now I'm afraid they insist.'

Justine wiped her eyes with a bunch of tissues. Had Matthew grassed her up? She hadn't believed he would, but then he was unstable and unpredictable. She wanted him arrested and yet the thought of it terrified her. If he was banged up, believed he had nothing to lose, he might provide a few authentic details about the Davis killing, details that hadn't been made public. Add a few lies of his own for good measure. Justine felt weak with fear, exhaustion and lack of food. In twenty-four hours she had had nothing but coffee and tea, a Milky Way and a few glasses of fizzy mineral water.

'Where are they?' she asked, her heart thudding with apprehension.

'In the ward manager's office. Through the doors on your right.'

'Adam, can you hear me?' Justine put her lips to his ear. 'I'm outside if you need me, I promise I won't be long. I love you!' She tenderly kissed his poor bruised cheek and forehead, gently squeezed his hand. Tears of desperation filled her eyes at the heartbreaking lack of response. 'I'll be back in a few minutes,' she whispered.

She hoped that was true.

Paula Casey sipped her tea and took a bite of ham sandwich as she stared at the television screen. 'Why do they put the poor woman through that ordeal?' she muttered indignantly as another shot of Chantelle Davis at the press conference flashed on to the screen. 'Won't do any good. They'll find that copper's murderer soon enough anyway.'

'Maybe she murdered him! Or had him stiffed.' Matthew laughed. 'All women are treacherous bitches,' he said loudly. 'Turn your back and they'll stick the knife in!'

Paula glanced warily at him. Matthew sat in his father's old armchair, munching crisps and ham sandwiches and gulping hot tea as he avidly watched the tail end of the news, eyes gleaming with laughter and excitement. He fidgeted and tapped his knee, bit his nails, couldn't keep still for five minutes at a stretch. It got on her nerves. He had taken a bath when he got up, using all the hot water. He wore newly washed blue jeans and a beige sweater, the black-and-yellow trainers. His blond hairdo looked ridiculous. Paula's nervousness increased as she stared at her son. She was more frightened of Matthew now than she had been of his drunken violent father. Genes will out, she thought.

'What are you fucking gawping at?' he barked, making her jump. He leaned forward and shoved the mug at her. 'Get us some more tea.'

Paula took the mug, got up and hurried to the kitchen. She no longer dared tell Matthew not to use the 'f' word. It was so quiet next-door, she thought, as she poured tea. She couldn't get used to the creepy silence. Of course Matthew's menacing presence in the house didn't improve the atmosphere.

The street had changed amazingly since the night of the fire. People smiled at one another, said good morning and good after-noon, lingered to chat. Chatting was easy and very pleasant when you knew a brick or stone wouldn't fly at your head, or an out-of-control pitbull at your throat. Paula had made the acquaintance of the little grey-haired frightened-looking woman who lived a few houses down. Her name was Alice Cameron, she had been a widow for six years and had a son and two grandchildren in Australia. People played up to the reporters and television cameras, talked sanctimoniously about what a horrific tragedy the Jackson fire was. But the truth was they were happy and relaxed now. They felt safe.

Paula wished she could feel safe. She couldn't come to terms with the fact that Matthew had murdered the Jacksons, felt ashamed of herself for being too frightened to tell the police and let justice take its relentless course. Even this hit-and-run doctor case: they were looking for a blond man driving a white Ford Fiesta! Surely Matthew couldn't have run over poor Dr Shaw? Of course not! It didn't make sense. It was just that he had been out at the time of the hit-and-run and normally he didn't crawl out of bed until lunchtime. It had to be coincidence, he didn't even know the man! But Paula was frightened and worried sick nevertheless, indigestion burning a hole in her stomach lining. She put three spoonfuls of sugar in Matthew's tea, wishing it was arsenic.

It was a shame Justine's fiancé wasn't dead, Matthew thought, but a coma was almost as good. Adam Shaw might die or end up a vegetable. Sooner or later the doctors would persuade Justine to allow his life support machine to be switched off. Even if Shaw woke up and remembered the hit-and-run, so what? Shaw wouldn't dare grass him up, knowing he'd witnessed Justine kill that plod!

Matthew giggled. Justine was alone now, terrified, vulnerable. His for the taking. He jumped up and swore. His laces were undone.

'Where are you off to?' his mother asked, surprised. 'I've got your tea here.'

'Mind your own business, you old cow!' He shoved her roughly against the wall and she gave a cry of fright. The tea slopped on to the carpet. 'Keep it shut,' he said threateningly, 'like I told you. Or . . .' He drew a finger across his throat and bared his teeth in a grin. His mother gasped with fear. He tied his laces, ran into the hall and slammed the front door behind him.

Paula didn't have a clue how or where Matthew spent his time, used up all his alarming new energy. Not trying to find a job, that was for sure! She went back to the kitchen and poured the heavily sugared, hot milky tea down the sink. Then she went upstairs and cautiously opened Matthew's bedroom door. She hadn't been in there since he had moved back.

The small room with its dingy woodchip wallpaper, child's wardrobe and ancient torn poster of the sulky topless blonde girl in ragged denim shorts smelled of aftershave and Camay soap. Paula didn't know what made her get stiffly down on her aching knees and pull the blue nylon suitcase out from under his bed. There was a neat pile of bitten finger and toenails on the bedside table, which he'd obviously forgotten to throw away. Matthew never clipped his nails, like normal people. She unzipped the suitcase, sighing heavily. Her indigestion was worse than ever today.

There was a videotape in there and an empty black leather wallet. A set of keys. Paula looked at them, puzzled. She couldn't play the tape because she had no video, although Matthew was talking about getting one. She picked up a few folded, stapled sheets of A4 paper and smoothed them out.

What was he doing with a photocopied curriculum vitae of some young woman named Justine Flynn? Paula studied the photograph. The girl was beautiful, had masses of lovely, light, curly hair and a warm humorous glint in her eyes. Surely someone like her wouldn't want anything to do with Matthew? She moved the paper aside and inhaled sharply.

A naked blonde girl smiled up at her from the magazine cover. The girl was on all fours, her legs spread wide and chained to some sort of iron bar, a naked man behind her about to . . .

'Oh, my God! Sweet Jesus!' Paula looked away, trembling with shock. Her heart thudded against her ribs. Another cover showed an Asian girl kneeling and blindfolded, her hands tied behind her back and her breasts bound with rope. She had some sort of red ball in her mouth. Wouldn't she choke?

These were worse than the ones Matthew had had before he left home, Paula thought, horrified. There was quite a collection. He had money for filth like this! No wonder women weren't safe when there were men around who wanted to do this kind of thing to them. She shut her eyes for a few seconds, took a deep breath. Her shaking fingers brushed something hard and scratchy.

'What the . . . ?' She lifted a coil of rope, a black leather dog collar entwined with it. Then she saw that it was too small to fit the average dog's neck. The collar had a steel loop at the front. What was that for? She flipped through one of the magazines until the answer to her silent question was revealed.

Another naked, big-breasted girl on all fours, a similar collar tight around her neck. Her hands were tied behind her back. One man had his thing in her mouth, another was doing it to her from behind. Paula gasped in horror as she saw a thin chain threaded through the collar loop, little clamps at each end of the chain squeezing the poor girl's nipples. She must be in agony! The man in front had grabbed a fistful of her blonde hair.

'Oh, dear God!' Paula dropped magazine, rope and leather collar, zipped up the suitcase and pushed it back under the bed. She had to get out before she fainted. She struggled to her feet, breathing hard and sweating, the blood hissing in her ears. A band of pain clamped itself around her chest. She staggered out of the room and shut the door, held tight to the banister as she went downstairs. Take it slowly, she told herself. Don't fall and break your neck because of that evil pervert!

In the kitchen she poured herself a big glass of sweet sherry and gulped it down. It wasn't wise, not with the indigestion, but she needed a drink after what she'd seen. Her breathing gradually returned to normal and the chest pain loosened its grip. Paula lit a cigarette, poured more sherry and went into the living room, sank trembling on to the sofa. She felt dirty, somehow, wanted to go to Confession and Mass so that she could cleanse her mind of that horrific filth.

She could understand the magazines, even though they shocked and revolted her. Magazines like that catered for inadequate men who couldn't attract women, sad men who had so little self-esteem that they needed to visualize women in degraded power-less subjection – and liking it! – in order to feel good about themselves. Paula shuddered and took another gulp of sherry, dragged on her cigarette.

It was the rope and leather collar that really gave her the creeps. Did Matthew plan to use them on some unsuspecting girl, like the one in the CV photograph? If he could murder the Jackson family, he was capable of anything. Her own son, her flesh and blood! She gave a little sob of fear. She stubbed out the cigarette, got up and went back to the kitchen for more sherry.

Who was this Justine Flynn? If Matthew planned to hurt her, she should be warned. Paula could do that much without putting herself in danger, surely? She didn't need to reveal her own identity. She went slowly back upstairs and into Matthew's room, opened the suitcase again and copied down Justine's Sefton Park phone number on a piece of paper. She struggled downstairs and picked up the phone, dialled 141 first. Justine Flynn's phone rang and rang. Why didn't she answer?

After a few seconds, Paula lost her nerve. She banged the receiver down and tore the paper into little bits, stuffed the pieces in the kitchen bin under some stale bread and damp teabags. She went back into the living room and collapsed on the sofa again, her thin body trembling with fear and exertion. She could call the police – if she dared – show them that stuff in the suitcase. But so what? Revolting and disgusting as it was, it didn't prove Matthew had committed any crime. Certainly not the murderous arson attack on the Jacksons. Paula's face crumpled as she thought of the dead baby girl, poor little Katrina. Why was it always the innocent who suffered most in this world? No religion, not even her own, could give an answer to that question! She'd asked the

199

priest once, and he'd got cross with her, told her to go away and count her blessings.

Matthew's luck would run out one day. He wasn't as clever as he liked to think. All right, so he'd got away with the Hayland Software fire, and now it looked like he might get away with torching the Jacksons. But one day he would be caught. And she would be crucified along with him.

If he didn't kill her first.

# Chapter Eighteen

'I'm Detective Inspector Stewart and this is Detective Sergeant Kiely. We'd like to talk to you in connection with the hit-and-run involving Dr Shaw.'

Justine was dismayed to see that the police officers were the two men who had witnessed the fight between her and Donna in the corridor a few minutes ago. She sat down in the ward manager's small cluttered office. DI Stewart, a paunchy, balding, bellicose man in his fifties, planted his heavy body in front of the door as if he thought she might try to escape.

'I was at home when it happened,' Justine said. 'I got a phone call from Rosemary Elliott, the Practice Manager at Adam's surgery.'

'Yes, we know.' DS Kiely sat on the desk and folded his arms. He was in his mid-thirties, slim and good-looking with wavy black hair, brown eyes and a cynical expression. He wore a dark blue suit. 'How's Adam doing?' he asked quietly. 'Still unconscious?'

Justine nodded and lowered her head, her eyes flooding with tears. John Kiely looked at her trembling, fidgeting hands plucking at her black-and-gold jeans and black sweater. He loved her oval face, beautiful, troubled dark blue eyes and mane of red-gold hair. He also felt sorry for her. But his immediate impression of Justine Flynn was that she was a woman who had something to hide.

'Can you think of anyone who might want to murder your fiancé?' Tony Stewart asked. Justine winced and put her hands over her face. 'Mrs Elliott and several other witnesses described a blond man driving a white Ford Fiesta,' he went on.

'As you know. Unfortunately nobody managed to get the car's licence number.' Too busy standing and gawping, he thought irritably. 'Have you any idea who this man might be?' He paused, sensing Justine's hesitation. 'There's a lot of aggression against doctors these days,' he commented. Some of it for a good reason, judging by the stories you heard. 'Of course we can't interview Dr Shaw at the moment, seeing as we don't know if he'll . . .'

'Survive?' Justine wiped her eyes and shot him a look of dislike. She wasn't sure what to say to them without incriminating herself. Who else but Matthew would have tried to murder Adam? Of course she couldn't tell them Adam had beaten him up, that Matthew had witnessed her kill Ronnie Davis. But she had to protect herself. Horror seized her as she remembered the knife and bloodied clothing in the bin bag under the sink. Why hadn't she got rid of them? She was cracked, a fuck-up! She gasped and closed her eyes, teetering on the verge of panic.

'Are you all right?' John Kiely slid off the desk and stood up.

'I feel a bit faint,' she whispered, playing for time. He quickly crossed to a small sink, filled a glass with cold water and handed it to her. Stewart looked impatient.

'Do you know of anyone who's got a grudge against Dr Shaw?' he asked. So far Ms Flynn wasn't being very helpful.

Justine took a sip of the heavily chlorinated water. 'A man's been stalking me for several weeks,' she said. 'I thought he might have done it. But he doesn't have blond hair, and I don't know what kind of car he drives. I've reported the stalking, there've been several incidents. My neighbours have seen him too. His name's Matthew, that's all I know.' She thought of Marinda threatening Matthew with her illegal handgun; what if the police found out about that? She hesitated. 'I think he might have murdered that family in Old Roan whose house was burned out. The Jacksons.'

Startled, the two officers glanced at one another. 'Can you prove that?'

'No,' she said in a low voice. 'But if you find him and arrest him for stalking me, you might find evidence. And . . .' she paused . . . 'I work for Brooks & Wilde, the advertising agency.

A colleague and a security guard were murdered there last week. I thought the stalker might have killed them too. Of course I could be wrong. He – the stalker – told me where he lived,' she lied, blushing. 'The police checked it out, but it was a false address.' Justine hoped she didn't sound like a hysterical accusing idiot.

'What makes you think your stalker is responsible for all those murders?' Stewart asked abruptly. Ruby Jackson's anti-social habits had gained her a lot of enemies. They were checking known arsonists but so far had come up with nothing. Some grudge-carrier could have lost it and gone too far, might now be horrified at what had happened. But when you poured litres of petrol through somebody's letter box and pushed a burning rag after it, you had to have some idea of the consequences! Stewart didn't know how the Brooks & Wilde case was progressing – or not.

'He could have gone to my office to ask about me. Anna – the receptionist – was always the last to leave. Something might have happened.'

'But why would he kill her and that guard if he's after you?' Kiely asked.

'I don't know,' Justine said desperately. 'I saw him on television the morning after the fire.' She shuddered. 'Outside the Jacksons' house. He was looking into the camera, laughing at me. It was like he wanted to prove something. Can you get hold of the TV footage?' she asked. It was on the regional breakfast news the other morning.' She stared at them, her hands clenched. 'I'm in terrible danger – he wants to kill me!'

If Matthew was arrested and charged with eleven murders, surely no one would believe him when he said she had killed Ronnie Davis? Justine hoped she was right. She had to accept the risk that Matthew might be able to provide authentic details about the killing; she was in more danger if he remained at large. She longed to rush home and get rid of the knife and clothing.

Stewart scribbled in a notebook. 'We'll find the footage and take a look.'

'I reported it. Maybe someone's done that already.' Justine doubted they had.

'Have you got anyone to be with you?' Kiely asked gently. 'At home, I mean.'

'My mother's staying for a few days. She came up from Manchester yesterday – for the wedding.' Evie would be roaming the flat, bored stiff and drinking all the booze. So what? Justine thought. At least I don't have to worry about her rooting in cupboards under sinks for cleaning materials!

'So you think this stalker tried to murder your fiancé?'

'I can't think of anyone else. Adam was so popular,' she said, wiping away more tears. 'He had no enemies.'

The loyal, loving, distraught fiancée. Stewart and Kiely exchanged another glance. Justine Flynn could be for real. But maybe the stuff about a stalker was intended to deflect them. Of course they would check it out.

'Did you and Dr Shaw have a good relationship?' Stewart asked, his squinting hazel eyes hostile.

'Please don't talk about Adam in the past tense! We were supposed to be married this afternoon,' she said coldly. 'I think I can safely say we had a good relationship! What are you getting at?' she asked, alarmed.

'Nothing.' Stewart looked at her hard. 'We have to ask, that's all. It's routine.' He didn't like Justine Flynn. She seemed too bloody perfect to be true.

'I suppose next thing you'll be asking if I took out a life insurance policy on Adam!'

'Did you?'

'No!' She glared at him. 'Have you actually listened to anything I've said? What are you going to do to catch that stalker? I'm in danger every minute he's out there, don't you realize that?'

'It's okay, Justine,' Kiely said quietly.

'Someone tried to murder Adam and he's in intensive care!' she cried. 'I'm being stalked by the man who might have done it. It is *not* okay!'

'I mean, try to relax.' He took the glass of water from her shaking hand, gently patted her shoulder. She was really frightened, he thought. Of the stalker? Or of being arrested for attempted murder? 'Take a breath.'

Kiely thought of the woman who had recently been imprisoned for fatally stabbing her husband on their way home from a night out: Amber Annette Donaldson had sat through interviews and televised appeals for information, weeping and apparently devastated, had provided an excellent description of the crazed thug she'd said had attacked and murdered her husband on a dark deserted country road. Turned out she was a jealous possessive bitch with a violent temper and a few ex-boyfriends alive to testify to that. Justine obviously hadn't carried out the hit-and-run herself but there were plenty of scumbags around who would stiff anyone for a few quid. Kiely didn't think Justine was another Amber Donaldson but they had to check her out nevertheless. She had no motive for wanting her fiancé dead. As far as he could see.

I've had enough, Justine thought suddenly. I have to get out of here.

'I've told you all I know,' she said, wiping her eyes. 'Can I go now, please?' She stood up, felt the weakness in her legs. 'I need to get back to Adam.'

'Sorry, but we're not finished yet,' Kiely said. 'Who was the woman in the corridor earlier?' he asked. 'Looked like the two of you were going at it hammer and tongs! Must have been something pretty important when your fiancé's in a coma in intensive care.'

'That's none of your business!' she stammered. Of all the bad luck! She blushed then turned pale. 'It's totally irrelevant.'

'Listen, love, we'll decide what's relevant in an attempted murder investigation.' Stewart was growing suspicious of Justine Flynn. 'Who was she and what were you rowing about?'

'If you're going to question me any further, I want a solicitor. You can't just walk in here and interrogate me like this.'

'Talking solicitors already, are we?' he asked aggressively. 'But yeah, love, you're right! You'll need a solicitor if you're charged with obstructing a criminal investigation.'

'That's crazy! I'm not obstructing anything!' Justine couldn't believe the way things were going. It was as if they suspected her!

'Was she a friend of yours?' Kiely had a charming smile. 'You want to cooperate with us, don't you? For Adam's sake, as well as your own.'

'Of course.' Justine sat down again. 'She was my best friend,' she whispered. 'But not any more. She told me she'd slept with Adam a few days ago, and when I asked him he admitted it was true. He said it had happened once and he didn't want anything more to do with her.' She bowed her head in humiliation. This was exactly what she had feared. Losing all privacy, her life spiralling out of control.

Kiely and Stewart looked at one another again. 'When did you find out he'd cheated on you?' Stewart asked brutally.

'The day before yesterday. Well, the night.'

'And you were still going to marry him?'

'Yes. No. I don't know!' she said helplessly. 'Donna – her name's Donna Gibson – came to say she was sorry just now, she begged me to stay friends with her. I told her to fuck off. That's what the row was about.' She stood up again. 'Can I go now?' she repeated. She had to stay calm, hold it together. But she was failing miserably.

Stewart didn't like women swearing. 'You must have been very hurt and angry when you found out he'd cheated on you,' he said, his beady eyes boring into hers. 'Devastated, in fact.'

'Not devastated enough to have him killed, if that's what you mean! I don't believe I'm hearing this,' Justine said wildly. 'How was I supposed to nip out at two in the morning and find someone to kill Adam by seven or eight? Even if I'd wanted to? I know you usually suspect the nearest and dearest, but you're barking up the wrong tree here. Stalkers often target people close to their . . .' She paused. She didn't want to say *victim*. 'Close to the person they're harassing.'

'There's something else,' Kiely said. 'Nothing to do with the hit-and-run. I take it you've heard about the murder of one of our officers, a Detective Constable named Ronnie Davis?'

Justine's mouth went dry as she stared into his cynical brown eyes. She nodded but couldn't speak. This is it, she thought. Next step some urine-stinking detention centre.

'The other night – on which such a lot seems to have happened! – you were in the same club as DC Davis,' Kiely went on. 'The Crystal Cave. We had a call from someone who knows you. Ronnie spoke to you several times that evening, didn't he? Before you even got to the club. We asked everyone in the Crystal Cave to come forward. Why didn't you?' he asked slowly.

The vinyl floor was grey with tiny yellow flecks. Justine felt freezing cold and was suddenly so dizzy she needed to sit down again. She turned, looking for the chair. Her peripheral vision misted and the only things in focus were the canary yellow flecks as they rushed forward to meet her. Then everything went quiet and she was falling down a black hole.

'Shit!' Kiely sprang forward and caught her as she fell. She collapsed in his arms, hair trailing. He smelled her perfume. 'Get some help!' he said urgently. 'Quick!'

'We're so sorry about Adam!' Charley Bluff had tears in her eyes. 'It's such a tragedy, so heartbreaking – I loathe these scum who go around wrecking decent people's lives!' she said fiercely, clenching her fists. 'The bastard who did this should be shot! I'd do it myself. I can't even imagine what hell poor Justine must be going through right now.'

'That's life, isn't it?' Evie Flynn puffed on her cigarette and took another swig from a bottle of lager. 'Full of little fuck-ups. Oh, dear!' She giggled at Charley's shocked expression. 'That may have been slightly inappropriate. I don't like hanging around this flat, that's all,' she said. 'I'm bored stiff and my partner, Swithin, is missing me.' She wished! 'No one thought to let me know the wedding was off,' she said crossly. 'I don't have a phone in my cottage, but they could have called the local pub. So I come here and land in the middle of a crisis. I'm no use to Justine.' She shrugged. 'She doesn't want me around. We hardly see each other, we've never got on.'

No wonder. Charley looked at the woman's silly hippie clothes, round red face and long coarse greying hair loose around her fat shawled shoulders. Evie had dark blue eyes like Justine's, but hers were bloodshot and filled with resentment. Even without the purplish nose, broken veins and alcohol-laden breath, Charley recognized a fellow tippler when she saw one. Poor Justine, she thought again. Even if Adam woke up, suppose he was brain-damaged? A lovely man like that! It didn't bear thinking about. Marinda was too upset to get out of bed.

'Well . . . I think I'll get back to my mother.' It was obvious this horrible callous bitch couldn't wait to slam the flat door in her face and get back to drinking the place dry. 'Tell Justine we're thinking of her, won't you? Let us know if there's anything we can do. Oh, and don't forget to watch out for that creep,' she called as she went down the stairs. 'He's dangerous. Phone the police if you spot him. Then me.'

'What creep?' Evie asked boredly, hanging on to the door.

'The man who's stalking Justine, remember? I told you. His name's Matthew and he's really scruffy-looking with . . .'

'Yeah, right. Okay, 'bye!' Evie shut the door and went slowly back upstairs. Mad bitch, she thought, wanking on about shooting people. She went into the kitchen and took a fresh bottle of lager from the fridge. She would start on the white wine later, she thought, peering at the bottles. Was that champagne? Lovely!

At least Justine and Adam's big warm comfortable flat was better than her own damp crumbling cottage beneath Manchester airport's flight path. Evie went up to the sitting room and swigged lager as she stared out at the park. The sun had set and the darkened sky was clouding over. It was cold and windy and there was a smell of burning leaves. She hoped Swithin would take the dogs out before he went down the pub, otherwise they'd crap all over the cottage. She strolled into the bathroom and sighed as she glanced at her reflection in the wall mirror. There was no good news about fifty! Swithin thought he was doing her a favour because he was six years younger. Men! They all thought they were doing you a favour. The doorbell rang again.

'Bloody hell!' Evie exclaimed irritably. 'It's like Victoria Station around here.' She hurried out of the sitting room and pressed the entry buzzer, not bothering to ask who was calling. She hoped it was a friend of Justine's who would stay so that she could piss off. Although Justine had said she didn't want anybody. Feet clumped up the stairs. Male, by the sound of them. Evie fixed a smile on her face.

'Evening!' The thin man with angry hollow dark eyes and short stubbly bleached blond hair looked warily at her as she opened the flat door. He wore clean, pressed blue jeans, a beige sweater and a brown leather jacket the colour of dog poo. The jacket was old-fashioned, with wide lapels, and smelled unpleasantly of some chemical. Formaldehyde, Evie thought, wrinkling her nose. Maybe it wasn't real leather. And who ironed jeans! He carried a tightly wrapped bunch of knackered pink roses.

'My name's Pete Smith,' Matthew lied. He blinked and coughed. 'I'm a close friend of Justine's. She phoned from the hospital and told me about the hit-and-run. I thought I'd come round, see if there was anything I could do to help.'

'Oh, right. Yeah. Come in.' Evie stepped back and opened the door wide. 'I'm Evie, Justine's mother. I forgot to ask who you were,' she giggled. 'Justine would kill me if I let a reporter in. Or that creep who's supposed to be stalking her.'

Matthew was taken aback, then angry. Was that how Justine talked about him? He followed Evie upstairs and into the sitting room. He stopped and stared at the white walls and plaster wedding cake ceiling, the three long sash windows and shiny parquet floor, the two burgundy leather Chesterfield sofas and the lamps on the tall grey marble mantelpiece. There were shelves crammed with books and CDs, a television in the corner by the fireplace. What was Justine's bedroom like? His heart beat faster. He laid the flowers on the polished cherrywood sideboard.

'They're nice,' Evie lied. 'Haven't you been here before?' she asked, seeing him stare around. Ignorant bastard! she thought, puzzled. Pete Smith didn't look like someone Justine would be friends with. He was a real sad act.

''Course I have.' Matthew blushed nervously. 'The furniture's been moved around, that's all.'

'Oh. Have you by any chance got a cigarette?' she asked flirtatiously. 'I just smoked my last one and I'll be desperate for another in about two minutes.'

'I don't smoke,' he said aggressively.

'Neither does Justine. Can't find an ashtray for love nor money!'

'How's Adam?' Matthew asked tightly. Stupid yapping cow! he thought.

'Still out of it. They don't know if or when he'll wake up. Of course it's terrible about the hit-and-run,' Evie sighed, shaking her head regretfully. 'People are so angry these days, their heads are so fucked-up. But I've got to admit, I never really liked Adam. Typical doctor – you know, arrogant and opinionated. Scorns alternative therapies, poisons his body with poor dead animals. I'm a healer, he thinks that's a load of old cock. Justine's not much better.' Evie drank more lager and held up the bottle. 'I'm not very hospitable, am I?' she laughed. 'Would you care for a little drinkie?'

Matthew looked at the bottles on the sideboard. 'Scotch.'

He couldn't believe Justine had this ugly old hippie for a mother. No wonder she had grown up to be a slut who screamed obscenities, wore provocative clothes and shagged any man who gave her the glad eye. He looked disgustedly at Evie's coarse grey hair, the saggy breasts beneath the long loose grey-and-blue patterned Indian cotton tent with tiny bells around the hem and sleeves. The irritating little bells tinkled as Evie crossed to the sideboard and poured him an enormous measure of Edradour. Or *The* Edradour, according to the label.

'Nice of you to call round,' she remarked, handing him the drink. 'That's my daughter!' she said gaily. 'Always got men falling over themselves to do things for her.'

Matthew frowned and blinked furiously, bit his lip. 'What men?'

'Well – no one in particular. Not at the moment anyway.' Evie laughed nervously. She wasn't sure why, but he was making her feel distinctly uncomfortable. 'I mean, that's the sort of girl she is. Popular,' she said lamely. 'That's the word I was looking for.'

'How long are you staying?' Matthew took a gulp of single Highland malt and coughed, his eyes watering.

'I'm out of here tomorrow.' Evie grimaced. 'Justine doesn't want me,' she said resentfully. 'I have to get back to my partner. We live near Manchester airport, were involved in protests against the building of the second runway.' There was a silence. Matthew obviously didn't give a toss about Manchester airport's second runway.

He had to get her out of the room for a few minutes. 'Have you got a vase for those roses?' he asked.

'Oh, yeah. Sure.' Evie walked to the sideboard and gingerly picked them up. They belonged in a bin, not a vase. What a cheap-skate, to buy such pathetic specimens! 'Better be careful, hadn't I?' she giggled. 'Don't want to get pricked like Princess Aurora and fall asleep for a hundred years. Although it'd be worth it to be snogged awake by the sexy young prince!'

Matthew looked at her blankly. What the fuck was she on about? He hated people who wanked on and never shut it. He felt like punching Evie in her fat ugly red gob. At the same time he was seized with excitement. He would ambush Justine and keep

210

her prisoner here, fuck, torture and humiliate her until he'd had enough. After that he would kill her. She had brought it on herself – it was what she deserved. He smiled. Evie smiled back uneasily, thinking it was for her.

'When will Justine be home?' he asked.

'Not for hours. She spends all her time at that hospital, I've hardly seen her. I'm not needed at all. That's why I'm leaving tomorrow.' Evie held up the bunch of flowers. 'I'll tell her you called,' she said brightly, hoping he would take the hint and piss off. It was irritating, the way he just stood there gawping and blinking.

'Don't tell her,' Matthew said urgently. 'I mean – don't bother her.'

'Oh, right. Well . . .' She held up the roses. 'I'll stick these in a vase.'

Evie disappeared and he quickly started to search the room, opening sideboard drawers and cupboards, running his hands along the high marble mantelpiece, the shelves of books and CDs. There must be a set of spare keys somewhere! He went on to the landing and paused at the top of the stairs. Below in the kitchen a cupboard door banged shut and water splashed into the sink.

He darted into another room. There was a big desk covered with papers and medical journals, a plant with waxy glossy leaves, a computer and printer. In the untidy spare room next door he got lucky. The keys lay on the unmade bed beneath Evie's smoke-stinking Indian cotton hippie rags. The key ring was black and gold, in the shape of Australia. Justine had been to Australia. They had to be hers! He grabbed the keys and ran out. Evie was coming upstairs carrying a white vase of drooping rosebuds. She looked at him, startled.

'Just looking for the bog,' Matthew explained, blushing.

'Door on your right,' Evie said slowly. She carried the flowers into the sitting room and set them on the coffee table, standing there uncertainly. Friend or not, Pete Smith was up to something. She wished she hadn't let him in. Better not tell Justine he'd been here. She would go ballistic.

Matthew ignored the toilet and crept into the bathroom, clicked the light on and gasped. The walls were white, like the other rooms, and had venetian blinds covering the window. The shimmery shower curtain had a pattern of clouds and birds. Next to the shower was an enormous old-fashioned bath with lion's-paw feet and shiny brass taps. The wall behind the bath was one huge mirror. There was a double sink and shelves crowded with bath oils, shower gels, deodorants, perfume bottles, and a basket containing miniature toiletries from hotels and airlines. Jars of face cream, a tiny jar of eye cream, bottles of body lotion.

Matthew stared at the things, picked up bottles and sniffed them, glanced at his own staring reflection. He imagined Justine stepping naked out of the bath or shower, her velvet skin wet and slippery. Had Adam fucked her in here? Soon it would be his turn! He buried his face in the perfumed folds of a thick white bathrobe hanging on the back of the door and groaned as his penis stiffened. He couldn't wait to get his hands on Justine, tie her up and make her beg!

'What the hell are you doing?' He jumped in shock. Evie was staring at him indignantly, her fat face flushed bright red. The tiny bells tinkled as her chest heaved. He let go of the bathrobe.

'Washing me hands,' he muttered, blushing and blinking furiously.

'Yeah, right! Look, I don't know what you're up to, but you can just get out now!' Evie stepped back. 'Go on!' she ordered. 'You're not a friend of Justine's. I bet you don't even know her.'

'Oh, I know her, all right!' Matthew said loudly. 'We go back a *long* way.'

'In your dreams!' Evie felt slightly dizzy, and wished she hadn't drunk so much lager. 'I'm pretty sure Justine wouldn't give a sad act like you the time of day! You're not her type,' she added unnecessarily.

Matthew clenched his fists as rage flared in him. Another cow with a gob as big as the Mersey tunnel, a bitch who picked up your every word and twisted it, looked at you like you were scum.

'Who are you anyway?' Evie cried. 'What do you want?' The doorbell rang and they both jumped. Matthew lunged at her and shuddered with revulsion at the feel of soft, fat sagging flesh as he shoved her violently aside. Evie screamed and staggered back against the wall.

'Bastard!' she shouted. Matthew ran downstairs and slammed the flat door behind him, ran down more stairs and into the hall.

He flung open the front door and pushed past a tall, dark-haired man standing at the top of the steps, a handsome man in his thirties who wore black trousers, a grey sweater and a black leather jacket. He carried a posh briefcase and a bouquet of perfumed white lilies wrapped in cellophane and tied with thin silky red ribbons.

'Hey!' Paul Melwood said sharply. 'Watch it!' Matthew stumbled on the steps, regained his balance and ran panting down the drive. Paul walked into the hall, shut the front door and went upstairs. Evie stood at the flat door, one hand clamped over her heaving chest.

'Good evening!' Paul smiled at her, felt in his jacket pocket and held out his card. Who the hell was she? he wondered. 'Paul Melwood. I'm a friend of Justine and Adam's. I hope I'm not intruding, but I heard about the terrible . . .'

'Jesus Christ!' Evie cried angrily. She crumpled the business card in her hand and threw it back at him. 'Not another one!'

Matthew lay sprawled on his bed, drinking lager and flipping the glossy magazine pages. All tied up and nowhere to go, being fucked every which way and loving it! That would be Justine tomorrow night. He couldn't believe he'd actually talked his way into the flat, managed to steal her spare keys! The leather collar lay on the floor. He couldn't wait to see it choking that smooth, slender throat.

Tomorrow the mad hippie mother would leave. Best to wait until dark before he went back to the house and let himself in. He imagined the look on Justine's face when she saw him.

'Surprise!' he shouted. 'It's the creep!' He dropped the magazine and rolled on the bed, convulsed with laughter. Downstairs in the hall Paula heard his laughter, and shuddered with dread.

'Your tea's ready,' she called, her voice quavering. 'Meat pie and chips.'

'About sodding time!' Matthew put the magazines and collar back in the suitcase and slipped Justine's keys in his jeans pocket. He got off the bed, stood up and stretched. He was starving.

After tomorrow Justine would be alone. She was cowering, terrified by the nightmare that was about to become reality. She knew he was watching, waiting, choosing his moment to strike. He had her in his power and there was nothing she could do to fight him now.

It was time.

# Chapter Nineteen

Her body felt heavy, weighted with exhaustion. It was all she could do to drive without falling asleep at the wheel. Orange streetlights and glowing red tail lights of other cars blurred her tired eyes. The rising wind had brought lashing rain and a sharp drop in temperature. The window wipers swished hypnotically.

Kiely and Stewart had gone, chased away by indignant medical staff after she had fainted in Kiely's arms. But they would be back. Of all the scenarios she had envisaged, being suspected of trying to have Adam murdered out of jealous rage at his infidelity was not one! Although when her story about Matthew checked out she would be in the clear. Hopefully! No one seemed to know what anyone else was doing, or supposed to be doing. Their stupidity and incompetence were terrifying. Justine had heard somewhere that the various police forces in England and Wales couldn't even communicate with one another via e-mail.

Her priority now was to get rid of the knife and bloodied clothing. Suppose the police searched the flat and found them? Who had told them she had been in the Crystal Cave club? She was upset, frightened, felt terribly shaken all the time. She couldn't believe she had killed a man, that she had narrowly avoided being raped and murdered. And there was Matthew, wasn't there? Maybe she wouldn't be so lucky next time. There would be a next time, she was sure of that! She was trying desperately to push the fear and trauma to the back of her mind so that she could concentrate on Adam, be there for him as well as keep herself together. But it was very difficult and she wasn't succeeding. It's too much, she thought, chewing her lip and blinking back tears. I can't deal with all this.

Waves of cold sweat broke out on her body as memories of the attempted rape and the killing suddenly flashed back full force. She gasped in panic and her chest constricted as she tried to draw breath. Her face burned, her trembling hands were icy. She smelled blood, felt the hardness of his blows, Davis' cruel hands kneading her cold bare flesh, ripping her stockings and underwear. The sting and the warm blood flowing as he slashed her thigh. The thrust of the knife as she plunged it deep into his evil heart.

Sobbing, she slowed the car and pulled over to the side of the road, trying not to hit any other drivers. Several blared their horns furiously as she swerved in front of them. She stopped in a busy street with a row of lighted shops and left the engine running as she sat there, sobbing bitterly, face buried in her hands.

'Hey, love! Are you ill?'

Justine cried out in fright. An old man in a tweed overcoat and black Russian fur hat was tapping on the driver's window, his kind face a mask of concern. She pressed the button and let the window slide down a couple of inches, shivered as rain and cold night air rushed in.

'What's wrong, love?'

'I had a shock, that's all.' She sniffed and wiped her eyes. 'I'm okay now.'

'You don't look it. There's a nice café over there.' He pointed a gloved hand. 'They do a good cup of tea. Come on, I'll get you one.'

'No, really. I'm all right.' She took a deep, shaky breath. 'I need to get home. But thanks very much anyway.' His kindness made her feel calmer.

'Listen, love, you look after yourself. I'm going to Mass in the morning,' he said solemnly. 'I'll say a prayer for you.'

She stared at him. 'Thanks,' she whispered. 'I'd really appreciate that.'

''Bye, love!' He stepped back. 'Take care, now.'

There are some good people, Justine thought, as she drove off. Hold on to that. Ten minutes later she pulled into the long, dark driveway and parked by the wall, got out and glanced fearfully around as she locked the car. She didn't dare garage the BMW and

216

walk back up the creepy, pitch dark cinder path. The cold rainy air smelled fresh and the trees creaked and rustled in the wind.

Inside the flat she swore as she sniffed cigarette smoke. The kitchen was a tip, the table and counters cluttered with empty wine and lager bottles. Breadcrumbs, butter-smeared knives, crumpled crisp packets, gnawed chicken legs, a lump of Blue Stilton. The box of Neuhaus chocolates was empty. Her mother had even opened a bottle of champagne. The sink was full of dirty plates and wet, blackened saucers that had been used as ashtrays.

'I thought you were never coming home!' Evie walked in smoking a cigarette and holding a beer glass full of champagne. 'Have you been at that bloody hospital all this time?' Her petulant whining voice was slurred.

'Where the hell do you think I've been?' Justine dropped her keys on the table and eyed the champagne bottle. 'Got something to celebrate, have you?' she asked sharply. 'That's nice.'

'How often do I get the chance to drink vintage champagne?' Evie was annoyed by her daughter's sarcastic tone and pale, miserable face. 'It's all right for you and his lordship! You can afford to swill it whenever you fancy.'

'Yes, you're right. We're rolling in love and luxury and it's not bloody fair, is it? You go ahead and enjoy. Adam's still unconscious, by the way,' Justine said dully. 'In case you're interested.'

'Oh. Sorry to hear that.' Evie stubbed out the cigarette in a rose-and-gold eggshell porcelain saucer. 'Listen, I can't hang around here any longer,' she announced. 'I need to get home to Swithin. I've been waiting for you to get back so you can give me a lift to Lime Street. There's a couple more trains to Manchester before midnight.' She belched loudly then giggled. 'Oh, pardon *moi*!'

'No use expecting you to give a damn about Adam, is it?' Justine pushed back her hair and looked bitterly at her mother. 'Express one crumb of concern for me. You never have and you won't start now. Keeping out of the way is what you do best! Not everyone has that talent.'

'It's my speciality.' Evie's blue eyes narrowed. 'You look stressed out, *dear*,' she said. 'Why don't you try some crystal healing?'

'I don't need crystal bloody healing!' Justine's voice trembled. 'I need Adam to regain consciousness. I need none of this bullshit ever to have happened!' She had constantly to drag herself back from the edge of hysteria and it was getting harder each time. 'I'm not fit to drive any more tonight,' she sighed. 'I'm totally exhausted, it was all I could do to get home in one piece. You'll have to take a cab to Lime Street.'

'Joking, aren't you? I can't afford bloody cabs,' Evie said, aggrieved. She drank more champagne. 'I haven't got money to burn, not like you and his lordship!'

'I'll pay.' Justine picked up the phone and dialled. 'It'll be here in fifteen minutes,' she said wearily when she replaced the receiver. She picked up her wallet and pulled out a twenty-pound note. 'This will cover the fare and you'll have plenty left. You can buy a drink at the station.' She glanced at the empties on the table. 'That's if you haven't had enough booze already.' She was afraid to be alone and wished Evie would stay another night, irritating as she was. Stephanie would stay, she thought. But she didn't want to put her friend at risk. Who knew what Matthew would do next?

'Oh, thank you! So generous – *not*!' Evie snatched the note and looked contemptuously at it. 'Can't you do better than this?'

'Sorry, I don't have much cash on me right now . . .'

'Your sort never do!'

Justine didn't have the strength to argue. 'Did anyone come round?' she asked apprehensively. 'Were there any messages? I didn't switch on the answering machine.' Matthew's message was still on the tape. She had to erase that. There was so much to do, so much to think about. She couldn't even fall apart in peace! She glanced at the cupboard under the sink.

'Let me think.' Evie swigged champagne and took another cigarette from the pack on the kitchen table.

'I asked you not to smoke in here,' Justine reminded her. 'The whole flat stinks.'

'Oh, for . . . !' Evie dropped the cigarette. 'Your cross-eyed Amazon neighbour with the big bazookas came round to offer her condolences,' she said abruptly.

'*Condolences?*' Justine winced and tears sprang to her eyes.

'You know what I mean!' Evie said impatiently. 'Anything she

218

could do to help, blah, blah. Looks like a shot putter, doesn't she? And *definitely* a pork pie short of the old picnic!'

'Charley's a good neighbour. She's helped me a lot.'

'Well, pardon me for daring to voice an opinion. Someone called Stephanie phoned, she wants you to phone her back. Oh, and you had a couple of gentlemen callers bearing gifts.' Shit! Evie thought, chewing her lip. I shouldn't have said a couple. She poured the last of the champagne. 'Have a drink,' she suggested. 'You look like you could do with one.'

'I don't want a drink. What *gifts*?' Justine stiffened. 'I told you not to let any men in here.'

'He's a friend of yours,' Evie said, hoping Justine wouldn't notice the switch from plural to singular. 'Your type with knobs on! He brought some gorgeous flowers. Come and see. Come *on*!' she laughed, as Justine hesitated. 'It's only flowers, for Christ's sake! They won't bite you.'

She turned and walked out. Justine nervously followed her upstairs, wishing she had never left her mother in charge of the flat. In the sitting room Evie indicated the vase of fragrant white lilies on the coffee table and picked up Paul Melwood's crumpled business card.

'*He's* a bit of all right,' she said lasciviously. 'Full of charm, bloody sexy and good-looking. Wouldn't mind a piece of that if I were fifteen years younger and four stone lighter. Not short of a few quid either. He said he'd be back.'

Justine took the card and smoothed it out, caressed it with the tip of her finger. It smelled faintly of aftershave and expensive leather. She thought of Paul's voice and his smile, the warmth in his grey eyes when he looked at her. A beam of light pierced her darkness.

'I see you've got someone to comfort you in your hour of need,' her mother remarked jealously. 'Don't blame you. Very sexy, your Paul! Very worried about you, too.'

'He's not *my* Paul!' Justine said furiously. 'It's not like that. I was going to marry Adam, remember? I love him!' She looked at her mother and froze. 'You said a couple of callers. Who was the other?'

*Shit!* Evie chewed her lip again. 'Look, okay, I admit I shouldn't have let him in without checking,' she began nervously.

'But he said he was a friend of yours and I had no reason to suspect him. Not at first anyway.'

'What's happened? What have you done?' But Justine knew already.

'Nothing! He brought flowers, I went to put them in a vase. I got back to find him hovering outside my room. He said he wanted the loo. Then I caught him snooping in the bathroom.' She watched Justine's angry expression turn to one of horror. 'I thought he was going to thump me, but instead he shoved me away and ran out. I binned the rosebuds, they were knackered. He was a right sad act!' She shuddered. 'I was pretty scared.'

'You let him in?' Justine breathed.

Evie looked puzzled. 'Pete Smith?'

'I don't know any Pete Smith! It was Matthew, the stalker. I warned you!' Justine said despairingly. 'He tricked his way in here, put his filthy hands on our things! He probably stole something.' Terrified, she looked wildly around the big room, trying to see if anything was missing. Maybe he had even planted a listening device or hidden camera. She had heard of stalkers who did that.

'Now, hang on a bloody minute!' Evie felt alarmed. 'You and loony knockers down the stairs told me this Matthew character was dark-haired. It can't have been him. The guy I saw was blond.'

'*Blond*? Are you sure?'

'I may not be an intellectual like you and his lordship,' Evie said indignantly, 'but I am capable of recognizing blond hair when I see it. His was bleached, though. Looked like he'd done it himself with a trowel.'

'Oh, no!' Justine sat on the sofa and buried her face in her hands. Having her suspicions confirmed made her feel worse, not better. There were some things you didn't want to be right about.

'What's going on?' Evie asked helplessly. Justine didn't answer. 'Jesus!' She shook her head, walked to the rain-drenched windows and peered down into the dark drive. It was a horrible night. 'Where's that sodding cab?' she muttered. She hoped the driver wouldn't be one of those sanctimonious gits who stuck *Thank You for Not Smoking* notices all over the place. She turned. Justine was on the phone, asking to speak to a DS Kiely or DI Stewart.

'Not there? Please tell them Justine Flynn called. It's urgent. Justine *Flynn*' she repeated, her voice shaking. She banged the receiver down and sat there, white-faced. 'They've got to help me now,' she whispered.

'Why are you calling the police?' Her mother stared at her.

'Don't you get it? You let in the creep who's been stalking me.' Justine stood up and ran her hands through her hair. She looked like a hunted animal, Evie thought. 'He tried to murder Adam!'

'*What?*' Evie stepped back, one hand to her mouth. 'Are you sure? He could have hurt me! Oh, Jesus!'

'Never mind Jesus. He only helps men.' Justine came towards her and held out her hand. 'Give me back my keys before you go,' she demanded. 'Otherwise I shudder to think who'll get their hands on them. I don't know how even you could be this stupid! I wish you'd never come here.'

'You're not the only one,' Evie said sullenly. She hurried into the spare room and shook out the quilt and pillow, looked under the bed and in the chest of drawers. No keys. She swore. She checked the bathroom and lavatory, ran down to the kitchen and opened her bag. Nothing. Justine appeared in the doorway.

'Where are they?' she asked fiercely. 'Come on, hurry up!' Typical that Kiely and Stewart weren't around when she needed them. She shivered with terror as she imagined Matthew snooping around the flat. Was Evie's presence an unwelcome setback for him? Maybe he had expected to find her alone. Or was he trying to frighten her again, prove he could violate her private space?

'I can't find the bloody keys,' Evie cried. 'I've looked everywhere. I left them on the bed, I know I did!'

'*He's* got them.' Justine stared at her. 'He must have taken them while you were down here. You let him steal my keys!' she gasped. 'What the hell am I going to do now?' The doorbell rang and she whirled round and gave a cry of fright.

'That'll be the cab – at last!' Evie picked up her scruffy bag. 'I'll leave you to your policemen and psychopaths, shall I?' she said angrily. 'I can't handle this. Look, I'm sorry about the keys, but it's not my fault, okay?'

She hurried out of the kitchen, went downstairs and unchained and unbolted the flat door. Justine followed, terrified and panicked. She had to get the locks changed before Matthew came back. Until then, bolts and a chain would have to keep him out. She hoped he wasn't hanging around in the driveway, waiting to pounce the minute her mother drove off. 'I won't come out with you,' she called.

Evie pulled open the front door and swore as a gust of wind and rain tore in, whipping her thin cotton dress up around her thighs. The cab was parked at the foot of the steps. The driver didn't bother to get out. Behind the cab was another car, raindrops sparkling on the roof and bonnet. A Mercedes. Justine turned her head away as cold rain blew in her face.

Evie didn't bother to say goodbye. She threw her bag on to the back seat, got in and slammed the door. The cab began to reverse. Justine stepped back, shivering with cold and fear, ready to slam the front door.

'Justine!' a man's voice shouted out of the darkness. 'Wait! It's me.' A tall broad-shouldered man got out of the Mercedes and ran forward. Justine stepped outside and gave a sob of relief as she recognized Paul Melwood. Cold rain beat on her face, hair and shoulders.

'Sorry to turn up like this,' he panted, sprinting up the steps. 'I should have phoned first but . . .'

'Shut the door!' she cried, panicked. 'Quick!'

Paul closed the heavy front door behind them and ran after her as she fled through the dimly lit hall and back upstairs. Only when the flat door was chained and bolted and they were in the kitchen did she let him take her in his arms and hold her shivering body, gently push back her damp hair.

'Don't go yet,' she sobbed. 'Please don't leave me!'

'Of course I won't,' he whispered. 'I'll stay as long as you want me to. What the hell's happened?' he asked. She was terrified. 'Is it Adam?'

She shook her head. Her cloud of hair was in his face. She smelled of perfume and the rain. Her short black sweater rode up and his hand touched the soft bare skin of her back. She was freezing. Paul hugged her.

'Tell me!' he said urgently. His heart pounded.

'It's the stalker – he came back twice the other night and I called the police, but he escaped. They don't care,' she sobbed. 'They won't take it seriously. Now he's been here again! He tricked his way in earlier while I was at the hospital, my mother let him in. Paul, he stole my keys! What the hell am I going to do now? I'm in terrible danger!'

Justine couldn't talk any more. She put her arms around his neck, clung to him and he held her tight while she cried like a child.


In the cold stuffy recesses of the vaults of the Joint Stock Innovation Bank on Tverskaya Street, Adriana Terekhova watched as the last of twenty-seven wooden crates stencilled with Cyrillic markings was lugged out and carried upstairs to the waiting lorries. It worried her that Paul Melwood had already found a buyer to sell the beryllium on to. But it was hardly likely that the customer would refuse the consignment, even if he discovered the contamination. Who was the mystery buyer? she wondered. Someone from India, North Korea, the Arab world? She shrugged. What did it matter? Soon she would have her two million dollars and a new life in America. She couldn't wait to leave Russia. Her daughters would love California. And if her mother didn't love it, she could go back to Moscow and rot.

The bank had closed years ago and no one came here now. Not for banking transactions anyway. There was no electricity and the men had to work by the light of oil lamps and torches. One lamp on an old wooden chair illuminated the slight hunched figure of her ex-husband Gregor, with his black beard and wild black hair. His long coat was pulled tightly around him. A regular Rasputin, Adriana thought. Without the intelligence or charisma.

Gregor was mean and little and greedy and ordinary. So ordinary he made her want to fall asleep. He was nervous now, smoking and pacing the length of the vault as he waited for his money. Adriana wondered again why she had ever been afraid of him, why she had let him beat and control her for years. He was nothing, a nobody. You didn't throw money at nobodies.

Gregor stopped pacing and turned to her. 'How much longer?' he asked irritably. He threw the cigarette down and trod on it, immediately rolling another. He didn't dare act too rude and aggressive, though, not now that she was surrounded by all these tattooed thugs of whom she was apparently in charge. There was no chance of getting back into her life now that she was a well-off Moscow businesswoman, he knew that. He had blown it with his ex-wife a long time ago. He would have to take his money – a fraction of what she would make from this deal, he thought resentfully – and think himself lucky. Scientists and academics were despised now, the new underclass. Anarchy reigned.

He looked at her again. Adriana wore a tight black dress and sheer black stockings, a black leather coat and black, high-heeled pumps. A diamond glittered on the third finger of her right hand; he hadn't noticed the ring before. The heels made her tower above him. Gregor hated her cool self-assurance. Adriana was so different now, so changed from the frightened girl he had known all those years ago. The bitch! he thought. I should have her money, her power.

'Be patient.' She glanced at him and smiled briefly. 'They haven't finished loading yet.'

'What difference does that make?'

'What's your hurry?' She shoved her hands in her coat pockets, felt the cold metal of the CZ 70 pistol. 'Are you planning to meet friends at a nightclub and drink French champagne at seven hundred dollars a bottle?' Her smile broadened. 'I don't think so!'

'I want my money!' he shouted. 'You've kept me waiting long enough.'

'Don't worry, Gregor,' she said calmly as footsteps hurried down the stairs and the two thugs who had supervised the loading reappeared. 'The waiting's over.'

The men grinned at one another. Tall and powerfully built, they looked like former athletes, as were many of the security thugs and racketeers in Moscow. Russian society didn't need athletes anymore. But the Mafia did. There were many jokes about 'organized sport', the phrase of which rhymed with 'organized crime' in Russian. They looked at Adriana and stood there silently, waiting for her order.

'What's going on?' Gregor asked nervously. Suddenly he felt very frightened.

'You didn't actually believe I would give you money, did you, Gregor? Not with your professed belief in logic and rationality?' Adriana shook back her blonde hair and gestured to the two men. They smiled at him menacingly, moved forward.

'No! Keep away!' Gregor charged and tried to dodge past them, but it was impossible to escape. They grabbed him, pulled off his coat and started to beat him. He grunted in pain, retched as their fists slammed into his solar plexus. The men punched him around the head and face, kicked him to the ground, then dragged him up and handcuffed him to an old office chair. The lamp shone on his pale, sweating, terrified face. Blood trickled from his nostrils.

'I could get my hired help to really hurt you.' Adriana could smell his warm blood and sweat in the cold stuffy dark vault. His fear. 'But I'm not a sadist. We'll do this quickly.'

'Let me go, Adriana!' he begged, struggling. 'Forget the money. Just let me go.'

'I can't possibly do that, Gregor.' She pulled the gun out of her pocket and he moaned in fear. 'You're a security risk, you see.'

'I'll keep my mouth shut,' he said wildly. 'I promise! I'm not stupid.'

'Your promise isn't good enough. And I'm afraid you *are* stupid!'

An idea came to him. 'Let me work for you,' he pleaded. 'I can get you things . . .'

'Please be quiet, Gregor. You're really starting to irritate me.' Adriana stepped sideways and levelled the gun at his left temple. 'Look at you now!' She laughed angrily. 'The almighty scientist who thought he could control the stupid little peasant girl from Sverdlovsk! Next thing you'll be telling me you love me.'

'I do love you! Don't kill me,' he shouted. 'Please, Adriana! No!'

'Shut your mouth!' She pulled the trigger and jumped back as the gun roared. Gregor's body twitched and his head slumped forward, dark blood flowing down the side of his face and neck and on to his chest, soaking his cheap, grimy white shirt. Blood dripped on to the stone floor. Ears ringing, Adriana lowered the gun and gazed at her dead husband. The diamond ring flashed white fire.

In a few days she would be rich enough to do what she liked for the rest of her life. She would never have to depend on any man again. Not for money, at least. She and her daughters would live thousands of miles away in the sunshine while Gregor's corpse rotted in this dank silent vault. Adriana loved that image.

His warm sticky blood dripped and rolled down the chair legs, pooled around her shoes. Adriana stood still and stared down at it.

She liked the idea of walking into a nightclub to drink champagne with her dead husband's blood staining the soles of her shoes. It was amusing and highly appropriate. She smiled. All she needed now was her two million dollars.

And Paul Melwood. She sincerely hoped she wouldn't have to kill him. This cruel world was sadly lacking in beautiful men. It would be a terrible waste.

'I got the best deal, Gregor!' she whispered.

# Chapter Twenty

'Thanks, mate.' The locksmith took the bundle of notes and stuffed them in his jacket pocket. 'Christ!' he exclaimed as he pulled open the front door. 'Look at this bloody rain! Night, mate!'

'Goodnight.' Paul Melwood stood on the wet steps beneath the light and watched as the van headed down the drive and paused at the gates. There was no sign of the stalker or his white Ford Fiesta. But it was too dark to be sure. Cold rain poured down, battering trees and bushes, and there was a fresh smell of earth. The van turned left and swished off down the wet road. Paul got into Justine's BMW, drove down the cinder path and put the car in the garage. He walked back up the path, flashing his torch to right and left, watching for movement in the bushes, tense in case someone loomed out of the darkness at him. No wonder Justine hadn't wanted to brave the pitch darkness of the large back garden. He felt scared himself. If only he'd known that the man he'd bumped into earlier that evening was the stalker! he thought again, frustrated. The bastard could have been sitting in a cell now.

Paul double-locked the front door and stooped to pick up a crumpled white envelope that lay on the mat. *Justine* was scrawled on it in black biro. It hadn't been there earlier, had it? He frowned and shook his head as he studied it. He couldn't remember. He stuffed the envelope in his jacket pocket.

He was stunned by the revelations Justine had sobbed out while they waited for the locksmith. They had even pushed Adriana, the beryllium deal and Sara out of focus for now. How could the police not realize the danger she was in? Another question went round and round in his head. How could Adam have cheated on her, hurt her like that? Paul found it incredible. It was an under-statement to say he didn't feel sorry for Adam any more, even though the guy lay unconscious in intensive care. He felt sorry for Justine because she loved Adam. She would stick by him now, sacrifice herself, and Adam didn't deserve that. Paul was glad Justine trusted him. Of course she wasn't in love with him, he had no illusions in that direction. He only wanted to help her.

'Did you see him? Is his car out there?' She came running down the stairs as he entered the flat and shut the door. Her hands were clenched in her jeans pockets. 'Aren't you going to put the chain on?' she asked anxiously.

'Well – okay. But the police will be here soon. No, I didn't see anyone,' he replied as they went back up to the kitchen. He laid the keys on the table. 'I put the car away.'

'Thanks so much! I'm really grateful.'

He won't know if you're home or not. And he can't get in now,' Paul said reassuringly. 'You're safe.'

'I don't *feel* safe.' She wiped her eyes on the sleeve of her sweater. 'I'm frightened all the time, whether I'm home or out somewhere.' Her face was pale, wild hair all over the place, and she wore no makeup. Paul looked into her long-lashed eyes then glanced away, staring at the shiny new keys on the kitchen table instead. He wanted to hold her again.

'How much do I owe you?' she asked. 'For the keys?'

'Don't worry about that.' He shrugged. 'Forget it.'

'But I want to pay you,' she protested, embarrassed. 'It must have cost a fortune to get a locksmith out at this time of night. I don't have much cash on me now, but I'll go to the bank in the morning and . . .'

'Justine, I said forget it! Okay?' He looked at her standing across the table from him, shivering and hugging herself. 'Don't mention it again.'

His sharp tone brought more tears to her eyes. 'I'm sorry.' Her voice trembled. 'You must be fed up! You come over to ask how I am and end up hearing about all this . . .' She stopped and looked down, laughed shakily. 'You certainly got more than you bargained for.' She couldn't bring herself to tell him about the attempted rape and how she'd killed Ronnie Davis in self-defence. Maybe because she couldn't quite believe it had happened, was unable to deal with it herself yet. There was a crazy sense of unreality about the whole terrifying event, despite the knife slash on her inner thigh and the bloody evidence hidden in the cupboard under the sink.

'Come off it, Justine! Of course I'm not fed up.' Paul's voice softened and he took a step towards her. 'I'm glad I could help. It's late,' he said. 'Why don't you try to get some sleep after the police have been? You must be exhausted.'

'I couldn't sleep.' The thought of spending the night alone with her demons – real and imaginary – terrified her. But it had to be faced. 'Don't worry,' she said as Paul looked at the empty wine and beer bottles, 'that wasn't me. I haven't been drowning my sorrows. My mother got bored waiting and had a binge.'

'Looks like it!' Some mother, he thought. 'Shall I make you something to eat?' he offered. 'That might help.'

She hesitated. 'Okay. Thanks.' She wasn't hungry, but it meant he would stay longer. 'Sure you don't mind?' she asked tentatively.

He grinned. 'You might, when you taste my cooking.'

'I'm sure it's not that bad.' Justine walked to the fridge and pulled open the door, very conscious of his closeness. She smelled his leather jacket, his aftershave, and suddenly wished desperately that he would hold her again.

'Eggs, spring onions, cheese, ham.' He smiled down at her. 'How about an omelette?'

'Fine.' She didn't care what she ate. Her stomach already felt like it had shrunk; eating an entire meal was unimaginable. Food was for happy people. She glanced at the bottle of Sancerre, one of the few Evie hadn't sampled. 'Fancy a glass of wine?'

'Just the one,' he said. 'I'm driving.' He took off his jacket, draped it over a chair and began to break eggs into a glass bowl. Justine uncorked the wine and poured two glasses. Drank hers too quickly. She sat at the kitchen table and watched as Paul grated cheese, chopped ham and spring onions and swirled butter around the warmed pan, waited for it to foam before he poured in the eggs. He was neat, methodical, absorbed in his task. Adam was like that too. She quickly poured herself more wine and gulped it down.

'I feel so vulnerable,' she said. 'Every time I come in or go out I feel his eyes all over my body. Whether he's watching me or not. The fear is *exhausting*.'

'You won't have to put up with that much longer. The police will get him soon.' Paul wished he could believe that.

'Will they? They act like I'm some kind of jealous, crazed *femme fatale*! I can't believe the way their minds work. Or *don't* work. Like lurid, overblown tabloid headlines.'

'I'm sure once they've checked out . . .' Paul stopped talking as the doorbell rang. They looked into each other's eyes. 'Don't be frightened,' he said quickly. 'D'you want me to get it?'

'No,' she said. 'It's okay.' She stood up, her legs feeling like lead. 'It won't be Matthew. He wouldn't bother to ring!'

John Kiely strolled into the warm kitchen and sniffed the savoury cooking smell, looked at the wine on the table and the omelette that would turn to rubber now that it couldn't be served and eaten due to his inopportune arrival. Cosy, he thought, looking at Paul Melwood. Flynn certainly didn't hang about.

'I called you over an hour ago.' Justine looked at him angrily, knowing what he was thinking. But she wasn't going to ask Paul to hide in the bedroom.

'Sorry it took so long but I was . . .'

'The stalker tricked his way in here while I was at the hospital and stole a set of keys while my mother's back was turned,' she said quickly. 'My mother said his hair was bleached. He must have dyed it since I saw him last. He tried to kill Adam!' Her voice trembled. 'There's no doubt.'

'Where is your mother now?'

'She went back to Manchester, left about an hour ago.' Kiely looked surprised, but Justine didn't want to launch into an explanation of her complicated relationship with Evie. 'He can't get in now,' she said. 'The locks have been changed.'

'I see. Good.' Kiely glanced at Paul. 'And you are . . . sir?'

'Paul Melwood,' he said stiffly. 'I'm a friend of Justine's.' He hesitated. 'And Adam's.'

'Melwood. That name sounds familiar.'

'Melwood Materials on the Dock Road. I own the company.'

'Oh, right, of course. Melwood Materials. Metals, rare earth products.' Kiely nodded. 'Interesting,' he said thoughtfully. He could tell by the way Melwood looked at Justine that he'd like to be more than friends. Maybe he'd get his chance now that she was alone and vulnerable. Her story about the stalker checked out, and they had got hold of the television footage that showed a scruffy unshaven dark-haired nutter outside the Jackson house, laughing at the camera and shouting her name, like she'd said.

Okay, so Justine Flynn wasn't an Amber Annette Donaldson. But Kiely still had a few questions to ask her. She had fainted just in time to avoid explaining why she hadn't come forward after being in the Crystal Cave club and talking to Ronnie Davis, though he didn't doubt that the faint was genuine, if highly convenient. He still wasn't sure the stalker had struck down Adam Shaw, although it seemed much more likely now. Life would be a lot easier if Adam could regain consciousness and identify his attacker.

'We think the guy lives in the Old Roan area,' he said. 'Probably in or around the street where the Jackson fire took place. We're checking it out.'

'That's all I ever hear – we're checking it out! Listen, I'm in danger,' Justine said fiercely. 'Don't you realize that? The bastard was here in my home only a few hours ago! What if I didn't know, hadn't had the locks changed? He wants to kill me, I know he does!' She shivered and hugged herself. 'He might even try again to kill Adam. Finish the job!' she said bitterly.

'There's no way he'll get into that intensive care unit. And we're keeping an eye on this place,' Kiely assured her. 'We'll get him.'

'That's what the other officers said!'

'We've got patrol cars driving past every hour.' Well, not quite every hour. They didn't have the manpower for that. 'If he comes back we'll be ready.'

Paul remembered the envelope and pulled it out of his pocket. 'This was downstairs,' he said, handing it to her. 'I can't remember if it was there earlier.'

Justine took the envelope and looked fearfully at it. She ripped it open, her fingers trembling. Inside was a photo torn from a magazine. A naked girl on all fours was being raped, sodomized and half-strangled by two masked men, a studded leather collar tight around her neck. There was a note with it scrawled in black biro on cheap lined writing paper. Of course it would be *cheap*. Justine read the note. Touching it made her skin crawl. Matthew's handwriting looked like a poisonous black hairy spider had dragged ink-stained legs across the page.

*This is you, Justine. I gave you loads of chances, but you rejected me and what we could have had together. You destroyed my love and now I hate you. You'll never know how much you hurt me, not even when you're screaming in pain and begging me to give you another chance. It's your turn to feel pain, feel my power. Get ready to take your punishment. You're evil and you should be wiped out. That's down to me. I'm going to destroy you.*

Justine turned white. Paul wished he had kept the bloody thing and torn it up. But it was evidence. The police had to take this seriously.

'That's not very nice, is it?' Kiely said gently, looking at her stricken face. He felt sorry for her. He stepped forward and took the note and photo, held them between thumb and forefinger. 'I'll keep this, thanks. Got a plastic bag for me?' he asked. 'Freezer bag, sandwich bag, whatever?'

'Yes. Somewhere.' Justine looked helplessly around the kitchen. She couldn't think straight, let alone remember where the plastic bags were kept. Horrible images of Ronnie Davis beating and threatening her in that dark alley, trying to rape her, flashed through her brain. The knife, his snarling, nasal, hate-filled voice, his warm blood soaking her. Now Matthew wanted to torture and murder her. There was no doubt, no more stupid crazy hope that maybe the nightmare would vanish, dissolve like autumn mist.

'A bin bag will do,' Kiely said, noting her confusion. He couldn't imagine Justine Flynn neatly labelling freezer bags of home cooked lasagne or meat-and-potato pie with cheese pastry, like his wife Lynette did, or making sandwiches to take to work. He moved towards the cupboard under the sink. 'In here?' he asked helpfully, stretching out a hand.

'No!' Justine gasped, horrified. 'Not there! Wait, I remember.' She darted around the kitchen table, knocking over her glass of wine, pulled open a drawer and grabbed a roll of freezer bags. She felt sick again. Paul glanced curiously at her, then took a yellow cloth and started to mop up the wine. She tore off two bags and handed them to Kiely.

'Thanks,' he said slowly. Of course she was freaked out by the note and photo. It couldn't be nice to know some creep wanted to rape and murder you. But something, he didn't know what, nagged at him. He took one bag and slid the note and photo into it, dropped that in the other bag. 'We'll need to check this place for fingerprints,' he said. 'We'll need yours prints and your mother's so that we can exclude them.' He turned to Paul. 'Yours as well, sir. Adam's too.'

'What? Right now?' Justine asked wildly. They might not stop at dusting for fingerprints. They would look around, find the knife and clothing. She was finished!

'In the morning. We'll send a forensics team.'

'I can't call my mother, she's got no phone.'

'If you give us her address we'll get someone from the local nick to call round. They can get her prints. We may want to interview her at some point.'

Matthew should be having his fingerprints taken, not her or Adam! It made Justine feel like a criminal. Poor Adam, having his fingerprints taken while he lay unconscious! I have to get rid of those things before tomorrow morning, she thought. Erase Matthew's message from the answering machine tape. What excuse could she give for going out? How long would Kiely stay? And Matthew might be out there. Waiting for the right moment. Justine didn't believe a police patrol car would spot him, not unless they were lucky or unusually observant. The phone rang and she snatched it up before Kiely could tell her to leave it for the answering machine. She didn't want him replaying Matthew's message.

'Justine? It's Stephanie. I phoned earlier, did your mother tell you?'

'I was going to call you back, but I haven't had a chance.'

'How are you?' Stephanie asked, her voice high and nervous. 'How's Adam?'

'Still unconscious,' Justine said quietly. 'I've been at the hospital all day. They made me come home to get some rest, said they'd phone if there was any change. Adam's parents are with him now. I'm going back first thing in the morning.'

'Poor you! And Adam. This is so awful! Justine . . .' Stephanie hesitated. 'I hope I haven't caused you any trouble, especially now, but I had to tell the police about the other night. Your hen night.'

'What do you mean?' Justine asked faintly. She turned her back on Paul and Kiely.

'Remember the guy who hassled you? Turned out he was Ronnie Davis, that policeman who got murdered. Did you hear about it? They were asking for anyone who'd seen him that night to come forward.'

'I saw something on television. I wasn't concentrating.' What now? Justine thought, closing her eyes.

'I saw him try to grab you as you ran out of the club. You must have been scared stiff! I couldn't get to you in time. Next thing he was gone too. I told the police what happened. Did he follow you outside?'

'I don't know, I never saw him again,' Justine lied. 'I jumped straight into a cab.'

'I made a statement,' Stephanie said breathlessly. 'You'll probably have to as well. I know it's a real pain at a time like this.'

Adam had guessed right. Of course Matthew had no intention of grassing her up. How could he get to her then? Justine saw the irony of the situation; it might be the kind, concerned friend who unwittingly got her banged up! Not her worst enemy.

'Have the police spoken to you?'

'Yes,' Justine said dully. 'Today.' She felt an invisible net start to close around her.

'I've been so worried! Why did you run out anyway?' Stephanie asked, curiosity getting the better of concern. 'You looked terribly upset. Something happened between you and Donna, didn't it? I asked her, but she wouldn't tell me.'

'Stephanie, I'm sorry, but I can't really talk now.'

'Of course, I understand. Justine, what can I do for you? Shopping, keeping you company? How about if I come over after work tomorrow? I'll cook for you.'

'Thanks, but better not,' Justine said reluctantly. She would have liked to see Stephanie, but was afraid Matthew might spot her friend, maybe try to harm her as well. Plus she couldn't face explaining about Donna. 'I'll probably be at the hospital. I'll phone you, okay?'

'Any time, don't hesitate. I'm thinking about you and I'm here whenever you need me. Take care of yourself, Justine,' Stephanie urged. 'Lots of love.'

'Thanks, Stephanie. 'Bye!'

She hung up and turned. Both men were staring at her and Justine suddenly felt very angry that she couldn't be alone, peaceful and safe. She sloshed wine into a fresh glass and sipped it, her mind in a whirl.

'If you come down to the station in the morning, we can take your fingerprints then,' Kiely said. 'And we'll get this place dusted, like I said. I also want to talk to you about the other night. Ronnie Davis, remember?' Justine flinched and looked away, sipped more wine. How many more times do I have to have that name flung in my face? she thought furiously. It was hard not to panic, burst out screaming and crying.

'Are you referring to that murdered police officer?' Paul asked, puzzled.

Kiely glanced at him as if to say, Are you still here? 'That's right.'

'What's his murder got to do with Justine?'

Good question. 'Ms Flynn and a group of her friends were in the same club as DC Davis the night he died,' Kiely said briefly. 'She saw him. Spoke to him.'

'So what? A lot of other people did too, I imagine. I realize your colleague's murder is very important to you, but don't you think Justine's got enough to worry about right now?' Paul asked angrily. 'And why is it necessary for her to go to a police station? You're treating her like a criminal!'

And you're treating her like your girlfriend. 'It's routine, Mr Melwood.'

Who did the arrogant bastard think he was, sticking his oar in? Just because he drove a flash git Merc S300 and probably flew to Zurich every week with suitcases stuffed with cash.

'It always is! What are you doing to ensure this stalker gets arrested before he murders somebody? If he hasn't already!' Paul crossed to Justine and put one hand on her shoulder. 'You saw that note,' he said. 'Do you think he's joking?'

'No. We're doing plenty, I can assure you.' Annoyed, Kiely turned back to Justine. 'Nine o'clock tomorrow morning, all right?' he said, shoving the freezer bag of evidence in his coat pocket. 'I'll expect you. Prints first, then talk.'

'Fine. I hope I don't get murdered before I can keep our appointment!' Justine saw him out, locked and chained the door behind him and went slowly back upstairs, her legs trembling. She swore as she heard the phone ring again. In the kitchen Paul held out the receiver.

'It's the hospital,' he said as she walked into the kitchen, his grey eyes anxious. Surely if Adam had taken a turn for the worse – or died! – they wouldn't tell her over the phone?

Justine grabbed the receiver, her heart pounding. She listened briefly then hung up and turned to Paul, eyes wide in her pale, anguished face.

'Adam's regained consciousness!' she whispered.

'Justine, wait! Adam may be confused, he might not recognize you. He's off the ventilator and can breathe by himself now, but we don't yet know if he's suffered any . . .'

Brain damage, the nurse was going to say. She watched helplessly as Justine raced ahead of her, pulled aside the yellow curtains and entered Adam's cubicle. He lay there still hooked up to the machines, eyes full of pain and fear and bewilderment.

'Adam!' Justine grasped his hand and stared down at his bruised face, choked with emotion. She breathed again as she saw recognition in his eyes. 'I love you,' she said. 'You're going to be all right, I promise.'

'Justine . . . *danger*!' he whispered frantically between cracked lips. 'Matthew ran me over . . . tried to kill me. He'll kill you . . .'

'No, he won't! Don't worry about me,' she told him, tears in her eyes. 'The police know everything now, they'll get him. You have to concentrate on getting better.' With the injuries he had suffered, it would be a long slow road to recovery, but Justine couldn't think about what lay ahead. To get through each day was enough of a challenge.

'I love you!' Adam whispered. He squeezed her hand hard, and she was glad. No nerve damage. 'I'm sorry about Donna. Never wanted to . . . hurt you.'

'Don't think about that.' She blinked back tears. 'Just get better, Adam. That's all that matters.'

'Don't blame you if you leave me . . .'

'I won't!' She kissed him, overwhelmed by love and pity. Her tense exhausted body was flooded with healing relief. She would stick by Adam now. The future could sort itself out. 'What's wrong?' she asked anxiously as he winced and groaned, tried to turn his head. He couldn't move.

'Pain,' he gasped. 'Agony all over. Like everything's broken.' His chest heaved.

Everything pretty much was broken, Justine thought furiously. Tears spilled down her face. Matthew had wrecked her life and Adam's, poisoned their existence. He was walking around, free to plan his next outrage, while Adam was stuck in here racked with pain and barely able to move. Matthew thought he had the inalienable right to do anything he liked to her and anyone close to her.

'The policeman!' Adam squeezed her hand again, his eyes full of alarm. 'Did you get rid of the . . . ?'

'Shh!' she whispered frantically, glancing around. She hadn't expected him to remember everything so quickly. 'I'm safe, Adam, I promise. Don't worry.'

It would have been intolerable if Ronnie Davis had survived; had raped her and got away with it. Especially while Matthew still menaced her. But Justine was already determined that the attempted rape wouldn't destroy her or give her years of nightmares and flashbacks, turn her insides to ice and drive away all healthy desire and longing. She was a survivor and she would fight back. She and Adam would get through this and be happy again one day. Whether they stayed together or not. She had to hold on to that thought.

Adam was given a shot of morphine and fell asleep a few minutes later. 'Go back home and get some rest,' the tired junior doctor urged her. Of course the big guns wouldn't turn up until the morning. 'It's nearly midnight, Adam will sleep through now. I know it's easy for me to say but try not to worry too much,' he added sympathetically.

Paul was waiting in the corridor, studying the wall of cards. He turned and came towards her.

'How's he doing?' He felt sorry for Adam again, despite his earlier reservations. No one deserved to be stuck in this place, hovering between life and death after being mown down by a maniac. 'Does he remember what happened?'

'Everything!' Justine's hands felt cold, but her face was flushed. 'He confirmed it was Matthew who tried to kill him. He's worried about *me* now,' she said, eyes full of tears. 'He was in a lot of pain so they gave him morphine. They say he'll sleep through the night and that I should go home and do the same.'

'I agree.' Paul put one arm around her. 'Would you like me to stay the night in your spare room?' he asked hesitantly. 'Just so you've got someone around?'

'That would be great.' She loved the idea of Paul's comforting presence in the flat. 'But what about your wife? Don't you want to get home?'

He took his arm away. 'I moved out a couple of days ago. I'm staying in a hotel in town until I find an apartment.'

'Oh.' She stared up at his handsome, troubled face. 'I'm sorry, Paul.'

'Never mind me,' he said abruptly. 'Worry about yourself.'

Justine wiped her eyes. 'Paul, he looks so helpless lying there! To think that bastard did this to him ... I can't believe it! Matthew's after *me* – it should be *me* in there! This is all my fault.'

'Hey, come on!' Dismayed, Paul wrapped his arms around her and she clung to him, her body shaking. 'Don't talk like that, Justine, please! It's crazy. Look, they'll arrest him soon and he'll go down for years.'

'Even if that happens, he'll get out one day,' she sobbed. 'And come after me again. I can never be free, never have peace of mind. It *is* my fault. I must have done something to make them ...' She gasped, bit her lip. 'Make *him* pick on me!' What happened to being a survivor? she thought in frustration. Why did she feel brave and determined one minute, overwhelmed with fear and irrational guilt the next?

'You didn't do anything! That's exactly what the bastard wants, for you to blame and analyse yourself, think it was your fault! Don't give him the satisfaction. And you will have peace of mind again,' Paul said firmly, holding her tight. 'You don't help yourself – or Adam – when you talk like this. For God's sake, don't feel guilty, especially about people or events you can't control. You've got more than enough to put up with. Don't be so hard on yourself.'

Justine laid her head on his shoulder and closed her eyes, drained and exhausted. He kissed her forehead, brushed his lips against her soft, fresh-smelling hair, his fingers gently stroking the back of her neck. She loved his comforting touch, didn't want him to let go of her. The double doors swished open and incoming footsteps stopped abruptly. Justine opened her eyes and turned her head to see Adam's parents, Christine and Eric, standing watching her.

Eric Shaw looked more shrunken and grey than ever, as if a layer of cigar ash had been rubbed into his skin. He wore maroon trousers and a tweed jacket. Christine wore a brown pinstripe trouser suit and the usual ton of makeup on her long thin face, her trembling downturned mouth painted pillar-box red. Her straight dryish hennaed hair fell around her shoulders. She stepped forward, dark brown eyes blazing.

'You slut!' she hissed. 'Don't waste any time, do you? I might have known! You're just like your ghastly mother!'

Was Paul asleep? Justine tossed and turned in the darkness, her heart racing. The radio played softly and the clock showed 3.10 a.m. In a few hours she faced the dreaded appointment with Kiely, the flat would be checked for fingerprints, and then – assuming she avoided arrest and detention – she would go back to the hospital. Justine was terrified that her fingerprints might somehow link her with Ronnie Davis. She couldn't refuse to have them taken, it would look too suspicious. And the police could probably force her anyway.

Right now she had to erase Matthew's message and get rid of the knife and torn clothing. It didn't matter how sick or frightened she felt, she just had to do it before it was too late. It almost had been! She slid out of the warm bed and began to get dressed in the dark. Lightning flashed and thunder growled, far off then suddenly right overhead. A shower of rain hit the windows.

Paul had been great with Christine, she thought, as she pulled on paint-splashed jeans that she hadn't worn for years, her oldest pair of trainers and a long, thick black sweater. He'd told Adam's mother politely but firmly to calm down, that he was simply a good friend. Though he certainly felt like more than that at the moment. She didn't know what she would have done without him tonight. The attraction she felt towards him had been there from the beginning, but she had ignored it. Now it was getting stronger. Maybe because she felt dangerously vulnerable. How could she think of Paul like this when Adam was lying in hospital barely alive? But he betrayed you, a tiny rebellious voice inside her said. Would you really have married him?

'Stop!' she whispered. She had to control the chaotic thoughts and emotions that whirled through her brain and made her feel as if she was losing it. She crept out of the bedroom, paused on the dark silent landing and glanced at the closed door to the spare room. No chink of light showed beneath it. She crept into the sitting room and erased the message on the answering machine then silently down to the kitchen, shut the door quietly and snapped the light on.

She had to wash the blood and fingerprints off the knife first. Just in case. She started to tremble. I can't do this, she thought. Tears rose to her eyes and she flinched with terror as the sound of Davis' voice, the force of his blows, the feel of his cruel, hard hands on her body, his blood flooding over her bare skin, flashed through her mind again. She clapped one hand to her mouth to stifle a cry. *Can't* wasn't an option. She put on a pair of washing-up gloves and filled the sink with hot soapy water, careful not to run the taps too hard. Then she stooped and took the bin bag out of the cupboard.

Justine was shaking and her breath came in short bursts. A wave of icy sweat broke out on her body as she slowly reached inside the bag, feeling for the knife. She drew it out and looked at it, feeling sick and faint. The blade and handle were sticky, clotted with dark, rust-coloured blood. Her skin crawled and the hairs on the back of her neck stood up. She dropped it into the sink and the water turned red. Nausea welled up inside her. She turned away and bent double, gasping for breath, trying to control the horrible sick feeling. Sounds of vomiting would definitely wake Paul.

After a few seconds she breathed more easily. Slowly she straightened up and turned back to the sink, steeled herself to wash the knife thoroughly. Tears dripped off her nose and chin and fell into the hot steamy water. Next she took out her small black leather handbag, emptied it of tissues and cleaned that. I should wash the clothes too, she thought. But she couldn't bring herself to. Besides, it would take too long. She poured the red water away and refilled the sink, reimmersed knife and handbag until no traces of blood remained. Then she dropped everything in a fresh bin bag, removed the washing-up gloves and put on her leather jacket and a pair of black leather gloves. She took her keys and the big yellow torch and shoved them in the jacket pockets.

Matthew might be outside, but she had to risk it. If he was, he would be watching the front of the house. She unlocked and unbolted the door that led to the fire escape and locked it behind her, paused at the top of the fire escape and looked fearfully down at the dark silent back garden. Holding her breath, she quickly went down the cast-iron steps and raced across the lawn to the garages. A minute later she was inside her BMW, bumping slowly down the cinder path towards the gates, headlights off and the doors locked, hoping no one would see or hear the car. It would be just her luck if the police chose this moment to cruise past!

At 3.30 in the morning Aigburth Drive was deserted. There was no sign of Matthew or his car. Justine put on speed as she headed for Southport and Formby, keeping to quiet roads off the beaten track. It took longer but it was safer. She constantly glanced in the driving mirror to make sure she wasn't being followed. There were few cars on the road. Twenty minutes later she was driving down a narrow dark track through pine woods that led to the beach, hoping there were no dossers, courting couples or psychopaths around. She got as close to the beach as she dared then switched off engine and headlights and wound down the window slightly. The bin bag was on the floor beside her.

Cold rain blew in her face. She could smell the sea, hear waves crashing on the beach. Wind whistled through the pine trees and distant thunder rumbled. She was reluctant to leave the warm safety of the car. 'Come on,' she muttered. 'Do it!' She grabbed the bin bag and got out, took the spade from the boot. She had to use the torch because it was pitch dark and the sea sounded alarmingly close.

She stumbled down the path and on to the beach, went as close to the pounding waves as she dared. She was terrified of being swept out. She emptied the bin bag. Knife, handbag, the torn bloody dress, stockings, shoes and underwear fell into the water, and she let the foaming waves wash over them, rush in and out and over the bin bags. The smell of salt and seaweed was strong in her nostrils, and she tasted salt on her lips. She jumped back as sea water swirled around her feet. The strong wind whipped her hair across her face.

When the things were rinsed, saturated and covered with sand she took them out of the water, dug a hole amongst the pine trees and buried them. The digging was hard, but it got rid of her nervous energy. The clothes would gradually decompose. So what if they were found? Who was going to be interested in old shoes, an empty handbag and a few odd bits of cloth? All sorts of rubbish turned up on beaches.

Justine dug a separate, deeper hole for the knife and gazed at it for a few seconds by the light of the torch. Ronnie Davis must be lying a mortuary fridge now, all neatly sewn up ready for display in the funeral parlour, her fatal stab wound in his cold dead heart.

'Rot in hell, bastard!' she cried. 'I'm still here – you didn't destroy me! No one will!' The wind tore the words from her lips and whirled them away into the darkness. She dropped the knife into the hole and covered it with sandy earth. Speaking those words and burying the knife was like a kind of vengeful ritual. It gave her temporary peace. She quickly strewed twigs and cracked branches over the place. The pouring rain would wash the sand off her trainers and car tyres. Even if the knife were to be discovered, who could connect it with her?

Wind and salty sea spray lashed her face and made her eyes sting. She was soaked, freezing cold. She turned, sprinted back to the car and drove off down the track. There was nobody about. The stormy weather would keep psychopaths and courting couples alike at home.

Justine drove fast and skilfully and got home within fifteen minutes. There was still no sign of Matthew or his car in Aigburth Drive. She garaged the BMW, raced panting across the lawn and back up the fire escape. Damn! she thought. I forgot to switch the kitchen light off. She unlocked the door and stepped inside.

Paul sat at the table, a mug of tea in front of him. He wore Adam's old navy blue bathrobe that was kept for guests, and his dark hair was tousled. His grey eyes looked tired. He studied her pale, frightened face and wild hair, the soaked jeans and muddy trainers.

'Hello', he said calmly. 'I couldn't sleep either. Fancy a cup of tea?'

'I went back to the hospital to check on Adam,' stammered Justine. 'I was worried.'

'Of course you were.' Why was she lying? Paul couldn't imagine what had driven Justine to brave the dark, stormy night alone, risk being attacked and murdered by the stalker. But he didn't believe it had anything to do with Adam.

'I know you would have given me a lift,' she said quickly. 'But I didn't want to disturb you.' She dropped the keys, pulled off her jacket and threw it on a chair.

'Sit down,' he said. 'You look exhausted.'

Justine collapsed on to a chair, picked up the bottle of white wine and gulped a few mouthfuls. Then she leaned forward, sighed and closed her eyes.

'Are you okay?' Paul asked slowly. 'I mean ... given the circumstances?'

'No,' she whispered. A tear glittered on her cheek. 'I am not okay!'

'Justine ...' He reached across the table and grabbed her cold hand. She gasped and looked up. 'Why don't you tell me what's really going on?'

'Believe me,' she sighed, 'you don't want to know!'

'Yes, I do.' He kept hold of her hand. 'I want you to talk to me.' He gazed into her beautiful, sombre eyes, overwhelmed by love and desire and the urgent need to protect her. 'I want you to tell me everything.'

'All right.' She brushed away the tear, looked down at his hand covering hers. Hesitated. 'Paul, what if ... what would you say if I told you I'd killed a man?'

# Chapter Twenty-One

'I'm going to stay with my girlfriend for a couple of days,'
Matthew announced importantly. 'I'll go after breakfast.'

'You what?' His mother glanced round in surprise as he bounded
into the kitchen. What the hell was he doing up at seven in the morning? She was exhausted after lying awake all night, groggy from
the sleeping pills that didn't start working until it was time to get
up. She remembered when she could pop one and go out like a
light, be dead to the cruel world for eight wonderful hours.

'Stay with my girlfriend, I said.' Matthew clenched his fist and
punched the air. '*Thick!*'

He had bathed and shaved: the terrible sweet smell of that
aftershave was enough to make your toes curl, Paula thought.
He'd brushed his teeth too even though all the toothpaste on the
planet wasn't going to brighten their dingy yellow shade. The
bleached stubble on his head already showed dark roots. He wore
yesterday's jeans and beige sweater, his last clean black T-shirt
underneath. Paula hadn't been able to do another load of washing
yesterday; she had run out of soap powder and didn't have the
energy to walk to the supermarket and lug back another heavy
packet.

The kettle boiled and she filled the teapot and moved her plate
of toast and marmalade from the table to the draining board. Too
late. Matthew snatched the toast and started munching it. He
attacked food like a wild animal tearing its prey, fearful that a
stronger predator would come along before it could fill its belly.
Paula looked out at the rainy back garden with its smoke-
blackened grass, the depressing low thick cloud layer. What was
there to get up for anyway?

Not even a skinful of Moggies and Valium could give her the peaceful night's sleep she craved. She was scared stiff, had terrible indigestion, couldn't stop thinking about the ghastly magazines in his suitcase. They were a silent, poisonous presence in the house, like leaking carbon monoxide. An invisible axe poised, ready to fall at any moment and hack apart her life. What *life*?

'You've got a girlfriend?' she asked, astonished and disbelieving. Then again, there was always someone daft or desperate enough. He'd lived with that Tracey, hadn't he? Until she'd regained her sanity and kicked him out.

' 'Course I have,' Matthew said aggressively. 'Why shouldn't I?' He grabbed her handbag and rooted in her purse. 'A fiver? Is that all you've got?' he grumbled. He folded the note and pushed it into his back pocket, crammed more toast into his mouth. 'Do us another few rounds,' he ordered. 'With bacon and two fried eggs. Baked beans.' He poured himself a mug of tea. 'Move your arse,' he said impatiently. 'I've got to go out soon.' He wanted to get to Justine's before eight o'clock. He wondered what time the mad hippie was leaving.

'Matthew . . .'. Paula couldn't remember the last time she had addressed her son by his Christian name. She faced him, clutched her pink wool dressing gown around her thin body. 'Don't do anything stupid, will you?' she pleaded. 'Don't cause any more trouble. I just want a bit of peace, that's all!'

'What are you on about, you demented old bat?' he shouted, startling her. 'Shut your face and get my fucking breakfast on! I'm already pissed off because I haven't got clean clothes for today.' He raised his clenched fist and she shrank back with a cry of alarm. 'You know what'll happen if you give me any crap! How many more times do I have to spell it out?'

'Leave me alone,' Paula whimpered, her eyes filling with tears. 'I won't say a word to anyone, you know that.'

'You'd better not. Keep it *shut*!' He pointed to the stained cooker. 'Breakfast!'

He turned and strode into the living room, switched the television on and flung himself into the armchair. Shame he couldn't let himself into the flat and grab Justine before she left for the hospital. But he had to wait until the mad hippie had gone. He'd

245

decided to kill Adam after he'd dealt with Justine, finish the job properly. He couldn't risk Adam waking up and not being a vegetable. He might remember everything, would certainly talk once he knew his precious slut was dead. Matthew grinned. He knew where he could get hold of a suitable weapon – and have some fun at the same time.

Paula brought his breakfast on a tray. He began to eat voraciously then sat up and stared as a photograph of the murdered policeman, Ronnie Davis, flashed on to the screen. Davis' plod mates were still appealing for witnesses to come forward. Matthew himself was the main witness in the '*murder*' case, of course. He alone knew the truth, had the power! He laughed with delight and slapped his thigh, causing baked beans to slide off his plate on to the tray.

After breakfast he went upstairs and grabbed his things, rushed out of the house and drove off, heading for Sefton Park. The rain was coming down hard, lashing the roads and pavements; he could barely see to drive. He pulled up at traffic lights and glanced at himself in the driving mirror. The dark roots were coming up nicely. He was already bored with being blond. People looked at him as though he was mental.

Paula slowly climbed the stairs, sighing and groaning at the indigestion that burned her throat and stomach and clamped her chest like an iron band. Was she imagining it or did her left arm and the fingers of her left hand feel a bit numb? She went into Matthew's bedroom, got stiffly on to her aching knees and pulled the suitcase out from under the bed. Unzipped it.

The rope and leather collar were gone.

The pissing rain rolled off the long dark green plastic mac that reached almost to his trainers. The mac was a relic from his sad bicycle days. He looked like a bloody monk, Matthew thought irritably, as he parked the Ford Fiesta and walked around the corner into Aigburth Drive. He didn't dare park too near Justine's house in case the police cruised past. The cracked Amazon with the tits was always walking that rottweiler, and her gun-toting old bat of a mother had nothing to do but gawp from behind the red velvet curtains all day.

Cold water droplets dripped off the hood's brim and ran down his nose and chin. He shivered and swore, grasped the crumpled white carrier bag. He hated the rain, but at least it meant he could disguise himself with the mac.

The big chestnut trees in the park and along Aigburth Drive were bright green in the rain. People hurried to their cars or headed for the railway station or the bus stop on the main road, careful not to poke out anyone's eye with their umbrellas. There were the usual diehard joggers and dog walkers, people who hadn't a clue what it meant to put in a day's work.

Matthew reached the house and strolled to and fro on the opposite side of the road, kept his head down and hid behind the chestnut trees. It infuriated him that he had to watch out for police cars. He would never forgive Justine for betraying him. That had sealed her fate. Calling him lowlife scum, screaming at him, rejecting him even when she knew he was the only one who could satisfy her. She would pay, by Christ she would! The photo and note he'd slipped through the letter box yesterday would give her an idea of what she was in for. She must be scared shitless now!

He sneaked up the drive of the neighbouring house, grabbed a tree branch and hoisted himself up on to the high brick wall. It was more of a struggle than he'd anticipated. But he didn't dare go up Justine's drive and across the front of the house where Amazon tits or her mad mother might spot him. He dropped over the wall and crash-landed in the bushes down the side of the house, a few feet opposite Justine's front door.

'Fuck!' he whined, biting his lip as pain shot through his right ankle. He bent to examine it. It wasn't broken or twisted, he had just landed awkwardly. He gripped the carrier bag and squatted amongst wet golden laurel and rosemary bushes, his back to the wall. Trees loomed above him, dripping rain. Sodden leaves drifted down, their colours changing to autumnal browns and gold. He pulled the hood further over his face. The mac blended well with the background.

He checked the bag's contents. Rope, leather collar, bread knife, the small bottle that contained about thirty sleeping pills. Paula swallowed the bloody things like sweets, had bottles of them all over the house. 'Mrs P. Casey' was typed neatly on the white label, together with Paula's address and last Wednesday's date, 11 September. Matthew frowned. If he were her doctor he'd give her a lethal injection, not sleeping pills.

Miserable old cow! He felt in his pocket for Justine's stolen keys.

A shiny black Mercedes S300 was parked a few yards away, wet leaves stuck to its roof and bonnet. Matthew frowned and blinked as he peered through the bushes. He'd seen that car before. Who did it belong to? Its presence nagged at him. He settled down and prepared to wait.

It would be hard to watch Justine come out of her front door, get into her poncy car and drive off. She might come out soon, give the hippie a lift to the station. Then he would go in. Stuck-up bitch! he thought furiously. She wouldn't be so full of it when he was fucking her lights out, choking her with the leather collar. He closed his eyes and heard her terrified, strangled cries, saw himself hurting her, triumphant at her pathetic, exposed helplessness. He would tie up her tits first, he thought, remembering the magazine article on Japanese bondage. Although the step-by-step instructions for tying a woman's breasts in a rope bra seemed quite complicated. But worth the effort! His penis stiffened.

Matthew slipped one hand beneath the wet mac, unzipped his jeans and closed it over his erection, beginning to feel warm and relaxed despite the cold rain. The pain in his ankle died to a throbbing ache.

The front door suddenly opened. Matthew clumsily tried to zip up his jeans. The zip stuck in his underpants. He freed his hand and cautiously parted the bushes to get a better look. Justine was coming out! She wore tight black pants which flared slightly to cover the tops of her flash New Balance trainers, a tight purple ribbed sweater that emphasized her tits – at least she wore a bra this morning! – and a long black silk raincoat. A black leather bag was slung over her left shoulder. Matthew couldn't believe she was only a few feet away from him, standing at the top of the steps across the narrow cinder path.

The damp rainy air made her hair look more curly, its colour rich in the dull, early-morning light. The blue of her eyes was intense, the lashes long and dark. Funny to have dark lashes and eyebrows with red-gold hair. She wore makeup, but not much. Sexy, shiny, red lipstick, not too red.

He crouched in the bushes, hardly daring to breathe. He slid his hand into the carrier bag and gripped the breadknife in case she spotted him. But Justine wasn't looking in his direction. Matthew started. There was somebody with her. A man! His heart pounded with shock and dismay.

She glanced up and smiled shyly as the tall, handsome, dark-haired man in the leather jacket, whom Matthew recognized from the day before, unfurled an umbrella and held it protectively over her. He held his breath and stared in horrified dismay as the man slid one arm around Justine's slender shoulders and hugged her to him, kissed her lightly on the cheek.

'I know it's nerve-racking,' he said. 'But I'm sure you'll be fine. Don't let them intimidate you.'

What was he on about? They came down the wet stone steps and walked quickly to the Mercedes. The man pointed a remote control device to unlock the car, held the passenger door open for Justine as she threw her bag on the floor and got in. He couldn't take his eyes off her!

Matthew groaned in agony and let the knife drop back into the bag. The Mercedes reversed, engine purring, and accelerated away. The bastard had fucked Justine, Matthew was sure. Over and over, all night probably. He'd given her that '*this is mine*' look. Matthew's chest heaved and his heart thudded with shock and fury at the terrible setback. How was he supposed to get her now? The slag didn't waste any time, he thought savagely. One man down, another taking his place in her bed before the week was out! She was evil, insatiable!

'Think,' he muttered, chewing his lip and blinking furiously. '*Think.*'

It would be all right, he decided after a minute. He'd go in now and if the hippie was still there, too bad. For her! If Justine came back alone, great. If not, that was okay too. The man might be tall and strong and tough-looking, but Matthew had the advantage of surprise. He could grab Justine, hold the knife to her throat and make the bastard swallow a handful of sleeping pills. It wouldn't take long before he passed out. Then . . . party time!

'Yes!' he breathed.

Matthew tilted back his head and laughed at the grey sky. Cold rain fell on his face and ran down his neck. He felt fantastic again, charged with new energy. He pulled Justine's keys from his pocket, bounded up the wet stone steps and kicked over the two pots of withered geraniums.

The first key wouldn't fit either of the locks. He swore and tried another. The second and third didn't fit either. He tried again. What was wrong?

'Come on!' he shouted, wriggling the key as he tried desperately to insert it.

'Fuck!' He kicked viciously at the door then tried again, wet fingers shaking with rage and frustration. None of the keys fitted.

Matthew couldn't understand it. Why the hell didn't they fit? He dropped them and snatched them up. Had he taken the mad hippie's keys by mistake? No way, José. They were definitely Justine's keys. He swore again as he realized he'd left the incriminating carrier bag in the bushes.

'Christ!' he shouted hoarsely. 'You're really bloody losing it, you are!' He turned and started back down the steps, tripped over a geranium pot and nearly fell headlong. He regained his balance and looked back at the door. He realized that the two locks were shiny and brand new, stronger than the old ones. The dark blue paint around them was slightly chipped and flaking. He couldn't get in because Justine had had the locks changed.

'No!' he roared, kicking the door. 'No! You fucking bitch, I'll kill you!' He felt he would go crazy with frustration at this second huge setback. Justine was still fighting, still thought she could beat him. She was laughing at him now, thinking how easy it was to stay one step ahead of *the creep*.

The police car pulled into the drive and screeched to a halt by the wall. A truculent, nervous-looking Charley Bluff opened her front door and stood waiting at the top of the steps, arms folded protectively across her massive chest. Two heavily built male officers jumped out and raced down the side of the house towards Matthew, truncheons and CS gas sprays at the ready. He stopped kicking the door and stared at them in shock.

'Who's this – Brother Cadfael? All right, soft lad!' one of them shouted. 'What the bloody hell d'you think you're doing?'

'I'm not doing anything!' Matthew tried to make a run for it but they grabbed him and twisted his arms up behind his back. 'Stop it!' he yelled in pain. 'You'll break me bloody arms, you bastards!'

'Oh, dear, sorry about that, sir!' one of the officers laughed. 'Maybe you'd care to file a complaint? Shut it!' he snarled.

Rain drummed on the soiled white carrier bag beneath the

golden laurel and rosemary bushes as Matthew was handcuffed and dragged to the waiting car.

'Paul? I'm at the warehouse.' Gary Jones, Head of Technical Supplies at Melwood Materials, sounded worried. 'We've completed the checks you ordered on the beryllium consignment.' He paused. 'The stuff's contaminated with enriched uranium.'

'*What*?' Paul sat up straight and gripped the phone. Adriana, sitting opposite, looked curiously at him. Rain pattered on the big windows and mist hung over Canada Dock and the river. The Mersey was as grey as the sky.

'Don't worry too much,' Gary said. 'I mean, this isn't an emergency situation. It's not dangerous.'

'Not *dangerous*?' Paul echoed angrily. 'What are you on, Gary?'

'I'm saying, it's not the whole consignment. At first we thought it was worse than it is. The level of uranium contamination is down to between one and two hundred grams. There's three tons of beryllium here. That's what I mean when I say it's not dangerous.'

'I see. Hang on a minute.' Paul glanced at Adriana sitting stiffly in her neat baby blue tight-fitting suit, a curtain of blonde hair over her shoulders. Her long legs were crossed and her arms folded. She tried to look bored but underneath he could see something else. She was apprehensive. 'Would you mind waiting outside?' he asked politely. 'I need to take this call in private.'

'Of course.' She got up and walked gracefully out of the office, taking her glass of mineral water with her. What was going on? she wondered. Another problem? She was fed up, desperate to get this deal closed. In the outer office she smiled at Paul's secretary. 'Terrible weather again.'

'The beryllium's been exported illegally,' Paul said in a low voice after the door closed softly. 'I had my doubts about the purchase order and export licence, but I thought it'd be all right. I should have realized it was too bloody good to be true.'

Of course Adriana knew about the uranium contamination. It explained her nervousness, her hurry. She wanted to get her two million dollars and disappear before the scam was discovered. The sample had been all right, but not the rest. Now he was stuck with a consignment of beryllium that he might not be able to sell on. Might not be able to do bloody anything with.

He could end up in jail for this. Or worse. Adriana Terekhova was almost certainly one of the faces of Russian organized crime. Did Ivanovich know? Must do since he had recommended her. Paul couldn't trust him now either. Adriana must have got hold of the beryllium from some down and out scientist at a clapped out nuclear institution, was trying to flog it and make big money for herself. Now he was as up to his neck in it as she was.

'Shit!' he breathed down the phone. He felt furious. Scared. He had to back out of this deal. But how? To go ahead could prove dangerous; to back out even more so. Gary waited silently. Geiger counters chattered as white-overalled men moved amongst the wooden crates in the chilly warehouse basement.

'The place needs to be de-contaminated,' he said finally. 'The stuff shifted. Fast.'

'I do realize that, Gary. Just get on with it, okay?'

'Shouldn't you call the police?' he asked. 'Or MI5? I don't know ... whoever deals with trafficking in nuclear materials? This stuff's probably been nicked.'

'All right, Gary,' Paul said sharply. 'I'll handle this. I'll get back to you later.'

'Okay. We'll carry on here.'

Paul hung up and leaned his elbows on the desk, rubbed his tired eyes. Then he swivelled round in his chair, lay back and stared out at the misty river. If he went to the police or MI5 he would be dead meat, he knew that much. After a minute he got up and opened the door. Adriana was sitting on the sofa in the outer office, calmly sipping mineral water. Paul wished that water came from Chernobyl! He had that feeling again, the sense of the black void that lay behind her smiling, beautiful, elegant façade. Adriana felt no compassion, no empathy, no warmth. *Nothing.* That was what frightened him.

'Sorry to keep you waiting.'

'No problem.' She smiled frostily and got up. He held the door open for her.

'I suppose there's no point in my asking you why you didn't tell me the beryllium consignment was contaminated with enriched uranium,' he said when they were seated again. 'And therefore not legally exportable even under Russian law.'

Adriana imploded with rage and panic. Paul Melwood had rejected her and might now try to reject this deal. It had to go through!

'I didn't tell you, Paul, because you didn't want to know,' she said evenly. She pushed back her hair and stared boldly at him.

He was uncomfortably aware of that. 'You've put me in an impossible position.'

'Come on!' She smiled. 'What's so impossible about it? You can still sell the beryllium and make a fantastic profit. More than I'll make,' she added, her blue eyes openly hostile for the first time.

'I don't think I can sell it now. Not legally, that's for sure. The deal's off,' he said abruptly. 'You can ship that stuff right back to wherever it was stolen from.'

'No!' Adriana gasped. She glared at him. 'You can't back out now. You owe me two million dollars.'

'You lied to me. I don't owe you anything. Look,' he said, 'don't worry, I'm not stupid. I won't go to the police or the security services, get myself in trouble as well as you. I don't want to spend the next fifteen years in Strangeways or wherever. I just want that stuff out of my warehouse. You can look for another buyer.' He paused. 'Another sucker!'

Adriana was silent for a few seconds. 'Exactly how much contamination is there?' she asked suddenly.

'As if you don't know! Between one and two hundred grams,' he replied. 'What difference does that make?'

'A big difference.' She sat down. 'Paul, that's nothing! The buyer won't care about that, he won't even notice. No one will know.'

'*I* know,' Paul said grimly. 'Gary Jones, my technical support manager, knows.'

'Gary Jones?' Adriana laughed. 'What a boring English name!'

'The deal's off,' he repeated. 'I want the beryllium shipped out.'

'Paul, please don't throw away this fantastic opportunity.' Adriana paused. 'Or your life,' she added slowly.

'Right, that's it.' He stood up, trying to conceal his shock and fear, and pointed to the door. 'Get out. Now!'

Adriana didn't move. 'And Sara,' she went on. 'You plan to divorce her, don't you? Not kill her. Or maybe you'd be happy if she died. You see, Paul, I know who you really care about.' She smiled, but her blue eyes were like ice. 'Who's that oh-so-beautiful lady with the wonderful red hair?' she asked softly. 'You spent last night with her. She's making me very jealous!'

For a few seconds Paul couldn't breathe or speak. How did she know about Justine? He stared at Adriana, his mouth dry with shock. She must have had him followed. Or tailed him herself.

'That lady is a friend of ours – Sara's and mine,' he said, as calmly as he could. 'She was in trouble and I helped her out. That's all!'

'Come on, Paul, you don't really expect me to believe that? Sara thought I was her when she interrupted our telephone conversation the other day, didn't she? Is your beautiful girlfriend really pregnant with your child? You must be very proud.'

'She's not my girlfriend and she isn't pregnant – certainly not by me! This is bullshit!' he said, turning pale. 'You've got it all wrong.'

'Have I? Then you won't care too much if anything happens to her. Is she the reason you rejected me? I hate her already!' Adriana teased.

'If you touch ... If you harm her, I'll kill you!' Paul said fiercely. He was horrified. 'I mean that. I don't give a damn about myself!'

'Don't be so melodramatic, Paul.' Adriana suddenly felt sad at the passion in his dark grey eyes, his obvious love for this woman, whoever she was, his dread that she might be harmed. No man had ever felt that way about her. 'There's no need for anyone to die. Nothing bad will happen – as long as you bring two million US dollars in cash to my hotel room on Friday. At twelve noon,' she said. 'That's a good time for me.'

Paul was silent, staring at the photograph of his grandfather. He had to go through with the deal now. He couldn't risk Justine or Sara being hurt, maybe killed. If he was murdered by the Russian Mafia or banged up for years, that was his problem. He had got himself into this mess and must bear the consequences.

He closed his eyes for a second as the painful, agonizing reality of his love for Justine crashed over him. He was already worried sick for her, especially after the terrible story she had spilled out to him last night, sitting at the kitchen table drinking wine. About how she had killed Ronnie Davis in self-defence and was terrified

254

of being arrested and accused of murder. Now she faced yet more danger. He couldn't bear the idea that she might be hurt, could even die, because of this bloody awful mess he'd got himself into! He had to protect her.

'Okay.' Adriana took her bag and stood up. 'I don't think there's anything else for us to discuss right now. It all seems pretty clear.' She smiled triumphantly at him, tossing back her hair. 'So, will I see you on Friday?' she challenged.

Paul didn't answer at first. Then he looked at her, his eyes sombre. 'You'll see me on Friday,' he said slowly.

'Excellent!' Adriana realized she'd been clenching her hands and forgetting to breathe, the way she always did when she was tense. Her neck and shoulders were stiff and aching. A good massage, she thought. That's what I need. She walked to the door and turned. 'You're an intelligent man, Paul. I knew you'd be sensible about this.'

It wouldn't hurt to give him a nudge, though.

Just to make sure he stayed sensible.

# Chapter Twenty-Two

The mesh-covered windows in the small interview room were too high for Justine to see out of and gave her a claustrophobic feeling. There was a green-and-black poster on the wall: *Have You Locked Your Car?* At least Kiely and his sidekick, a thirty-something detective constable named Bernadette Doyle, were not chain smoking and calling her '*love*'. Justine wondered what had happened to Stewart; maybe he had more important things with which to occupy his valuable time. Bernadette Doyle had a sharp face and a pale complexion, calm brown eyes and long straight brown hair. She wore a sad beige suit with a white shirt underneath. She kept staring at the glittering diamond engagement ring on the third finger of Justine's left hand.

'So,' Kiely said briskly, 'according to your statement, DC Davis approached you early in the evening in question and asked if he could buy you a drink. Which you refused.' Justine nodded, feeling scared and irritable. 'He and his mates then turned up at the next pub you and *your* mates went to – and you later saw him in the Crystal Cave nightclub in the city centre. Where you watched a striptease act,' he finished flatly.

'That wasn't my idea. I didn't want to watch strippers.' Justine realized that sounded feeble. 'It was a hen night, my friends had arranged everything.' She didn't want to think about that night, let alone answer questions about it.

'You later left the club in an upset state after your friend, Donna Gibson, confessed to you that she'd had sex with your fiancé, is that correct?'

'You know it is! How many more times do I have to explain this?' Justine asked angrily. 'The entire Merseyside police force must be splitting their sides laughing over my violated private life!'

'No one's laughing at you.' Kiely sat next to Bernadette Doyle, wearing a dark suit and sipping coffee. He liked Justine's ribbed purple sweater, or what he could see of it. She'd kept her black raincoat on and clutched her handbag as if it were a good luck charm. Or as if she expected to walk out at any minute. Her hair was slightly damp from the rain.

'Look, I'm sorry, but I really can't summon up much interest in your murder inquiry,' Justine said impatiently. 'For the simple reason that if you don't arrest that stalker soon you'll have to launch another one – for *me*. How much longer is this going to take?' she asked. 'I need to get back to Adam. You wanted me to make a statement and now I've done it.' She tapped her right foot against the floor and played with the handbag strap as she fought to stay calm. She was horribly on edge. A cigarette would have come in handy, but of course she didn't smoke any more! Her fingertips were stained with ink. Looking at them made her feel humiliated.

'Your friend Stephanie said Ronnie Davis was hassling you.' Bernadette spoke with a quiet Belfast accent.

'Okay, so he was hassling me. It happens, doesn't it? Occupational hazard of being female, or so we're encouraged to believe. Don't tell me you wouldn't have laughed me out of the nick if I'd reported that! He wanted me to dance with him but I said no, I had to leave. That was the last I saw of him. I ran out of that dump and took a cab home.' Justine thought of Davis' dead weight in the pitch black alley, the blood, the rain, the curious cab driver, how she couldn't stop shaking – and felt stirrings of panic. 'I didn't watch the news, I didn't even know this Ronnie Davis had been murdered at first.' She looked down at her hands, at the sparkling diamond ring on her finger. 'I had other things on my mind,' she said darkly. 'As you know.'

'We think something happened,' Kiely said. He and Bernadette looked closely at her. 'Something you're not telling us.'

For a second Justine experienced the curious suffocating feeling again, the frightening sensation that she wouldn't be able to catch her next breath. Her hands went cold and she felt light-headed. What the hell was wrong? It's panic, she told herself. Breathe slowly. She raised her head and looked at them.

'I've told you – I can't remember how many times! – I never saw the guy again after I'd left the club. I wish I'd never gone out that night,' she said bitterly.

'Did you have a lot to drink?' Bernadette Doyle looked at Justine's clenched hands. 'On your hen night?'

'There's no way I was drunk, if that's what you mean.'

'Why won't you tell us the truth?' Kiely asked angrily. This was going nowhere and he was losing patience. 'DC Davis followed you out of that club. He must have caught up with you . . .

'He didn't! I never saw him!'

'Maybe you saw his killer. You could have been the last person to see him alive. Why won't you cooperate with us?'

'I am!' Justine cried, panicked. 'I didn't see anything and I don't know anything. Except that I'll end up murdered as well, if you don't arrest that stalker!'

Kiely looked at her distraught face and wondered whether or not to believe her. 'Snow White', Stewart had sneeringly labelled her. They had no leads, nothing to go on. Not even a murder weapon. Only Justine Flynn, who was oddly reluctant to talk about her hen night. 'What were you wearing that evening?' he asked suddenly.

'What?' she gasped. '*Why*? Don't you dare try to say I provoked him into hassling me!' she said fiercely. 'That argument went out with the Stone Age, or hadn't you heard? Although I realize the police and the entire British legal establishment can't seem to move on from that distant period in history!'

'I wouldn't dream of saying you provoked him!' Kiely's anger mounted. Because he was a policeman, she automatically assumed he was a reactionary, sexist dinosaur. 'There's a perfectly valid reason for my question,' he said sharply. 'So please answer it.'

'I wore a black dress and black shoes. A longish dress,' she said defensively. What was Kiely getting at? She struggled to think straight, control her panic.

'Thank you.' He picked up a pen and scribbled something she couldn't read upside down. 'Was it a tight dress?'

'Close-fitting!'

'Did the shoes have high heels?'

'High-ish,' she admitted sullenly. 'I suppose.'

258

'Right. So, wearing a long, close-fitting dress and high heels, you could walk or run faster than a six-foot tall, *fit* man who followed you out of a club?'

'*I never saw him again!*'

'So you keep saying. We'd like to take a look around your flat,' he said. 'See the dress and shoes you wore that night.'

'No way!' She went icy with fright again as she pictured the dark, stormy beach where her bloodied clothes were buried. 'Not unless you have reasonable suspicion of something – I can't think what! – to obtain a search warrant. And you have no *reasonable* suspicion. You've dusted the place for fingerprints, and that's where it stops!'

Fortunately, her wardrobe contained several other black dresses and pairs of high-heeled shoes that she could produce if they insisted. The dress she had in mind was shorter than the one she'd worn that night, and had a different neckline. But nobody would know, not even Donna, Stephanie or the others. Who ever remembered the exact details of another person's clothing? Most people weren't that observant, especially in a dark crowded nightclub with a few drinks down their necks, desperately seeking the partner of their dreams. Justine stood up.

'I've had enough of this,' she said abruptly. 'I'm not wasting any more time here. I want to get back to Adam.'

'Even after he cheated on you with your best friend?' Bernadette asked softly. Justine ignored the remark, wouldn't look at her.

'Would you like to read over and sign your statement before you go?' Kiely pushed a pen towards her. 'Or possibly tear it up?'

'I don't need to read it over.' Justine scrawled her signature, flung the pen back at him and walked to the door, hoping they wouldn't try to stop her.

'We may need you to come back and talk to us again,' Kiely called. He winced as the door slammed. Bernadette gathered her papers and looked at him expectantly.

'D'you still think she was the last person to see Ronnie alive?'

'Yes, and I still think she saw something. Of course I can't prove it.' Kiely frowned, looked at her. 'You didn't like Ronnie, did you?'

'I didn't have much contact with him. But, no.' Bernadette shook her head. 'To be honest, I thought he was a bit of a creep.

He was friendly enough, I'll give him that. But I had the feeling it was all an act.' She thought for a second. 'Maybe Ronnie caught her up and hassled her again. Or worse! Or maybe she saw someone attack him and now she's too scared to tell us in case she gets herself into trouble.'

'She'll get into more trouble if she doesn't,' Kiely said grimly. 'She knows something, I'm sure. I'd like to take a look around that flat, just out of curiosity. But she's right, there's no grounds for a search warrant.' He paused. 'Maybe she murdered him.'

'Yeah, right!' Bernadette laughed. 'A six-foot tall, *fit* man . . .' she mocked.

'Okay, okay! We'll try some more people Ronnie got sent down,' Kiely sighed.

'There's a few lined up for a chat. One's a real hard case, Danny Easton, he got out of Strangeways last week. He made a lot of threats against Ronnie.'

'What about Flynn's stalker?' Bernadette asked. 'You'd better pick him up quick-sharp if you want to talk to her again.'

'We're working on it.'

Justine walked quickly out of the police station. I'm dead! she thought, giving in to panic. I'll be murdered by Matthew or else go down for killing Ronnie Davis. They'd never believe it was self-defence, certainly not now. She shivered with horror and burst into tears, imagining the police searching the flat, putting their hands on her and Adam's private, personal, intimate things. It made her sick to think of it; it was as bad as Matthew being there. She wanted to talk to Paul again. He would listen, help her. She realized she was starting to depend on him emotionally.

An auburn-haired woman in blue jeans and a black puffa jacket sitting smoking near the entrance stared after Justine as she ran out. She got up, trod on her half-smoked cigarette and followed.

'Hey, love!' she called as Justine stumbled down the rainy concrete steps, pulling her mac tight around her. 'You all right?'

Justine stopped and turned, her face streaked with tears. She looked at the woman with amazement.

'You're Ronnie Davis' wife! Sorry . . . widow,' she corrected herself quickly.

'Chantelle.' She couldn't believe she was actually seeing,

meeting this woman about whom she'd thought and wondered so much over the past few days. 'I saw you on television,' she said. 'The press appeal.'

'Yeah,' Chantelle said grimly, coming down the steps towards her. 'Right bloody celebrity I am, and enjoying every minute.' She had a husky voice and her Scouse accent was strong. 'Shame I haven't got the cash to go with it. I'd love to go mad in Tesco Village, get me kids anything they wanted.'

It wasn't exactly clever to talk like that but Ronnie's death did make it seem like Christmas, even with his grief-stricken parents and brothers looking at her as if they thought she was the one who should have been stiffed in a dark alley! Chantelle also felt drawn towards this lovely-looking woman. Why was she so upset? A woman who ran sobbing out of a police station might be on her side, and Chartelle desperately needed someone on her side. Someone she could talk to.

'What are you doing here?' Justine asked curiously.

'I was supposed to come and collect a few of Ronnie's things,' Chantelle explained, reaching in her bag for cigarettes. 'They probably thought I'd want them to weep over! I know he had a photo of me and the kids on his desk.' She grimaced. 'Trying to give the impression he was human. It was taken in between kickings.' Justine flinched. Chantelle lit the cigarette and took a drag. 'They've kept me waiting ages, so sod his bloody things.' She blew out smoke. 'This sounds mad,' she said, looking at Justine, 'but I feel like I know you.'

'Well, I'm a bloody celebrity too. Or will be, once I've been murdered.'

'Eh?' It was Chantelle's turn to flinch. 'What d'you mean?'

'Nothing,' Justine said awkwardly, backing off. They stared at one another. 'My name's Justine Flynn,' she said. 'I'm the fiancée of the doctor who was badly injured in a hit-and-run incident. I don't know if you heard about it? Maybe someone took my picture, there have been journalists sniffing around.' Not only journalists.

'Yeah, I heard about that.' Chantelle nodded sympathetically. 'It was terrible. How's he doing, your fella?'

Justine blinked back more tears. 'Not so good,' she muttered. 'At least he's regained consciousness. I was terrified that he'd . . .' She bowed her head, couldn't finish the sentence.

'It gave me the creeps, seeing you run out crying like that. What have those bastards done to you? What's up?' Chantelle asked.

I stabbed your husband to death in self-defence and now I'm terrified I'll be done for his murder! What could she say to this woman? Justine looked into Chantelle's reddened hazel eyes, saw the sorrow, fear and anguish there. Chantelle had a coarse, pale complexion and pale lips, a tiny crescent-shaped scar on her chin. There was another scar high on her right cheekbone, one that had needed stitches. It's true, Justine thought. Her life with that man was hell. But did Chantelle love him? Many women loved the men who abused them. She had a wild desire to spill out the truth, talk and talk until Ronnie Davis' widow knew everything. At the same time she wanted to run away.

'Why don't we go for coffee? Or a drink?' the other woman suggested, seeing Justine hesitate. 'Give you a chance to calm down.' She smiled as she exhaled smoke. 'I know I could do with a drink, a good big vodka. Haven't had one in ages.'

'I can't.' Justine wiped her eyes. 'I haven't got time.' Talking to this woman might be very dangerous.

'Go on,' Chantelle urged. 'You can spare half an hour, can't you, love? You'll feel better after a drink.'

'I don't know,' Justine muttered. 'I suppose so.'

'That's right.' Chantelle gently took her arm. 'Come on, let's get out of this bloody hole.'

The two women walked past the rows of parked police cars and out into the rainy city street.

In his office overlooking the car park Kiely impatiently grabbed his ringing phone and listened to the nervous, halting voice at the other end. A voice that anticipated trouble. Kiely leaned back in his chair and closed his eyes.

'Run that past me again,' he said slowly. 'You've only just realized *what*?' Bernadette Doyle turned away from the window and looked at him, her arms folded. 'Who was responsible for that?' he shouted furiously. 'I'll have their guts for garters! Bloody idiots! Right, I'm on my way.' He slammed the receiver down, jumped up and grabbed his jacket.

'What's happened?' Bernadette asked, startled. She'd never seen John Kiely anything but cool, calm and completely collected.

'Justine Flynn's stalker was finally picked up this morning,' he said grimly. 'Outside her house. A neighbour called the police. He must have been in here while we were taking Flynn's statement and talking to her.'

'*Been* here? What's with the past tense?'

'Some stupid bastard only let him go, that's what's with the past tense!' Kiely shouted, his face red with fury. 'A breakdown in communications, as they had the bloody nerve to say. Charged him with loitering and let him walk out of here, right under our bloody noses!' He glared at her. 'If that bastard's not banged up soon there'll be egg on my face and shit splattered all over the fan!'

'And Justine Flynn will be dead,' Bernadette said quietly.

Matthew was wet, cold, starving and totally peed off. His mother had better not nag him when he got home unexpectedly or he'd land her one. Miserable old bat! Pity they didn't burn witches any more. He got off the bus and walked back to where he'd left his Ford Fiesta. It was cold, still pouring with rain.

He couldn't believe the police had let him go. A fair-haired, long drink of water called Sean had solemnly warned him to behave himself from now on. Thank Christ he hadn't had the carrier bag on him when he'd been arrested! He had to get it back before someone discovered it. Rope, leather collar, breadknife, bottle of sleeping pills . . . even the plods would be able to work that one out. But he didn't dare go near the house again until dark. That bloody Amazon with the tits had spotted him and grassed him up, even though he'd been ultra careful. She and her old bat mother must be keeping a twenty-four-hour vigil. Neither of them had a man, of course. What man would want anything to do with the likes of that? The pair of them were like something out of *Night of the Living Dead*.

He would go home now, watch telly and get something to eat, take a nice hot bath to get the chill out of his bones. Pray no one found the bag before nightfall. It made him sweat with fear to think of it lying there. He walked around the corner into Aigburth Drive. He couldn't stay with his mother any longer either. The plods had released him by mistake, he felt sure. He was due to appear at the Magistrates Court in a few days' time, but there was no way he was going to keep that appointment! After that they would come to pick him up, now that they knew his address. He reached his car, stopped and stared with dismay.

'Christ! Jesus *Christ*!' The driver's window was smashed and the radio gone. Broken glass was scattered over the slashed seats and cold rain poured in, soaking the car's interior. Looked like they'd used a Stanley knife. The tyres were okay. He felt shocked, assaulted, full of rage. Kids or filthy, lowlife smackheads must have done it. This was Justine's fault too! He'd get her tonight. There would be no more fuck-ups.

He drove back to Old Roan, wind and rain blowing through the smashed window and freezing his arse off. He'd have to tape plastic over the window. He had no money for garage repairs that would cost a fortune. He had no bloody money for anything.

The house was cold and stale-smelling and there was no sound of radio or television. He dropped his wet mac on the hall floor and marched into the sitting room.

'*Bastards* did me bloody car in . . .' He paused at the sight of his mother. 'What's up with you?' he asked roughly.

Paula lay slumped in the middle of the sofa, still wearing her pink wool dressing gown and dirty slippers. She was grey-faced and sweating, her mouth open and her right hand clutched to her chest. Her thin chapped lips were blue.

'Can't . . . breathe!' she gasped. Her terrified dark eyes stared up at him. 'Terrible pain here.' She moved the hand on her chest, spread the fingers slightly. Her features creased in agony. 'Left arm's numb.' She made a huge effort. 'Call ambulance. Quick!'

Pain like she'd never known clamped her chest and body, crushed and suffocated her and made her break out in waves of sweat. She didn't know why her left arm had gone numb, but she knew the agonizing chest pain meant a heart attack. What luck Matthew was back so unexpectedly! She had never imagined she would be glad to see her son. Now for an ambulance, an oxygen mask, paramedics patting her hand and calling her love and telling her not to worry because everything would be fine. Another wave of sweat broke out on her body and her bowels heaved.

'Toilet!' she gasped. Although she didn't know how she'd get upstairs, not even with Matthew's help. He flinched and stared at her in disgust.

'I'm not taking you to the toilet, you dirty old cow! You must be joking!' He studied her and grinned suddenly. 'You're having a heart attack, aren't you?'

He felt nervous and excited. If he did nothing, his mother would die soon. All by herself without him having to lift a finger. He took a step towards her, his fists clenched.

'You never wanted me,' he said angrily. 'You ruined my life. You can die right there on that crappy old sofa. Don't think I'm shelling out for your funeral either. I'll get the council to throw you on the tip.'

Paula clutched one clawed hand to her chest and mewed frantically. She was filled with terror as the realization dawned that Matthew wasn't going to call an ambulance, he was just going to stand there and do sod all. Her blue lips moved, formed words that didn't come. She was helpless, her left arm lying uselessly by her side. He really hates me, she thought, seeing the fierce triumphant gleam in her son's eyes. But not as much as I hate him! The pain spread to her neck and jaw, made her thin body as stiff as a plank.

Why hadn't she killed him? It would have been so easy to empty a bottle of sleeping pills into his tea – he took so much sugar he wouldn't have noticed. Why hadn't she told the police about him? She had been afraid and now it was too late. Her body was gripped by a series of spasms and her bowels voided. She slid sideways, still staring up at him.

'You've shit yourself!' Matthew shouted, his face twisted with disgust. 'You filthy old bitch!' He strode to the window and glanced up and down the street, partially drew the curtains. Her face was as blue as her lips. It wouldn't be long now. Paula's eyelids fluttered and her eyeballs rolled upwards, showing the whites. He gasped with fear and ran out, slamming the door behind him.

He needed a drink. In the kitchen he opened cupboard doors and banged them shut, swearing furiously. He found a half-full bottle of cream sherry in the cupboard under the sink and gulped it, wincing at the sweetness. It wasn't strong enough, but it was better than nothing. It warmed his empty stomach and relaxed him. Bottle in hand, he stared out at the back garden, at the blackened patch of earth where he'd burned Ruby Jackson's garbage and the block of wood he'd used to murder the security guard. He glanced at the clock on the wall. Twenty-past twelve. He'd give his mother another fifteen minutes. He switched the radio on and paced the kitchen, gulping sherry.

When the fifteen minutes were up he walked out of the kitchen and hesitated outside the living room. Fear, revulsion, tremendous reluctance swept over him. How could you be sure someone was dead? Take their pulse, listen for breathing, hold a mirror to their lips? He could never locate his own pulse on the few occasions he'd been curious enough to attempt it. He'd have to touch his mother and he hadn't done that since he was a toddler. Except to feel the back of her hand. He shuddered, grimaced, blinked furiously.

He opened the door and walked slowly into the room. His mother's eyes were wide open, staring at the ceiling. Her face was blue and there was a horrible stink of shit. He bent over her, holding his nose, gingerly took her wrist and pressed three fingers to where he thought her pulse should be. Her flesh was cold and clammy. He felt nothing, no throb of life in her knotty veins. He dropped her wrist and pressed his hand to her flat chest then jumped back, sweating with fear. He felt sick.

She was dead all right. She wasn't going to wake up and ask when he was going to get a good job and look after her, give her money, a daughter-in-law, Sunday lunch with a lovely joint of roast lamb and a couple of grandchildren. Matthew started to laugh and went on laughing until he nearly choked. The old cow had got what she deserved. Fate kicking in to give him a break at last. His run of bad luck was over.

He ran upstairs and started carefully packing his suitcase. It was a shame he couldn't stay here by himself. But that was too risky, and of course he had no cash for rent, bills, all the expenses that went with living in your own house.

The old bitch was dead. He jumped up and punched the air with his fist. '*Yes!*'


'So they're not bothered about that bastard stalking you and sending you dildos and filthy pictures? Trying to murder your fella?' Chantelle shook her head in disbelief. 'They're hassling you because they think you could have been the last person to see Ronnie alive?'

'That's right.' Justine forced down another mouthful of the slice of Sachertorte Chantelle had persuaded her to eat, and sipped her second espresso. She didn't know what the hell she was doing here, except that she was too tired and desperate to think straight anymore. The café down the tiny side street near the Mersey smelled of chips, coffee, cigarettes and the day's special, home-made chilli chicken. The lunchtime crowd was pouring in; none of the hungry office workers took any notice of the two women sitting at a table by the window.

'Look, sorry to sound thick, but . . . I don't get it.' Chantelle lit another cigarette. 'I know Ronnie hassled you and you told him to get stuffed. But why do they reckon you were the last person to see him alive? I mean, he was with a gang of mates, and he must have spoken to other people as well. Why *you*?' She jumped as Justine's cake fork clattered against her plate. 'What's wrong?'

'Nothing!' Justine blanched, terrified again. 'I don't know, he . . .' She paused. 'Apparently he left that club right after I did,' she stammered, avoiding Chantelle's puzzled gaze. 'One of my friends saw him and made a statement. The police know he hassled me during the evening, and they think he followed me out of that club. But I never saw him again,' she lied shakily. Funny how she had suddenly lost her desire to confess all! Was she crazy, having a conversation with the widow – albeit merry widow – of the man she had killed in self-defence?

'What did Ronnie say to you?' Chantelle blew out smoke. 'No, don't tell me, I can guess. Wasn't exactly a smooth talker, eh? Came straight to the point, I bet!' Justine nodded, refusing to look at her. 'You were lucky,' she said, staring at Justine's white face and downcast eyes and wondering . . . what? 'When Ronnie doesn't – ha! – *didn't* get it handed to him on a plate, he usually took what he wanted.' She paused, dragged on her cigarette. 'By force.' Justine was silent, strained, fighting back tears. 'Are you sure you're all right, love?' asked Chantelle.

'I'm fine.' She glanced at her watch. 'Actually, I should be going now.'

'They asked me if I knew anyone with a grudge against Ronnie,' Chantelle went on, as if she hadn't spoken. 'They're chasing up ex-cons he put away, fellas who got out during the past couple of months.' She smiled. 'They won't get much joy there.'

Justine looked at her. 'Why not?' she asked tightly.

'Because I'm pretty sure it wasn't some sad old lag killed Ronnie.' Chantelle took another hungry drag on her cigarette. 'His mates, his family, all thought the sun shone out of his arse. But I was Ronnie's wife,' she said huskily. 'I knew different, didn't I? Same old, same old!' She gently touched the scars on her chin and cheekbone with a ragged, bitten fingernail. 'I didn't get these walking into doors when I'd been on the sauce. Though that's what Ronnie told everyone. What a stupid cow, eh?' she grimaced. 'Not fit to be let out. You wouldn't think people believed crap like that nowadays, would you? But they did. Gave them a right giggle.' She picked up her glass of red wine and took a swig. 'Shame they don't have vodka here,' she remarked.

'So . . .' Justine could barely breathe. 'What do you think happened that night?'

'I think he attacked some girl or woman, tried to rape her.' Justine flinched and turned pale again, tried to hide her shocked reaction. But she didn't quite succeed. Chantelle stared at her again with a flash of intuition. 'She wasn't the first, and she wouldn't have been the last. 'He'd taken his knife with him, and that was always bad news. But this time he picked the wrong one. Someone with guts who fought back. I don't think she meant to stiff him, but I'm glad she did. I hated the bastard! I'm chuffed he's dead. So are the kids.'

Justine jerked her head up and stared back at her. Tears glittered in her eyes.

'She was clever enough not to leave the knife there,' Chantelle went on slowly. 'Didn't think the police would believe it was self-defence. Couldn't face all the crap she would have been put through. They keep saying things have changed but . . .' She heaved a long sigh. 'Yeah, she fought back. Not like me all these years,' she said bitterly, crushing out her cigarette in the cut-glass ashtray. 'Bloody soft girl, that's what I was! Bought meself a new dress from Dorothy Perkins, got some lipstick and eyeshadow in Boots, went clubbing and fell for a fucking psycho!'

'Don't blame yourself, for Christ's sake!' Justine reached across the table and grasped Chantelle's hand. 'Any woman would be terrified of a man like that. What about your family and friends?' she asked gently. 'Were you too frightened to tell them, ask for help? Did none of them suspect what was going on?'

'Me mam and a couple of mates – I've lost touch with most of me mates – guessed Ronnie landed me one now and then. But they didn't realize how violent he was, and I was too scared and ashamed to tell them. They had their own problems. Besides, you don't like telling people your husband beats the crap out of you! You feel like it's your fault, like you were a bloody idiot for not realising what he was before you got manacled to him. Anyway,'

Chantelle said briskly, 'let's get back to you.' She lit another cigarette and sipped her wine.

'You're supposed to sit tight and hope this stalker doesn't murder you?'

Justine shrugged tiredly. 'The police tell me they'll pick him up soon, that they're keeping an eye on my house. Of course they can't do twenty-four-hour surveillance,' she said. 'I realize that.'

'Be nice if they could just do their job, eh?'

The whole conversation had an air of unreality about it. She and Chantelle were sitting talking as if they were close friends, had known one another for years. But it felt that way. Justine kept glancing at the spare chair on which they'd dumped their bags, imagining Ronnie Davis' bloody corpse slumped there, accusing her like Banquo's ghost at Macbeth's dinner party.

'Listen,' she began. She picked up the tiny espresso cup and put it down again. 'It's been . . . interesting to meet you, but I really have to get to the hospital. Adam will wonder where I am.'

'Hang on a minute!' Chantelle dragged on her cigarette and pushed back her rough auburn hair. 'You're the first person I've been able to talk to in ages,' she said, hazel eyes pleading. 'I'd like us to be mates, Justine. You won't, will you?' she asked suddenly. 'Let that bastard murder you?'

Justine looked warily around the café. 'If it was down to me, I'd murder *him*!' she said in a low voice. Her eyes flooded with tears. 'I hate seeing Adam lying in that bloody hospital bed! He's got weeks, maybe months of treatment ahead. He's in pain all the time, but of course they can't give him too much morphine. He's frantic with worry about me. Now his bloody stupid mother's probably going to tell him I'm having an affair because she caught me getting a comforting hug from a friend! She never liked me.' She stared out of the window. 'God knows what'll happen now!' she sighed. 'It's such a mess and I'm so frightened and sick of it all. Sometimes I wish . . .'

'That he'd murder you and get it over with? No, you don't!' Chantelle said sharply. 'This is fate,' she said, tapping ash from her cigarette. 'Us meeting like this.' She stared at Justine, wondering if she was wrong after all, if she was about to make a holy show of herself. 'Do you believe in fate?'

'I don't know what I believe anymore,' Justine said wearily.

269

She took her wallet from her bag and looked round for the waitress. 'I really have to go now. Let's get the bill, okay?'

'You helped me.' Chantelle decided to follow her gut instinct, that strange flash of intuition. Shame she hadn't had one of those when she'd first met Ronnie. 'If I'd killed Ronnie I might have got twenty years,' she said. 'If he'd murdered me he could have pleaded nagging bitch and been out in less than three. You saved my life.' She swallowed the rest of her wine.

Justine stiffened. 'What the hell are you talking about?' she asked slowly.

'I thought the bastard would kill *me* with that knife!' Chantelle said, looking into her eyes. 'Every single bloody day I was married to him I was terrified. He murdered my baby girl.'

'*What?*'

'Kicked me in the stomach while I was pregnant. She was dead, but I still had to be induced, give birth to her. They let me hold her for a while, say goodbye before they took her away. I told her I was sorry. For everything. She was a lovely little thing. Perfect.'

'Oh, Chantelle –!' Justine looked at her, anguished.

'Ronnie said he'd kill me if I told anyone what he was,' she went on tonelessly. 'I knew he meant it. There were times when I wouldn't have minded being killed. But he wouldn't have done it quickly. He got off on causing pain, you see. He loved that. He raped and beat up other women besides me. Thought he could get away with anything, did our Ronnie. He got more than he bargained for the other night, though.' She smiled at Justine, a ghastly smile. 'Didn't he, love?'

Justine started to tremble. Her hands shook so much that she dropped her wallet on the flowered china plate, scattering chocolate cake crumbs. 'I don't know what you're . . .'

'Oh, I think you do.' Chantelle's eyes bored into hers, studying her reaction. 'It's all right, you don't need to be scared. Not of me anyway. He raped you,' she stated quietly. 'You thought he'd kill you that night. You got the knife and–'

'Shut up!' Justine caught her breath and looked away. 'I don't know what the fuck you're talking about! He didn't rape me,' she said fiercely. 'No way! And I didn't –' She stood up, scraping the chair back. 'I won't sit here talking to a crazy woman!' she hissed. 'I knew this was a mistake.'

'I'm no more crazy than you are. Okay, so he didn't rape you. But he was going to, wasn't he? He attacked you.'

'*No!*' Why was she bluffing? It was too late for that. She might fool the police, but she couldn't fool this woman who had known her dead husband better than anyone. When had Chantelle guessed? Probably the minute Justine had denied seeing Ronnie Davis again. Her terrified, furious reaction spoke the words she couldn't bring herself to say aloud.

'I want to thank you for saving my life,' Chantelle said relentlessly. 'I owe you one.' The cigarette smouldered in the ashtray, sending smoke spiralling into their faces. The buzz of conversation in the café seemed to fade into the distance.

'You killed Ronnie,' she whispered, 'Didn't you?'

# Chapter Twenty-Three

'You've run out of cigarettes *again*?' Melissa Jones, sprawled on the chintzy sofa watching television, looked irritably at her stocky, dark-haired, bespectacled husband as he pulled on his dark green jacket and zipped it up. 'I don't believe you, Gary! You only bought the last pack this morning. When are you going to stop smoking?' she demanded.

'Oh, Christ, the record's stuck again! I'll stop smoking when you stop nagging.'

'I'm sick of it and so are the kids. I'm just grateful they haven't followed your bad example. As far as I'm aware,' she added darkly. 'I mean, what do I know? I'm only their bloody mother!'

'Don't start, Melissa, okay?' Gary warned, checking the contents of his wallet. Forty-five quid. 'I'm stressed out at work lately.' What did smoking a few fags matter, he thought ironically, after he'd spent the day checking that contaminated beryllium consignment from Russia? He should be glowing green in the dark! He'd see if he got any funny looks on the short walk down the road to the off-licence.

'You're not the only one who's stressed! Of course you're also stressed out by smoking.' Melissa yawned and sat up. She wore a dingy white bathrobe and had a blue towel wrapped around her head. 'Smokers think nicotine relaxes them, but it just makes them more tense. I wish you'd read that,' she said, nodding at the book on the coffee table: *How to Stop Smoking*. 'Might even make a diehard like you think twice.'

'I can't stand that American self-help, Pollyanna complex bullshit. It's irritating.' Gary looked at her critically. 'Your legs could do with a shave,' he remarked.

'Don't try and change the subject.' Melissa's wide velvety brown eyes, the crow's feet around them shining with moisturiser, were accusing. 'I'm a nurse–'

'Aren't you just!' he interrupted, bored. 'Saint Melissa Jones, national treasure.'

'Shut *up*!' D'you know the first question those sodding smokers always ask when they come round from the anaesthetic? 'Nurse, when can I smoke?' It's unbelievable! They'd light up on the ward if they were allowed, they don't give a toss about anyone else. This bloody woman today – she'd just had a lung removed, for Christ's sake – insisted on being wheeled to the smoking room. Where she fainted, of course! You wouldn't believe the number of patients who faint in that smoking room. Blood all over the floor and I had to drag her out, trying to make sure the drip didn't get dislodged.' She paused for breath. 'What's the point in wasting NHS resources on such morons?'

Gary frowned. 'That's a very dodgy path to go down, Melissa, denying people medical treatment because you don't happen to like their lifestyle.'

'You totally refuse to see my point,' she said indignantly. 'As usual.'

'Never mind. At least we still talk to each other after sixteen years of marriage.' He grabbed his keys off the mantelpiece. 'Shall I bring you back a fix of smoky bacon crisps?' He smiled at her. 'Although you do realize you may be denied a heart bypass one day, if the surgeon finds out you ate them?'

Melissa leaned back on the sofa. 'I'll have a couple of packets,' she said sullenly. 'And a Crunchie.' It was useless to argue with Gary, but she couldn't help herself. 'Your smoking costs us at least a hundred and eighty quid a month, d'you realize that?' she asked angrily. 'I've worked it out.'

'Good thing I'm a technical support manager with Melwood Materials then, isn't it?' he said pleasantly. 'We can live in a nice detached house in Childwall, provide our two point four teenage nightmares with all the designer sports gear, foreign holidays and computer equipment that their acquisitive little hearts desire – and still have cash to spare for my sad old vice!' He walked out of the living room. 'See you in about ten minutes.'

Melissa grunted then looked up. 'Hey, hang on!' she called. 'What's a Pollyanna complex?' Too late. The front door slammed

273

and she sighed and sank back against the sofa cushions. *Panorama* had just started, a report on the potential dangers of dodgy wiring in aircraft. Melissa picked up the remote and switched channels. Who wanted to think about *that* when they next flew off on holiday! She yawned and closed her eyes, stretched her tired, aching limbs. I'm knackered, she thought drowsily.

'One hundred and eighty quid a month,' Gary mused as he came out into the dark quiet road with its elegant thirties detached houses, trees and high hedges. 'Mmm. That *is* quite expensive.' The night air was chill, but at least it had stopped raining. He walked briskly past a parked Ford Mondeo with two men sitting in it, then paused and glanced back. The men didn't look at him but down and then at each other, as if they didn't want to be recognized. Burglars? he wondered uneasily. There had been a couple of break-ins recently. Undercover police officers? The driver was young, in his twenties, and had a shaven head. Gary caught the gleam of a gold earring. The other man was older, with a moustache and dark curly hair.

Gary shrugged and walked on. He could have taken the car, but it wasn't worth it for such a short journey and he got little enough exercise anyway. That was another thing Melissa was always nagging him about. He wondered if Paul Melwood had done anything about the beryllium consignment. He didn't understand what was going on. Paul was usually extremely careful who he did business with, but he'd definitely messed up on this one.

He came to the roundabout and the row of shops at the end of the road, and went into the off-licence. He bought two packs of Embassy Regal, a new blue plastic lighter, and a Crunchie for Melissa. The shop didn't have her favourite smoky bacon crisps, so he bought two packets of prawn cocktail. Outside he tore the cellophane off one pack, pulled out a cigarette and lit it, drawing the smoke deep into his lungs. He coughed. Melissa was right, he should give up smoking. He would one day. The truth was, he just bloody liked it too much.

Gary walked quickly back up the road, taking swift drags on his cigarette. He realized he felt tense because of the presence of the Ford Mondeo and its occupants. Who were those men? What were they doing there? He'd never seen them before. Once he got home he would go up to the front bedroom and take a look; if they

274

stayed there much longer he would phone the police. They were up to no good, he felt certain. So what if they turned out to be undercover police officers? Better to make an arse of himself than let a preventable crime take place. Melissa's prawn cocktail crisps crackled in his jacket pocket.

He took another drag on his cigarette as he neared his house and the parked Ford Mondeo. Then he stopped. The two men were gone. He smiled at the relief he felt. You're bloody paranoid, he chided himself.

'All right, Gary lad!' The shaven-headed man with the gold earring stepped out from behind a hedge. Gary flinched with fear, went cold as he saw the gun in the man's hand, some sort of revolver. He backed away, eyes riveted on the gun, and collided with the other man.

'Where d'you think you're going, Gary?' The man shoved him in the chest and he staggered backwards. 'Eh?'

'Who are you?' he stammered, terrified. 'What d'you want? How d'you know my name?' He dropped his cigarette and the stub lay glowing on the wet pavement. 'What the fuck's going on?'

'Questions, questions.' The man shoved him viciously again. 'Keep it shut!' he hissed. He gestured towards Gary's house. 'Otherwise your wife gets it. Right,' he said. 'Give us your wallet.' Gary handed it over, silent and trembling. Seconds later he lay dead, bullets lodged in his heart and brain.

Melissa, fast asleep in front of the television, didn't notice that Gary was long overdue, as were her crisps and Crunchie. Corinne Jones, back early from an unsuccessful blind date fixed up by her friend Emma, was the first to discover her father's lifeless body sprawled in the driveway. Her panicked screams woke her mother and set curtains twitching in nearby houses.

Melissa never did get to find out what a Pollyanna complex was.


'Aren't you taking poor darling Whitney out?' Marinda Bluff, dressed in a heavy peach satin robe, shook her sleeping daughter who was stretched out on the sofa snoring her head off. 'It's almost midnight. Got no consideration, have you?'

Charley opened her eyes and sat up. 'Nearly *midnight*?' She rubbed her eyes.

'That's what I said. You've had too much of that cognac again,' her mother scolded. 'You'll get cirrhosis of the liver, the way you knock it back. Look at her,' she said indignantly, cuddling the restless, whining dog. 'She's longing for her walk. Get your fat arse off that sofa. Bloody hell!' She grimaced in pain as she slowly straightened up and rubbed her back and arms. 'This arthritis is beyond a joke.' She picked up the remote control and switched channels. 'That film was rubbish. Sickmaking bloody mawkish sentimental *bloody* rubbish.' She stroked the rottweiler's broad back. 'Wasn't it, darling? Grandma loves you,' she murmured, kissing the dog's head and glaring at Charlie. 'Go on, move!'

'All right, all right! I'm going.' She swung her legs off the sofa.

'Not scared of that stalker, are you?' Marinda laughed. 'He's probably spent the day receiving electric shocks and having cigarettes stubbed out on his private parts. After which they'll have given him a nice cup of tea and locked him in a cell for the night.' She grinned and picked up her brandy glass full of Cointreau. Her thin, dry yellow hair was loose around her bony shoulders.

'Let's hope you're right.' Charlie yawned hugely and staggered out of the red velvet drawing room into the hall. Her head felt like it was stuffed with cotton wool and she was ready for bed, not the park. But Whitney needed a pee and a run. She put on her parka and zipped it up, took the dog lead and her torch from the polished hall table and opened the front door. Whitney yelped excitedly.

'Steady, baby doll!' She pulled up the fur-lined parka hood and clipped the lead to the dog's collar as they went down the steps. Whitney barked at the wind and flying leaves. Rain poured down again and it was freezing. Autumn with a vengeance. Charley shone her flashlight down the dark drive, flicking it to left and right as they reached the gates. The rottweiler barked again, strained at her lead.

'All right, darling! Take it easy, okay? Mummy's a bit nervous tonight.'

Charley looked across the wide road into the park. There was no moon; it was black as pitch except for the weak lamps that lit the paths leading to the lake. She remembered Matthew's glare of hatred as he was bundled into the police car that morning. He knew she had called them. He knew about Dad's gun.

Don't be stupid, she chided herself. Mum's right, he's locked

276

up now. And even if he wasn't, there was no way he'd dare come back, not with Whitney ready to rip his throat out. Charley longed to talk to Justine but she didn't answer her phone or doorbell, had been out all day and still wasn't back. She spent nearly all her time at the hospital. Poor Adam! Charley thought sadly. It was a miracle he had survived the terrible hit-and-run.

Her head spun with cognac and cold night air. I must cut down on the booze, she thought. I'll stick to beer and wine for the next two weeks, keep off the hard stuff. She crossed the road and nervously entered the park by her usual route.

'God damn it!' Marinda tutted irritably as the door bell rang loudly. 'She must have forgotten her keys.' Charley never did that, but she was a bit on edge lately. She put down the glass of Cointreau and heaved herself out of the armchair by the fire, all the while staring at the television. Another thriller, the unsuspecting heroine returning to the house where a psychopath lay in wait. She stuck the cigarette in her mouth while she tied the belt of the robe, then walked out of the drawing room and down the hall, sighing and swearing under her breath.

Charley drank too much, that was the plain truth. Marinda didn't know how her daughter managed to drag herself out to work in the mornings, change the old dears' nappies and feed them their breakfasts, checking the cereal bowls for sets of false teeth afterwards. She shuddered. Imagine being stuck in a *care* home, at the mercy of the likes of that! The bell rang again as she shuffled down the hall.

'All right, all right!' she screeched. 'I'm coming. Can't get five minutes' peace with you around!' She opened the connecting door, stepped into the cold tiled porch and opened the front door. The porch light had gone out; cold wind and rain blew in her face. 'What the bloody hell d'you think you're playing at?'

A dark, monk-like figure loomed at her and a hand shot out, pushing her in the face. She inhaled a gust of nauseatingly sweet-smelling aftershave. Marinda staggered backwards and flung up her arms, too shocked and surprised even to cry out. The cigarette dropped on the tiled porch floor. She bit her tongue and tasted blood in her mouth as she fell and smashed the side of her head against the door jamb.

'Where's the gun?' Matthew shouted. He slammed the front

door behind him and put the chain on, then grabbed Marinda and dragged her into the hall. The old bitch was stick thin, had bones that would snap like a chicken's. He spun her round and gave her another enormous shove, this time in the small of her back. She went flying again and slammed into the wall, slid to the floor and collapsed in a heap. He laughed.

Marinda rolled over and lay stunned and gasping for breath, her head whirling with pain and shock. She stared at Matthew in terror, at the knife gripped in his hand. Was he going to rape her? A lot of old women got raped. It had nothing to do with your age or how you looked or what you wore. She prayed she would pass out, that Charley and Whitney would get back soon. But they'd only just gone. He must have been waiting.

'The gun!' Matthew yelled again. 'Where is it, you old cow?' He had to hurry up before melon tits and the rottweiler got back. 'Tell me!'

When his foot slammed into her side, Marinda knew her right hip was broken.

'In the fridge,' she whispered between bloodied lips. 'In a cake box.'

'*What*? It had better be,' he shouted. 'Or you're dead.'

He raced down the long hall. To his left was a study with book-lined walls and a rolltop desk. On his right a big bathroom done in puke pink. Further down, the door to an old-fashioned pantry stood open. Wooden shelves were crammed with tins and jars, and sacks of rice and potatoes were propped against the walls. A tea chest held a Mount Everest of stained, battered novels, the covers depicting gruesome aliens emerging from gleaming steel ashtray spaceships and terrified women fleeing from sweating, wild-eyed men, heaving bosoms popping out of Wonderbras as they ran. Matthew grabbed two tins of red salmon and one of tuna chunks in oil and shoved them in his mac pockets. He would have liked to steal more, but there wasn't time.

The old kitchen had a red-tiled floor, ancient stone sink and scrubbed, bleached wooden drainboard, the only evidence of millennium existence being a computer-controlled fridge freezer as tall as himself. He opened the fridge and grabbed the cake box, tore off the pink ribbon and picked up the heavy, chilled revolver that the old bitch had menaced him with the other night. How many people had been shot with it? he wondered. The fridge was a good hiding place. He would never have thought to look there. He ran out of the kitchen and dashed back up the hall.

Marinda lay helpless, agonizing pains shooting up and down her right leg and hip. She had a blinding headache and her head was spinning. Is this it? she wondered as Matthew ran towards her, gun in hand. Is he going to kill me? I don't care. I might see my darling David again. Or death could be just a state of non-feeling, like before I was born. Suits me fine either way. Better than snuffing it in a geriatric ward. Charley would be strolling around the park lake, smoking and fantasizing about men she'd never have, while Whitney did her business. Charley was always home when she wasn't wanted and never home when she was. Story of her bloody life.

'Old cow!' Matthew stamped on her face, broke her nose and kicked her a few more times. Marinda passed out with pain and shock, lay choking and gurgling as blood flowed down the back of her nose and throat. He rushed to the door and unchained it, thought of something else and rushed back.

'Hey!' He squatted beside her and shook her roughly. Marinda's head rolled to one side and she coughed blood. 'Bullets,' he shouted in her ear. 'Where are they?' He prodded her in the ribs with the gun. 'Come on!'

She opened her eyes. Two men leaned over her, two snarling men with thin faces, bared yellow teeth, rabbit jaws and bleached blond hair dark at the roots. Two pairs of hate-filled, dark staring eyes. She realized she was seeing double. Why didn't Charley and Whitney come back?

'Drawer,' she croaked. She could hardly speak for pain, for the blood filling her nose and mouth.

'Where? What drawer?'

'The study.' She paused, made a big effort. 'Top drawer,' she gurgled. 'Desk.' Matthew leapt up and ran into the study, wrenched open the top drawer of the desk and took out an old cardboard box of bullets. He wasn't sure how to load the gun or even use it, but it couldn't be that difficult. Any moron could shoot somebody. He stuffed gun and bullets in his pockets and ran out. Marinda had lapsed into unconsciousness. He ran down the hall, flung open the front door and slammed it behind him. He didn't think melon tits would call the police; he was sure she kept the gun illegally.

279

He raced round to the side of the house and furiously rang Justine's bell. No answer. He had to get her, she had to die soon! When Justine was dead he could start a new life with someone else. A beautiful, kind, sweet girl who would love and respect him and do anything he wanted. In bed and out.

He ran down the steps and scrabbled around in the wet bushes, searching for the carrier bag he had left there that morning. He gasped in fear, swore.

The bag was gone.

# Chapter Twenty-Four

'Shh, baby doll! Please!' Charley could barely restrain the excited rottweiler as she stuck the key in the front door and turned it. 'Damn!' she muttered crossly. 'Bloody porch light's gone out, I can see sod all. I only replaced the bulb ten days ago. Typical.'

She switched on the flashlight. Her hands were wet and slippery with rain, and her boots crunched broken glass on the step. How the hell did glass come to be there? She shone the flashlight upwards and gasped. The porch light hadn't given up the ghost after just ten days. It was smashed.

'Oh, my . . .!' Charley whirled round and shone the torch down the wet steps and into the dripping bushes. It's him! she thought. He's back. He was still around, judging by the state of Whitney. She trembled with fright.

'If you come anywhere near us, my rottweiler will rip your throat out!' she called boldly into the darkness. There was no sound, no movement. Only rain, the wind rustling trees and bushes, the distant swish of tyres on wet tarmac. She turned and hurried inside. Whitney dashed ahead of her, barking furiously. Charley cried out in fear as she saw the peach satin heap crumpled on the floor outside the drawing room.

'Mum! Oh my God! Oh, *no*!'

Whitney stood over Marinda, whining and yelping as she licked her bloodied face and nuzzled her shoulder.

'Mum!' Charley pounded down the hall and knelt over her mother, breathing hard. 'What happened? I've told you not to drink too much,' she said despairingly. 'You can't take it at your age.' Although how could a drunken collapse, a possible stroke or heart attack, cause all this bleeding, the terrible state of Marinda's face? Drunks usually fell about like rag dolls, didn't hurt themselves. She smelled the blood as she pushed the whining rottweiler away. Marinda opened her eyes and her chest heaved as she coughed up more blood. Her nose and eyes were swelling.

'He did it,' she whispered.

'What? *Who*?'

'The lowlife . . . Justine's stalker.'

'Jesus *Christ*!' Charley looked wildly up and down the hall. 'How did he get in?' she shouted, panicked. 'Is he still here?'

'Gone. I let him in . . . thought you'd forgotten your keys. He punched me, stamped on my face. My hip's broken.' Marinda paused, panting for breath, squeezed her eyes shut with the pain. 'Call an ambulance.'

'Yeah. Yeah. Right. Hold on, okay? Just hold on, you're going to be fine.' Charley got to her feet, trembling with rage and fright. 'That lowlife!' she shouted, her eyes filling with tears. 'He'll go down for this, by Christ he will!'

'No!' Marinda panted, opening her eyes. She raised her head slightly then let it fall again. 'No police!' she hissed.

Charley stared down at her. 'Why the hell not?' she cried. 'Look what he's done to you!'

'No police!' Marinda whispered frantically. 'He's got your father's gun – that's what he came for. They mustn't know about the gun.'

Her head lolled sideways and she passed out again. Whitney whined and barked, sensing Charley's panic, Marinda's hurt. Charley dashed for the hall phone. The bastard had Dad's gun! What in the name of God did he want that for? 'Stupid bloody question!' she muttered. Why did anyone want a gun! She couldn't call the police, but she had to warn Justine. Why didn't she come home? A cab had driven up earlier and driven away again before she could get outside. Could that have been Justine?

'Ambulance, please,' she said, her deep voice shaking with panic. 'My mother's unconscious, she's had a terrible fall. I think her hip's broken.'

Justine watched, white-faced, as John Kiely carefully examined the contents of Matthew's wet, soiled carrier bag in his office. Kiely had worked until nine, nipped home for a late dinner and an early night, and had now been called out again. Lynette wasn't happy. The desk lamp shone on the rope, leather collar and knife. Justine stared at the horrible things, cold with fear again as she imagined how Matthew must have planned to use them on her.

'I took a cab home from the hospital and its headlights picked out this in the bushes opposite my front door,' she said quietly. 'I didn't go inside. I grabbed the bag, got back in the cab and came straight here.'

She was cold, starving, trembling with exhaustion. She had spent another long afternoon and evening at the hospital, witnessing Adam's pain and feeling helpless to do anything about it. Christine hadn't said anything to Adam about Paul Melwood yet, but she would. Then there was the mindblowing meeting and conversation with Chantelle Davis; the bizarre – no, *crazy* – offer Chantelle had made once Justine's shaky denials, her bluffs, had fallen apart. Justine didn't know what to think about that incredible offer, how to respond. She could barely take it in. To top it all, though, to really make her day, there was the carrier bag in the bushes – its contents providing further stark, terrifying evidence of Matthew's intentions.

'He's obviously been to my house again,' she said. 'He must have been lying in wait.' She paused. 'I don't know why he went away but I'm sure he'll be back!' The idea of a restraining order, an injunction or a jail sentence deterring someone like Matthew was so ridiculous it would have made her laugh if she hadn't been so frightened. The police *had* to get him soon.

She blushed as a sudden thought occurred to her, and was glad that Kiely stared silently at the things on the desk and didn't meet her eye. Matthew must have seen her come out of the house with Paul this morning. He probably thought Paul was her lover! Now he would be more angry, even more filled with hatred. How had she become the focus of such hatred? Bad luck, being in the wrong place at the wrong time? What had he and Ronnie Davis seen in her that she herself couldn't see? Intellectually, she knew that she shouldn't blame herself in any way. Emotionally, that wasn't so easy. The questions went round and round in her head.

Kiely raised his head and looked at her. 'Have you touched these at all?' He put the things back in the bag and stripped off his latex gloves.

'No,' Justine said, shivering with fear and revulsion. 'I looked inside, but I didn't touch anything. I didn't want to!'

'Good.' He sat on the edge of the desk. 'We know who this guy is now,' he said. 'His name's Matthew Casey and he lives in Old Roan. Right next-door to the burned-out house, as a matter of fact.'

'Oh, my God!' Justine pushed back her hair. 'I told you he murdered them.'

'We've got no evidence to prove he was responsible for that arson attack,' Kiely warned. Although they might find something soon. Casey didn't appear to have any form, but that meant sod all. 'He wasn't home when we got there,' he said, 'but his mother was. It's her name on that bottle of sleeping pills. We found her dead.'

'*Dead*?'

'Natural causes,' he said hastily. 'Looked like a heart attack. Of course an autopsy will have to confirm that. We don't know if Casey is aware of his mother's death. Or if he'll be back. He seems to have taken most of his stuff.'

'So he could be anywhere?' Justine turned away and stared at the dark, rainy window. 'Well, that's great!' she said bitterly. 'What am I supposed to do now?'

'If he turns up at your house he's nicked.'

'He wasn't earlier, was he?'

Kiely felt embarrassed. 'We are giving this urgent priority now.'

'Oh, such a relief!' Justine exclaimed, her voice heavy with sarcasm. 'I'll sleep easier now.' She stared at him. 'Hang on a minute! How do you know his name and where he lives? How did you find out?'

Kiely pulled on his black coat. 'He was picked up outside your house this morning,' he said reluctantly, hating to have to admit the awful cock-up. 'He was questioned and charged with loitering, released after a few hours.'

'*What*?' Justine went cold with horror. 'You had him in custody and you let him go? I don't understand! How . . .?' She shook her head in despair, lost for words.

'Not me personally.' He glanced away. Shit! he thought. 'I'm very sorry,' he said awkwardly. 'It was a breakdown in communications.'

'One that could cost me my life! How the hell could this happen? Stupid question!' she hissed. 'No one's shown any interest or competence since the start of this nightmare.'

'I wasn't made aware of the mistake until after he'd been released.' Kiely shrugged. 'We went straight to his house but, like I said, he'd done a runner. I'm very sorry,' he repeated helplessly. 'But at least we now know who he is—'

'Not as sorry as me!' Justine's eyes filled with tears. 'What do I do now, sue you for incompetence from beyond the grave? For Christ's sake! Don't you realize the danger I'm in?'

'Of course we do. Look, it won't happen again. Casey will be picked up within twenty-four hours.' Otherwise it would be a Chief Constable's inquiry and goodbye to his career. Not to mention what could happen to Justine Flynn. He locked Matthew's bag away for the night and picked up his car keys. 'You said you came here in a cab. Can I drop you somewhere?' he offered.

'I don't suppose you're going to offer to put me up in a five-star hotel suite, with round-the-clock protection!'

'Budget doesn't run to that, I'm afraid,' Kiely said regretfully. 'Where would you like to go?' he asked. 'Home?' He couldn't ask her more questions about Ronnie Davis, not at the moment anyway.

'Yes.' Justine stood there, hugging the black silk raincoat around her slender body, her beautiful blue eyes accusing him. Kiely tried not to stare at her. She was the most gorgeous woman he had ever seen.

Justine longed to see Paul again and felt like going straight to his hotel. But she couldn't let Kiely drive her there. Besides, it was late and Paul might be asleep. She wondered if he'd tried to call her. She had resisted buying a mobile; worried about headaches and brain tumours. Even though she might be murdered by a stalker any day soon!

'Right,' Kiely said, smiling at her. 'Home it is. I'll let you know as soon as we've picked Casey up. We'll do all we can to protect you, but until he's arrested you really have to watch your back.'

'I'd never have known if you hadn't told me!' She could sue them for harassment, incompetence, you name it. But that would take years, cost time and energy she didn't have, and lead nowhere. All Justine could think about was surviving the next twenty-four hours.

Charley Bluff came running down her front door steps as Kiely's navy blue Golf GTI reversed and drove off, Whitney panting and growling behind her. 'Justine!' she called urgently. She ran up, big breasts bouncing beneath the unzipped parka. She wore baggy blue jeans stuffed into pale grey moon boots. 'Thank God you're home!' She glanced at the police car parked outside the gates. 'They got here a few minutes ago. They're watching the place – at last! Justine, something terrible's happened! I wanted to warn you . . .'

'What now?' Justine shivered in the cold night air, her keys clutched in one hand. The police car's presence didn't make her feel any safer. She longed to get inside and lock the doors. 'It's him, isn't it?' she asked fearfully.

'He got into our house – he beat Mum up, broke her hip and nose!' Charley gave a sob of terror. 'She's in a terrible state. She answered the door while me and Whitney were in the park, thought I'd forgotten my keys. The ambulance took her away about fifteen minutes ago. I'm off to the hospital now. I wanted to wait a bit, see if you came home.'

'My God!' Justine breathed, horrified. 'But why would he hurt Marinda?' she asked wildly. 'She's got nothing to do with . . .'

'He knows I phoned the police this morning. They caught him trying to kick your front door in. I was so relieved when he was dragged off, I thought, that's it, we'll all be safe now.' Charley glanced round again, lowered her voice. 'He stole Dad's gun,' she whispered. 'And the bullets. That's what he came for. I can't tell the police – it's an illegal handgun. Imagine the trouble we'd get into if they found out we'd had it all these years.' She seized Justine's arm. 'Take care, for God's sake! Why the hell did they let him go?' she asked tearfully.

'Some idiot who didn't know about my case charged him with loitering then released him. Now they're looking for him again.' Charley's grasp hurt; Justine pulled her arm away. 'Don't you think we should warn the police he's got a gun?'

'I told you, we can't! It's me and Mum who'll end up in prison, not that scum. You knew about the gun too, they might say you're an accomplice. Besides, what have the police done for us?' Charley asked furiously. 'Sweet FA, that's what!' Her beady eyes glittered with rage. 'I totally refuse to be banged up because that bastard stole the gun my father intended me and Mum to have for our protection! I want it back, Justine. Dad shot an escaping SS officer with that revolver. It's part of our family heritage.'

Justine hadn't taken Charley's wild utterances seriously before, had thought of her as an amusing eccentric. But at that moment she understood exactly why Adam considered Charley Bluff a disturbed individual. She felt desolate again that he wasn't waiting for her upstairs, to share talk and laughter, make love. She was alone. Terribly alone.

'I can't imagine you'll get the gun back. But what about Marinda?' she asked nervously. 'Will she be all right?'

'I don't know. She's a mess, Justine. She sank a bottle of Cabernet Sauvignon with dinner, then half a litre of Cointreau. They can't do a lot with her until the effects of all that sauce have worn off!' Charley wiped her eyes on her sleeve and patted the rottweiler. 'I have to go,' she said. 'I'll see you tomorrow. Take care!' She tugged at the dog's lead. 'Come on, babe.'

She hurried off and Justine dashed for her front door. This is my fault, she thought. Matthew stole that gun because he wants to kill me and Adam with it. Beating the crap out of Marinda was part of the fun. What if Marinda died or ended up permanently disabled?

The phone was ringing as she let herself into the dark cold flat and snapped on lights. She locked, bolted and chained the door then ran up to the kitchen and grabbed the receiver. Evie's empties still littered the table and counters and there was a lingering smell of cigarettes. The place looked a depressing mess. The police had been here, dusting for fingerprints. Matthew had been here. It didn't feel like home any more. Justine forgot about food and drink; her stomach felt like it had a big stone in it. Paul, she prayed. Let it be you!

'Bitch!' Matthew hissed. 'Slag!'

Justine nearly dropped the phone in terror. Then she took a breath, tried to control herself. She couldn't let this psychopathic bastard know how frightened she was, get more sick pleasure from her fear. Where was he? she wondered.

'Sorry to hear about your mother,' she said softly, playing for time. 'Was it really a heart attack? Or did you murder her, like you murdered the Jacksons?' There was a brief, stunned silence at the other end.

'How'd you know about my *mother*?'

'From the police, of course. They know all about you now. Including the moron who let you walk this morning. They're searching your house and they've got your carrier bag. Not very

287

clever to leave it outside my front door,' she commented. 'Really thick, in fact.' Justine didn't want to warn Matthew that she knew he had a gun. If he thought an armed response team was after him, he might barricade himself in somewhere, take a hostage. She might be that hostage. Or even Adam.

The police had his carrier bag? Matthew shook with fear as he gripped the greasy phone and stared up and down Lark Lane. He had spent the afternoon and early evening in the city centre, merging with crowds in cafés, pubs and burger bars. He had his latest giro and the fifty-six quid from Paula's purse, but that wouldn't last five minutes. The plods were watching Justine's house and he had nowhere to go. He felt under seige and was furious. One obstacle after another had stopped him from getting his hands on this betraying bitch! But his chance would come.

'Lost your voice?' Justine asked, listening to the harsh breathing. 'They also know you tried to murder Adam,' she said. 'He identified you.' She paused to let that sink in. 'You're fucked!'

'No!' Matthew got his voice back. '*You* are,' he shouted, panicked. 'I saw you get felt up by that copper, you slag! I'll say you murdered him.'

'When you're banged up, is that when you'll tell? Who do you think's going to believe a psychopathic arsonist with eleven murders under his belt? One of them a baby! Or is it twelve, if we count your poor old mum? Oh, yes,' Justine said quickly, 'they know you murdered my colleague Anna, and that security guard.' If they didn't, they surely would soon. 'As I said . . .' she breathed her hatred down the phone at him '. . . you're *fucked*!'

'No!' Matthew yelled. Why didn't the bitch sound scared? She should be terrified, begging and pleading with him not to hurt her, to forgive her for betraying him. Even though she knew it was too late for that. He wanted, *needed* her fear. Beads of cold sweat prickled his body. 'Lying bitch!'

'Yeah, right! Believe what you like.' Fear dropped away as Justine burned with hatred. Let the end come, she thought, whatever it is. The waiting's over.

'You're on the run now,' she said viciously. 'You're the victim. You'll be stalked and hunted down and cornered like a sewer rat. And then . . .' She paused, thinking of Chantelle Davis, of the chilling words that had tripped and stumbled out of that pale mouth with its broken teeth. She remembered Paul's words: *He doesn't get it and he never will.* 'You're going to die!'

She crashed the phone down and stood shivering and breathing hard, hands pressed to her mouth. Then she dialled 1471 and swore as the pompous voice informed her that the caller hadn't been thick enough to leave his number.

Years in prison wouldn't make Matthew Casey give up, she thought. He would build muscles on that puny body, keep going on vengeful, murderous fantasies. When psychiatrists deemed him fit for release – without bothering to ask her opinion, of course – he would come after her again. This time better equipped to fight. She brushed away tears, snatched up the bottle of white wine and took a swig.

She had to flush Matthew out, force him to make a fatal mistake. It was a hugely dangerous risk, but one she had to take. She had no faith in the police and no belief that she would get justice, legal or moral. Unless she took it for herself. Everything was clear now. Terrifyingly clear. The phone rang again and she grabbed it, her body trembling.

'Justine?' Chantelle's gravelly voice was hushed; Billy and Yasmin were asleep upstairs. 'I know it's dead late,' she apologized, 'but I phoned a few times and there was no answer so I got worried. Are you okay?' she asked anxiously.

'Not really.' Justine swigged more wine. Her body ached with exhaustion. 'I'm glad you called,' she said calmly. 'I've decided to take up your generous offer.' No one would humiliate or terrify her ever again. If she was going to die, she would die fighting. 'Although I must be crazy!'

Chantelle was silent. 'You're not crazy,' she said at last. 'You're doing the right thing.'

'Am I? I certainly hope so. Look, I'll see you tomorrow, okay?' Justine had a question for Chantelle, but didn't trust herself to say any more at that moment. Besides, you never knew who might be eavesdropping. 'We'll talk then.'

She hung up and dialled Paul's city centre hotel. He answered on the first ring.

'Paul? It's Justine.'

'Thank God!' he breathed. 'I've been trying to reach you for hours.' Adriana had guessed he loved Justine. Was it so obvious? He was more worried for her than he was for Sara in that fortress farmhouse. But he didn't believe Adriana would bother with his wife now she knew how he felt about her. 'What's been happening?' he asked. Are you all right?'

'Yes, for now. The police are watching the house.' Justine was too tired to rehash the day's events over the phone, and wouldn't tell Paul about Chantelle Davis. She just wanted to see him. Very much. 'I'm sorry to phone so late, but I only got home about five minutes ago. Did I wake you?'

'No, of course you didn't. Listen,' he said urgently, 'I want you to get out of your flat tonight – now! Don't let anyone see you, not even the police. Can you do that?' One more day until Friday, when the beryllium deal would be done and Justine would be safe. From that ruthless bitch Adriana, at least. He felt torn by guilt and anxiety.

'I think so. But why?' Justine glanced round the untidy kitchen, felt a stab of fear.

'I want you to be safe. I've found somewhere for you. Go and pack a bag now, get out of there so that no one sees you. Make sure you're not followed. Don't use your car or Adam's and don't come to my hotel, it may not be safe. Take a cab into town and phone me from a call box. I'll tell you where to go next. You've got to trust me,' he said. '*Please!*'

She was silent for a few seconds. Instinct told her to grab a bag and go; reason told her to stay put, let the police watch out for her. Instinct won hands down. 'Okay,' she said finally. 'I'll trust you.'

'Good!' Paul let out his breath. 'Go now,' he said. 'Take care. I'll wait for your call.'

Justine ran upstairs and threw clothes and toiletries into a nylon flight bag. She ran back down to the kitchen and switched off all the lights, unlocked the fire escape door and crept down the metal staircase. She grabbed the key from beneath the flowerpot, raced across the garden, unbolted and unlocked the door in the wall and closed it. She put the key in her pocket. She would return it when she got a chance.

In the suffocatingly dark alley that ran between the houses she was suddenly seized with panic again. Bad things often came in threes: would Matthew be lurking, or perhaps another psycho with a knife and a raving personality disorder? Third time unlucky? She ran, gasping for breath, her heart pounding in fear. She wasn't sorry to be leaving the flat and didn't care if she never went back.

How could she ever wind down if she survived this nightmare, get used to normal daily existence again? She must have enough adrenalin stored in her heart muscle to cause palpitations for years to come! On the main road opposite the closed Chinese takeaway she hailed a cab which had just disgorged a bunch of laughing drunken clubbers.

In Aigburth Drive the two police officers, sitting bored and stiff in their patrol car outside the house, saw the lights in the top flat go out. So did the two men in the Ford Mondeo further down the dark road. The shaven-headed young driver with the gold earring grinned.

'Goodnight, babe,' he murmured. 'Sweet dreams!'

Half an hour later a different cab dropped Justine off outside a renovated Georgian house in the city centre, now converted into luxurious apartments. Paul's was at the top of the house. He opened the door and she caught a glimpse of white walls, wedding cake ceilings, an expanse of shiny wooden floor, and beyond the big windows city lights glittering like jewels. Paul wore black trousers and a slightly rumpled blue collarless shirt. His jacket lay on the hall floor.

Justine realized she loved his grey eyes beneath their thick, straight brows, his dark brown hair, his thin, tanned face. She knew she would give in to this attraction, the desire she felt for him, that she couldn't hold back any longer. And she didn't want to hold back. This would be a catharsis, a way of wiping Ronnie Davis' abuse, violence and sexual assault from her mind – from her body – and replacing it with something wonderful, healing. Like burying the knife on that dark, stormy beach, making love with Paul would be another way of proving to herself that Davis hadn't destroyed her, couldn't go on hurting her from beyond the grave.

'Thank God you're safe!' He shut the heavy door, locked it and took her in his arms. 'No one can find you here. You weren't followed?'

'I'm pretty sure I wasn't. I sneaked out the back way, took two different cabs.' Justine looked up at him, her eyes shining with tears. 'I wanted to see you,' she whispered. 'I missed you, Paul!'

Her words soothed his tortured soul and he felt vast relief. Each time they parted he wondered if there would be a next time. Sentences formed in his head and dissolved as he searched for words to describe and explain this crazy situation. But he said nothing, only held her beautiful face in his hands and looked into her incredible eyes. Justine stared back at him. Then he leaned her gently against the wall and kissed her, sliding his tongue between her lips, exploring her mouth, his hands buried in her soft mass of curls. He wanted her, body and soul.

Justine moaned and kissed him back hungrily, put her arms around him and held him tight. It felt so good to hold him. She closed her eyes, guiltily banished Adam's wavering image from her mind. Her body melted, opened like a flower as it responded to the sure touch of this man who was as desperate for her as she was for him.

'I love you!' Paul whispered. He started to pull off her clothes.

# Part Three

# Chapter Twenty-Five

'The bastards murdered Gary, shot him right outside our house! They killed my darling husband for forty-five sodding quid!' Melissa Jones was screaming, crying, hysterical. 'Corinne found him – she'll never get over it! I don't believe this! How could anyone be that callous?'

'Melissa, *who* shot Gary?' Paul stood in the centre of Adriana Terekhova's Adelphi Hotel suite, gripping his mobile, overcome with horror at this terrible news. Gary Jones hadn't turned up for work that morning and now he knew why! He looked across the big room to where Adriana stood by the window, wearing an elegant, figure-hugging black trouser suit and calmly sipping vintage champagne instead of her usual mineral water. Sunlight slanted across the walls and dusty rose pink carpet, illuminating her blonde hair. She appeared mesmerized by the stream of traffic crawling along Ranelagh Street. His open briefcase lay on the desk near the bed, filled with neat stacks of US dollars. Blood money.

'It was muggers, I told you!' Melissa shouted. 'They just took his money, shot him and drove off. A neighbour saw two men drive away, but he didn't see Gary's body in our driveway, didn't realize what had happened until later. Never thought to get the number, of course, stupid sod! The police said the car was probably stolen anyway.'

'My God!' Paul's eyes filled with tears. Gary's death wasn't a brutal mugging, no way! Although it was meant to look like that. Thank God Justine was safe now, hiding at the apartment he'd rented yesterday. They had worked out a complicated scheme for getting to and from it without being tailed.

'Gary's last memory was of me being pissed off with him,' Melissa wailed. 'I feel so bloody horrible, I was such a cow! I've got to hang up now; she said suddenly. 'I have to tell more people, I'm supposed to organize the funeral. I can't go on without Gary!' she shouted. 'I need Gary, I love him!' Someone whispered something and her wails receded into the background.

'Hello? I'm Melissa's mother,' an older woman's voice informed him. 'My daughter's not fit to talk at the moment, she's in shock. Well, we all are. There's a lot to do just now,' she said. 'It's chaos here. Could you phone back tomorrow sometime?'

'Of course.' He swallowed. 'I understand. My name's Paul Melwood,' he stammered. 'I'm – I *was* – Gary's employer.' Murderer, more like! Or as good as. 'Please let me know what I can do to help,' he said urgently. 'Melissa's got my number, but I'll call back anyway.'

'All right. Thanks for ringing, Paul. I know Gary thought a lot of you. Goodbye for now.' The phone went dead, leaving him crushed with guilt and despair.

'My *God*!' he repeated, stricken. He brushed away tears. He felt stunned, needed to sit down alone in some quiet place and try to absorb the enormity of this dreadful, shocking event. But what was there to think about? Gary was dead, purely and simply because of *his* greed. End of story.

'Come on, Paul! Don't look like that,' Adriana said sharply. 'So pale, so shocked. What did you expect? This is your fault.' She waved her champagne glass at him. 'I had to make sure you'd honour our agreement.'

'You knew I would! The money's all there.' He threw down his mobile and pointed to the briefcase on the polished cherrywood table. 'Why the hell did you have to have him murdered?' He felt sick.

'Gary Jones was a threat to us,' she said calmly. 'You told me so yourself.'

'For Christ's sake, I just happened to mention that he knew about the beryllium contamination! After I'd talked to him on the phone. I didn't mean . . .'

'That's exactly what you meant,' she interrupted. 'You were very unhappy with him, that much was obvious.' Adriana smiled although she felt angry. She resented Paul's stunned expression, his obvious horror and revulsion at this simple little damage limitation exercise. He should have been happy, relieved. *Grateful*. 'I only did what you thought about but didn't have the guts to do,' she said contemptuously.

'I *never* thought about murder! I never wanted anyone dead.' Paul picked up the mobile and stuck it in his jacket pocket. 'That was his wife I talked to,' he said bitterly. 'Gary's got – he *had* – three kids, all at school. His daughter found his body last night! What the hell are those children supposed to do now? How will they ever get over losing their father – knowing he was murdered?'

'I really don't know. Life is full of pain. We all have to learn that. Some sooner than others.' Bored and irritated, Adriana strolled back to the bedside table and refilled her glass. 'Why don't you give them some of your money?' she suggested, smirking. 'An application of money can heal practically anything, after all. I know many people aren't comfortable with that truth. *Little* people,' she added softly.

Paul stared at her. He was in no position to look down from lofty moral heights. There was no point in talking any more. The deal was done and he had to walk out of here, try to rid himself of the horrible taint, the dark shadow Adriana Terekhova had cast over his life. And not only his life. Sara or Justine might have been murdered too! He took a deep shuddering breath.

'It's done,' he said flatly. 'Finished. You've got your money. I'm out of here.' He turned and headed for the door.

'Wait!' Adriana ran after him and grabbed his arm. Champagne spilled on the thick carpet and he recoiled as a cloud of her sweet, cloying perfume hit his face. Its smell made him feel sick again, took him back nineteen years to the hot July day his grandfather was buried. The body had been brought to the house just before the funeral, and his mother had bustled around spraying copious amounts of lemon air freshener to mask the sickly smell of decaying flesh that permeated the downstairs rooms. Adriana spent a fortune only to smell like a lemon-scented corpse! But that was appropriate. She had death in her eyes and all over that beautiful body he'd never had the slightest desire to touch.

'You're being very stupid,' she cried. 'We've worked well together, Paul, don't you think?' Her blue eyes glittered. 'This is only the beginning. The next deal could be even bigger than this one.'

He shook his head in disbelief. 'You must be bloody joking!' He wrenched his arm free. 'Gary was one of a long line, wasn't he?' he said. 'You're right, it is my fault he's dead. I as good as pulled that trigger. I'll never forgive myself.'

'*What?* You're crazy!' she hissed. Paul moved away. He wanted to hit her.

'Think what you like.' He strode to the door.

'Your beautiful girlfriend is sleeping very late today,' Adriana called desperately. 'I don't know why, because you didn't spend the night with her.' Paul Melwood hadn't been near the woman with the red-gold hair lately. Maybe she really was just a friend of his and his drunken wife, although Adriana found that hard to believe. 'She might have found another man to fuck,' she taunted. 'What do you think?'

'I don't know and I don't bloody care!' Paul stopped and turned, stared into Adriana's cold blue eyes. Then he let his gaze travel slowly over her body, lingering on her breasts, her slender legs in the close-fitting trousers, back up to her pink, gloss-slicked lips. The contemptuous, appraising stare reminded Adriana of the way punters used to look when they were deciding whether or not they wanted her business. She blushed with anger, then embarrassment. Paul smiled at her unease.

'She's not my girlfriend,' he said. 'I haven't got a girlfriend. I rejected you for yourself, not some other woman.' Where had he said that before? 'If you can't deal with it, tough! You've got your money, I can only hope I get mine. After what we've done, we're lucky not to be starting indefinite jail sentences. Be happy with that. Take your two million dollars and fuck off back to wherever you came from!'

He went out and slammed the door, strode down the narrow carpeted corridor to the lift. His body trembled with shock and fright – and relief. Adriana's words proved that her hired help hadn't followed him or Justine. They thought she was sleeping late, didn't realize she'd fled. She and Sara would be safe now. Adriana might hate him for rejecting her, but she had no reason to harm him or anyone now.

Poor Gary! he thought, his throat tightening again. He would make sure Melissa Jones wanted for nothing, although no amount of money could compensate for the loss of her husband and the father of her children. Gary had been cheerful, humorous, efficient, bitingly sarcastic with idiots. Everyone had liked him – except the idiots. Going down in the lift Paul's mobile rang.

'Hello, Han speaking.' The Korean businessman had a smile in his voice. 'I'm sorry to be late with my call. The buyer was completely satisfied,' he announced triumphantly. 'I have your money.'

'What? That's fantastic!' Paul breathed, closing his eyes.

'Shall we say four this afternoon at your office?'

'That's fine. I'll see you then. And thanks a lot. *Kam-sa-ham-ni-da.*'

Han chuckled. 'Thank you too!'

Paul stepped out of the lift and crossed the lobby. Uncertainty and fear dissolved; his life suddenly seemed to shift into sharp focus. His divorce would come through in a few months. Sara, armed with a big settlement, would stop drinking herself stupid and get a life. She could keep the farmhouse with its ghostly monk and the ghost of their toxic married life. Andrew and Rebecca didn't give a flying damn about anything as long as they got their allowances. He could give up Melwood Materials tomorrow if he wished, go anywhere, do anything. And what of Justine? He pushed through the Adelphi's revolving door and paused at the top of the steps, jostled by a coach party of pensioners eager for their three-course hot lunch.

He loved Justine and he wanted her to leave Adam. Last night had been a revelation, the culmination of months of frustrated desire, a shattering release of unbearable tension. Justine had been as hungry for him as he was for her. He drew in his breath as he recalled the feel of her soft, slender naked body, the look in her eyes when she came, their moans and cries as they clung to one another. She had fallen asleep in his arms and he had held her for a long time, looking at her beautiful face as she slept. Thinking about how he wanted her. Forever.

'Not over yet, Paul,' Adriana murmured, watching from her window as he hurried down the steps and strode to his parked Mercedes, the sun shining on his dark brown hair and broad shoulders. Paul Melwood had proved himself weak, dangerously soft, and she was hurt and humiliated and very disappointed. But most of all she was angry. Despite the two million dollars and the prospect of a new life.

'*I* say when it's over.' She turned and hurled the glass across the room. It smashed against the far wall, fizzing tiny 1990 vintage bubbles. 'Not you!' She clenched her fists. 'Never you!'

'Where have you been? It's almost lunchtime.' Adam watched as Justine walked into the sunny ward. 'I missed you.'

He felt a stab of jealousy as the departing Registrar, a good-looking man in his late thirties, stopped in his tracks and gave a startled glance back at her. Justine looked beautiful, although pale and tired. She wore a short black leather jacket and a tight black v-necked Joseph top with cropped, dark blue jeans. She had on the soft leather ankle boots he thought were so sexy, with the high heels and zips up both sides. Her curly hair was all over the place as usual, and he could smell her sensual flowery perfume. He longed to touch her.

The mental agony was as bad as the physical – lying here, he had nothing to do but think. He was desperate for the police to arrest the stalker so that Justine would be out of danger. But what if she was arrested for the murder of that policeman? It might still happen. They couldn't even begin to deal with their own personal disaster until this nightmare ended.

Another question nagged him more than the pains shooting up his legs and back: Was it true what his mother said about Justine having an affair with Paul Melwood? Christine had never liked her. But Adam refused to believe Justine would bring her so-called lover to the hospital and snog him in the corridor outside the intensive care unit. Hurting the one you loved, destroying faith and trust and happiness in one crazy blow, was his speciality! Paul Melwood fancied Justine, Adam was sure, might perhaps try to take advantage of her vulnera-bility. He hoped to God the bastard didn't succeed. He was tortured by the thought of losing Justine. If that happened, he had only himself to blame.

'Sorry I'm so late.' Justine threw her big grey duffel bag on the armchair by the bed and leaned over to kiss him. 'I overslept, I was exhausted. How are you this morning?' she asked, stroking his cheek, trying to smile. 'You look a bit better.'

She could still feel Paul's touch on her body. Her nipples were tender, her breasts ached and she felt slightly sore inside. The astonishing intensity, the ferocity of their desire, had over-whelmed her. Beyond that, she couldn't think about last night.

Except that it shouldn't have happened. She blushed fiercely as Adam grasped her hand and kissed it.

Justine found it hard to take in what Paul told her about the beryllium deal and the Russian woman, Adriana, who had had him tailed. It seemed fantastic, like something out of a movie or novel. She had even laughed at first; she was already in so much danger, what did another threat matter? But it was very real to Paul. They had to be ultra-cautious until the deal was done, he said, make sure they were not seen together. Last night had been like a dream. This morning she felt terrible again; she was cold and shivery and had a headache, as if she was coming down with flu. That horrible leaden fear was back, like a stone lodged firmly in her stomach. In her mouth, the fresh minty taste of Paul's long, slow, parting kiss. And the taste of her own guilt.

Adam kept hold of her hand, kissing her fingers one by one.

'I'm about as well as anyone with a smashed leg and pelvis and broken ribs and Christ knows what else can be!' He grimaced in pain. 'Do you realize how hard it is to pee when you're lying down? By the way, you just missed my mother,' he said, looking closely at her.

'I did?' Justine shrugged. 'Can't say I'm gutted about *that*.' She had tried to get on with Christine Shaw, failed, and wasn't going to pretend any more. Things like not getting on with your fiancé's mother belonged to a world where people had a realistic chance of making it through the next twenty-four hours. Soon she would meet Chantelle Davis and together they would search for Matthew. And when they found him . . . what then? She shivered. This is crazy, she thought. I'm not really going through with it, am I? I can't! 'I brought you *The Times* and the *Independent*,' she said. She gently pulled her hand free, turned and rooted in her bag. 'And that novel you said you might like to try.'

'Thanks. Look, never mind me, how are *you*?' Adam asked anxiously. 'I don't suppose the police have arrested Casey yet?'

'No, but they'll pick him up soon.' She hoped that sounded convincing. 'They're looking for him as we speak. It's only a matter of time.'

'But how much time? Useless bastards! I feel so helpless lying here encased in plaster,' he complained. 'I can't do a damn' thing to protect you.'

'Don't worry about me,' Justine said guiltily. 'I'll be fine.'

'Will you? I can't help worrying. About you, about us. How I hurt you.' He had tears in his eyes. 'I worry about absolutely bloody everything!'

'Adam, please listen. You're out of intensive care now and you're going to be fine. I can understand you're pissed off at the pain and at being stuck in here, but try to concentrate on getting better, okay?' Justine glanced around the busy ward. 'Take your medication, smile at the nurses. Eat. Sleep. Do what they tell you.' She smiled. 'Do what *I* tell you!'

'Justine . . .' He reached for her hand again, touched his lips to her fingers. 'I don't care about my pain – I hate the pain I've caused you. I hurt you so much, I've been such a bastard! I wouldn't blame you if . . .' He stopped. A tear rolled out of the corner of his eye and dripped on to the white pillow. 'If you find someone else, if you leave me, it's what I deserve.'

Justine stiffened, and her face burned again. She got up, drew the flowered curtains around the bed, and sat down. 'Adam, I–'

'My mother gave me a load of old bollocks earlier,' he muttered, sniffing. 'Some crap about you snogging Paul Melwood outside the intensive care unit the other night.' He mimicked Christine's earnest, bossy voice. '*I know you're ill and vulnerable just now, darling, and maybe it's not the right time to tell you, but Justine's not the girl you think she is and the sooner you realize that, the better. She's nothing but a slut, like that awful mother of hers!*' He kissed Justine's hand again, gazed into her eyes. 'I told her to fuck off.'

'Good. Adam, I was freaked out about you that night!' Full of remorse, Justine stood up and leaned over him, covered his injured face with kisses. 'Paul gave me a hug, he was just trying to comfort me. That's all it was, I swear!' She had the power to hurt Adam as much as he'd hurt her. But she couldn't bear to do that. Suppose things went wrong? She might never see him again after today. If so, she wanted his last memory of her to be a good one. 'Christine saw us and was only too delighted to jump to the wrong conclusion.'

'I can imagine. I guessed it was something like that.' Adam smiled crookedly as she plucked a tissue and gently blotted his tears. 'You've got more class than I have,' he muttered. 'That rich sod fancies you rotten though, doesn't he?' he added. 'I could tell the minute you introduced him to me in that restaurant. The way he looked at you . . .'

'Lots of rich sods fancy me!' Justine said lightly. 'Poor sods, too.' She crumpled the tissue and dropped it in the brown paper bag sellotaped to the bedside locker. 'But you're the only one I love, Adam Shaw.'

'Do you mean that?' A spark of hope gleamed in his dark brown eyes. 'Are you sure you don't just feel sorry for me?'

'I feel sorry for both of us, Adam!' she whispered, her eyes wet. 'But yes, I mean it. I do love you.' It's true, she thought. I don't want to stop loving him. So why should I? Why let Donna win? It sounded crazy, but it was as if the night with Paul had crystallized her feelings, made her realize it was Adam she wanted. Despite everything. She had wavered and now she was steady. She only hoped it wasn't too late.

'I couldn't bear it if we let everything that's happened pull us apart,' he said.

'Neither could I.' Justine bent her head towards him and they kissed, a long deep passionate kiss. They hadn't kissed like this since before Donna, before the ghastly encounter with Ronnie Davis. Before Paul! It felt gentle, healing, arousing. She closed her eyes. Her soft hair tickled his bare shoulders.

'That feels like coming home. I never thought I'd do it again,' Adam said shakily when they drew apart. He slid a hand beneath her top and gently stroked her breasts. Her tender nipples hardened instantly. 'I love you so much! Hey, what's wrong?' he asked anxiously, seeing her tears.

Paul had kissed her, touched her like this, only hours ago. Scenes from their lovemaking flashed through her mind. Moonlight on pale, rumpled sheets, the glittering city beyond the big windows, the salty taste of his skin and the feel of him inside her, her cries as she came. I am a slag, she thought, hearing Ronnie Davis' snarling voice again, thinking of Matthew's note. They're right. Maybe that's what they sensed in me.

'I feel so guilty!' she whispered.

'About *what*, for Christ's sake?' Adam's voice rose.

'First I get Matthew stalking me – then another man tries to rape me! How could I be so incredibly unlucky? What made them pick on me? I must have done something!' she said, wiping her eyes. 'If it hadn't been for Matthew stalking me, you wouldn't be lying here injured, you wouldn't nearly have died–'

'Stop that right now!' he said fiercely. '*You* nearly died the other night – what were you supposed to do, let the bastard rape and murder you? You fought back and he got what he deserved. Now he can rot in hell! So will Casey when they catch him.' He paused, lowered his voice. 'You can't possibly hold yourself responsible for what they did, blame your looks or your clothes or God knows what. That's crazy – and it's fucking tragic! Some men prey on women the way one wild animal preys on another – it can be any woman, anywhere, any time! You had the misfortune to run into two of them. That's not your fault! It's bloody heart-breaking the way you torture yourself with guilt instead of putting the blame where it lies – with *them*. You're not a victim, Justine. Don't act like one, please don't think like one!' He lay back, exhausted.

'You're right.' She sat taking in his words. Of course I'm not to blame, she thought, conviction growing and strengthening. How could I ever think I was? She had been telling herself that, but not truly believing it. It was time to rebuild her self-esteem. Put the blame where it truly lay, as Adam said. Suppressed rage at Ronnie Davis and Matthew bubbled up from deep inside her. Davis hadn't raped her, hadn't stabbed her with his ghastly knife. He wouldn't stab her with his words any more! And as for Matthew . . . well, he had it coming! Her mouth set in a grim line.

'I wish I'd killed Casey the other night,' Adam whispered, his eyes full of bitterness. 'Beating the crap out of him only made things worse. I should have listened to you. He wanted revenge and he bloody got it, didn't he?'

'Take your own excellent advice and don't blame yourself for that!' They kissed again. Justine put her arms around him and laid her head on his chest. A minute later she straightened up. 'Adam, I'm really sorry, but I have to go now.'

'Already?' he asked, disappointed. 'You've only been here five minutes.'

'The police want to see me,' she lied. If they didn't want to now, they soon would. Kiely wasn't going to leave her in peace.

'What is it this time?'

'I don't know. They said it was just routine.'

'Yeah, right! Don't take any shit from them,' he warned. 'Phone a solicitor if you think you need one. I know a guy . . .'

'Knock-knock!' A young, dark-haired nurse in a white uniform stuck her head through the curtains. 'Got your lunch tray here,

Adam. Vegetable curry, like you ordered. I didn't know you were a veggie.'

'I'm not,' he replied. 'The vegetarian dishes here are marginally less disgusting, that's all.'

The nurse grinned at Justine. 'He looks a lot more cheerful than he did at breakfast,' she commented. 'I suppose that's down to you.'

'I'd like to think so.' She slid off the bed, leaned over and gave Adam a last kiss, hoping it was the last for now and not forever. 'I'll see you later, okay?' she whispered as the nurse drew the curtains. 'I have to go shopping after I've talked to the police – the fridge is empty and there's nothing but ice cubes in the freezer.'

'Why don't you stay home after you've done all that?' he suggested. 'Watch TV, have a good dinner, get an early night. You need the rest. Unplug the phone. But call me first, let me know you're all right.'

'I'll do that,' she promised, and hesitated. 'I wish I could stay with you,' she said. 'I don't feel like going anywhere.'

'I wish you could too. But we'll have all the time in the world once this bullshit is over.' Adam hadn't believed that this morning but he did now. Justine still loved him! He didn't deserve her love, but he had another chance and he wouldn't blow it. He frowned suddenly. 'Take care, for God's sake!' he warned. 'Until they've arrested that bastard. And remember what I said about the police.'

'I will. I know it's easy for me to say, but try not to worry.' She kissed him again. 'I love you!'

'I love you too.' He watched her as she walked away. The patient in the next bed, a middle-aged man, rolled his eyes and whistled. Justine smiled back at Adam, waving as she walked out of the ward. She hated to leave him.

Outside she found herself in floods of tears. In a hospital, that didn't attract too many curious glances. She went down seven floors in the lift, walked through the lobby and out into the big car park, glancing around her as she went. That was second nature now.

There was no sign of Matthew, no reporters or photographers hanging around. Now that Adam wasn't going to die, the hit-and-run doctor case was no longer sufficiently tragic or exciting to warrant further coverage.

Chantelle sat waiting at the wheel of a dark blue Ford Sierra.

305

She wore her jeans and the black puffa jacket again. She gazed at her reflection in the driving mirror as she combed and fluffed her dry hennaed hair. Justine put on a pair of black leather gloves, opened the door and slid into the passenger seat.

'Where did you get the car?' she asked. She pulled out a tissue and dabbed at her eyes. Chantelle took a last drag on her cigarette and tossed it out of the window.

'It's Ronnie's,' she said matter-of-factly, turning the key in the ignition. 'Courtesy of Merseyside Police.'

'You're joking?' Justine stared at her in consternation.

'No worries.' Chantelle smiled. 'I have to hand it back tomorrow – they'll give it a lovely spring clean, inside and out, before it goes to the next lucky copper on the list. Adam not too good this morning?' she asked, looking at Justine's tear-stained face.

'No, he actually seems better today.' Justine sniffed and wiped her eyes. 'At least he was after I'd managed to cheer him up a bit.'

'Good.' Chantelle put on a pair of sunglasses and reached for another cigarette. 'Now all we need is for you to cheer up. Me mum's picking the kids up from school and taking them to her place for their tea,' she said. 'They're staying the night. I'm having a quiet evening at home but if I decide to go out, whose business is that? I'm all yours.' She lit the cigarette and blew out smoke.

'Are you sure you want to help me do this?' Justine asked abruptly. There was a brief silence.

'I told you,' Chantelle said quietly, 'you saved my life, Ronnie would have killed me. I couldn't stop him killing my baby girl. But maybe now I can make sure this stalker doesn't get you. Like I said – I owe you one!'

Justine buried her head in her hands. 'I can't do this!' she moaned. 'I can't!'

'Okay,' Chantelle said calmly. She switched off the engine and leaned back, took a long drag on her cigarette. 'All right.'

'Would you put that fucking thing out? It stinks in here!'

Chantelle wound down the window and threw the cigarette away, took off her glasses and squinted in the sunshine. She looked across at Justine. 'Drop you off home then, shall I?' she asked huskily. 'It's okay,' she added. 'I understand. Well, I don't really.'

'I'm scared,' Justine confessed. 'Bloody terrified! What if it all goes wrong?'

'So what if it does? What's the alternative?'

Justine was silent. Then she took her hands away from her face. 'You're right,' she said finally. 'There isn't one.' She looked at Chantelle. 'I'm ready. Let's go.'

'You sure?'

'I'm sure,' Justine said firmly. 'Freak-out's done.'

Chantelle looked down. 'Love the boots,' she remarked. 'But they're a bit . . .'

'No problem. I've got that covered.' Justine unzipped the boots and pulled a pair of muddy old trainers out of her duffel bag. Chantelle waited while she laced them.

'And you can see all that curly hair a mile off. Even at night.'

'Got that covered too.' Justine took out a black baseball cap and tucked her hair carefully beneath it. Then she fastened her seat belt. Chantelle put her dark glasses back on, started the engine and drove out of the hospital car park.

'I checked,' she said, in answer to Justine's sudden anxious look. 'No CCTV around here.' She grinned. 'That's reserved for the doctors' and consultants' car park!' Justine smiled slightly, shook her head. They paused, waiting for a gap in the stream of traffic. 'Mind if I smoke another fag?' Chantelle asked. 'I'll keep the window open.'

'Have a whole bloody packet, why don't you?'

'Thanks. I might just do that.' She lit another cigarette and glanced at Justine. 'Come on, love,' she said quietly. 'Cheer up.'

'And why the hell should I *cheer up*?'

Chantelle blew smoke out of the open window. 'Because today's the day you get your life back.'

# Chapter Twenty-Six

At the top of Bold Street was the bombed-out church, St Luke's, its roofless blackened shell illuminated by orange light. The church had been left that way as a memorial to the 1941 May Blitz. St Luke's and its beautiful, peaceful gardens were now closed off, due to dangerous falling masonry. Matthew glanced nervously around as he followed the woman. She was middle-aged and wore a headscarf and a long black belted coat, carried an umbrella. A black handbag was slung over her left shoulder. Her high heels tapped the pavement as she walked. The September afternoon sunshine had changed to gloomy twilight and now it was dark and raining yet again, orange-grey clouds bunched overhead. The cold wind blew raindrops in his face. Bold Street was deserted now that the brightly lit shops were closed.

He drew the loaded revolver from his pocket and gripped it; the gun felt heavy in his hand. He had loaded it earlier, sitting in the car. He had abandoned the Ford Fiesta and suitcase in the Lime Street station car park that afternoon: now that the police were looking for him, it was no longer safe to drive around in it. And he couldn't walk the streets dragging a suitcase. He had only a plastic carrier bag that contained socks and underpants, a spare pair of jeans and his good white shirt, the tins he'd stolen from the Bluffs, and two bondage mags salvaged from his collection.

Matthew had spent last night in his car, uncomfortable and shivering with cold. He had woken up from time to time and driven around, furious at not being able to go near Justine's house because of the police car parked outside. This morning the car had gone, hopefully for good. He had cruised past a few times, but there had been no sign of her. What was the bitch up to? How would she spend her last day on earth?

He hadn't shaved or bathed, and wore yesterday's jeans and beige sweater, the mock leather jacket. He felt dirty, like a dosser, and hated it. There was nothing worse than not being able to take a hot bath or shower whenever you liked, put on clean, fresh clothes. He didn't dare go back to his mother's house. He shuddered as he recalled her lying on the sofa, stiff and stinking. She would be in some mortuary fridge now.

He looked round again, checking that no one else was about. The woman turned left down a side street and stopped by an illegally parked Nissan Micra. He heard the jangle of keys. Now! he thought. Just do it. He dashed forward and thrust out the gun.

'Give me the keys!' he shouted, menacing her. 'Come on!'

The woman whirled round and dropped her umbrella. Matthew had a glimpse of furious dark eyes in a pale face. She flung out one arm and something hit him in the solar plexus, winded him so that he staggered backwards and dropped the gun. He clutched his stomach and gasped for breath.

'Get away from me!' the woman shouted hysterically. She swung her heavy bag again; this time it caught him on the side of the head. Dazed by the blow, Matthew sank to his knees on the wet pavement, the carrier bag's contents scattered around him. 'I didn't survive a car crash and a hysterectomy to be threatened by scum like you!' Her face was contorted with rage and fright. 'Get away from me, you filthy bastard! Help!' she shouted. 'Someone help me! Call the police!'

She stumbled away screaming, deafening piercing screams that reverberated down the street and went right through his aching head. Matthew grabbed the gun, pushed his belongings back into the carrier bag, and fled. He was panting and trembling and his heart pounded in his chest. He hated running and of course he wasn't fit. He remembered his contempt for the joggers in Sefton Park.

He fled down another side street. A young man in jeans and a denim jacket was getting out of a silvery Vauxhall Corsa. He carried a briefcase in his right hand. Matthew ran up to him and gestured furiously with the gun.

'Keys!' he gasped. 'Or I'll kill you. Now!'

'Okay, mate! Take it easy!' Terrified, the man tossed the car

309

keys at him and backed away, eyes riveted on the gun. 'Take it easy, all right?' he implored. He dropped the briefcase and flung up both hands. Matthew picked up the keys, opened the car door and stuck them in the ignition. He started the engine and tossed the carrier bag on the passenger seat.

'Wallet!' he shouted, levelling the gun at the man's face. 'And get back – right back. Over there!'

'Okay! Whatever you say, mate.' The man threw a leather wallet at him. He caught it and stuck it in his jeans pocket. The man backed further away, raised his arms higher. He was scared shitless, Matthew thought, gratified. That was how it should be. He jumped in the car, slammed the door and drove off at speed. He would have preferred a BMW or a Mercedes, something flash, but this would do. At least the windows were intact and the petrol tank full, no broken bits of glass pricking him in the arse.

The nerve of that stupid bitch, he thought as he drove, wanking on about a car crash and a . . . whatever *that* was! Dirty, screaming cow! She'd reacted like a maniac. Had she even noticed the gun? Women were all the same, even women who looked quiet and respectable. He recalled Justine shouting insults, kicking him, screaming at him to leave her alone. Making him feel like dirt. His face burned.

The guy was probably on the phone right now reporting his car stolen, but stolen cars weren't exactly high on the plod priority list. Then again, looking for someone with a gun just might be! In Duke Street he pulled over and checked the wallet. It contained some pound coins and small change, a bank card and one hundred and twenty quid in ten-pound notes.

'Nice one!' He grinned. The sight of the money reminded him that he was starving, had eaten only a packet of crisps and a couple of custard cream biscuits hours ago. His empty stomach growled in protest. He drove around until he came to a McDonald's, parked in the sheltering, anonymous car park and stowed the carrier bag in the boot.

After two quarter pounders, chips, a cheeseburger and chicken nuggets he felt better. He drank a Coke and a large coffee, sweet and milky. The people there looked crazy. Dossers, drug addicts, stinking pissed nutters who carried on long, rambling conversations with themselves. A fat woman in red leggings, her hair a brittle, bleached frizz, shouted at a brat in a Nike sweatshirt. The brat had his own mobile phone, for Christ's sake! They should all be shot, Matthew thought disgustedly, rounded up and exterminated like the vermin they were. He wiped his mouth, got up and carefully emptied the colourful cardboard wreckage on his plastic tray into the bin. In a nearby pub he ordered two large Scotches and a pint of lager.

'What's this?' he asked aggressively, pulling a disgusted face as he sipped the flat lager. 'Drip tray Special Old Piss?' The landlord, a tall, bearded, perspiring man, his grubby checked shirt strained over a huge paunch, shrugged. He kept a baseball bat behind the bar.

'You don't like my lager, mate?' He looked at Matthew menacingly. 'You know what you can friggin' well do! Thanks for the tip,' he said, keeping the sixty-five pence change. 'Very generous of you.'

The pub had dark panelled walls with black-and-white photographs of battleships and ocean liners. Matthew returned the fat bastard's menacing stare, weighing him up, then decided not to argue. He left the lager on the bar and retreated to a corner table to nurse his Scotches, glaring at a group of laughing girls as he drank. They were talking loudly and chain-smoking, tossing back glasses of red wine. Students, by the sound of them. A couple of the girls looked pissed already. They would go on to a club, find men to fuck for the night.

Justine was like them. She was beautiful – and educated, for all the good that had done her! She looked like an angel. But she was a demon who had to be obliterated. She would beg him for death! He finished his Scotch, jumped up and strode out, glaring at the girls as he left. They looked at him and pulled faces at one another, burst into wild laughter.

Matthew felt better with the food and Scotch inside him, full of manic energy, the way he'd felt the night he torched the Jacksons. He got back in the stolen car and drove to Sefton Park, his confidence rising. He switched on the radio and turned the volume high as he raced along, weaving amongst the traffic heading out of town. He laughed loudly as drivers blared their horns in alarm. The gun lay beside him on the passenger seat. It felt like a friend. If some wanker tried it on with him, they'd get the shock of their sad life!

Aigburth Drive was dark and quiet, the wind rustling the

chestnut trees. There were a few diehard dog walkers and lone women scurrying home late, lugging plastic bags full of groceries. Matthew cruised past the big Victorian house, saw that it was in darkness. The police car wasn't back. It looked like there was no one home. The long velvet curtains in the ground floor flat were closed. Had melon tits and her rottweiler gone to bed already? It was only 9.30. He hoped her old bat mother was dead. He cruised as far as the park gates, reversed and drove back.

He swore and banged his fist against the window, hurting himself. Where the hell was Justine? She could be home, of course, cowering in the dark, but he didn't think so. The bitch went out a lot, flaunting herself, hunting for men to fuck. He parked the car on the opposite side of the road, got out and walked very slowly back towards Justine's house, ready to disappear into the park if anyone spotted him.

He passed a dark-coloured Ford Sierra with a woman and what looked like a teenage boy sitting inside, the tarty-looking woman smoking and gazing indifferently out of the partially open driver's window. The boy could be a girl, of course. Sometimes it was difficult to tell. He or she had a black baseball cap jammed over the ears and one arm pressed against the window, obscuring the face. The head was bent low over what looked like an A-Z of Liverpool. Tourists, Matthew thought scornfully. He wouldn't tell them they were miles from the Albert Dock or the Tate bloody boring Gallery or Cavern Walks, because he couldn't be arsed. Plus he didn't want to draw attention to himself. The Ford Sierra suddenly accelerated away, tyres screeching. The woman's sparking cigarette stub flew out of the window and landed glowing in the centre of the road.

'Stupid bastards,' Matthew murmured. He gripped the gun in his pocket, trying to get used to its unwieldy weight, and stood behind his favourite chestnut tree. It seemed a long time since he had stood there. He swore at the rain blowing in his face. His wet hand slid on cold metal. Tree branches creaked overhead. He pulled the loaded gun out of his pocket and peered at it in the dim light.

He would wait for Justine. As long as it took.

He wasn't going anywhere.


'Love the jacket!' Chantelle commented as she brought the car to a halt further down Aigburth Drive, out of Matthew's sight. 'He looks a real sad case, doesn't he?' she said wonderingly. 'Hard to believe he's a . . .' She stopped.

Justine's face was grim and frightened. She glanced nervously up and down the dark road. A young couple, their arms wrapped around each other, strolled past the car, heading in the direction of Lark Lane.

'If I could get him up to the flat and kill him there, I could claim self-defence.' She spoke in a hushed voice, like a scared little girl. 'There wouldn't be any doubt then. I'd be in the clear.'

'No way!' Chantelle looked horrified. 'That's far too dangerous. He might kill you first. I still think we should ambush him, clobber him with the baseball bat and get the gun, like we planned,' she argued. 'Take him down the docks and shoot the bastard there, sling him in the Mersey.'

'Then the police will know it was murder! And who's got the best motive? Yours truly! No. They already suspect me of knowing something about your dear departed husband's untimely demise. I'm in enough trouble as it is. My way's better.'

Chantelle shook her head. 'It's too bloody risky!'

Justine stared at her. 'He won't shoot me straight away,' she said softly. 'If at all. I'm certain of that. Manual strangulation is his preferred method.' Her eyes glittered. 'And there's no way he'll let all those fantasies go to waste,' she added, recalling the magazine picture of the naked girl on all fours being raped and half choked by two men. 'He wants his fun first, doesn't he?'

'Oh, my God!' Chantelle whispered. She lit another cigarette, her fingers trembling. 'I don't like it.' She frowned, exhaling smoke. 'I still think we should jump him – batter him before he realizes what's going on. Otherwise, no chance! We could both end up dead or in the slammer.'

'Chantelle, I can't sit here and argue any more. Let's just do it, okay? Before I lose my nerve completely. I'm going to get out of the car and walk back to the house. Let him see me.' Justine's face was pale in the darkness. She pulled off the baseball cap and stuffed it in her bag, shook out her mass of curly hair. 'He'll be right behind me. I need to know *you're* right behind him.' She paused. 'Okay?'

'Okay!' Chantelle sighed. 'If that's the way you want it.'

'If you don't want to do this, if you've changed your mind, you

313

can back out now,' Justine said quietly. 'Go home to your kids. I'll understand.'

'Shut up, will you?' Chantelle reached under the seat and pulled out the baseball bat. 'Ronnie kept this here all the time,' she said. 'Imagine driving around with a baseball bat under your seat! Lucky for me he kept it in the car not the house, eh?'

'Here's the keys.' Justine unbuckled her seat belt and swung open the car door. 'I'm going now,' she whispered. 'Don't lose sight of me, will you? Please!' Her mouth was dry with terror and she didn't know if her legs could carry her the short distance.

'I won't,' Chantelle promised. 'You'll be fine!' She hoped that was true. 'Go on,' she said. 'I'm right behind you.'

Justine got out of the car and closed the door quietly. She started to walk back to the dark house. Cold rain wet her hair and shoulders; the chill night air smelled of autumn. Wind sighed through the trees. Her legs, her whole body, trembled with stark terror. What if she was wrong? she thought suddenly. Matthew might just shoot her after all. How could she predict what he would do? She slowed as she drew level with the chestnut tree on the opposite side of the road, behind which he was hiding. You're crazy! she told herself. Get away now. *Run!*

Justine's heart was pounding, battering itself against her ribs. Her breath came in gasps. It took all her self-control not to break into a screaming, panicked, desperate dash for safety. Out of the corner of her eye she saw a thin dark figure emerge from behind the tree's broad trunk, stand still as if uncertain what to do next. The streetlight, half hidden by swaying branches, gleamed briefly on his cropped, bleached hair. She gasped in horror, thinking of Ronnie Davis. Matthew darted back into the shadows. A few seconds later he stepped out again, dodged between two parked cars and started to cross the road.

Justine gripped her keys as she walked trembling up the drive and across the front of the house. She climbed the steps to her front door and stuck the key in the lock. Turned it. Footsteps behind her broke into a run, pounding the gravel, and she heard hoarse breathing.

This is it, she thought. She had deliberately exposed herself to horrifying danger, taken this enormous risk. Now it was too late.

314

Every nerve in her body screamed as she braced herself for impact, pain, terrible injury. Death.

She had never felt so vulnerable.

He couldn't believe his luck when he saw her walking along, bold as brass, the cold misty rain soaking her hair and shoulders. Justine mustn't get inside and lock the door, escape again. This longed for moment had finally arrived, the culmination of all his dreams and fantasies. The past was stone dead, like his mother. The future was crap. Only now mattered. He gripped the gun, holding it ready. He caught her at the top of the steps.

'Don't move, you bitch!' he said hoarsely. Justine's face looked washed out beneath the overhead light, her eyes wide with shock and terror. He smelled her perfume, the even more delicious smell of her fear. 'I've got a gun – I'll fucking kill you right here if you don't do what I say!'

He pressed the gun to her left temple and grabbed a handful of soft damp hair, yanking her head back. Justine gasped, gave a choked cry of pain. He shoved her into the dark hall and kicked the front door shut. He twisted his hand in her hair, tightening his grip, and forced her up the stairs to her flat. 'Open the door,' he grunted. 'Come on, move your arse!'

Justine did as he said, praying he wouldn't notice the chain and fasten it once they were inside. The sweet musky smell of his awful aftershave hit her face and turned her stomach. His sad, shit-brown leather jacket reeked of some other foul odour, like formaldehyde. The smell reminded her of the hospital. And she could smell alcohol on his breath. That was bad news.

Inside the flat the phone was ringing. She wondered who it was. Adam? Paul? Stephanie? The police? She recalled Adam's face earlier that day, the look in his eyes, the words he had spoken: '*I love you. We've got all the time in the world.*' Had they? I love you, Adam! she thought. She wanted to cry, but not in front of this bastard. She wouldn't give him the satisfaction.

'That your new boyfriend?' Matthew snarled, kicking the door shut. He slammed her against the wall and jammed the gun to her head as he grasped the chain and fastened it.

'*No!*' She groaned with terror and her heart sank. How could Chantelle get in now, especially without being heard? What was she going to do? Think! she told herself. Don't panic. Matthew grabbed her again and dragged her upstairs.

'Couldn't bloody wait, could you?' he panted, yanking her head back as he twisted his hand in her hair. 'Fucking slag!'

They reached the landing and he kicked her legs viciously from under her. Justine fell, hands outstretched, hair tickling her eyes and nose. She tried to curl her body up, but he grabbed her right ankle with his free hand and dragged her towards the bedroom. Hands flailing desperately, she shook strands of hair out of her eyes as she tried to wriggle free. The phone stopped ringing.

'Why me?' she gasped, trying to establish the dialogue that experts in these situations said was so necessary. 'What did I ever do?' The answer was a kick in the stomach that winded her, then made her retch. Matthew let go of her ankle and she doubled over clutching her stomach, saliva hanging in strings from her mouth. Through watering eyes she saw his jeans and purple-and-yellow trainers, caught another whiff of sickeningly sweet aftershave. Matthew pulled her up by the hair and thrust the gun barrel into her mouth. At that moment Justine thought she would die.

'Don't you like that?' He laughed as she stared up at him, gagging and choking on the cold gun barrel. Her eyes were frantic. '*Don't* get me going on what you've done!' he shouted, angry again. 'Or I'll really lose me rag.' He dragged her to her feet and shoved her into the bedroom. 'Get in there!' he panted. 'I've been here before, remember? I know where you fuck all the men! You wouldn't look at me,' he snarled. 'You betrayed me. You made me feel like bloody *nothing*!'

Another inferiority complex. Was there no end to them? You *are* nothing, Justine wanted to say but didn't dare. He clicked the light on, sent her stumbling towards the unmade bed.

'Get your kit off,' he ordered, levelling the gun. 'The lot. *Do it!* Or I'll kill you now, you bitch!'

Her unread thrillers and the heavy Inishbofin quartz stone lay on her bedside table, the clock radio and Adam's copies of the *Lancet* and the *British Journal of General Practice* on his. Adam's bathrobe and some of her clothes were draped over the sofa. The bedroom looked so normal, a place where they had talked, laughed, slept in each other's arms, made love. Now it looked like a place where she might die. Even if Chantelle got in, she would be too late. Matthew might kill her as well. Justine fought back her terror, tried to focus on a tiny calm space deep inside her. She had to play for time, grab the opportunity when it came. If it came. She backed away, retreated to her side of the bed.

'I said, *strip!*' He levelled the gun at her, his hands trembling. Justine was terrified he might fire it accidentally.

'Don't you want me to get my black stockings first?' she asked breathlessly. 'Put some sexy shoes on? The heels are so high I can hardly walk in them! But they're not meant for walking in, are they?' She tried to smile. 'Let me put some makeup and perfume on as well. Get ready for you properly.'

Matthew stared at her, relaxed slightly. This was more like it, Justine being submissive, wanting to please him. This was how it should be. Of course it didn't mean he trusted the bitch an inch.

'Go on then.' He stepped back, keeping the gun levelled. 'Hurry up. And don't try anything!' he barked. He glanced around the bedroom. He'd need something to tie her up with.

Downstairs, Chantelle leaned her weight against the partially open flat door. The chain didn't give. She cursed silently. There was only one thing to do.

Justine pulled a pair of black stockings from her dressing-table drawer, moved to the wardrobe and took out high-heeled black shoes with ankle straps. Matthew stared at her, the gun trembling in his hands, his eyes glittering with murderous lust. She moved slowly back to the bed, laid the stockings and shoes on the quilt.

'Hurry *up*, you bitch!' he said hoarsely. 'Strip!' He was getting hard.

She took off her leather jacket and black top and tossed them on the bed, stood looking at him. She tried to breathe, keep thinking, not give in to panic. Matthew stared, mesmerized, at her full, round breasts with their rosy erect nipples. She had beautiful soft skin. This was what he'd dreamed of: Justine standing there naked, her blue eyes full of fear. But she wasn't naked yet.

'I need the loo,' she said suddenly. 'I really have to go.'

'*What?*' Matthew shouted, furious and disgusted. His erection subsided. He hated any mention of bodily functions. Especially female ones.

'It's nerves. I'm frightened about what's going to happen,' she said. 'What you're going to do to me. You can understand that, can't you?'

Matthew looked at her with loathing. 'You don't need to go,' he

317

shouted. 'You're a lying bitch! No more tricks!' He moved forward and snatched up one of her black stockings.

'Get over here!' He beckoned with the gun. 'Turn round and put your hands behind your back.'

'I need the loo,' Justine persisted, on the verge of panic. She was trembling, her eyes filled with tears. She couldn't stall him any longer. 'No!' she gasped as he came towards her. 'Don't touch me.' Her bare skin made contact with the hard edge of the bedside table. Her shaking fingers groped behind her, closed over the heavy white quartz stone.

There was a sudden crash from downstairs as the flat door flew open and banged against the wall, wood splintering as the chain gave way and snapped. Shocked and startled, Matthew glanced over his shoulder. In that split second, Justine lunged forward and brought the stone crashing down on the hand that held the gun. He gave a yell of agony and dropped the weapon, clutched at his wrist. She kicked the gun across the room and it slid to a halt by the door. Chantelle rushed upstairs, gripping the baseball bat.

'Fucking *bitch!*' Matthew screamed. He grabbed Justine and smashed her across the face. Dazed, she dropped the stone and fell back on the bed. Desperate to retrieve the gun, he dashed for the door and collided with Chantelle.

'What the fuck?' He recognized the woman who had driven off in the Ford Sierra. What the hell was she doing here? He'd seen her somewhere else, too, he was certain. He saw the hatred and fury in her eyes as she swung the baseball bat. The blow smacked agonizingly into both his palms as he caught the bat and wrestled her to the ground, both of them clinging on for dear life.

Chantelle got on top of Matthew, but he kicked her and rolled her over. The room resounded with their furious grunts. Justine got off the bed and grabbed her stone again. Matthew climbed astride Chantelle and pinioned her with his knees. He leaned down and sank his teeth into her left hand. She screamed in agony and revulsion, slackened her grasp on the baseball bat. Matthew punched her viciously in the face, then lunged for the gun and grabbed it. *Now!* he thought triumphantly. Both these bitches were going to get it!

There was a sickening thud as Justine brought the white quartz stone crashing down on his skull. Matthew reeled as he knelt there, half turned and stared at her, his eyes full of shock and surprise. He felt a sensation of exploding stars and flashing lights, time being suspended. The bloody bitch! he thought. Justine had tricked him again. His mouth fell open and he drooled saliva.

He couldn't understand what was happening to his body. He wanted to lift the gun and fire it, blast Justine's beautiful face to a bloody pulp. But his hand, his whole body, felt numb. He was drained of strength, had no control any more. He felt helpless and terrified.

'Don't!' he mumbled thickly. 'Don't kill me. Please don't!' Chantelle scrambled to her feet, her hand and nose bleeding. Matthew dropped the gun and sank on to all fours, crawling on his belly like an injured dog.

'What do you expect me to do, you bastard!' Justine screamed. 'Drive you to Casualty?' She raised the stone and brought it crashing down again. Rage and terror, the unbearable tension of the past weeks, lent her strength. 'Die!' she sobbed. 'Leave me in peace!' She cracked him on the head a third time, smashing his skull with all her strength. Chantelle gripped the baseball bat and watched silently.

The third blow fractured Matthew's skull. He collapsed, arms and legs splayed. Blood trickled from his nose and ears. Chantelle pulled a supermarket carrier bag from her jacket pocket and wrapped the baseball bat in it, fished out a handkerchief to wipe her bleeding nose. Justine gently laid the heavy quartz stone on the bed. Its pure whiteness was stained with Matthew's blood.

'Check the pulse,' Chantelle said urgently. 'Better if I don't touch him.'

'I can't!' Justine gasped. She hugged her bare breasts, shivering with shock and revulsion. She stared disbelievingly at the body on her bedroom floor.

'We have to make sure he's dead.' Chantelle looked at her anxiously. 'Come on, Justine, please! You can fall apart when the police get here.' She picked up Justine's black top and threw it at her. 'Put this back on.' She ran to the wardrobe and pulled out a long, loose-fitting purple sweater. 'And this.'

Justine put on the top and sweater then gingerly knelt over Matthew. She was terrified of his staring eyes and unable to believe he wouldn't suddenly sit up and grab her. Icy with fear, her breath coming in gasps, she pressed three fingers to his wrist and then to the artery in his throat. His skin felt rough, still warm. She waited a full minute, both women holding their breath. Rain lashed the windows.

'No pulse,' she said finally. 'He's dead, all right!' She jumped to her feet and ran out of the bedroom, thudded downstairs to the kitchen. Chantelle followed.

'Give me five minutes to get clear before you phone the police,' she said. 'I'm sorry I can't stay. Have a big drink and a bloody good howl!' She put her arms around Justine and hugged her tight. 'We can't meet again, but I'll be thinking of you.' She brushed Justine's hair back from her face. 'You're safe now, love.' She smiled. 'It's over!'

'I don't know what to say,' Justine mumbled. 'Except, thank you!'

'I wasn't much use.' Chantelle looked at her injured hand. 'Better get meself a tetanus jab for this,' she said grimly. 'Don't fancy death by lockjaw!'

'Oh, my God!' Justine's eyes were filled with tears and she couldn't stop shaking. 'I can't believe he's lying there . . .'

'He's *dead*, Justine!' Chantelle grabbed her by the shoulders. 'He can't hurt you any more. You've got your life back. Promise me you'll get over this – and what Ronnie did – and be happy again?' she said urgently. She glanced through the open door at the stairs. 'Being cracked on the head with a stone was too good for the bastard!'

'I promise,' Justine whispered. 'I'll be happy.'

'Good. Right, I've got to go.' Chantelle backed away. 'Take care of yourself, Justine!'

'I will. You too.'

'No worries!' Her footsteps sounded gently on the stairs and the flat door closed softly behind her. Then Chantelle was gone, leaving Justine alone in the silent flat with Matthew Casey's dead body.

Charley Bluff woke up and blinked at the autumn sunlight slanting across her pillow, a miracle after last night's endless rain. She sat up and looked out of the window; the back lawn gleamed with dew. Whitney snorted and stirred in her sleep. Charley lay down again and stared at the blue sky. Last night she had downed several large brandies, taken a sleeping pill and gone to bed just after the nine o'clock news headlines. She still felt groggy from the sleeping pill.

She wouldn't go to work today, she decided. Or tomorrow either. Stuff the old dears, with their incontinence pads and lost false teeth and all their bloody pills! She needed a couple of days off after the trauma she'd been through. Marinda had a broken hip, a broken nose and was suffering from shock. A few weeks in hospital would give them a chance to wean her off the booze, the doctor said. Old ladies weren't supposed to go staggering around drunk. It was difficult enough to avoid broken hips at Marinda's age without that. Charley looked at the gorgeous clear sky, felt Whitney's warm comforting weight across her legs. Marinda was already giving the nurses and doctors hell. Good! Let someone else take it for a change. She had enough to worry about. She was scared stiff.

Did the creep plan to come back and shoot her? The hideous irony of being injured or even killed by Dad's gun! The creep might even hurt Whitney. Tears pricked at her eyes. She got up, put on the acrylic leopard print dressing gown that Marinda had bought her last Christmas, and went to phone Mrs Harris at the Greenlea Residence.

'Good morning, Mrs Harris, Charley here. I'm sorry to leave you short handed, but I'm afraid I can't come in today. Maybe not tomorrow either.' She held her nose for good effect. 'I've got this awful cold and I wouldn't want to pass it on to any of the residents . . .'

She was in the kitchen making a cup of Earl Grey tea and wondering what to do with the hours of delicious freedom that lay ahead when the doorbell rang sharply. She gasped and dropped the teabag in the sink, went stiff with fear. She walked slowly down the hall and into the drawing room, drew the heavy red velvet curtains. Light flooded into the room and a car drove off, just out of sight. Charley looked nervously out of the windows. There was nobody on the front steps as far as she could see. She didn't dare answer the door.

'Who the hell is it?' she muttered angrily. When would the police arrest that creep? She loathed the awful tension, the dread of what might happen next. The young, red-haired postman cycled up the drive and she sighed with relief at the sight of a familiar, friendly face. She quite fancied the postman although he was too young for her of course, only in his early twenties. She hurried into the hall and switched off the alarm system, unlocked and unchained the front door. The postman was coming up the steps.

'Morning, luv!' he called. Bloody hell! he thought, startled at the sight of Charley's bulk encased in the leopard print dressing gown. What *does* she look like? One of the older postmen, Alan, actually fancied her. But Alan was a bit kinky. He handed Charley two brown envelopes.

'Looks like bills,' he said airily. 'Chuck them in the bin, that's what I'd do. Life's a bitch, then you die. Hey, look!' He stooped. 'Someone's left you a prezzie.'

A parcel lay on the doorstep. It was giftwrapped in gold foil and tied with thin gold ribbon. The postman picked it up and gave it to her, then hurriedly backed off as Whitney came growling to the door to join her mistress.

'Heavy, that,' he commented. 'Must be those diamonds the Sultan of Brunei promised you, eh? Right, see you, love! Not going to work today?'

'No, I . . . I thought I'd take the day off,' she said slowly. 'I don't feel too good.'

'Sorry to hear that. You're right, best thing to have a day off. You look after yourself,' he grinned. 'Don't let the bastards grind you down, eh? Ta-ra!'

''Bye! Thanks.' Charley went back inside, locked and chained the door behind her. She dropped the letters on the hall table and stood holding the package, feeling its weight. It was oddly shaped as well as heavy.

'All right, darling!' she said to the impatient dog. 'Walk in the park in five minutes, I promise. Just let Mummy check the post and get dressed.'

There was no stamp, no name, no address. Charley hesitated, then tore the package open and cried out in astonished joy. Whitney barked.

It was Dad's gun. Complete with box of bullets.

# Chapter Twenty-Seven

'What was that noise?'

The tanned, muscular young blond man rolled off Sara Melwood's naked, sweaty body, sat up and looked fearfully around the oak-beamed, lamplit bedroom. The curtains were open and rain beat against the mullioned windows. Heavy branches outside swayed and creaked in the wind. 'It's like *Wuthering Heights* or something round here,' he said nervously.

'I'm amazed you've heard of *Wuthering Heights*. Kieran, what are you *doing*?' Sara groaned. 'I was just about to come.' She turned over and reached for her cigarettes and lighter on the bedside table. There was an empty champagne bottle and a half-full glass of warm, flat gin-and-tonic. 'You're imagining things,' she said irritably. 'I didn't hear any bloody noise.'

'That's because you're pissed!' Kieran looked at the old wooden latch door. 'It came from downstairs,' he said. 'Sounded like breaking glass. How come you don't have a couple of dogs?' he asked. 'Living out here in the sticks?'

'I can't stand dogs!' Sara lit her cigarette and took a long drag. 'They're dirty, smelly nuisances that take up more time than kids. And they cost a fortune.'

'You could afford it,' Kieran said resentfully. He kept his eyes on the oak door. 'It's so bloody quiet out here,' he complained. 'Gets on me nerves. Is this place haunted?'

'Oh, for . . .! Darling, this house is hundreds of years old.' Sara sat up and caressed his shoulders, rubbed her breasts against his back. She wouldn't tell superstitious, Neanderthal Kieran about the ghostly monk, that would only upset him more. She'd never seen it anyway. 'You hear all sorts of noises,' she laughed. 'That's

normal for an old house. Especially on a stormy night like this.'
She drew her long crimson nails lightly down his bare back,
making him shiver. 'If you're going to move in with me, you'll
have to get used to it.'

'Is it the timbers creaking?' he asked. 'Or your bones?' And
grinned at his wit.

'Right little charmer, aren't you?' Sara missed Paul although
she wouldn't admit it to herself or anyone. She hated being alone
and wanted a man around the place, in her bed. She had no
illusions about Kieran Mulholland, the thuggish-looking barman
she had chatted up while out clubbing one night, but he would do
for now. Kieran liked cars and sci-fi movies and the *Sunday Sport*,
labels that he couldn't afford – or pronounce correctly. Football
too, of course. He was the classic cliché himbo. But Sara wasn't
interested in what lay between his ears.

'It's haunted,' Kieran stated sullenly. He turned back to Sara,
studied her face and breasts. She wasn't a bad shag for her age,
and he wouldn't mind having the run of this place, the use of her
Porsche and credit card. Sara Melwood was alone, loaded and
gagging for it. He could give up bar work. But Kieran hated the
creepy silence of the countryside, the pitch blackness of the non-
light-polluted night sky. He wanted the reassuring noise and chaos
of the city streets, the drunks, the dossers, pissheads screaming
and fighting outside clubs and pubs, the wail of police and ambulance sirens. He listened for another few seconds, then relaxed.

'Lie down,' he ordered, shrugging her hand off his shoulder.
Sara dropped her smouldering cigarette in the ashtray and obeyed,
her eyes gleaming with anticipation. Kieran parted her legs and
stared at her slim, tanned body. She could bloody well wait for it,
he thought. Horny bitch! Why should she come more often than
him? He knelt over her face and held his stiffening penis to her
mouth.

'Get me going again,' he ordered. 'Then I might let you come.'

He was a bit of a sadist, Sara thought. Definitely a sexual
fascist. But he excited her – so far. She moaned as Kieran roughly
stroked her breasts. She couldn't caress him because her arms
were imprisoned by her sides. She gagged slightly as he forced
himself further into her mouth. He stared down at her, lips slightly
parted. Sara closed her eyes and concentrated on her task. She
prided herself on giving an excellent blow job.

324

The bedroom door latch clicked. Sara's eyes flew open and she stared in shock as a man and woman appeared, the man middle-aged and dark-haired with a moustache, the woman youngish, blonde and blue-eyed. She wore an expensive camel coat and her blonde hair fell around her shoulders like a silk sheet. She and the man both held guns. The sub-machine guns looked like Uzis, the kind carried by the *Carabinieri* Sara had seen in Rome. A 9 mm pistol with an effective range of 100 metres, one handsome young officer she'd flirted with had proudly informed her in broken English. It could fire six hundred rounds per minute. Sara arched her back and dug in her heels, started to struggle frantically.

'Stop it, you bitch!' Kieran hissed angrily. 'I'm not ready yet.' He grabbed a handful of her hair and twisted it. 'D'you want a slap or what?'

Who are you? Sara wanted to scream at the man and woman. What do you want? But she was choking, gagging, couldn't breathe. Her eyes watered. She kicked out furiously again, tried to turn her head. She looked down the gun barrels, saw the elegant blonde woman's mocking smile, Kieran's furious little pale brown eyes.

'What are you playing at?' He pulled away, raised one hand and gave Sara a stinging slap across the face. The woman laughed. Kieran turned and saw them, saw the Uzis. His stupid face went blank with shock.

'What the *fuck*?' There was a flash and a deafening roar. Kieran went rigid for a second then collapsed across Sara's naked body, blood pouring from gaping bullet holes in his head, back and buttocks.

Sara was covered in blood and screaming, smelling the metallic tang and the smoke from her smouldering cigarette. She tried frantically to scramble out from under Kieran's twitching body. Away from the murderers with guns.

'I don't understand!' she screamed. 'Who are you? Don't kill me, please don't kill me! D'you want money? I can get money – just give me a chance!'

'I don't want your money.' The blonde woman looked angry. 'I want your husband. Where is he?' Paul Melwood hadn't checked out, the receptionist at his hotel informed her, but he hadn't been in all day. The hired help had lost him. They had gone to his so-called girlfriend's house, but he wasn't there either. The place was

325

surrounded by police cars and incident vans. He wasn't at his office; the trail had gone cold. Adriana was furious at being tricked, outwitted.

'Where is your husband?' she repeated. She stepped forward and smashed Sara across the face with the gun butt. Sara fell back on the bed, choking blood. Adriana looked contemptuously at her small breasts and thin legs.

'Don't . . . know!' Sara could only mumble in dazed shock. Blood poured from her left temple and split lower lip, and she bit on something hard as she ran her tongue around her blood-filled mouth. It was a piece of tooth, one of the laminated porcelain veneers she'd had bonded over her front teeth a few years back. Two hundred quid for that veneer! she thought stupidly. Her cheekbone was smashed too, judging by the agonizing pain on the left side of her face.

'My husband moved out,' she gasped. 'I don't know where Paul is, I swear! What is this? Please!' she begged, terrified. She struggled to sit up. 'I don't understand.'

'Don't you?' Adriana had been worried about Sara Melwood, wondered if she knew or suspected anything. It didn't look like it. So what? She had to die anyway. 'No, I don't believe you do,' she said. 'And because this isn't a movie, I won't bother to explain why I'm going to kill you.' She glanced at the dark-haired man. 'D'you want to fuck her first?' He grimaced, shook his head.

'No. I didn't think so,' Adriana laughed. 'Paul will know why you died,' she said to the shaking, bloodied, terrified woman on the bed. 'That's all that matters.' She glanced at the man again and nodded. They both raised their guns.

'No!' Sara screamed. She covered her breasts with her bloodied hands, trying pathetically to protect herself. 'Why?' she screamed at them. 'Why?'

'Shut your mouth, you scrawny old whore!' Adriana said icily.

Bullets smashed the windows and the three-sided dressing-table mirror to smithereens, ripped into the old timbers and plaster walls. Into Sara's naked body, tearing flesh and bone and sinew. She was flung back against the headboard and collapsed, dragging the bloody sheet with her as she fell across Kieran's body and lay sprawled with her legs open, her blue eyes staring at death. Adriana lowered the gun and frowned. Her thirst for revenge was only partially slaked. This wasn't much good, but it was better

326

than nothing. Paul Melwood would know he was to blame for his wife's death, would have to live with that. He was lucky to be alive. Now it was time to go.

'All right,' she said abruptly. 'Drive me to the airport.'

'So what if Casey had murdered me?' Justine brushed away tears as she sat at the dressing table, fluffing out her damp hair. The lamplit bedroom was warm and tidy, all traces of last night's horror removed. She would never forget the sight of Matthew Casey being zipped into a body bag and lugged out. She wondered if she would ever get back the Inishbofin quartz stone from the police. She wasn't sure she wanted it back. It was no longer an object of pleasure but an instrument of death. She could never again look at it without being reminded of evil. She glanced around the bedroom. The flat gave her the creeps more than ever now.

'I had to force it to end – one way or another! I couldn't take it any longer.' She picked up the cup of tea Paul had made her and took a sip. 'I'm so tired and freaked out,' she said morosely, '*sick* of police stations and hospitals and interrogations! Jail's probably next on my list of major life traumas. What's the point of living if I have to go through all this shit?'

'Come on, you don't mean that! The way you feel now is a reaction to last night – to the past few weeks. And there's no way you'll go to jail.'

Paul wanted to say more, but the hairdryer roared. He got up and strolled to the bedroom windows, parted the curtains and looked out at the stormy night. The weather echoed his mood. Justine had narrowly escaped being raped and murdered by that policeman, and last night she could have suffered the same fate at the hands of the stalker. It was mindblowing, horrifying! Now she didn't want to talk about any of it. Shutters down, subject closed. Simple as that. He strode back, snatched the hairdryer from her and yanked the plug out of the socket. Justine gasped and stared up at him.

'Sorry,' he said, feeling guilty at her startled look. 'But I need you to talk to me. This is doing my head in! I get back to the apartment and find you've gone without even leaving me a note. Then it turns out you took an *insane* risk, deliberately came back here alone last night!' His voice rose. 'What was in your mind? What

327

the hell did you think was going to happen? For Christ's sake, Justine! The bastard could have murdered you.'

'Stop saying that!' She flinched and turned pale. 'I told the police I believed I was safe because I assumed they were watching the house. I wasn't to know the patrol car had gone, was I?' She sighed. 'Paul, I've spent most of this morning and afternoon going over last night with them. How there was a struggle, how I managed to break away and slam the flat door on him. How he kicked it in. I've just got back from the hospital, I had to tell Adam everything too. He was freaked out, as you can imagine!' She stood up and turned away, pulling the belt of the white bathrobe tight around her waist. 'It's over,' she said tiredly. 'Matthew Casey's dead. I know I'll have to start dealing with my emotions and all that stuff at some point, but right now I only want some rest and peace and so-called *normal* existence. Can't you understand that?'

She would never tell another living soul the truth about last night, what she and Chantelle had done. It was their secret and that was how it would stay. Let Adam and Paul and the police and everyone think she was crazy! Matthew Casey was dead, back where he belonged, roasting in hell with other demons. She had survived.

'Of course I can. I'm sorry,' Paul repeated. 'I can't begin to imagine what you've been through.' He wrapped his arms around her and she stiffened. 'But you took such a crazy risk!' He hugged her, lifted the mass of damp, fresh-smelling hair and kissed the nape of her neck. 'I love you,' he murmured, his lips against her warm, soft, perfumed skin. 'You just went off without telling me. I was frantic, I couldn't stand the thought of you in danger! I want to be with you, protect you.'

'Paul.' Justine gently disentangled herself from his embrace and turned to face him, her arms folded. 'Would you mind leaving now, please?' she asked awkwardly. 'I'm sorry to throw you out like this, but I really need to get some sleep.'

'You want me to leave?' he asked, hurt and dismayed.

'That's right. I'm sorry.' She blushed and took a few steps back.

He stared at her. 'Okay,' he said slowly. 'If that's what you want.' There was a brief silence. 'D'you think you can sleep here alone after what's happened?'

'I don't know, but I'll try.' Justine glanced around the big bedroom and shivered. 'I won't be here much longer. The renovation work on the Childwall house is finished now. I'd like to move in as soon as possible, get things ready for whenever Adam leaves hospital.'

'I see,' Paul said, his handsome face grim. He felt devastated. 'That's the plan, is it? You're going to turn yourself into a suburban doctor's wife. A *betrayed* suburban doctor's wife! You can do better than that for yourself, Justine,' he said bitterly. 'Much better. Of course I don't mean me, necessarily.'

'Paul, you're helped me so much.' She looked at him pleadingly. 'I don't know what I would have done without you these past weeks. The other night was fantastic,' she said sadly, 'but it shouldn't have happened. I blame myself.'

'You blame yourself for everything! You know I love you,' he said. 'Now that all this shit is over, I was beginning to think we had a chance at last. I want you, Justine,' he said urgently. 'You're all that matters to me.'

'Please don't say that,' she whispered, anguished.

'Why not? It's the truth.'

'Adam's not even out of hospital yet and he's been through so much. I can't leave him now – I don't want to! Certainly not tell him about us. I could never hurt him like that.'

'He hurt you,' Paul said, stung. 'Or has that nasty inconvenient little fact been rationalized away and banished to some dark recess at the back of your mind?'

'No.' She looked at him, her eyes full of tears. 'And it won't be – not for a long time. Look, I wish none of these terrible things had happened! But they did and I couldn't stop them. I can scarcely believe they're really over, that I survived! All I want now is to get on with my life. And that means staying with Adam. I still love him, Paul.' She looked away and twisted her hands together, played with the belt of the robe. 'I've been really unfair to you, I know that. I should never have made love with you.'

'You keep talking about what you should and shouldn't have done,' he interrupted, shocked and stunned as his hopes and dreams crashed around him. Sure, he had money. He had bloody everything! Except the woman he loved. 'What is it with you, Justine?' He moved towards her. 'Why do you blame yourself for every bad thing that happens? You even thought you were to

329

blame for being stalked.' She gasped, but he couldn't stop the words spilling out. 'Why don't we talk about what Matthew Casey shouldn't have done?' he asked furiously. 'Or poor, vulnerable, traumatized Adam? He shouldn't have fucked your best friend a few days before you were due to marry him. *Should* he?'

'Stop it!' She was crying now.

'You'd never have looked at me if he hadn't betrayed you. You loved and trusted him, you believed he loved you.'

'Adam *does* love me!' she cried. 'You don't understand.'

'Damn' right I don't! You were so hurt and devastated, you didn't know what to do,' Paul went on. 'You could have coped better if you hadn't had his betrayal to deal with on top of everything else. Why can't you admit it, Justine? Adam made you feel more frightened and torn apart than that stalker did!'

'No!' she shouted. 'Stop!' She flung herself on the bed and curled up, put her hands over her ears. 'I don't want to listen to this.'

'I know you don't,' he said brutally. 'But you're going to.' He sat beside her and took her in his arms. 'I love you, Justine,' he said, stroking her hair. 'I'd never betray you with some sad, jealous, greedy slapper who hates you because you're the real thing and she's a piece of crap and knows it.'

'Adam never meant to do what he did . . .'

'Fuck your best friend!' Paul leaned over her. 'You can't say it, can you?'

He smelled her perfume, her newly washed hair, her warm body. He undid the belt of her bathrobe and pulled it open, slid one hand up her satin-smooth thigh and over her flat belly. He stroked her soft breasts, the nipples tight and hard against his palm. Justine moaned, tried to twist her body away. She squirmed and cried out as his exploring hand slid between her legs.

'You do want me,' he murmured, kissing her smooth belly, feeling her wetness on his fingers. 'I know you do.' He was suddenly shocked at himself. What the hell did he think he was doing? He was no better than a rapist!

'I'm sorry,' he said, abruptly letting go of her. 'I shouldn't have done that.' He carefully tucked the bathrobe around her naked body. Justine curled up, closed her eyes and they lay still for a few moments. Then Paul raised himself on one elbow and looked down at her, his grey eyes full of sadness.

'Don't you feel anything for me?' he whispered. He smoothed back her hair, traced the curve of her lips with one finger.

'Of course I do.' Justine gazed at him. 'But I've made up my mind,' she said calmly. 'I've realized that I love Adam too much to let everything that's happened destroy us. I truly believe he feels the same way. It's not only about Donna.' She paused. 'I know this doesn't exactly sound politically correct, but she really threw herself at Adam. She fancied him for ages, was determined to get him. All the while pretending to be my best friend! *That's* what I call betrayal,' she whispered, her eyes wet.

'I take your point. But Adam gave in to her. How can you live with that?'

Justine pulled his head down and they kissed, a long sweet kiss. 'Same way I can live with *this*,' she whispered when they drew apart. She smiled sadly. 'Adam and I are quits now.'

'No way!' Paul said fiercely. 'We're different and you know it.'

'Maybe, but –' She broke off and tensed in his arms as the doorbell rang, long and loud. 'Who the hell is that?' She glanced at the clock radio. 'It's nearly nine.'

'Ignore it.' Paul kissed her forehead. 'Let me stay with you tonight,' he pleaded. 'I don't think you should be alone here. Better still, come back to my place. We won't make love if you don't want to.' He hoped she would change her mind. He was agonized, gutted by the fact that she still wanted Adam. Especially after the other night. But he loved her and he wouldn't give up. Not yet.

Justine jumped in fear as the bell rang sharply again. 'My car's parked outside.' She sat up and tied the belt of the robe. 'Whoever it is knows I'm home.'

'So what?' Paul asked, furious at the interruption and at the nerve-racked state into which it had thrown her. Justine scrambled off the bed and ran out on to the landing, picked up the entry phone. A second later she came rushing back.

'It's the police again,' she said, whitefaced. 'Kiely and that Bernadette woman. Why can't they leave me in peace? I've only spent half last night and most of today answering their *fucking* questions!' She threw off the robe and dragged on dark blue denim jeans and a black cashmere sweater, pushed her bare feet into purple leather, wooden-soled mules. Paul got up and put his hands on her trembling shoulders, turned her to face him.

331

'It's okay,' he said gently. 'Everything's going to be fine. Casey's dead and you won't go to jail. I know the police are a pain in the arse at the moment, but that's all they can be! You're alive, you're safe. Think of that.'

'Yes, you're right. Will you stay in here?' Justine asked, blushing. 'I'm sorry, but I really don't want them to see you right now. They'll think . . . God knows what!' That she was jumping into bed with another man while her fiancé lay badly injured in hospital? Hadn't she done exactly that?

'Your private life is your own business!'

'Yes, I know. Will you tell them or shall I?' She gasped and whirled round as the flat doorbell rang.

'Take it easy,' Paul said anxiously. 'You'll be fine.' Justine ran out of the bedroom, slamming the door behind her. He sat on the bed and looked around the big, dimly lit room, at her clothes flung over the sofa, at the dressing table cluttered with her perfume, make-up and little jars of moisturiser. Adam's presence was everywhere too, from the white bathrobe draped over the sofa to the pile of medical journals by the bed. On the dressing table was a bottle of *Opium* for men, next to a comb with dark hairs entangled in it. The warm bedroom smelled of perfume, sex, intimacy. Paul sighed. He was an intruder in a private place.

He had no right to feel this sadness, the terrible hurt and disappointment. He felt it anyway. He couldn't even say he had lost the woman he loved.

Justine had never been his to lose.


'Nice flat you've got,' Bernadette Doyle said, glancing around the big sitting room. 'You can't swing a rat in my place.'

An unpleasant analogy. Justine didn't smile or reply. Kiely looked handsome and well-groomed in a dark suit and the black overcoat, Bernadette smart in a pinstripe trouser suit. Shame about the dove grey pashmina wrapped tightly around her broad shoulders like some Victorian scullery maid's shawl. Justine didn't invite them to sit down, but they did anyway.

Bernadette was disappointed not to be offered coffee; she bet Justine Flynn was the type who only drank it fresh ground. But it was late and Justine looked fraught, eyes restless and filled with anxiety. It wasn't surprising. She must be very tired and still in shock from fracturing her stalker's skull with the beautiful white

Inishbofin quartz stone. Bernadette imagined Justine picking it up on that windswept island off the Connemara coast, weighing it in her hands, never dreaming that one day she would kill somebody with it. It remained to be seen whether or not Flynn would face a manslaughter charge over Casey. And not only Casey.

'We've got some news for you,' she said. 'We've evidence that suggests Casey was responsible for the arson attack on the Jackson home.'

'That's not exactly news!' Justine sat down. 'Not to me, anyway.'

'We also found a missing videotape from your office – it shows Casey entering the premises. He had a photocopy of your curriculum vitae in his possession.'

'So that's how he knew where I lived! And other things.' Justine stared at Bernadette. 'Did he kill Anna and the security guard?'

'We believe so,' Bernadette admitted reluctantly. 'Of course Casey's home is still being searched by the forensics team and more tests need to be carried out.' She wouldn't mention the half-burned block of wood with which he had battered the security guard, the magazines depicting extreme bondage and sexual torture of women. Justine Flynn probably had enough nightmares to be going on with.

'I'd like to ask you a question,' Kiely said, wanting to get off the subject of Casey for the time being. 'Several, in fact.'

'Can't it wait until tomorrow?' She asked. 'I'm exhausted.' Matthew Casey was everything she'd suspected. So what? She hadn't been able to stop him murdering twelve people. If it hadn't been for Chantelle Davis, she would be number thirteen. She had her life. Now there was only liberty to worry about!

'Look,' she said, 'obviously neither of you has much of an existence outside your local nick – but I do!' She wondered where she had left the telephone number of Adam's criminal law solicitor acquaintance. 'I'd like to be left in peace to get on with my life. I want you to stop harassing me!'

Kiely leaned forward and studied her, his dark eyes brooding. 'I wouldn't describe our behaviour as harassing, any more than I'd describe yours as cooperative,' he said calmly. 'Where have you been for the last couple of days?' he asked. 'Or nights, more like? It's a bit pointless having a patrol car parked outside your house when you're not home. Wouldn't you agree?'

Justine was silent. They hadn't mentioned that until now. She couldn't tell them she'd been at Paul Melwood's secret apartment, making illicit love with him. Or cruising the streets and suburbs of Liverpool with Chantelle Davis as they searched for Matthew Casey, discussing how best to kill him once they had flushed him out. She looked down, twisted her hands together.

'I was at the hospital,' she stammered. 'With Adam.'

'Were you?' Kiely glanced at Bernadette Doyle.

'Of course!' Justine's nervousness increased. 'Where else?'

'We'll come to that later. Let's talk about the night Ronnie Davis was murdered,' Bernadette broke in. She played their new trump card. 'Why did you get the cab driver to drop you off in Lark Lane? You never mentioned that, did you? Lark Lane's a good ten minutes' walk from here.'

The cab driver, Justine thought. The bloody cab driver. 'I wanted to walk,' she said desperately. 'I was upset.'

'Thank you.' Kiely smiled at her agitation. 'We weren't sure you were the distraught young lady he picked up shortly after DC Davis was murdered. You've now confirmed that. Although he'll have to identify you formally, of course.' Justine gasped and stood up. 'Yes, you were upset, weren't you?' he continued. 'About your fiancé and your best friend getting together.'

'They weren't *getting together*!'

'What would you call it, then? The cab driver said you were more than upset. You were panicked, in a right state. Enough to want to walk for ten minutes on a dark night in the pouring rain. Wearing heels and an evening dress. Weren't you afraid Matthew Casey would be hanging around?'

'I didn't think about him,' Justine said sullenly, cursing herself for falling into their trap.

'No? Same as when you walked home alone last night, eh? Amazing, the risks you take without even thinking!' Kiely shook his head wonderingly. 'I can't decide if you're very brave or very stupid.'

Justine looked at him. 'I know what you are!'

Bernadette stood up and walked to the mantelpiece. 'DC Davis followed you out of the club. We've got several witnesses who'll testify to that. Including your friend, Stephanie. He must have caught up with you. What happened then?'

Justine sat down again, shook her head wearily. She couldn't take much more of this. '*Nothing!*'

'Did you see something?' Bernadette demanded. 'Are you afraid to tell us?' Her tone softened. 'Look, Justine, we're not thick! You couldn't possibly have reached Hope Street and got into that cab without him catching you up.'

'I'm sorry if it doesn't fit the jigsaw you've constructed, but –'

'Did he attack you, try to rape you? Maybe you had a knife,' Bernadette suggested. She'd been thinking about that. It was just possible Flynn could have stabbed Ronnie in the heart if a struggle had broken out. He probably wouldn't have expected her to fight back. 'Lots of women carry illegal weapons.'

'Do they really? I wonder why!' Justine said bitterly.

'Is that why you're afraid to confess? You had a knife because you were frightened of Casey. Do you admit you carried a knife that night?'

'No, I don't!' Justine glared at her. 'I'm not thick either,' she said. 'If I'd stabbed Matthew Casey in self-defence, I'd have been done for using unreasonable force, being in possession of an illegal weapon. Not him for stalking and attacking me! I could still get charged with manslaughter even though he ambushed me on my own doorstep and tried to rape and murder me. After you lot let him go! Why don't we talk about *that*?'

'You either killed DC Davis – you probably didn't mean to kill him, we realize that – or you saw something,' Kiely stated, frustrated by the fact that there was nothing else to go on. 'If you don't tell us the truth you could be charged with withholding vital evidence, obstructing a murder inquiry, carrying an illegal weapon and failing to report a criminal offence. You could even be looking at a murder charge.' He paused. 'What did you do with the knife?'

Justine sat still, her body frozen. She saw detention centres, prison, trial by media. Editors loved stories about women who killed men. She would be tabloid headlines, deadly female aggression personified. Any chance of regaining control over her life would disappear. No way! she thought fiercely. Davis had beaten her, tried to rape her, and she had killed him in self-defence. He would never hurt another woman. Same with Matthew Casey. That was enough. It stopped here.

'I never carried a knife.' She stood up and faced them,

straightened her shoulders. 'I never saw anything or killed anybody. I know it was raining that night, and I wasn't exactly equipped for a weekend in the Lake District,' she said sarcastically, 'and that I should have remembered my very own personal stalker nightmare and been suitably terrified and cautious. I'm sorry my behaviour doesn't conform to your expectations.' Tears filled her eyes. 'But all I could think of was my best friend and my fiancé screwing each other's brains out! That's the *truth*! And now you can bloody well leave me alone!' She turned away, her shoulders shaking. Bernadette glanced at Kiely and shrugged.

'You still haven't told us where you've been for the past two days and nights,' he said sharply, angered and frustrated by Justine's defiance. 'D'you want to be charged with perjury as well as murder?'

'What are you on about now?' She turned on him. 'Do *you* want to be charged with harassment and criminal neglect of duty?' she flashed. 'If Matthew Casey had murdered me last night, you'd have been to blame. You had him in custody and you let him go! First I'm a hysterical joke to be brushed off. Now you're trying to fit a murder on me, or make out I've witnessed a killing I'm too frightened to talk about. Or that I go around with a handbag full of illegal knives! *You're* the joke!'

'Where were you yesterday afternoon?' he shouted, seeing any prospect of promotion for the rest of his working life dissolve into thin air. 'You lied to your fiancé as well as us. You told him you had to talk to the police, that it would take a few hours. Routine, you said. Oh, yes!' He nodded at Justine's shocked expression. 'Adam would have given you an alibi if he could. But he was as gobsmacked as us. Where were you?' he repeated.

'I won't answer any more questions,' she said, her voice shaking. 'Get out of here!' she ordered. 'If you want to talk to me again you can do it in a formal interview with a solicitor present.'

'That's a very good idea.' Kiely nodded, breathing heavily. 'You're going to need a solicitor.' He tried again. 'If I don't get some answers – *now!* – I'm going to throw the bloody book at you! A manslaughter rap's just for starters. Did you murder Casey too?' he barked. 'Cracking him over the head with a stone three times! How do we know that was self-defence?'

'Now we're really into the realms of bullshit!' Justine felt the blood drain from her face again. They could speculate all they liked, she reminded herself. Proof was what counted, and Kiely wouldn't be this angry if he had any. It didn't stop her feeling terrified. She looked him in the eye. 'I'm asking you to leave!'

'*I'm* asking you again, where were you yesterday afternoon and the other night?'

'That's totally irrelevant and none of your bloody business!' In a minute she would collapse, Justine thought. Confess everything, tell them whatever they wanted to hear, so that the questions would stop and she could get rid of them. Except she wouldn't get rid of them.

Bernadette Doyle stared at Justine, eyes narrowed, trying to get the measure of her. She didn't know what to think. Except that they knew sod all.

'If you don't answer, you'll be arrested and formally charged with wasting police time. And then you'll be charged with . . .' Kiely broke off and the three of them turned simultaneously as they sensed another presence.

Paul Melwood stood in the sitting-room doorway, his hands in the pockets of his leather jacket. He looked calm and confident.

'Justine was with me yesterday afternoon and the night before,' he said quietly. 'At my apartment. We were making love.'

# Chapter Twenty-Eight

'What a slapper!' Kiely said furiously as he and Bernadette Doyle left Justine's flat and walked to their waiting car. 'Screwing Melwood at his apartment while her fiancé's stuck in a hospital bed, high on morphine with half his body encased in plaster!' They got into the car and slammed the doors. 'No wonder she's been so cagey all along – of course she didn't bloody want anyone to know where she was!' He thought of Lynette, imagined the heart-wrenching pain and humiliation if his wife cheated on him with another man. Pain or not, she would find herself in a divorce court before she had the chance to get her knickers back on.

'There may be one thing we've overlooked in all this.' Bernadette fastened her seatbelt. 'A missing link.'

'And who or what might that be, Sherlock?' Kiely glanced at his watch and drummed his fingers on the wheel, staring out into the darkness. 'To think I was actually sorry for her!' Justine Flynn had made a right prat of him, he thought.

'If Ronnie had raped her she would have needed urgent medical help,' Bernadette reminded him. 'Tests for HIV and STDs. There's no record of her visiting any A&E departments. Or her GP.'

'She could have gone to a private clinic. But they wouldn't report it, and it'd take forever to check them all out. Or maybe Shaw treated her. He might have been covering up for her all along. He must have known if she'd been raped, you could hardly keep *that* secret from your nearest and dearest!' He sighed and rubbed his eyes. 'So what's your missing link?'

'Matthew Casey. Flynn could be telling the truth,' Bernadette argued. 'Casey was stalking her. He could have followed her that

338

night, got the raving hump when he saw Ronnie hassling her. He murdered those other people – and he tried to murder Adam Shaw. He probably had a knife on him. He wouldn't have thought twice about killing Ronnie.'

'You could be right,' Kiely said slowly. It was a possibility he hadn't considered, one that suddenly seemed very obvious. The sexist dinosaur, so eager to portray Justine Flynn as the deadly female that he'd overlooked the bleeding obvious? He instantly dismissed the uncomfortable thought. 'D'you think Flynn knows?' he asked. 'Or guesses?'

'No way! She would have told us – we might have picked him up sooner then. The more I think about it . . . yeah!' Bernadette nodded. 'It makes sense. Okay, we didn't find a knife in his house or car, or that car he nicked. And the knife in that carrier bag's not the murder weapon. He must have got rid of it. But forensics can check the body again for hair, fibres and stuff. Plus his clothes and the Ford Fiesta. What do you think?' she asked excitedly.

'Yep.' Kiely nodded. 'Let's do it. Although we may never find out what happened,' he said moodily, 'now that Casey's dead.' He put his foot down and the car lurched forward, narrowly missing one of the crumbling stone gateposts.

'Watch it!' Bernadette shrieked in alarm. Kiely's crap driving scared the hell out of her.

'Sorry. It's a shame,' he mused. 'There's a lot of questions I would have liked to ask that bastard!'

'What about Flynn now?' Bernadette stared straight ahead. She didn't feel sorry for Justine any more either. She couldn't imagine screwing another man if her own boyfriend was stuck in hospital, suffering from terrible injuries. Had Flynn been banging Paul Melwood all the time Adam Shaw was in a coma? The thought of it made her shiver. It also made her wonder what else Flynn might be capable of.

'We haven't finished with her yet,' Kiely said grimly. 'She could still be looking at a manslaughter rap. For Casey, if not Ronnie Davis.'

'Casey has to be self-defence, surely?'

'She hasn't quite explained how she managed to break free and brain him three times with that stone. Not to my satisfaction anyway. She was damned lucky he didn't carry a knife last night,

339

wasn't she? Strange, that he took no weapon to threaten or murder her with.'

'Maybe it shows how cocky he was. D'you think you can make manslaughter stick?' Bernadette asked.

'I don't know.' Kiely smiled, an unpleasant smile, his eyes fixed on the road. 'But I'm going to have a bloody good try!'

The cold grey late-September morning smelled of dead leaves, exhaust fumes and distant woodsmoke. Paul stood under the hot shower in his hotel suite, exhausted and hungover, trying to come to terms with the fact that he and Justine were finished before they had even started. He had come straight back here after the police had left Justine, unable to face a night alone in the apartment, smell her perfume and body on his rumpled sheets. He was devastated when she again begged him to leave, told him it was best that they didn't see each other for a while. At least she wasn't crass enough to come out with mawkish clichés about staying friends.

Paul couldn't accept that they were finished. Not yet. Justine still had feelings for him, he was certain. But she was still in shock, sledgehammered by trauma, and it might take a long time for her to get over what had happened, sort out her feelings. He had to be patient now, not pressure her. Otherwise Justine would fall straight back into Adam Shaw's arms. He ignored the mocking little voice that told him that was exactly what had happened.

He stepped out of the shower and wrapped himself in a big towel. A thought occurred to him. Where *had* Justine been during those stolen, mystery hours the police now believed had been spent making love with him? She had gone off by herself, she'd said. She'd wanted solitude, time to think, to get away from craziness and danger for a while. Fortunately Paul had met Han at his apartment instead of the office, thinking it was safer and more discreet. Han was back in Paris now. There was no one to challenge the alibi he had given Justine.

He strolled back to the bedroom, dripping water on the blue carpet. His breakfast had arrived; he nibbled a croissant and poured himself a cup of coffee. He would check out this morning and go back to the farmhouse to collect more stuff, move into the apartment properly. Face the fact that Justine wouldn't be moving

340

in with him. She was safe now, that was the most important thing. So was he. Adriana Terekhova had gone.

Paul dialled the Mawdsley farmhouse, steeling himself for a shouting match with Sara. Maybe he shouldn't warn her he was coming. She might carry out her threat to burn the rest of his clothes and papers. If she hadn't already. Paul felt stunned with misery as he listened to the endlessly ringing phone. He only wanted to be with Justine. But she didn't want him and there was nothing he could do about it. For now.

He hung up after twenty rings and got dressed. Jeans, a grey cotton sweater, his leather jacket. It was nearly nine, Sara probably wasn't awake yet. She must have disconnected her bedroom phone. He would go and collect his stuff and to hell with her if she and her hangover woke up and made a scene!

Paul left the city and its suburbs behind, drove as fast as he dared along the narrow, twisting country lanes that led to the farmhouse. Fallen branches were scattered everywhere, the aftermath of last night's storm. The low, thick cloud layer didn't look like it would break anytime soon. The Mercedes bumped up the track to the farmhouse. Paul stopped the car and switched off the ignition. He got out and stood there, puzzled, instantly apprehensive. The iron-studded, oak front door was wide open.

'Sara?' he called, looking up at the stone house. He frowned. No matter how pissed Sara was, she never forgot to shut the front door when she staggered in at night. What was going on? He walked into the cool hall, looked up the polished oak staircase.

'Sara?' he shouted, gripping the smooth banister. No answer. He walked down the hall. The kitchen light was on and the blinds drawn. There were two empty champagne bottles on the counter and a spilled packet of unshelled pistachio nuts, greasy glasses in the sink. He went back along the hall and climbed the creaking stairs. At the top he looked down the narrow uneven passage that led to Sara's bedroom at the back of the house. Was she with a man? he wondered uneasily. He didn't want to burst in on them like some sad bastard in a B movie. He walked slowly down the passage and stopped. Her bedroom door was ajar.

'Sara?' he called. 'Are you there?' He walked into the room and stopped, gave a choked cry of horror. He grabbed at the door as his legs buckled under him.

The bedroom looked like a slaughterhouse. There was blood

341

everywhere, huge splashes on the white walls and carpet, on the flowered bedclothes that had been dragged to the floor. The lamps were on, the windows and dressing-table mirrors smashed. The ancient plaster gaped where bullet holes had torn through. Paul could smell death. It was a massacre.

He looked at the bodies on the floor, the young, muscular blond man, his body rigid and pale, eyes staring at nothing. Sara lay sprawled on top of him, covered in rusty, dried, clotted blood, her legs obscenely splayed. They didn't look like people any more. Just cold, stiff, dead meat. He saw another empty champagne bottle on the bedside table, Sara's half full glass of gin-and-tonic. Condoms spilled out of a blue packet. There was a faint smell of the disinfectant-like perfume he hated, even though it was supposed to be one of the most expensive brands in the world. The lace-trimmed ice blue satin knickers and suspender belt Sara had discarded were splashed with dark, dried blood.

Paul rushed for the bathroom and vomited, crouched low over the lavatory, tears pouring from his eyes. He was shaking uncontrollably. A minute later he flushed the lavatory and straightened up, breathing heavily. He leaned against the cool smooth wall. He was covered in icy, prickling sweat. In the garden a few birds sang, and he could see a dirty red tractor belching puffs of smoke as it crawled across a distant ploughed field.

He sat on the edge of the bath and started to cry. Sara would never again drink champagne, wear satin lingerie, go clubbing, fuck another man, worry about not being rich enough or if she would still be able to pull after the menopause. Think about new career possibilities. Her existence had been callously and brutally cut short.

Paul didn't need to ask himself what the hell had happened. He knew.

His fault.

'No more lies, Justine!' Adam sank back against his pillows, exhausted and crushed with misery. The lunch trays had been cleared, and the ward was quiet. Justine had drawn the curtains around his bed, and they talked in whispers. 'All that morphine hasn't softened my brain, you know! There's only one reason Melwood gave you that alibi,' he stated. 'You *are* fucking him! No!' He raised a hand as she opened her mouth to protest. 'Don't deny it anymore, don't treat me like I'm a bloody idiot. Did he help you kill Casey?' he flashed. 'I mean, you wouldn't be stupid enough to walk back to that house alone in the dark, not when you knew Casey would be waiting to rape and murder you. As he very nearly did!'

'Adam, I *told* you, I thought I was safe – that the police car would still be there,' Justine said desperately. She had been naïve to think she could keep her brief affair with Paul secret from him. Or the police, for that matter. Guilt suffocated her, and she was terrified at the thought of hurting Adam, putting the boot in when he was already down. It wasn't only the guilt; she felt shaken and upset most of the time, and was constantly on the verge of tears.

'Yeah, right!' He looked at her disbelievingly. 'You hadn't been home for two days, you were staying with Paulie. The police aren't going to hang around protecting someone who's not even bloody home, are they? Tell me the truth next time,' he said bitterly. 'Then I won't make a total arse of myself in front of the police, and unwittingly force you into revealing all the intimate personal secrets you need to keep from me!'

'I didn't want you to think –'

'What, exactly?' Adam grimaced in pain as he struggled to sit up. 'That you and Paulie were screwing each other up a tree every minute you weren't sitting by my bed playing the loyal, distraught fiancée? Must have been a hell of a strain,' he remarked. 'No wonder you look knackered!'

'That's not fair! It wasn't like that!' she said fiercely.

'What was it *like*, then? Don't get me wrong, I'm glad he helped you. Christ knows what would have happened otherwise!' Adam turned his face away as tears stung his eyes. 'I'm no bloody use to you stuck in here,' he said brokenly. 'No bloody use, period!'

'Paul Melwood did not help me kill Casey!' Justine clenched her fists. 'No one did. It was self-defence! I could have ended up murdered, it freaks me out just to think about it – and all you can do is go on about some stupid alibi!'

'I'm *going* on about you and that bastard screwing each other's brains out!'

'I could be charged with double manslaughter, I might be looking at years in jail! Don't you care about *me*?' she hissed.

Adam stared at her beautiful unhappy face and felt desolate, aching, agonizing loss. This was one pain a morphine shot couldn't cure. He smelled her leather jacket, her perfume, gazed into her angry, guilty eyes.

'Of course I bloody care about you,' he whispered. 'It freaks me out, too, what happened to you. What could have happened! But I want the truth, Justine. You fucked your great friend Paulie, didn't you?'

Justine was silent, her eyes downcast, hair falling across her face.

'All right,' she said in a low voice. 'Yes. But only once.' There was no relief in having it out in the open. All it did was make her feel ten times worse.

'*Only* once? Christ! You sound like me.' Adam sank back on his pillows again. 'Well, now I know what it feels like, don't I?' he said shakily. 'How much it hurts. Congratulations, Justine!' he whispered, tears rolling down his cheeks. 'You really showed me.'

'Oh, Adam, I didn't want to *show* you! I never meant it to happen,' she stammered, almost in tears herself. 'I swear, the last thing I ever wanted was to hurt you!'

'I've no right to feel hurt.' He turned his face away again, didn't bother to wipe his flowing tears. He had been hugely relieved to hear of Casey's death, despite his horror at Justine's ordeal. Today he had finally started to feel better, something almost approaching human. No more. He was crushed, devastated, in despair.

'I've lost you,' he said, tasting salt tears on his lips. 'It is too late after all.'

'No!' Justine took his hand. 'Adam, please, I –'

'Look, just go now, will you?' He pulled his hand away. 'Let me make an arsehole of myself in private.' He looked at her. 'Do you love him?' he demanded. 'Come on, tell me! Might as well know the worst.'

'I was attracted to Paul,' Justine said reluctantly. 'And I care about him. But I don't love him, Adam, certainly not the way I love you.'

'Oh, right. Thanks a whole bloody lot for that! Why did you have to come out with all that bullshit the other day?' he asked, his voice choked with emotion. 'About moving into the Childwall house, getting things ready . . . telling me you loved me and how you wanted us to be together. Go!' he begged, agonized. 'Leave me alone, Justine, please. I've lost you and I know it. It's all my own fucking fault.'

'Adam, don't say that. It's not true!' Her tears dripped on to his hand.

'The bastard took advantage of you when you were alone and vulnerable – and it's my fault you were vulnerable,' he went on. 'You're not to blame. I messed everything up.' Adam shook his head despairingly. 'There's nothing more to be said.'

'There is! I love you, I want us to get married. Be together like we planned. I mean what I say, Adam, I swear!'

'Do you?' He wiped his eyes. 'I suppose you've told Paulie that?'

'Yes! I told him the other night shouldn't have happened. I was frightened and vulnerable, like you said. I shouldn't have slept with him, I wish to God I hadn't! It was a mistake.' She grimaced. 'Sorry to sound like you again!'

'Don't worry about it. Look, I can understand why you slept with him,' Adam muttered. 'You were alone, terrified, you must have felt terribly betrayed, thought I didn't love you any more after what I'd done. Otherwise you'd never have looked at him, not seriously anyway.'

'That's what Paul said,' she whispered.

'Did he, indeed?' Adam bit his lip. The idea of Justine talking intimately with Paul Melwood, revealing her thoughts and feelings, tortured him more than trying to imagine their lovemaking. The bastard! he thought again, taking advantage of her. His throat tightened.

'What are you going to say now?' she asked nervously. 'That you've lost faith, don't trust me anymore?'

'No! I may be a stupid bastard, but I'm not a hypocritical one. I don't deserve you,' he said sadly. 'I never did.'

'Adam . . .' She hesitated. 'Do you still want me?'

'Of course I bloody want you!' He grasped her hand and kissed it. 'I love you, Justine. But I feel as though I've lost you.' He stared up at her. 'Are you sure you still want *me*?'

'I'm sure. But I'm frightened we might split up after all,' she said disconsolately.

'I love you, and you still love me.' He smiled through his tears. 'You've made me believe in miracles! How the hell can we split up now?'

'If I get charged with manslaughter – or murder – there might be a lot of publicity. I'll be every tabloid editor's fantasy made flesh,' she whispered fearfully. 'We'll have no privacy, our lives will be ripped apart. When a man goes to prison, his partner usually sticks by him. Most female prisoners are abandoned and forgotten about.'

'So you think I'll abandon you? No way! Look, stop talking about bloody tabloids and going to prison!' he whispered fiercely. 'Come here.' Justine leaned over him. Adam put his arms around her and kissed her. 'You'll be all right,' he whispered, hugging her to him. '*We* will. You're not going to prison! I love you more than anything or anyone. Nothing will change that. We'll never lose each other now!' She laid her head on his shoulder.

The knowledge that Justine had slept with Paul Melwood was indescribably painful to Adam. Even though he knew that it served him bloody right! It was unbelievable what she had been through, what she might still have to go through. But Justine loved him and wanted to stay with him. He was incredibly fortunate. He would get out of hospital soon, Adam promised himself, and they would build a new life together. He kissed her soft lips, looked into her eyes, caressed her beautiful hair. This time he would take care of her. Forever.

He still hated Paul Melwood's guts.


Paul walked into his apartment, poured himself a giant measure of Scotch and collapsed on the sofa. A tragic incident, a grim and terrible example of the increasing violence in rural areas. Or so it seemed. Only this time the householder and her young lover had been shot, rather than the intruders. He could tell the police what little he knew about Adriana Tereshkova, but he was under no illusions that they would trace her, wherever she had flown off to. He was the one who would face charges of trafficking in illegal nuclear materials, conspiracy to murder person or persons very well known. Although shocked, horrified and torn with guilt and remorse, Paul wasn't ready to face a stiff jail sentence. Lose his company, money, reputation, everything he had. He finished the Scotch and poured more.

As Sara's husband he was suspect number one, of course, statistically speaking. Most murdered women were victims of husbands or partners. It wasn't robbery because nothing was missing. Neither Sara nor her lover had been sexually assaulted, although Sara had been struck around the face and head with some blunt object. It appeared to be a mystery. The police would dig and dig, though, and maybe they would find something. Maybe not.

Paul tried to put himself in their investigating shoes. Sara had had many affairs, they might reason; something could have snapped. But he had moved out, started divorce proceedings, offered her a big settlement. Why bother to go to those lengths if he had murder on his mind? Or was that a diversionary tactic? Either way, they couldn't prove anything. So far. He had to sit it out, stay dumb.

He thought of Justine. She knew about the beryllium deal and its tragic consequences for Gary Jones, would realize why Sara had died. She wouldn't say anything to the police. Paul only hoped Justine wouldn't condemn him. She knew his secret and he knew hers. It was an intimate situation, like being lovers. Except that Justine didn't want him as her lover. Pain stabbed his heart again, despite the shock and remorse at Sara's appalling murder. He had no interest in her lover, Kieran something. Sara's credit card had been found in the man's jacket pocket.

Sara's parents had died years ago, and her younger sister, Kate, was on holiday in Thailand. He couldn't reach Andrew or Rebecca, but had left messages on their answering machines. They must have gone away for the weekend. They would be shocked to hear of their mother's death, but Paul didn't think they would miss her very much once the shock had worn off. As parents, it had been down to him and Sara to fight the battle for communication. They had lost that battle. Another failure.

He swallowed Scotch and stared out at the city lights, the Mersey glittering in the distance. Disjointed thoughts and questions raced through his brain. Tears filled his eyes and he wiped them away. He could put the farmhouse on the market now. *May your wishes come true and curse you!* Whether or not anyone would want to buy a house where a woman and her young lover had been brutally murdered by one or more unknown assailants, was another question. He didn't care; he would give it away. Or shut it up forever, leave it to the mice and spiders and earthbound souls of medieval monks.

'I'm sorry, Sara,' he whispered, choked with anguish. 'I'm so sorry!' He gulped more Scotch and started to sob, big, broken sobs that racked his body. He couldn't shake the terrible image of his wife's naked, blood-splashed corpse in that house of death, her wide open pale blue eyes, so horribly devoid of expression. Where was Sara's soul now, her spirit? Cursing him from some other dimension? Or at peace, beyond the petty and wearing range of pointless human emotion?

The Scotch bottle was empty and there was nothing else to drink. A full yellow moon broke out from behind the clouds. Justine didn't pick up her phone, and the answering machine was switched off. Paul imagined she had had more than enough of answering machines. She was probably sitting by Adam's bedside, holding his hand while they talked about their future together. He had no future. He didn't care if he got arrested and banged up. So fucking what? He deserved it, didn't he?

Paul realized he was drunk. But not drunk enough. He picked up his car keys then dropped them, walked slowly into the hall and pulled on his jacket. He would go out and drink more Scotch in some bar, then wander the city streets until he was too tired to think any more. Maybe he would be mugged, get his head kicked in, be stabbed and thrown in the Mersey. He didn't care.

Anything to anaesthetize the unbearable pain, the guilt that would torment him as long as he lived. The love he felt for a woman he could never have.

All his fault.

# Chapter Twenty-Nine

The house was warm and there was a savoury smell of cooking, a welcome refuge from the cold misty December evening. The sound of a Chopin concerto drifted faintly from the sitting room. Justine frowned as she shut the front door. She didn't like Chopin much, and found classical music depressing lately. In the dining room the table was set, polished glasses sparkling in the candle-light. She took off her coat and dumped her briefcase in the hall, walked into the brand new fitted kitchen of the big old house. She felt exhausted, drained. And apprehensive.

'Hi there!' The kitchen was a mess and Adam looked flushed and happy. He wore black jeans and a navy blue sweatshirt with the sleeves pushed up. She went into his arms and they kissed. 'How are you?' he asked, stroking her hair. 'How's the new job going? Did you have a good POETS day?'

Piss-off-early-tomorrow's-Saturday. 'It was all right. I ran out of steam around four o'clock. The job's fine.' She smiled. 'It's me that's the problem – I get lost in thought sometimes, completely lose track. Luckily that hasn't happened in a meeting! The people there know about me, but I haven't had any awkward questions or comments. So far. What's this?' she asked, looking at the steaming pans. 'You should be resting. I know you're going back to work next week, but –'

'I wanted to surprise you. I felt better today and got sick of sitting around the house reading the papers and watching crap television. You wouldn't believe the shit programmes they put on during the day.'

'I would!'

'Anyway, I had to go out this afternoon. To the physio.'

'Oh, yes. How did you get on?'

'Not too bad. Bit painful today, but I'm just relieved I don't need those bloody crutches any more.' Adam let go of her and took a bottle of champagne from the fridge. 'Have a drink,' he said. 'Then we'll eat. I'll wait on you for a change. I've done *boeuf bourguignon* with ribbon noodles – I saw it on a cookery programme,' he grinned. 'Giant grilled prawns on a bed of salad for starters. At least that's easy.'

'I'm impressed! The noodles smell great.' The cork sploshed and she took the glass of foaming champagne he handed her. 'Adam . . .'

'Yep?' He slid one arm around her waist and smiled, thinking how sexy she looked in the tight purple suit with the black top underneath. He felt violent desire as he looked at her. He couldn't get enough of her since he had come out of hospital. Their laughter and closeness, every minute they spent together, each time they made love, felt like a miracle to him; Justine felt the same way, wanted him as much as he wanted her. The nightmare was receding. Although not quite. Adam could scarcely believe that she still loved him, that they had survived the terrible whirlwind that had almost torn their lives apart. They certainly hadn't emerged unscathed. He worried about Justine all the time, and both of them had days when they were laid low by fear, anxiety, depression. But that was to be expected after what had happened. With time and a peaceful, happy life, those feelings would disappear.

'I had a phone call this afternoon,' she said hesitantly. Adam took his arm away as she removed her jacket and draped it over a chair. The skirt was short and close fitting around her curved waist and slender hips. 'From Paul Melwood.'

'*What?*' Adam frowned, and his handsome face darkened ominously.

'He asked if he could see me tonight and I said yes. I'm meeting him at that bar near the Albert Dock. He wanted to have dinner, but I told him I'd rather just make it a quick drink. His trial starts next week,' she said. 'He knows he's looking at a long stretch.'

'Good!' Adam turned away, furious and filled with anxiety.

'Adam, don't be like that! He only wants to say goodbye. I tried to call you, but you were out. And I didn't know you were cooking or I'd have . . .'

'Well, this is great!' He dumped his glass of champagne on the table. 'The bastard's got a bloody nerve!' he said furiously. 'He knows we're back together, living in our new house – that we're getting married just before Christmas and he's *not* on the guest list! Why can't he fuck off?' That was what scared him about the miracle, he realized. The fact that any second of any day it might blow up in his face.

'He did fuck off,' Justine said, pained. 'I haven't heard from Paul for almost three months.'

'And you've been all the better for it!'

'He only wants to say goodbye,' she repeated. 'Look, I can understand you're not happy about it,' she said anxiously, 'but it's one drink! It won't take long.'

'Justine.' Adam sat at the kitchen table, grimaced at the sudden pain in his lower back. Some days he felt more like eighty than thirty. He had physiotherapy twice a week now, instead of every day. But it was a long haul. He wondered if he would ever feel normal again. 'We're talking about a corrupt, so-called busi-nessman who's facing charges of conspiracy to murder and trafficking in stolen nuclear materials,' he said quietly. 'He may not be guilty of murder, but he certainly got himself mixed up with some very dodgy people. And I don't mean MI5! If that woman, Melissa Jones, hadn't looked in her dead husband's diary, read what he'd written about that contaminated beryllium consignment and called the police, our Paulie would have got away with it. I can't understand how the hell he managed to get bail!' He paused, gulped a mouthful of champagne. 'You told me what a great friend he was, how he helped you . . .'

'He did!'

'But he could have got you killed.' Adam stared at her. 'He got his wife killed, didn't he? And his employee, Gary Jones. He may not have killed them himself, but he's responsible. The same thing could have happened to you! That's why I hate him,' he said slowly. 'Not just because you and he . . .'

She blushed and he glanced away. There was an awkward silence. 'You've been through hell this past couple of months,' he went on. 'You've had an agonizing wait, not knowing whether you'd face manslaughter charges in respect of Casey or Ronnie Davis. You've just heard from the CPS that you won't be charged. But now everything's fine, *we're* fine. Of course you still feel bad

351

now and then, you haven't come to terms with all the trauma. That's going to take time, maybe a long time. Talking to Melwood again certainly won't help your recovery.' He stood up, pushed back his chair. 'The police have refused him protection, but that doesn't mean he's not at risk. He'll have to give evidence at his trial, won't he? Do you think it's a good idea even to be seen with him?'

'It's only a drink,' Justine repeated sulkily. 'I'm not going to sleep with him again! Don't you trust me, Adam, is that it?'

'Of course I trust you! That's not what it's about. You've been better these past few weeks, less jumpy and anxious, not looking over your shoulder every minute when we're out. Having nightmares about blood and knives and stalkers, being terrified whenever the phone or doorbell rings. I'm worried that if you see Paul bloody Melwood it might upset you all over again, cause a setback.'

'I can't not do things because they may or may not upset me,' Justine argued. 'That's the perfect way to stay traumatized for life! But yes, you're right,' she said abruptly. 'It probably isn't wise to meet him. I'll phone and cancel, take a shower. Then we'll have dinner.' Adam had voiced all her fears; she was very reluctant to meet Paul and talk to him. Even if it was for the last time.

'Never mind the bloody dinner,' Adam sighed. He wrapped his arms around her again. 'Go on!' he whispered, kissing her. 'Say goodbye to him. Just promise you'll come back to me. I'm still terrified of losing you,' he confessed shakily. 'I get crazy sitting around the house all day, wondering if you're all right. I have to stop myself phoning you every half hour, turning up at your office to have lunch with you or drive you home every day. You're so precious to me!' His luminous dark brown eyes were anxious, troubled. 'I can't stop thinking how I don't deserve you, how I couldn't bear to lose you!'

'When a man says he doesn't deserve you, believe him!' Justine teased. 'The sooner you get back to work, the better.' She stopped smiling and hugged him tight, stared into his eyes. 'I love you,' she whispered. 'I'll always come back.'

'Will you?' Adam was kissing her lips and smooth throat, unhooking her bra, pulling off the stretchy black velvet top. His warm hands stroked her bare back, her breasts. He manoeuvred her out of the kitchen and into the sitting room, where they

352

collapsed on the sofa. He dragged the tight skirt up over her hips, pulled off her tights and pants. Justine groaned with pleasure as his fingers slid inside her, stroking gently at first, then harder.

'D'you want me?' he murmured, kissing and sucking at her breasts. 'Tell me you want me, Justine, I need to hear you say it!'

'I want you, you know I do!' She moaned with pleasure as he flicked his tongue over her hardened nipples. 'You're doing this deliberately,' she gasped, as he gently parted her thighs, stroking the soft skin. 'You want Paul to smell you all over me, don't you?'

Adam was deep inside her and she was crying out and clinging to him, lifting her hips to meet his thrusts and moving her head from side to side as her body melted, shuddered on the verge of orgasm. Adam's fingers slid through her silky hair, held her head still for a second. He looked into her eyes.

'He'd better not get that close!' he whispered fiercely.


'Justine! It's great to see you.' Paul stood up as she entered the dark, smoky bar near the Albert Dock and walked to his table, shrugging off her soft black leather coat. Her tight purple suit looked creased and rumpled, and her beautiful curly hair was wild. He smelled her familiar perfume. Justine didn't smile back and he felt hurt when she quickly turned her face so that his kiss landed on her cheek instead of her mouth.

'I got you a drink,' he said, indicating the glass of Sancerre.

'Thanks.' She sat down and sipped it. 'I can't stay long,' she said, looking at him for the first time. Paul wore a dark grey suit and a white shirt, no tie. He looked thinner, she thought, pale and unhappy. 'Adam was cooking dinner for us. I didn't know, otherwise I would have cancelled tonight.'

'I see.' He didn't want to hear about Adam, visualize unbearably cosy domestic scenes of food and wine and sex on the sofa. 'How are you?' he asked. 'You look great.'

'I'm doing okay.' She hesitated. 'I get bad dreams and I feel anxious sometimes. It's not over in my head. But I'm getting there.'

'Of course.' He wanted to grab her and pull her into his arms. She took another sip of wine and set the glass down again.

'I'm very sorry about Sara,' she said. 'Her death must have been a terrible shock for you. And for your family.'

'Yes. They don't speak to me any more,' he said abruptly. 'Not that I blame them. Thanks for your condolence card – and the letter. It helped.'

'Did it? I'm glad.' Paul was so lonely now, she thought, so isolated. Ostracized by his family and friends, his business ruined, facing years in prison, tormented over the deaths of Sara and Gary Jones. He was ruined now. But alive.

'I'm sorry I upset you that night,' he said in a low voice. 'I shouldn't have said those things.'

'Forget it.' Justine sat with her arms and legs crossed, her hair partially concealing her face. Her body radiated tension.

'Are you happy?' he asked. He took a gulp of Scotch. 'I mean, with Adam.'

'Yes.' She shook back her hair, looked into his eyes. 'I am, actually.'

'Good. I just wanted to know. I love you,' he said. 'I miss you like crazy!'

'Don't, Paul!' she begged. 'Please!'

'It's okay, no worries.' He smiled crookedly. 'I'm not going to bombard you with letters and visiting orders from the nick, beg you to wait for me. There's no chance for us, there never was. I know that.'

'I care about you,' she said desperately. 'We can stay in touch.'

'No,' he said. 'You've got your life. Adam. I'll be in jail.' He took her hand, felt the smoothness of her skin, stared at the glittering diamond ring on the third finger. 'I might get time knocked off for good behaviour,' he said gloomily. 'As if you've got a chance to do anything else in prison!'

'You don't belong in prison. You're not a murderer, you never wanted anyone to die.'

'I was too greedy, got mixed up with the wrong people.' He squeezed her hand. 'I'm to blame for what happened.'

'Can't you get away?' she asked suddenly. 'Make a new life somewhere?'

'I thought about it. Briefly. They've taken my passport and frozen my assets. Sounds painful, doesn't it? I only have enough for food, rent and petrol.' He smiled slightly. 'But I suppose I could get round that, if I really wanted to.'

'Then why don't you!'

He looked at her and she saw the warmth in his grey eyes. 'Would you come with me?'

She glanced away, lowered her head. 'No.'

'I didn't think so. Anyway, there's no point,' he sighed, holding on to her hand. 'I don't want to go on the run for years. I'd rather do the bird, or whatever they call it, and get it over. I just wanted to see you one last time before the trial starts,' he said. 'Make sure you were okay. Let you know . . .' he lowered his voice '. . . that I'll never breathe a word to anyone of what you told me that night. About Ronnie Davis.'

Justine stiffened. 'I know you won't.' Suddenly she needed a drink. She picked up her glass of wine and drained it. 'I should go,' she said. 'Adam will be waiting.'

'All right. Promise me you'll look after yourself?' He stroked her face, traced the outline of her lips with one finger.

'I promise,' she whispered. 'You too! I won't forget you, Paul.'

'Justine?' She gasped and looked round. Adam stood by their table, hands clenched in the pockets of his fleece-lined, denim jacket. His thick, dark hair was tousled, his face grim as he looked at them. She wondered how long he'd been there. Paul didn't let go of her hand; she had to pull it out of his grasp.

'I thought you might like a lift home,' Adam said. He glanced at Paul, a hostile glance, then back at her. 'I mean, that's if you're ready to go home, of course?' His eyes were anxious as he looked at her.

'Yes.' Justine smiled at him as she stood up. 'I'm ready.'

'Good.' Adam smiled back at her as he helped her on with her coat and slid one arm around her shoulders. He lifted her hand, the hand with the diamond ring, and kissed it. Then he glared at Paul Melwood.

'I hope you rot in hell, you bastard!' he said, his voice cold and full of menace. 'You took advantage of Justine, put her in danger.' His arm tightened around her shoulders. 'She could have been killed!'

'I never put Justine in danger,' Paul said calmly. He stood up. 'And what did you ever do for her?' he challenged. 'I mean, when you weren't taking the law into your own hands and making a bad situation worse?' He glared at Adam. 'Or shagging away from home!'

Adam drew in his breath, picked up a wine glass and smashed it on the table. Justine grabbed his arm. The crowded bar fell silent as people looked round at them. Someone laughed drunkenly. A barman pushed his way through the throng.

'Outside, lady and gents!' he said loudly. 'Right now, please. Otherwise you can talk this through with the officers of the law!'

'We're leaving,' Justine said. 'Adam, come *on*.' She pulled at his arm and they left the bar, people quickly parting to let them through. Paul grabbed his coat and followed, shaking with anger. His last meeting with Justine, and Adam bloody Shaw had to ruin it for him! The bastard couldn't keep away. He was disappointed that Justine had told Adam where she was going.

The mist had lifted and it had turned cold. The moon and stars were out, the moonlight reflected in the glittering river Mersey. They could smell the river and the not so distant sea, traffic fumes and fast food. Papery curled leaves drifted across the slippery stone flags of the quay and clustered around their feet. Adam stopped and looked down at her.

'I'm sorry,' he said. 'I shouldn't have come here like this.'

'Adam, I'm glad you did. Really.' She kissed him. 'Let's go home, okay?'

Paul grabbed Adam by the shoulder and swung him round. 'I hope she doesn't regret her decision to stay with you, you . . .'

'Stop it!' Justine cried. 'Leave him alone!'

The powerful Harley-Davidson roared out of nowhere, startling them.

'What the hell is he doing?' Adam jumped in shock. 'He'll run us over!' He shoved Paul away and grabbed Justine's hand.

The bike weaved its way between the empty stone troughs on the concrete flags. It slowed suddenly and the pillion passenger stretched out a bulky, leather-clad arm.

'Run!' Adam yelled, dragging her by the hand. 'This way!' They raced for a nearby wall and he pushed her down, threw himself on top of her. Justine fell, her long hair entangled in his fingers. She screamed in pain. The cold concrete flags ripped her stockings and scraped her knees. She was freezing, paralysed with shock and terror. They scrambled frantically behind the low wall, Adam holding her tight, his breath in her ear.

Paul's body jerked and twitched as the bullets slammed into him. He staggered backwards and fell. The shots sounded like thuds, he thought; the gun was fitted with a silencer. He felt stinging jolts to his left shoulder, his chest, his neck. He collapsed and put a hand on his stomach, felt warm, sticky wetness. He rolled on his back, his chest heaving. The bike roared off and there

356

was only the sound of distant traffic, the river slapping gently against the quay.

'No!' Justine sobbed. She struggled to her feet and ran to him. Paul stared up at her, tried to speak. A dark stain spread out from under his body. Moonlight and massive blood loss made his skin ashen.

'Paul!' she cried, kneeling over him. 'Don't die, please don't die. Somebody help!' she shouted. There were big buildings nearby, full of lights and presumably people. Why didn't somebody come? She started to cry. 'Adam, help him!'

Paul's lips moved and he gave a little sigh. Then his eyes clouded over and his head rolled to one side, blood trickling from his mouth.

'No!' she cried again, sobbing bitterly. Shocked and sickened, Adam crouched over Paul and felt for the pulse in his neck.

'I'm afraid he's dead,' he said quietly. 'There's nothing I or anybody can do for him now. Don't!' he said sharply, as Justine stretched out a hand. 'Don't touch him. He lifted her gently to her feet, held her so that she didn't fall. 'I told you, he's dead. We can't help him.'

'Are you sure?'

'Yes.' She was shaking with panic, her face streaked with tears. 'Whoever killed his wife and Gary Jones didn't want him put on trial,' he whispered in her ear. 'Didn't want to risk letting him give damaging evidence.' Adam was unnerved and trembling with shock. 'That could have been us lying there!'

'I know,' she gulped. 'I know.'

Adam kissed her, hugged her tight. People ran towards them, shouting urgent questions.

They stared down at Paul's body sprawled on the flags, moonlight shining on the dark pool of blood that surrounded him.

# The Hit
## Denise Ryan

*The most compelling debut since Martina Cole's*

To the world, Shannon's father-in-law is a pillar of the Liverpool community. Only she suspects that Bernard is the monster responsible for raping and murdering a local girl.

No one, including Shannon's CID detective husband, believes the head teacher capable of the horrific crimes she accuses him of. The only person who takes her allegations seriously is Bernard himself – and he decides it's time to silence his troublesome daughter-in-law for good.

Terrified for her life, Shannon realises there's only one way to stop herself becoming Bernard's next victim. It isn't legal. It isn't moral. But it's certainly permanent!

'This is Denise Ryan's first novel and it is a powerful offering'
*What's On*

'A cracking debut novel'                    *Publishing News*

'racy, fast-paced thriller'                  *Lancashire Life*

'Realistic crime novel from a north west author'
*Manchester Evening News*

# Dead Letter
## Jane Waterhouse

A Garner Quinn mystery by the author of *Shadow Walk*

A crazed fan is stalking true-crime writer Garner Quinn, sending letters thick with sexual and violent overtones to her remote, *unlisted* address which she shares with her young daughter and elderly house-keeper. Garner is right to be concerned. The fan has read all her books, taped every one of her television appearances, and, what's worse, knows her every move.

The only way to protect her family is to find the stalker before his words become actions. Pushed to the edge, she hires Reed Corbin, founder of a prestigious security firm, who takes a personal interest in the case – and in Garner. Together they embark on a quest to learn whether the threats to Garner are personal, or more far-reaching than they could ever have imagined.

Praise for Jane Waterhouse and *Shadow Walk*:

'A well-crafted page-turner' *The Times*

'This is thriller writing without a wasted word'
*The Good Book Guide*

'A quest for justice story in the style of Patricia Cornwell and Kathy Reichs' *Bookseller*

'First rate. Garner Quinn is a memorable creation'
*Chicago Tribune*

'Make no mistake: Jane Waterhouse is a writer to watch'
*Booklist*

# Shooting at Midnight
## Greg Rucka

'Crisply written, hard-bitten, all-action stuff'
*The Times*

Bridgett Logan is a tough New York City private investigator with a history she doesn't talk about – not even to some-time lover, Atticus Kodiak.

But now Bridgett's friend, Lisa, has been accused of killing an abusive drug dealer and Bridgett is forced to face her past. For it seems the only way to solve the murder and prove Lisa innocent is to go undercover as a dealer herself. And while gaining acceptance into a gang of hardened criminals won't be easy, it will be child's play for Bridgett compared with constantly being around the seductive white powder her body still craves...

Praise for Greg Rucka and *Smoker*:

'Tough and edgy' *Sunday Telegraph*

'Twists with aplomb...' *Guardian*

'A can of narrative worms so deftly deployed that the readers will bite nearly every hook' *Publishers Weekly*

The very best of Piatkus fiction is now available in paperback as well as hardcover. Piatkus paperbacks, where *every* book is special.

The prices shown above were correct at the time of going to press. However, Piatkus Books reserve the right to show new retail prices on covers which may differ from those previously advertised in the text or elsewhere.

Piatkus Books will be available from your bookshop or newsagent, or can be ordered from the following address:

Piatkus Paperbacks, PO Box 11, Falmouth, TR10 9EN

Alternatively you can fax your order to this address on 01326 374 888 or e-mail us at books@barni.avel.co.uk

Payments can be made as follows: Sterling cheque, Eurocheque, postal order (payable to Piatkus Books) or by credit card, Visa/Mastercard. Do not send cash or currency. UK and B.F.P.O. customers should allow £1.00 postage and packing for the first book, 50p for the second and 30p for each additional book ordered to a maximum of £3.00 (7 books plus).

Overseas customers, including Eire, allow £2.00 for postage and packing for the first book, plus £1.00 for the second and 50p for each subsequent title ordered.

NAME (block letters)_____

ADDRESS _____

_____

I enclose my remittance for £_____

I wish to pay by Visa/Mastercard          Expiry Date_____

| | | | | | | | | | | | | | | | | | | | | |
|---|---|---|---|---|---|---|---|---|---|---|---|---|---|---|---|---|---|---|---|---|---|